"Chief," Wally Benson said, "we've got a situation." He handed her his radio.

"This is Chief Hooper," Abby said into the radio. "What's up?"

"We got us a body, Chief."

"A body?"

"Yeah, a teenage girl, maybe thirteen, fourteen, something like that. On the bank of Watermark Slough."

"Can you tell what happened to her?"

"Looks to me like she might have drowned, except for the fact that she's on the shore. Thing is, she's naked as a jaybird. Not a stitch of clothes on and none around. Could be a homicide."

Abby felt a twinge in her gut. "You don't recognize her?"

"Can't say that I do, Chief. I got the site secure, though. And the county lab people are on the way. I knew you'd want to know."

"Yeah, thanks." Abby thought for a moment, aware of both Frank and Wally listening in. "Where did you find her?"

"At Frank Keegan's place."

Abby looked over at Frank, who'd heard every word. His brows rose right along with hers.

R.J. Kaiser "scores a hit with this action-packed Caribbean-based adventure."
—*Publishers Weekly* on *Payback*

Also available from MIRA Books and
R.J. KAISER

PAYBACK

Watch for R.J. Kaiser's newest blockbuster

FRUITCAKE
March 2000

JANE DOE

R.J. KAISER

MIRA

ISBN 1-55166-510-7

JANE DOE

Copyright © 1999 by Belles-Lettres, Inc.

Look us up on-line at: http://www.mirabooks.com

Printed in U.S.A.

To Amy Moore-Benson, with thanks.
Your care, passion and vision
always make the difference.

Saturday
February 15th

The pounding sounded like it was coming from the inside of his skull, but he wasn't sure. The only certainty was that his head ached like hell, the pain cutting through his frontal lobe with the subtlety of a laser. His stomach didn't feel so hot, either. It was a pool of bile, his whole body a vat of poison. At that moment, death didn't seem like such a bad idea.

Frank Keegan slowly opened his eyes. He saw a ceiling. It looked familiar. It was *his* ceiling, and he appeared to be in *his* bed. That was promising, though he wasn't sure what it meant. Groaning, he rubbed his head, only then realizing the pounding was coming from somewhere out there in the great void. Yes, he could hear it plainly now—loud knocking, and a voice, somebody shouting.

"Frank!" came the muffled sound from outside. "Frank, you home?"

He would have said, "No, I'm dead," but opening his jaw took real effort and he wasn't sure he could get a sound past the cotton in his mouth. The banging on his door continued, but he didn't much care. If he was being warned of fire, well, fire he could live with. Moving, breathing, thinking—those were a problem. Christ, if he ever took another drink, he'd shoot himself.

As the intrusion became more insistent, Frank realized he would have to deal with it. He reached down to find the covers, only to discover he was on top of them and naked from the waist down. That gave him pause. What was he doing in a shirt but no pants?

"Frank!" came the man's voice from outside the trailer. "I don't have all day! Wake up!"

Frank sat up, sending the room spinning. He had to brace himself to keep from toppling over. If he was going to respond to the banging, he'd have to find some pants. There was a pair on the floor, the pant legs inside out. He must have been in a hell of a hurry to get out of them. Not bothering with the wadded-up shorts nearby, he fumbled to get the trousers right side out, then pulled them on. As he stood the room started to spin again, but he managed to button the waistband and zip up the fly. Then he staggered through his dreary mobile home to the front room, fighting to keep his gorge down.

He opened the door to the blinding light of day, though it was, in fact, gray and drizzly. Toad Lopez, Kay Ingram's main bartender down at the River Queen, stood there in a rain slicker, his blue-black bangs scalloping his forehead, his grin as wide as the hood.

Toad got his nickname because of the warts on his fingers. Some people called him Fernando—not because it was his real name, which it wasn't—but because he looked like Fernando Valenzuela. Toad also was a lefty, though he bowled instead of pitched. His average was only 167, but he'd bowled four perfect 300 games—one while he was dead drunk, though the story was suspect because there were only three witnesses and they were drunk, too. His real name, as best Frank could recall, was Juan.

"Jesus, Toad," he said, squinting at him, "what are you doing here?"

"I brung you your pickup, Frank," the man said, gesturing over his shoulder at the beat-up Toyota. "Kay left me a note saying I should drive it over first thing."

It took Frank a moment to process what Toad had said. With the mention of Kay, the first hazy memories of the night before began to return. It was Valentine's Day and he'd gone to the River Queen to see his former ladylove because he didn't have anyone else to call on and because Valentine's Day without a woman was even worse than Christmas without a kid. Kay had finally spoken to him. That was a victory of sorts. Relations between them had been strained since their breakup, and they hadn't spoken at all since he and her daughter, Abby, had gone head-to-head for the Riverton police-chief job. The trouble was, he couldn't remember much of their conversation—only that it was tentative at first.

Frank glanced up at the leaden sky, shivering in the damp air. "What time is it, anyway?"

"A little after ten," Toad replied.

"That late?"

"Don't you mean, that early? Kay said you'd be in bad shape, but criminy, you still look shit-faced, Frank. And what's that on your shirt? Blood? Looks like you cut your face." Toad drew a line across his own cheek with the tip of his finger to show him the place.

Frank peered down at himself, seeing spatters of blood on his chest. "Christ, I don't know." The gray outdoors did a sort of half turn and he had to grab the door frame to steady himself. "You tell me, Toad. Did I get into a fight last night?"

"Beats me. I was off."

Frank searched the murky recesses of his memory. Toad was right. Kay had tended bar and Belinda Ramsey had waitressed. He had drunk margaritas until he couldn't see straight.

In honor of Saint Valentine. No recollection of a fight came to mind, though he remembered wanting to punch out Mort Anderson. Of course, he *always* wanted to punch out Mort Anderson.

"Who brought me home?"

"Don't got any idea."

Frank recalled Kay taking away his car keys as a condition for getting another drink, but everything after that was a complete blur. "You got the keys?" Frank asked.

Toad dangled Frank's key ring from his finger, then put it in his hand.

"Thanks, amigo. I'd invite you in for a cup of coffee, but the *casa*'s a mess and, anyway, I've got to barf."

"I don't want no coffee," Toad said. "But I could use a ride back into town."

"Oh, Jeez," Frank said as it hit him. "I wasn't thinking. I guess you don't want to walk, do you?"

"Not in this muck."

"Come on in," Frank said, stepping back. "My apologies." He staggered toward the bedroom, leaving Toad to close the door. "I'll just get my shoes on and find my wallet."

"Don't be too long, huh, Frank?" Toad Lopez called after him. "I gotta open the Queen."

Frank stopped at the bedroom door, steadying himself on the frame. "I thought Kay always opened up."

"Usually she does, but she left for San Francisco early this morning."

"San Francisco? What did she go to the city for?"

Toad hesitated before responding. "Mort," he finally said, looking sheepish.

Kay had taken up with Mort Anderson after she and Frank had broken off, which was difficult for Frank because all of Riverton knew that he and Mort hated each other's guts. Their mutual contempt began with a bad real-estate deal years ago and blossomed with their rivalry for Kay's affections. Frank couldn't stand the son of a bitch, especially when Mort started gloating over having won Kay's heart.

Frank went off, his stomach heaving. He hoped if he had a little breakfast, he might feel better, though the thought of food was enough to make him vomit. But after he dropped off Toad at the Queen, he'd go over to Thelma's for a bite. The town's favorite hangout for chow was officially the Riverton Café, but Thelma Foley had been running the place for a hundred years, so everybody called it Thelma's.

Ducking into the bathroom, Frank took a look in the mirror to see what Toad had been talking about. Damn, if he didn't have a long gash across his cheek. The blood had dried. It wasn't a serious wound. But the hell of it was, he didn't have the slightest idea how he'd gotten it. Not the slightest.

Delta Lanes
Riverton, California

At two o'clock, Abby Hooper pulled up in front of the bowling alley in her Bronco. It was raining so hard that the Delta Lanes sign was a blur and the puddles in the parking lot looked deep enough for waders. Abby groaned. She'd rather have stayed in bed. But she'd promised Mae Brown she'd be an alternate on her bowling team, and she simply couldn't let Mae down.

Things in the department were at that critical stage. Loyalty and friendships were being defined. Little things meant a lot, respect won or lost. Besides, what kind of woman would let menstrual cramps get her down? To the world, Abby Hooper was gutsy, unflinching. A woman with brass balls to go with her porcelain smile.

The being a woman part was the real complication. She had been Riverton's police chief for a month, but she was only the second sworn female ever to serve on the force. That created a special burden. Half the town was pulling for her to succeed. Half was expecting her to fall on her face—her enemies, Chet Wilsey in particular, actually hoping for it. What that meant, of course, was that she had no choice but to succeed. She owed it not only to herself but to all the other women who were watching to see how she'd fare with the good old boys.

Mumbling, Abby pulled the hood of her Riverton Police Department rain slicker over her head, grabbed her bowling bag and made a dash for the entrance. It was a short run, but she managed to get soaked from ankle to thigh just the same. Water dripped from the end of her nose. Her head hurt. And the place where she'd been shot in the thigh a few years back throbbed like it always did in the cold and damp.

Abby paused just inside the door, letting the water drip onto the worn rubber mat that protected the carpeting, which, in all honesty, was beyond protecting. The Delta Lanes was one of those old-fashioned alleys that hadn't changed in thirty years. It smelled like a closet and had the familiar feel of an old grammar school. And there was something about the signature sounds—the whir of ball on wood and the hollow thump of pins clapping together—that Abby found stirring. Maybe it was association. She'd lost her virginity after a bowling date, and thereafter had always connected bowling alleys with new beginnings. She'd been sixteen; the sex, as she remembered it, neither good nor bad, the young man memorable primarily for his clumsiness.

Abby took off her rain slicker and, glancing up, saw Chet Wilsey, of all people, staring at her. Chet, her predecessor as police chief, was at the shoe-rental counter along with Dix Fowler, the sergeant of the force and her number two in command. Dix and Chet remained close, and Abby had little doubt where Dix's true loyalties lay, though he played the role of company man to a fault.

Giving her slicker a last little shake, Abby strode toward

Chet as though everything was fine. He maintained eye contact as she approached. So did she. Chet was sixty-five, quite tall, with only a hint of flab on his sinewy body. He stood out in a crowd because of his snow-white hair and imposing demeanor. Chet's hawkish features went well with his big-fish-in-a-small-pond brand of arrogance. Abby didn't like him because of his antipathy for her—which she could attribute to nothing more than the fact that she was a woman.

"Well, hello, Miss Hooper," he said, managing somehow to make the mere recitation of her name cause for amusement. He really was an ass.

"Good afternoon, Chief Wilsey. Dix."

Chet motioned toward her bowling bag. "Your gear looks new, Miss Hooper," he said. "You a novice at bowling, too?"

She decided to meet the issue head-on. "Actually, I have a bit more experience with bowling," she replied dryly.

"That a fact?"

"Yes. I bowled in a women's league in Sacramento for about six months. With a team of female police officers. 'Lady Cops' was our team name."

"Nice," Chet said. He nudged Fowler with his elbow. "Isn't that sweet, Dix? 'Lady Cops.' I like that."

Abby refused to be annoyed. Even if Chet Wilsey was an out-and-out misogynist, which she doubted, he was definitely of the old school that believed women had no place in police work—except maybe as clerks and coffee monitors. It was more ignorance than malevolence, which she concluded was deserving of her pity, not her wrath. Then, too, Chet had lost his wife in the past year and had that pain to deal with. It was a shame the loss hadn't made him a more compassionate human being. People, she'd learned, were often hard to predict.

Dix Fowler, to his credit, looked uncomfortable. He was in his late fifties, badly overweight and in terrible physical condition. But he was closing in on retirement and intended to hang on to his pension at all costs. In a way, Abby felt sorry for him. His job commanded one loyalty, his friendship another. He mumbled something incoherent and turned back to the clerk, leaving Chet to torment her alone.

"That girl I hired for the force a few years back liked to bowl, too, as I recall," Chet said. "Her problem was she liked to ball even more, pardon my French. Left when she got pregnant. But I suppose I mentioned that, didn't I?"

"Yes, a couple of times, I believe."

She hadn't intended to be as snide as she sounded, but Chet deserved it. What annoyed her most was she'd bent over backward to be as respectful toward him as she could during the transition from his administration to hers, but he was still unwilling to give her any credit for it. Oh, he'd managed rudimentary politeness at times, but his bitterness was never far from the surface. He'd taken the setback personally, believing that he—with the compliance of the town's old guard—should name Frank Keegan his successor. Much to his chagrin, the rebellious majority of City Council decided otherwise.

"I take it you're both on the other city team," Abby said, looking back and forth between the two men.

"That's right," Chet said. "My retirement hasn't disqualified me. Or if it has, nobody's said so."

"The two city government teams are playing each other tonight?" she asked.

"That's affirmative," Chet replied. "City One versus City Two."

God, she thought, just my luck. The only thing worse than bowling against Chet Wilsey would be bowling with him. "Well, may the best team win," she said. "Now if you'll excuse me, gentlemen…"

She walked away, her cramps bad enough that she'd have given a day's pay to bend over and take a deep breath. But

Abby couldn't afford the slightest falter. Not in front of Chet Wilsey. Or for that matter, any man.

At the top of the stairs she stopped to look for Mae, badly needing a friendly face. Abby didn't like being the lightning rod for the town's divisions, but that's what she'd become. Hardly anyone was neutral toward her. She was either a champion or villain, depending on who you talked to.

"Abby! Abby! Down here!"

She saw Mae Brown waving at her with a white towel at the far end of the row of lanes. Mae, a short, athletically built woman, doubled as head dispatcher and ex-officio office manager of the Riverton Police Department. At five-four, Abby and Mae looked straight across at each other, but Mae had twenty pounds on her. She and her husband Judea, employed in the Public Works Department, and their teenage daughter were one of only six African-American families in town. Mae had the highest average of any woman in the Saturday Afternoon League and was in the top ten of men and women combined. She, Abby had heard, was a stud.

When Abby got to the lane, Mae showed her the spot at the end of the extra ball racks where people hung their coats. Abby hung her slicker on a hook and carried her bowling bag to the bench.

Judea, who was putting bowling shoes on his huge feet, glanced up at her. "So," he said, pushing back his horn-rimmed glasses, "this is our secret weapon, huh, Maisie?"

"If Abby is half as good with a bowling ball as she is with her service revolver, you and me can coast tonight, sugar."

"Don't count on much from me," Abby said. "I haven't had a bowling ball in my hand since before Christmas. Plus, I'm not feeling very well today."

"Lord, that when I do my best stuff. Helps you focus. Bet you shoot over your average."

Abby sat down next to Mae to put on her shoes. Chet and

Dix arrived, greeting the Browns before going to the bench opposite them.

"So, you've called up the reserves, eh, Judea?" Chet chortled.

"This here's our secret weapon, Chief Wilsey," Judea replied, jerking his thumb in the direction of Abby. "Hate to say it, but you don't got a prayer."

"We'll see, Judea, we'll see."

The other bowlers arrived and greetings were exchanged. Abby listened to the banter with growing apprehension. About the only way this day could turn out all right was if she won the match in the last frame by throwing a strike. To be human was to be inferior if you were both a boss and a woman. Just thinking about that, she lowered her face to her hands, pushed back her short brown hair and wished she could throw up.

Frank Keegan had hung out at Thelma's as long as he could without it looking like he had no life whatsoever—a possibility that occasionally concerned him. Trouble was, he found rainy Saturdays depressing. Like a lot of folks in Riverton, when he couldn't fish, he headed for either the River Queen or the Delta Lanes. Not feeling up to the smell of booze, he opted for the bowling alley. The Saturday Afternoon League would be going at it, so he'd find Chet and some of the other boys.

As he entered the building, Frank took off his Giants hat and, removing his jacket, shook the water from it. Walking past the counter, he nodded at the boy manning the cash register. "Hi, Donnie."

"Mr. Keegan, how's it going?"

"About the same as always," he said, feeling like a damned liar. Frank rarely drank the way he had last night and was rather embarrassed about it. There'd been a couple of comments from people over at Thelma's that he wasn't looking his best, but he'd mostly passed the morning and early afternoon in painful anonymity, slouched in a rear booth.

The worse part was he still hadn't figured out what the hell had happened to him last night, except that he'd gotten roaring drunk and somehow ended up at home with a cut on his face, his shirt bloody and his pants off. As the hours passed, bits and pieces of the evening had come to him. He remembered making a pass at Kay—a stupid trick only a drunk would pull. He recalled her chiding him, but not exactly rebuffing him, which was strange because she'd been cool toward him for months. He also had flashes of memory of screwing in the dark, but he was damned if he could say who with and whether the recollections were real or imagined. He'd have said Kay was the likely candidate—particularly if his recollections were of the imagined variety—but it was hard to believe she'd have actually gone to bed with him, given her relationship with Mort.

Either way, Frank was completely baffled. It wasn't the sort of predicament a man liked finding himself in—not knowing how he'd spent the night and with whom. "What lane's Chief Wilsey on, Donnie?" he asked the kid.

"Let me see…" The boy checked his list. "City One's on lane eight, Mr. Keegan."

"Thanks."

Frank gave his jacket another shake and ambled off. After the bowl of soup at Thelma's, he'd started feeling human again. But only marginally.

Reaching lane eight, he spotted Chet Wilsey, but he was surprised to see that one of the bowlers on the other team was his recent adversary, Abby Hooper. Though they'd been in competition for the same job, Frank didn't regard her as an enemy. What struck him most was the irony that she was the daughter of his former lover. But bizarre things happened in small towns, where, in one way or another, everybody was connected to everybody else. In Riverton politics and business, incest was rampant.

The thing that made the situation with Abby and Kay especially unusual was that mother and daughter were estranged. After her parents split up, Abby had been raised by her father, Ty Hooper, the scion of one of the oldest landowning families in the region. Kay had left the Delta soon after the divorce and didn't return for fifteen years. By then her second husband had died, leaving her with enough money to buy the River Queen. On one of the few occasions when Kay discussed her child, she told Frank she'd made overtures to Abby, hoping for reconciliation, but had been turned down flat.

It had all happened long before Frank had come to town, but he'd heard that Ty had died when Abby was away at college. She hadn't returned to Riverton until the police chief job opened up. Her decision to apply for the position surprised a lot of people, including Kay. Abby had been a deputy with the Sacramento County Sheriff's Department and, though her record was excellent, at thirty-three she was on the young side.

Frank himself had been a reluctant candidate, tossing his hat into the ring only because he'd been pressured by Chet and W. C. Joyner, the mayor. They didn't like it that Abby was the only candidate, and Chet in particular didn't like it that she was a woman. Frank felt no real passion over the issue. He didn't even know Abby until they began competing for the job. In fact, they met for the first time at a City Council meeting.

The battle over the police-chief job had been pure politics. In truth, neither Abby nor Frank had been especially qualified. Both were outsiders to the force and had limited administrative experience. But they were the only candidates, which was no surprise, considering the job only paid $37,500. Abby's advantage was that Frank had been out of police work for a few years and she was still in it. She'd attained the rank of sergeant, a commendation for bravery, had completed all the requisite course work and had superlative test scores and a folder full of recommendations.

Frank had been a detective on the Stockton police force some years back—a talented one, according to his superiors—and a Vietnam vet. If he and police work had run afoul of each other, it was because his career had run afoul of his ex, Arlene. Actually his entire life had pretty much run afoul of Arlene, whose outstanding characteristic was her overarching disapproval of him. In her eyes, nothing he stood for was worthy—until he volunteered to become her ex-husband, of course. That, she liked.

Had it not been for Beth, the decision to divorce would have been a slam dunk from the get-go. But they'd both decided it was in their child's best interest to subject her to a shitty marriage, so the poor kid had to endure them at each other's throats until common sense finally prevailed. Naturally, Frank had gotten the short end of the stick, because Arlene had taken their daughter off to San Francisco, making him an every-other-weekend daddy, a slowly fading star in the firmament of his child's life. To this day, he regretted that it had worked out that way. He'd never spent as much time with Beth as he'd have liked. And now that she was dead, it was too late.

Since moving to Riverton five years ago he'd operated a little security-and-investigation business, raised pears and spent a lot of time fishing. With Arlene hardly more than a bad dream that only occasionally came to mind and his daughter gone, Frank was free to live as modestly as he chose, a luxury family men didn't have. Mostly he kept his head down and passed each day as pleasantly as he could, either alone or with his friends. His ill-fated sortie into politics was the first high-profile venture he attempted since coming to Riverton. And Abby Hooper, bless her heart, had made sure his march to the White House ended before it got started.

While his defeat was a humbling experience in a way, he hadn't taken it too seriously because it wasn't so much about him as it was about town politics. The real difference between him and Abby was she had no political baggage, and therefore three council-member votes in her corner to his two.

The one conversation of consequence they'd had was at City Hall the night her selection was announced. "You may have done me a favor, Miss Hooper," he'd told her honestly. "I don't think I've got the stomach for city politics." After shaking hands, he'd wished her luck and that had pretty much been it. He'd run into her in town a time or two and they'd said hello, but mostly Abby Hooper was a stranger.

Which was not to say he was indifferent toward her. The truth was he rather liked Abby, finding her genuine, forthright and more than a little attractive. The attraction was somewhat unsettling because of his and Kay's past relationship. To the best of his knowledge, Abby was unaware of the affair, but he could only imagine how disgusted she'd be if she knew his feelings for her.

Frank settled into a seat at the observation level, above the lanes. Abby's turn had come and she took her bowling ball from the rack and approached the lag line. Frank couldn't help noticing she had a nice ass. It was narrower, tighter, rounder than her mother's. No surprise. Kay was sixteen, seventeen years older than her daughter.

On the other hand, Chet Wilsey, who had always had an eye for the ladies, didn't think much more of Abby, the woman, than he did Abby, the cop. The night of the City Council vote, when he and Frank had broken out a bottle of bourbon to lament their loss, they'd talked about the new chief's sexuality. "I'll give you odds she's a lesbo," Chet had said with mild disgust. "Has to be."

"Why do you say that?"

"Shit, look at her, Frank. Struts around like that gun of hers is a cock. Never been married. No known boyfriends. You ever seen her in a dress?"

"Your generational bias is showing," Frank had told him. "Women are like that nowadays."

"What makes you the expert? You're not exactly generation X yourself."

Frank had laughed. "I watch a lot of television, what can I say?"

Chet, who was no dummy, picked up on Frank's interest in Abby. "If you've got ideas, I'd think twice, my friend," he'd warned. "You're better off screwing her mama. Kay Ingram can be tough as nails, but she's a real woman."

God knew, there was no arguing about Kay's appeal. But this feeling for Abby was something else altogether. The strangest thing about it was that it was based on nothing. He hardly knew the woman. He certainly had no hard feelings toward her for whipping his butt. And though he'd never told Chet, losing had come more as a relief than a disappointment—hell, he'd have voted for her himself had he been on the council. Still, he had this thing for her he couldn't explain and hated to think it might have anything to do with the fact he and her mother had once been lovers. That was a little too kinky.

The other possibility was he was having some kind of midlife crisis. Abby was a kid compared to him. The women in his life had always been in his age group or, in a couple of cases, a bit older, like Kay. But there was something about Abby Hooper.

The bowlers had finished their line and were regrouping for the next game when Chet spotted him watching the action. "Keegan, you old turkey, I thought you'd sworn off bowling forever. Or has it become your spectator sport?"

Frank laughed. "What else is a guy going to do on a rainy Saturday? Football season's over. The weather's too shitty for fishing. If I stayed home, I'd have to clean house, and you know how I love housework.''

''Christ, I know the feeling,'' Chet lamented. Then he took a closer look at him, frowning. ''What happened to your face? Looks like you got on the wrong end of some woman's wrath.''

Frank shrugged. ''I don't know. Had an accident. No big deal.''

Behind Chet, Abby had turned around and, seeing Frank, nodded. He gave a weak wave. ''Hi, Chief,'' he called to her. ''You teaching this old cop humility?''

She gave a slight smile. ''We're trying.''

Chet, his back to her, grimaced. Frank could see from the overhead projection of the score sheet that it was a close contest. Abby seemed to be doing well, which probably galled Chet. The former chief returned to the lane and the final game got under way. Frank settled back to watch Abby. Her vulnerability beneath the plucky facade drew him to her—the urge to protect, probably. He had to laugh at the thought. Wouldn't Chet love that!

Down on the alley, it was Abby's turn. She made her approach, the ball swinging back, then coming off her hand as smooth as soft butter on bread. Frank didn't see the ball strike the pins. His eyes were on her. Shit, maybe Valentine's Day had hit him harder than he thought.

Abby figured it would come down to the last two bowlers in the last frame of the final game, and it had. The pressure was on her, making her feel like the whole town was watching, even though the only spectator was Frank Keegan. The funny thing was she'd have preferred if it were a hundred strangers rather than Frank. The man was harmless enough— sort of a nice guy, even—but something about him made her feel self-conscious.

''You can do it, baby,'' Mae called out over the clunk,

clank and clatter of the alley. "Get a strike now and you've got two balls to get your eight pins."

Abby forced her mind back to the task at hand. She dismissed the notion that Frank was watching and didn't look at Chet. But as she lifted her ball she heard Chet say to Dix, "Now we'll see if she's got nerve."

Knowing it was gamesmanship, she ignored him. Instead, she focused on the ten pins standing at the end of the lane, sixty feet away. Her stomach was one big knot, but Abby decided to make the pain work for her, like Mae said. She started her approach. As the ball swung down in an arc it lofted slightly, and she knew immediately that she hadn't thrown well. When all was said and done, the five and seven were left standing. It was not an impossible split, but for a bowler of Abby's caliber, it was a serious challenge.

"You can do that, baby," Mae called. "Pick it up."

"Shoot 'em down, Chief," Judea added. He clapped, encouraging her.

Abby stared at the two lonely pins. The odds had shifted radically. The pressure of hitting one pin would be bad enough, but two so far apart...

Chet had to be gloating. She couldn't hear him, but she didn't need to. She moved forward on her approach to the line. This time her ball rolled true.

"Yeah, baby, yeah!" Judea hollered.

"Come on, come on!" This from Mae.

The ball smacked the five pin on the right side, sending it flying. It just barely clipped the seven pin, which tottered like a drunk before falling on its side with a thud. Screams of joy echoed down the alley.

"You've got another ball, Miss Hooper," Chet Wilsey said when the din had subsided.

"Eight more pins, Abby," Mae said. "Just eight more."

Everybody returned to their seats. Abby watched her ball coming back along the return track. She rubbed her hand on her pants. All she had to do now was roll decently. Good would do.

Abby advanced. It was a clean release. The ball looked good...yes...bam, it hit the pocket flush, sending pins flying. Only the ten remained standing. She'd done it!

Her teammates were on her, slapping her back and, in Mae's case, planting a kiss on her cheek. Abby, feeling great, turned to their opponents for the first time. Chet got up without making eye contact and stretched.

"Looks like this time I owe you the steak dinner, Judea," he said blandly.

"You bet your ass you do, Chief."

Abby allowed herself to glance Frank Keegan's way. His eyes felt as tight on her as a new pair of panty hose. She turned her attention to Chet, who pointedly said nothing to her. Instead, he strolled back to talk to Frank. Abby didn't care about being snubbed; she'd gotten what she really wanted.

As she removed her bowling shoes, she noticed Chet had gone off in the direction of the bar, leaving Frank Keegan alone in the gallery. When they made eye contact again, he gave her a thumbs-up, which made her smile. No, Frank wasn't a bad guy, despite the company he kept.

Abby was looking for her street shoes under the bench when she heard a scream, followed by a crash. Everyone turned toward the entrance. There were more shouts. A couple of guys ran to the main door. She heard somebody holler, "Fight!"

Abby instinctively felt her hip, but her weapon was in the Bronco. Not bothering to put on her shoes, she headed to the lobby, breaking into a jog as people gravitated in that direction. Over the general din of voices, she heard more screaming, the voice of a girl.

Arriving where a small crowd had gathered, Abby saw two young men trading punches, one, the bowling-alley clerk, with blood running down his mouth. The girl who'd been screaming was on the far side, terrified.

"Somebody do something!" she cried as more punches were exchanged. "Somebody stop them!"

Abby pushed the man in front of her aside and moved toward the combatants. "All right, that's enough!" she shouted. "Police! Break it up!"

The words had no effect, so she grabbed the arm of the nearest boy, half turning him. Without really looking at her, he swung his arm, catching her flush on the cheek. The blow knocked her backward and Abby fell, landing on her butt. She scrambled to her feet, realizing she needed more than moral authority to put a stop to this.

"Call 911 and tell the dispatcher to send over the patrol officer," she told the woman behind her. Then she looked around at the faces in the crowd. "A couple of you guys help me separate them." Figuring she had to lead by example, she jumped on the back of the fighter right in front of her just as his opponent landed a punch, knocking both the kid and Abby to the floor.

A couple of men moved forward, grabbing the young man who was still on his feet. The boy she had hold of writhed, managing to shake her off just as another figure moved forward, brushing her aside and, taking the kid by the shoulders, slammed him to the floor.

"Hold still, Donnie, before I break your arm."

It wasn't until he had the kid pinned with his knee in the boy's kidneys that Abby realized it was Frank Keegan. Another man emerged from the crowd and stood next to her. Abby, on her back, peered up at Chet Wilsey.

"You have your cuffs, Miss Hooper?" he asked with calm disdain. "Frank could use them."

"No," she said, getting to her feet. "They're in my vehicle with my weapon."

"A little pointer," Chet said, his voice indulgent. "Carry

your cuffs with you, even if you don't have your weapon. They're good for slapping a perpetrator up the side of the head.''

The crowd had fallen silent. All eyes were on Abby. "Thanks, Chet," she said. "I'll remember that."

"It's all Donnie's fault," the girl lamented. "Emilio didn't do anything."

"That's a lie!" the boy under Frank's knee shouted.

"Shut up!" Chet roared. "All of you!"

There was another stunned silence. For a second the purr of the air coming out the heating vents could be heard. Abby knew she had to take charge. "Thanks, Chet," she said. "I'll take care of this now." She moved to the middle of the arena, between the boy on his feet and the one Frank still had pinned to the floor. "Get him up, Frank," she said.

Frank complied, lifting the kid to his feet, but he kept the boy's hands behind him. Abby stood between the combatants. "I could run you both in," she said. "The fact that you're beating on each other is bad enough, but when an officer orders you to quit, you damned well better listen." She got in Emilio's face. "And in case you're not aware, that whack you gave me was an assault on a police officer."

"I...I didn't know...who you were," the boy stammered, wiping his bloody mouth.

"I identified myself as police. That's all you need to hear."

"Sorry. Jesus, I didn't know."

Abby turned to the other kid. "You work here?"

"Yeah."

"You better learn to avoid confrontations."

"But he cussed me out."

"I don't care what he did. Are you eighteen?"

"Nineteen."

"You're coming down to the station Monday and giving me a statement. Are you of age?" she asked the other boy.

"Yes, ma'am."

"Then I want to see you, too."

The front door flew open and Wally Benson, the officer on patrol duty, rushed in, his rain slicker glistening. He approached Abby. "What's up, Chief?"

"Wally, check the IDs of these two kids. This one's getting back behind the desk, and this one's going home as soon as you get the information from him. I'm going to see them both down at the station Monday."

"Right, Chief."

"Okay, folks," she said, addressing the crowd, "the show's over. Go on home."

People began disbursing. Wally had the clerk behind the counter and Emilio was with the girl, jerking his head away as she kept dabbing his cut lip. Chet stood with his hands on his hips, looking like he wanted to say something, but was fighting it. Finally he grumbled, "Nice job, Frank," and to Abby he said, "I'd put some ice on that cheek, if I was you, Miss Hooper." Then he walked away.

Abby watched him go, her face burning with embarrassment and anger. She'd given Chet the opportunity to make her look bad and he'd grabbed it. She had to salvage what dignity she had. To Frank she said, "Thanks for your help."

"Hope I didn't step on your toes."

"I asked for assistance."

After an uncomfortable hesitation, he said, "There's a reason linemen are bigger than quarterbacks, Abby. I wouldn't make anything of that."

His kindness didn't alleviate her embarrassment, however well intended it was. "You don't have to make excuses for me," she said. "I wasn't as prepared as I should have been. But you live and learn."

"It's only my opinion, but you don't have to apologize for the way you handled this. They pay you to think, Abby, not knock heads."

"Frank, you'd have made a worse chief than me," she said. "You're too softhearted."

"I don't know whether to take that as a compliment or an insult."

"Suit yourself."

He contemplated her, weighing his response. "Buy you a cup of coffee?"

Abby was in no mood for socializing, so she was inclined to turn him down. On the other hand, he'd been nice and she didn't want to hurt his feelings. And she did sort of like the guy. "I do have to get home," she said, "but I can probably spare the time for a cup of coffee."

He looked down at her stocking feet. Abby realized she wasn't exactly ready for a coffee date.

"I'll just run back and get my gear," she said.

It only took a minute to get her shoes on and gather her things. When she returned, Frank was leaning against the counter chatting with Wally Benson. Abby felt awkward to be going off with a guy right in front of one of her officers, even if it was only for coffee.

"You okay here, Wally?" she asked.

"Yep. All done. I'll just see these kids to their car."

"I'll finish this up Monday," she said, glancing at each of the boys in turn. "I'd better see you both, or there'll be hell to pay."

Each grumbled their assent and Abby followed Frank in the direction of the snack bar.

"Were you like that when you were a kid?" she asked.

"Worse. Being in trouble was a state of bliss."

"Must be in the chromosomes," Abby said.

"That's an easy one to plead guilty to," he replied.

Abby smiled and they walked in silence to the snack bar. There was one customer at the counter, otherwise the place was empty. Frank led her to a corner table, saying he'd get the coffees. Abby watched him, trying to decide what she thought of the man. Something about him was very comfortable and likable, even if he did seem more uneasy in her presence than not. He returned to the table, setting one of the paper cups filled with coffee in front of her.

"Oh, I forgot to ask," he said. "Cream or sugar?"

"No, this is fine."

Frank sat, his movements a bit ginger. His skin was sallow, his eyes sunken and he had a nasty scratch across his left cheek. The man did not look well. It was either the flu or a hangover, she couldn't tell which.

Abby didn't know Frank Keegan, but she liked his quiet, unassuming manner. Yet he had a presence that kind of simmered under the surface like a secret. That appealed to her. Men with secrets could be interesting.

Frank was younger than Chet. If she had to guess, she'd say he was twelve or thirteen years her senior, which put him at forty-five or -six. She knew little about his past other than what she'd seen on his résumé. There was nothing to indicate his life had been exceptional, but he seemed out of place in Riverton, as though maybe his body was there, but he'd left his soul somewhere else.

Best of all, there was something about his looks she really liked. Frank was above average height and his thick brown-blond hair had the sort of body that made a woman jealous. His blue eyes were too intense to be friendly and had a curious snap to them—when he was feeling well, anyway. His mouth was probably his most attractive feature and accounted for his sex appeal.

He sipped his coffee. "I've been meaning to tell you I'm sorry Chet's such an asshole when he's around you. You shouldn't take it personally, though. He's having trouble adjusting to his loss of power."

"I know he's pretty much had his way in this town for a long time," Abby said. "It can't be easy for him to be on the outside looking in."

"You're more understanding than he deserves."

"Well, I'm not losing any sleep over Chet Wilsey," she replied. "But I appreciate you saying what you did."

He peered into her pale gray eyes. "I'm sure Chet will come around in time. To be honest, I think he's still struggling with losing Sally. A guy can't be soft in every facet of his life, you know. If you cry at night, you gotta show your balls in public or you start doubting your manhood."

She listened carefully, then said, "That what it is?"

"It's my theory."

"I wish I could be that charitable. I think the whole problem is that I'm a woman."

Frank, she noticed, did not rush to deny it. He took another sip of his coffee. She took a sip of hers.

"I'm hardly one to give advice," he said, "but if there's a trick to dealing with sexism, it's not to let it get to you. When a guy like Chet sees he can't put a dint in your armor, he eventually backs off."

"I'll have to remember that." Abby heard the touch of snideness in her tone and wondered if it was excessive. Men loved to give advice, and she couldn't help but feel defensive when they did because the implication was that women needed help, which wasn't necessarily true. Frank was probably innocent because there was no doubt he meant well. It was hard to make exceptions and hard to back away, once you'd gone in that direction. Being too nice was as much a problem as being too harsh, and it was something she always had to guard against, which was a hell of a commentary on modern life. "So, what happened to your face?" she asked, changing direction. "Looks like you've had a run-in with someone or something."

"Yeah," he said, "it sure does." He fingered his cup. "I'm embarrassed to say I don't know what happened. Last night I had a few too many and after a certain point I don't remember a thing." Then he added, "That's not normally my M.O., but I'll sometimes stray on a special occasion."

"So, what was the occasion?"

He gave her a bemused grin. "Yesterday was Valentine's Day, Chief."

"Oh, that's right," she said, flushing.

"Seems like your love life is about as exciting as mine."

Abby felt herself color even more, hiding behind her coffee cup. "Personal subject," she said.

Their conversation came to an awkward pause, and Abby rued the fact that social situations had never been her forte. She didn't enjoy dating, at least at first, before she got to know the person well enough to relax.

"You haven't ever been married, I take it," he said.

"From one personal subject to another," she replied.

"Sorry."

Abby thought better of her response. "But to answer your question, no, I haven't. How about you?"

"Oh, yeah. Married for fifteen years, divorced for ten. We've each moved on to better things. Arlene married a gynecologist after we split. They live in the big house in Seacliff in the city, drive the fancy cars, do the big social number. You know the story. She got what she really wanted."

Abby detected acceptance, maybe even relief in his voice. "Have any kids?"

Frank shifted uncomfortably. "We had a daughter."

She could see instantly she'd gotten into a sensitive area, but didn't expect what he said next.

"Beth drowned out at Ocean Beach when she was fifteen. Goofing off with friends. It was nobody's fault. Poor judgment."

"Frank, I'm sorry."

"Not a subject to dwell on," he said, his pain evident.

She watched him take his own turn hiding behind his coffee cup and knew she was getting her first good look at his soft underbelly. It wasn't often she had conversations like this with men, certainly not since returning to Riverton. But his suffering did make her feel closer to him—something she was quite sure he couldn't appreciate. Hell of a way to live, when you stopped to think about it.

Just then Wally Benson appeared at the entrance to the café. Spotting them, he hurried back to their table.

"Chief," he said, "we got a situation."

"What kind of situation?"

"Sandy Mendoza is out at Watermark Slough and asked for assistance. I told him you were here and he said he'd like to talk to you." Wally handed her his radio.

Sandy Mendoza was a big good-looking Latino, a Jimmy Smits type, but with a real soft manner. He had a cute little blond Anglo wife and three darling kids, age two, three and four. He was a solid police officer and her favorite. "This is Chief Hooper, Sandy," she said into the radio. "What's up?"

"We got us a body, Chief."

"A body?"

"Yeah, a teenage girl, maybe thirteen, fourteen, something like that. On the bank of Watermark Slough. Just inside the city limits unfortunately."

"Can you tell what happened to her, Sandy?"

"Looks to me like she might have drowned, except for the fact she's on the shore. Thing is, she's naked as a jaybird. Not a stitch of clothes on and none around. Could be a homicide."

Abby felt a twinge in her gut. "You don't recognize her?"

"Can't say that I do, Chief," Sandy's voice crackled over the radio. "I got the site secure, though. And the county lab people are on the way. I knew you'd want to know."

"Yeah, thanks." Abby thought for a moment, aware of both Frank and Wally listening in. "Who found her, Sandy?" she asked.

"Sam and Bert Aspeth. They'd just launched their new boat at the ramp and were headed up to the river for a test run."

"Where, exactly?"

"At Frank Keegan's place."

Abby looked over at Frank, who'd been listening. His brows rose right along with hers.

"The body was by his boat," Sandy went on, oblivious to Frank's presence on the other end. "I went over and banged on his door, but nobody's home."

"Yeah, I know," she said. "As a matter of fact, Frank's here in town with me. Hold the fort and we'll be right out."

"Roger."

Abby handed the radio back to Wally. "Head on out there," she told him. "Frank and I will be along."

Benson gave Frank an uncertain look, then went off. Abby stared at Frank. After a minute he shook his head, seemingly reading her thoughts.

"I have no idea," he said. "None."

"Well, let's hope it has nothing to do with your bad night."

Abby got to her feet and so did Frank, looking very somber, indeed. She had a sick feeling in her gut, the kind that really hurt. Worse even than cramps.

Watermark Slough

Frank stood atop the levee, watching Abby and the technicians from the county crime lab at work on his dock and boat. His hands were in his pockets. The collar of his jacket was turned up against the wind that whistled across the Delta from the Carquinez Straits and San Francisco Bay beyond. The rain had stopped and the gray clouds were beginning to clear.

An opaque plastic tarp had been placed on the body about

fifteen minutes ago. Until then, the slender corpse had lain forlorn and naked at water's edge, looking more like a clay sculpture than the dead body of a young girl. Even at a distance he could see signs of rigor mortis and lividity, the localized discoloration of the skin. The position of the body had not allowed him to see her face clearly, but there were other bits of evidence that this had been a person—light brown hair flowing lavalike from the cranium, matching sets of washboard ribs under the pallid skin of the torso, knobby knees and long narrow feet, still too big for the body, a small dark patch at the pubis, two little breasts scarcely more than puddles of flesh.

This was clearly not someone who'd been dead for a very long time, and yet he was glad he was some distance from the body. Even the first hours after death did not present a pretty picture. Frank was glad they'd covered her for another reason, though—Beth.

His daughter had been in the mortuary by the time they'd gotten word to him. Her body hadn't been badly ravished by the sea, but enough damage had been done that Arlene had refused to have the casket open. He never saw his child in death and so their final goodbye had been impersonal, based entirely on what he'd been told. It didn't matter, though, because his imagination was vivid. Too damned vivid, actually.

Beth's panic—the terror she must have felt in the waning moments of her life—was the unbearable part. He hadn't handled that well and this was a harsh reminder.

Frank gazed up the slough in the direction of town in an attempt to get his mind off the morbidity of the situation. Were it not for the remote location, a crowd would have gathered. As it was, he was the lone observer and Sandy Mendoza the lone sentry. Wally Benson had left to take care of an automobile accident on the bridge in town.

Before he and Abby had arrived, Sandy had sent the Aspeths home. Bert, who was in his eighties, wasn't feeling well, and his son, Sam, wanted to get him out of the cold. Sam was the current proprietor of the Aspeth Drugstore, having taken the reins from his father, who'd taken them from his father thirty years earlier. The chances that they were involved in the girl's death were negligible. The thought wouldn't enter anyone's mind.

At the Delta Lanes, when they'd walked to their cars, Abby had scarcely said a word. He couldn't blame her. Did she treat him like a colleague or a suspect? As Frank drove home, Abby following, he realized how badly he needed to assure her he was no more involved than the Aspeths—because if he was, he would have remembered something. Surely.

At the foot of the rough-hewn steps leading down to the dock, the technicians and Abby continued their examination of the scene. Frank looked off to the southwest in the direction of Mount Diablo, rising conelike beyond the far edge of the Delta. Nearer, a huge military cargo plane circled lazily on its lumbering approach to Travis AFB. It was from there that thousands of GIs had taken off for Southeast Asia twenty-five, thirty years ago, Frank among them. Sitting in his boat in the slough or up on the river, he often saw the planes, though he didn't always think of Vietnam. But the dead girl and this particular plane had conspired, it seemed, to bring back seldom visited memories.

He had not had a horrible war, as wars went, having seen a lot of action in only four of the twelve months he was in country. He'd been wounded, but his injuries weren't serious. He'd seen some things he wished he hadn't seen. And, like most everybody who'd gone, the experience of war had changed him.

The senselessness of it had gotten to him more than anything. In ways, the quieter months had been the worst. His base had been the target of frequent mortar and artillery attacks, which was more insidious. Survival turned almost entirely on chance; skill and caution having little or nothing to do with it. The experience had taught him the necessity of ignoring those things you're powerless to affect.

The scratch on his face hardly seemed to fall in that category. Ultimately he had no reason for concern because, drunk or sober, he was not the kind of man who would hurt anyone—especially not a young girl.

Sandy Mendoza, who'd been moving about the perimeter of the crime scene with guard-dog diligence, joined him at the top of the levee. "What do you make of it, Frank?"

"I haven't a clue. Any sign of how she might have died? Any obvious trauma?"

"Not that I could see. Just scratches."

Frank restrained himself from touching his cheek.

"I hate it when something like this happens to a kid," Sandy said, his tone philosophical. "Makes me think of my own."

Frank could empathize with that. God, could he ever. Sandy had no idea about Beth, he was sure, or he never would have made the remark. Frank kept his personal life, especially the past, pretty quiet. Kay knew more about him than anyone. Chet and a few others in town were aware of his daughter. Mostly he was known for who he was now— a private investigator of sorts, a pear farmer of sorts, and the failed candidate for police chief.

Sandy ambled off without saying anything more and Frank stared down at Abby, who was talking to one of the technicians. Ironically, he found her cute, even when she was doing her police-chief thing. He liked looking at her.

The thing he hated most about this—apart from the fact he didn't know what the hell had happened last night—was that Abby was cop and he was suspect. That wasn't exactly an ideal formula for friendship, or anything else.

Not that there was any percentage in thinking in those

terms. Eventually Abby would find out about him and her mother and that would be it, assuming he had a chance with her in the first place.

Frank couldn't say he regretted his relationship with Kay Ingram, though, even now. Whatever else may have been lacking, he had to admit the woman understood him. Actually, their friendship had not been easy to define. They'd gotten acquainted the first year he was in town, and their mutual appreciation of margaritas and cribbage led in time to margaritas and cribbage at his place. The affair lasted a couple of years. Throughout the months they played cribbage, whether at the Queen, at his kitchen table or in bed, he had kept track of wins and losses. That is, until the day Kay announced that seeing all those marks on his little red spiral pad made her feel old. Frank did a final tally before tossing the notebook. Kay's last victory put her ahead 175 to 174. "That's a lot of fucking," she said. "You've had me more than some of my husbands." To hear Kay talk about it, you'd have thought she'd been married a dozen times, though it had only been three.

The turning point in their relationship had come that same day. After another margarita she'd told him she was good for one more shot at marriage. Later she'd regretted it, even apologized. But with that statement, she'd tipped her hand. Though the affair lasted another three or four months, things were never the same.

Even dropping by the Queen hadn't been easy, especially the past month or so after the police-chief thing had come up. Frank had made himself particularly scarce after his loss, partly due to embarrassment at losing, but also because he knew Abby was an awkward subject for Kay.

The thing he found perplexing was why Kay and Abby's alienation continued. As far as he knew, Abby had never been to the Queen. Once he'd asked Chet if he knew what was behind their problem. "If I had to guess," Chet had said,

"I trace it back to Ty and his feelings about the divorce. He and the girl were real close." Beyond that, it was a mystery.

Another aspect of the Kay-Abby issue that was little discussed was how it fit into town politics. Because of Kay's connections with the business community, which had controlled the town for years, she had been associated with the coalition that supported Frank and was, by implication, against the one that supported her daughter. Kay had kept a low profile, but it was no secret whose side she was on. What people talked about most wasn't that Kay and Abby were in different camps, but rather that both behaved as though the other didn't exist.

The issues were personal, true, but the demographics played a role. Riverton had more than one identity. Abby, three of the five council members and most of the town's rank-and-file voters, especially those who lived in the Bottoms, were associated with one faction. Kay, Chet, the Chamber of Commerce and the folks who lived in the tonier Grove section of town were associated with the other.

There was also a division along gender lines. Riverton, being small and fairly isolated, had embraced women's issues with less alacrity than the urban areas. Abby's election, in a subtle, indirect way, had been a feminist shot across Riverton's paternalistic bow, though nobody had characterized it that way. The women's revolution, if that was the right term, had come to town quietly, like the proverbial thief in the night. Frank's biggest regret was that he had been forced to take sides on the issue.

All that paled aside the circumstances he found himself in now, though. The thing that bothered him most was knowing Abby had to be suspicious of him. And he wasn't looking forward to the time when Kay would be brought into it as a material witness, if in no other capacity.

Down below, Abby had finished her conversation with the technician and was headed up the steep steps he himself had cut into the bank of the levee. Frank watched her wind her way up the rocky slope. She was evidently in good shape because she wasn't breathing hard when she arrived at the top, but her cheeks were rosy from the cold air, her eyes glistening.

Without saying anything, she handed over a Polaroid shot of the girl's face that Sandy had taken before the technicians had arrived. Frank, his stomach knotting at the thought this, too, had happened to his own child, examined the photo. Except for the puffiness around the mouth and flatness beneath the lids of the eyes, it could have been a photo of a girl dozing on the beach. The hair looked dirty and brittle, but the brows and lashes appeared normal. She was pubescent, but the promise of womanly beauty was already in her features.

"Ever seen her?" Abby asked after a few moments.

He shook his head. "No."

"Nobody else has, either. She must not be local."

Frank stared at the photo. "Somebody's going to miss her soon."

"Yeah, she probably won't stay a Jane Doe for long."

The two of them stared across Tyler Island at the fallow fields and largely treeless landscape, their hands in their pockets. Tyler Island, like all the others in the Delta, was reclaimed swampland, protected by a system of dikes and levees. These vast tracks, some actually below sea level, were islands in the sense they were surrounded on all sides by either a river, a slough or a lake. In winter, especially, the landscape could be stark. He noticed Abby give a little shiver.

"Any idea how she died?" he asked, knowing they would have to talk about it eventually.

"She might have drowned. They're certain she was in the water. But she could have been dead before going in."

"You're saying it wasn't an accidental drowning."

"The autopsy will tell us more," she replied. "There are no obvious signs of trauma. And there's the little matter of how she got out of the water. Dead people don't crawl out on their own."

"Are you saying homicide, then?"

Abby looked at him pointedly. "I'm not saying anything just yet, Frank. Let me put it this way. The fact that she's naked, it's the dead of winter, and there are no clothes around, is suspicious."

"How long do they think she's been dead?"

"We've got rigor mortis and fixed lividity. I saw the technician press the livor marks. There was no blanching. If it was today she died, it was very early today."

"As, for example, last night."

"For example."

Frank didn't need to be a genius to see where this was headed. Even his hangover couldn't spare him. The obvious was pretty obvious.

"They're certain she was moved," Abby went on in the matter-of-fact tone of a professional, though the unpleasantness of the conversation she couldn't hide. "And probably not just from the water to the shore. The patterns of the discoloration and lividity indicate she might have been moved more than once."

"Did the Aspeths pull her out of the water?" Frank asked.

Abby shook her head. "They didn't touch her. They never even got out of their boat. She was lying just like she is now when they first spotted her."

"So we know somebody else was involved," he said. "The question was if it was before she was dead or after."

"Or both."

"Yes," he agreed, "or both."

Abby stared down at the technicians who continued with their labors. Frank watched, too, his uncomfortable feeling getting decidedly more uncomfortable. He knew this was only the beginning.

"What else do they have?"

She drew a long, slow breath. "There are some pretty heavy abrasions on her heels."

"Her heels? That's not an injury that's going to kill anyone."

"No, they're theorizing she may have been dragged. Like maybe down these steps here."

"And by implication killed somewhere else."

"Possibly," Abby said. "They also found traces of blood on the lower steps."

"Which is consistent."

"It appears most of it was washed away by the rain, but there were collectable samples."

"That's good."

"Frank," she said, looking at him darkly, "it wouldn't be good if the blood was from someone other than the victim."

"Do you know it isn't?"

"Not yet," she said.

She looked at the gash on his face, making him all the more uncomfortable. "Well, no need borrowing trouble," he said, trying hard to sound upbeat, but without much success.

"My job is to look for trouble," she said. "You know that."

He sensed it was time to start getting specific. "You trying to say something, Abby? If so, you might as well spit it out."

"I'm going to be asking you some questions," she replied. "Under the circumstances you might…"

"Wish to have an attorney present?"

She winced.

"If you're concerned about procedure, don't be," he said. "You've advised me of my rights. Consider it done."

"This is no laughing matter," she said.

"Look, neither of us has a problem unless I did something to that girl down there, and I didn't."

"You know that for a fact?"

"I have no recollection of her whatsoever."

"That's not the same."

"It's true I don't remember a thing after drinking at the River Queen, but that doesn't mean I committed a crime."

"It doesn't mean you didn't, either."

"Sounds like you have some physical evidence down there. That ought to help determine things one way or the other."

Abby turned her back to the wind and gazed silently into the middle distance. Below them, on the leeward side of the levee, his trailer house lay in shadow, a mute witness to God knows what. Behind it, his eighteen acres of pear trees spread out as far as the water table would allow, their branches winter naked, a tiny army of tuft-headed soldiers, too few in number to be formidable, but sufficiently numerous to provide a tax write-off for their liege lord.

"I don't like this any more than you," she finally said to him.

Frank stared at the bleak landscape beyond his orchard, painfully aware of the body lying cold and lifeless under the tarp down at water's edge. "You know what the worst thing about this is, apart from the kid dying?" he said.

"What?"

"Knowing you've got suspicions."

"Frank, it's my job to be suspicious, you know that. Anyway, I'm the least of your problems. It'd be one thing if you knew how you got that cut on your face. It's another thing completely that you don't."

"I want to be constructive," he said. "What can I do to help?"

"I plan on questioning you formally, but it doesn't have to be right now. How about Monday morning?"

"Before or after the kids from the bowling alley?"

Abby actually smiled, despite herself. "I'll work you in, Frank, don't worry. And bring your lawyer if you want."

"I don't need one."

"That's your decision." She shifted uncomfortably. "Do you mind if I have Sandy take a picture of those scratches on your face?"

"No, be my guest."

She nodded as though his answer pleased her. She called to Sandy Mendoza to bring his Polaroid. He got the camera from the patrol car and ambled over.

"Chief?"

"Frank and I would like you to take a couple of shots of his face."

Mendoza blinked. He turned his handsome head back and forth between them.

"We're both cops," Frank explained, "which means we have a preference for physical evidence and a natural aversion to oral testimony."

Sandy nodded, though Frank was certain he didn't understand. Frank took off his cap and Sandy took four shots from different angles. The three of them examined the results.

"God," Frank said, gazing at the pictures, "I look like shit."

Abby handed the photos to Sandy, along with the one of the girl. "Take these and put them in an evidence bag and label it," she said.

"Right, Chief."

They watched Mendoza head off.

"Suppose he's ever worked a homicide scene?" Frank asked.

"Considering there hasn't been a homicide in Riverton for eighteen years, I doubt it. Dix Fowler's probably the only sworn personnel I've got who remembers that one, and he's squeamish about the sight of blood."

"Dix is a good old boy," Frank said, "but he worshiped the ground Chet walked on. You should bear that in mind."

"Thanks for the advice," she said, "but Dix Fowler also happens to worship his impending pension. And I can affect that a lot more than Chet at this point."

Frank shrugged.

"But to get back to the matter at hand," she said, "I really would consider hiring a lawyer. It's no time to be macho."

"Are you saying that because you care?"

She gave him a look of disapproval. "Don't be flip," she said. "I'm treating this very seriously and you should, as well."

"All right," he said, "point taken. Any other advice?"

"Yeah. Find out from your drinking buddies what you did last night and who brought you home. I want to talk to everybody concerned, even if that means camping out at the River Queen." She did not mention her mother's name. She didn't have to. "Unless you have some questions yourself, Frank, I'm out of here."

"No questions, Chief. But I do want to say something before you go."

She waited.

"I'm sorry this got dumped on you," he said. "And I'm sorry we're on opposing sides again. Really sorry about that."

She zipped up her jacket to her chin. "Believe it or not, Frank, so am I."

Tyler Island

Abby lay in her bed at last, thankful to be off her feet, thankful this miserable day was almost over. Across the room the TV set was on, but the sound was off. She tended to turn the damned thing on for company, which wasn't a good reason. Often she didn't bother looking at the set, but the flickering images did offer comfort, sort of like burning logs in a fireplace.

It was raining again, the tattoo on the windowpane making her glad for the warmth and shelter of the house where she'd grown up. Drawing her knees up to her chest, Abby listened to the low roll of thunder somewhere off across the Delta and clutched the hot-water bottle more firmly to her abdomen. As was so often the case when she was blue, she wondered if returning to Riverton had been a mistake.

During the three months she'd been back, her feelings had vacillated between satisfaction and uncertainty. The new job was a career opportunity, yes, but hardly a spectacular one. Maybe it was the challenge that appealed to her—the need to disprove the old saw that you can never go home again.

Of course, Riverton was a far cry from the town she'd once known. Her father was gone now and her mother had returned. That was probably the central irony of the whole business. Kay Ingram, a mover and shaker, on the turf that had once belonged exclusively to her and her father. It almost seemed obscene.

Abby had struggled mightily to convince herself that Kay would not be a factor in her decision. But, in spite of that, her mother's presence had probably been a bigger factor than she was prepared to admit. Abby knew there were deep passions surrounding her childhood, whether or not she'd convinced herself they'd been laid to rest.

In fairness, though, there were other elements involved that had nothing to do with her family life. She had spent so much time on her own, fighting the fight of a woman in a man's world, that she could hardly turn her back on the challenge posed by Chet Wilsey and his cronies. It was still too early to tell how that one would play out, but she was fully committed to the struggle.

Now, though, she had this Jane Doe case to contend with. It was her first big challenge involving police work, as opposed to administration. Everybody would be watching her closely, which was fine because this was her career and she wanted to do well. Her immediate problem was Frank Keegan. She hated to think he was involved in foul play, not only because she liked the guy, but because there were a whole bunch of political implications. People wouldn't have to use their imaginations much to perceive her as vindictive.

Justice, however, was her primary concern. Abby knew that a suspect's innocence or guilt was rarely in doubt as far as the investigator was concerned. But this drowning was an instance where her instincts had told her nothing. Frank could be in big trouble. Manslaughter or even negligent homicide were serious offenses. That scratch on his face was not a good sign. And she was stuck in the middle. She could no more ignore it than she could rush to judgment. The field was littered with land mines.

Abby groaned, turning to her other side and adjusting the hot-water bottle. She glanced around her room, realizing she still wasn't used to being back in her childhood home. Her father had been alive the last time she'd lived here, and after so many years away, she'd forgotten how isolated the old Hooper mansion truly was.

But country life was in her blood. When she'd been quite young, of an age when most kids hungered for playmates, Abby had found the isolation appealing. There wasn't another dwelling within half a mile, yet the seeming seclusion had led to a false sense of security. Once, when she was in high school, her father had caught a group of boys parked over on the road with a telescope mounted on a ladder in the bed of their pickup. They'd been watching her undress in her second-floor room for weeks and, considering all the time she spent in her underwear, or even naked during the heat of summer, she'd been absolutely mortified at the discovery.

Though her father had lived in the Victorian all his life, he had lost interest in the place after Abby had left home. In his waning years, he'd allowed the structure to sink into a somber melancholy. After his death, she had let the house sit vacant, though the farmland had been leased out. A few months before she'd made her decision to return, Abby decided to rescue the old house. She'd had the exterior painted a cheerful violet with white trim, and extensively renovated the interior. And even though it was not the sort of home a young woman alone would be expected to choose for herself, Abby found it suited her.

In the midst of her reminiscing, the phone rang. She crawled over to the bedside table. "Chief Hooper," she said, affecting her usual businesslike tone.

"Good God," came a woman's voice, "you actually answer the phone that way?"

The voice was familiar. "Crystal?"

"Yeah, you got it in one. What's with the Chief Hooper business?"

"I thought maybe it was somebody at the department calling," Abby explained. "Nobody normal ever phones at this hour."

"I never claimed to be normal," Crystal said with a laugh. "Lesbians aren't by definition, you know. Just ask Pat Robertson."

Abby laughed. "Thanks, but I'd rather not."

Hearing Crystal Armstrong's voice raised her spirits. Months would go by between phone calls, but it never seemed to make a difference to their friendship. Crystal was one person with whom she could banter and still feel perfectly at ease. Her friend could be outrageous, even profane, but Crystal was nothing if not loyal. The fact that her best friend was a lesbian was an advantage, as far as she was concerned. Talking to Crystal was a little like talking to a man, but without the disadvantages.

When they'd first met, there'd been some feeling out on Crystal's part, but once Abby had made it clear what she was and was not interested in, the underlying tension had gone away. "You know what I like best?" Crystal had once told her. "Having somebody who's straight accept me for who I am." There'd been tears in her eyes when she'd said it.

"I know I've been a real flake for not calling to see how you're doing," Crystal said, "but you know me, I tend to wait until I need something."

There was a hesitancy in Crystal's voice, a wariness. "Don't tell me," Abby said. "You're pregnant."

Crystal barked her amusement at the suggestion. "Even better. I've become a prizefighter, kiddo!"

"A what?"

"A prizefighter, Abby. You know—Rocky, Ali, Tyson, Evander. Left, right, left, right...pow, down for the count."

"Crystal!"

"The other girl's down for the count. Not me. That's what I meant. Hell, I'm unbeaten. Of course, I'm not having my first fight until next Thursday."

"Are you serious or are you smoking something?"

"Dead serious. I'm an official member of the Women's International Boxing Federation, lightweight class. That's 135 pounds, in case you're wondering."

"Crystal, why?"

"For the same reason you wanted to be police chief. You know—it seemed like a good idea at the time."

"Yeah, well, what if you get hurt?"

"What the hell, I don't like my nose, anyway. The only problem is I'm sort of alone in this thing. I've got nobody to buck me up. I'll admit it, Abby, I'm kinda scared."

"What you need is somebody to take you in to have your head examined," Abby said.

"Not you, too!"

Abby heard the pain, the disappointment, in Crystal's voice and felt terrible. "Hey, I'm sorry," she said. "It's just that the thought of you in a boxing ring is a little hard to fathom. What prompted you, if that's not too indiscreet a question?''

"Fame and fortune, I guess. Abby, there's girls who make forty, fifty, sixty Gs a match. Not in Sacramento yet, but it's coming. And when the big money's there, I wanna be a contender. Is that so ridiculous? Hell, I can't sing or hit a baseball. I can't act. What's left?"

Abby absently rubbed her stomach. "I can see you've thought this through."

"Can you think of a better way for a thirty-year-old to put a little zest in her life?''

"For me, prizefighting would come a little farther down the list," Abby said. "But pray tell, when did all this happen?"

"I been training three months."

"And the fight's Thursday."

"Yeah, at Memorial Auditorium. I'm on the undercard for a couple of male junior lightweight contenders. It's the real thing, Abby, and I'm nervous as hell. I haven't told too many people, but I was sort of hoping you could come. I could use a screaming fanatic pulling for me."

Abby was touched. "Sure, I'll come to see you fight. Barring an emergency."

"Great. Perfect. You made my day."

Abby looked over at the flickering TV set. The late local news was coming on, and she was curious to see how they'd report the Jane Doe case. Two mobile news crews had shown up at the crime scene late that afternoon. She'd been interviewed for about fifteen minutes, but if her previous experience was any indication, that would be good for maybe fifteen seconds of airtime.

"There's another reason I called," Crystal said, bringing her back. "I got a message for you from Darren." There was a wary pause, then she went on. "The little twit's back in town and wants to know if he can see you. I said I wouldn't give him your phone number, let alone your address, without checking with you first.''

For a second Abby was stunned. ''What does…he…''

''Want? I don't know. Sex, probably. Do jerks like my brother ever change?''

Abby was rarely surprised at anything Crystal Armstrong said or did. She had never hesitated to take Abby's side against Darren, even though she loved him like he was her own child, and would defend him with her life.

Darren had once told Abby that when he and Crystal were teenagers, growing up in the mean streets of North Highlands, Crystal had jumped into the middle of a knife fight and kicked butt to save him from getting his throat slit. Then, when they got home, she'd damn near killed him for getting into the situation to begin with. That, in a nutshell, was Crystal Armstrong.

''Seriously,'' Abby said, ''what's going on?''

''Well, the little bastard shows up out of the blue and says he's home. In the next breath he's asking about you. I tell him you're married and have six kids. He says, 'So when's her husband's poker night?' Hell, Abby, who knows what's up with him? Your guess is as good as mine.''

''What happened to Shelly?''

''Still in L.A., I guess. Darren probably got tired of screwing her. That's the way it is with guys, isn't it? Hell, you'd know better than me.''

Abby didn't like it that the mention of Darren Armstrong sent a twinge through her. She'd conditioned herself to hate him and here she was having twinges. Why did Crystal have to bring him up? But then it occurred to Abby the reference to Darren—or for that matter, the call—wasn't all that innocent. Another shoe was about to drop, she was sure of it.

''Oh, but speaking of Darren…'' Crystal said.

Abby's heart gave a lurch. She knew it. This was the real point of the call. ''Yeah, what about him?''

"I know you don't want to hear this, but he really wants to see you."

Abby groaned. "The feeling's not mutual."

"That's what I figured," she said lightly. "So tell me to tell him to go to hell."

Abby hesitated. "All right. Tell him to go to hell."

"Okay, fine, I will. And can I tell him about his getting you pregnant?"

An icy sensation went through her. The pregnancy Crystal so indelicately brought up was something Abby had pushed from her consciousness with such grim determination that sometimes she wondered if it had really happened at all.

"No," she said. "Absolutely not."

"Uh-oh."

Abby had a sinking feeling. Suddenly she knew. "You told him."

"I didn't mean to," Crystal moaned, "but we had this big fight…and, well, it just kind of slipped out."

"Shit," Abby said.

There was another rumble of thunder, this one closer than the last. Abby glanced at the window, which a couple hours ago had been a blur of diaphanous silk. It was now a mirror.

"Crystal," she said, "I could just kill you."

"So cheer for Mulroney Thursday night. I deserve it."

Abby tried to sort out the implications. "Tell me what Darren said when you told him."

"Nothing," Crystal replied. "He was shocked. Asked me if you'd had an abortion and I said yes, the weekend he told you *hasta la vista* and took Shelly to Tahoe."

Abby moaned. "That secret was supposed to die with you, Crystal Armstrong."

"I know. I'm a total airhead. What can I say?"

Abby thought for a moment. "I have a feeling this is all leading somewhere," she said, "so just spit it out."

"Well, under the circumstances Darren says he absolutely,

positively has to see you. Dumping somebody is part of life—he says he doesn't owe you an apology for that. But the pregnancy, the abortion, what you went through, calls for an apology."

"Tell him I don't want his apology." Abby heard Crystal put her hand to the phone. There was mumbling, and she realized that Darren Armstrong was there.

Crystal came back on the line. "Guess who just walked in?"

Abby was furious. She considered hanging up but knew that was too immature. "Put the sonovabitch on," she grumbled.

There was more fumbling. Then she heard his voice, the man with the golden loins, the man who'd taught her the hard part about being a woman. It was a voice she hadn't heard in three and a half years. "Abby? Hello, you there?"

Her stomach fibrillated like a dying heart. "Hello, Darren."

"I just have this one thing to say," he said. "I'd like ten, fifteen minutes of your time, max. At your convenience."

"First, it's unnecessary, and second, I don't want to see you."

"Every sinner's entitled to his penance," he said hastily.

"Not at my expense."

"Dinner," he said. "Just dinner."

"Darren, I just said no to ten minutes of my time. Now you're asking me to dinner?"

"It's a negotiating ploy."

She could see that white-tooth smile and the cute-as-hell grin lines as vividly as if he had just walked into the room. From the day he'd swooped down in that medevac chopper and whisked her and her dying partner to the Med Center, the male of the species had been an entirely different and often daunting proposition. The blue eyes and Brad Pitt hair. The narrow hips. The shoulders. The boots. The headphones.

The droopy fistful of flowers as he stood at the foot of her hospital bed the next day. That goddamn grin. Of course she was going to fuck him on their first date and every date thereafter. Did she really have a choice?

"No," she said.

"I'll beg."

"Fuck you, Darren."

"I'd say we're making progress."

"No."

"Please."

"No."

"I need, really need, to tell you I'm sorry."

"No."

"I have your address."

"No, you don't."

"I beat it out of my punch-drunk sister."

"I don't want to see you, Darren."

"There's nothing in it for me but an easier conscience."

Abby thought of what one of her instructors at the academy once said—never draw your weapon unless you're prepared to shoot. Darren Armstrong needed to be shot. Calmly, coolly, she hung up the phone.

Watermark Slough

Frank had warmed up some canned stew in the microwave, but he hadn't eaten much. And three hours later it made him sick to look at the bowl, still sitting on his kitchen counter. The thought of food wasn't any more appetizing now than it had been at dinner. It seemed his stomach hadn't recovered from the previous night. That, and the fact that he'd been nervous as a pregnant cow, waiting for Kay Ingram to return his call. Surely she'd gotten back from San Francisco. It was damned near eleven o'clock.

Frank flushed the contents of the bowl down the garbage

disposal and stuck it in the dishwasher. He did a little more cleaning up in the kitchen, then went into the front room and dropped into his favorite chair. After a minute he got up to turn on the TV, then thought better of it and dropped back down into the chair. There was no point in watching the news again—once was enough.

His name hadn't been mentioned in the coverage of the Jane Doe case, though Abby had been interviewed. She'd sounded calm and competent. That was good for her and good for Riverton, but he couldn't get it out of his mind that he was a suspect. Worse still, he couldn't be sure himself he was innocent, though to have actually hurt that girl seemed impossible.

The problem was that the evidence against him was mounting. After Abby left, he'd gone back inside his mobile home and taken a good look around. He'd found semen stains on his bedsheets, and that wasn't good. It might even be devastating, since he hadn't had a woman there in months. Those shady recollections of having sex were apparently based on fact, not fantasy.

His concern was that Jane Doe might have spent time in his bed before ending up naked and dead on the beach beside his dock. How it could have happened with him drunk out of his mind was beyond him. But he couldn't come up with another likely candidate for sex, other than Kay, and she wasn't returning his call.

If Jane Doe had had intercourse before she died, evidence of it would likely turn up in the autopsy. Forensics being what they were these days, he'd be implicated or cleared. But that would take time.

Frank fought the urge to phone Kay again. He had no way of knowing whether she'd already heard about the girl, but he hoped not. The chances, he reasoned, were better of getting a straight, unemotional response if she didn't know about the body by his dock. The other possibility was that she *had* heard about the incident and was too horrified to return the call.

Frustrated, he got up to turn on the TV again when the telephone rang. "Thank God," he murmured. He snatched up the phone. "Hello?"

"Frank?"

He instantly recognized Kay's voice. "Oh, good, it's you."

"I called my answering machine," she said, "and there was an urgent message from you. What's wrong?"

The innocence in her voice hit him hard. On the one hand, it meant she probably hadn't heard about the girl. On the other, it was not the tone of a woman who'd had sex with him the night before. Had they been intimate, she'd have been embarrassed, tense. Still, he managed to gather himself, forcing calmness.

"Kay, please tell me what happened last night."

"Last night? You mean you don't remember?"

"I remember getting drunk at the Queen and I remember us talking. You took my keys, and after that I assume I had a few more margaritas. From that point on it's almost a complete blank."

Kay cleared her throat. "Well, you got obnoxious and I finally had to run you out. Actually, I escorted you out myself."

"How'd I get home?"

"I drove you, Frank, in your truck. Don't you remember that, either?"

"No."

Several moments of silence passed. "Well, I guess you were worse off than I thought," she said.

"Kay, what did we do when we got to my place?"

There was a long silence.

"Kay?"

"What did we *do?*" she asked disdainfully. "Nothing. I dropped you off and I left. Didn't Toad return your truck?"

"Yes, this morning, but he couldn't tell me anything about last night."

"That's because he didn't work last night."

"I know that," he said. "But I'm trying to piece things together and I'm not getting much help."

"What do you expect from me, Frank? A blow-by-blow account of your evening?" Her voice had turned sharp.

"Look," he said, "I apologize. I'm not accusing you of anything. I'm frustrated."

"Maybe there's a lesson in that."

"Please," he begged. "Tell me exactly what happened. Did you drop me off up at the road or what?"

"No, you were too drunk. I took you to your front door. You couldn't get your key in the lock so I opened it for you."

"Did you go inside with me?"

Again she hesitated. "No. You told me you were okay and I decided that was good enough. So I closed the door and left."

Frank's heart sank.

"Is there a problem?" she asked.

"Possibly. I don't know yet."

"What do you mean?"

"Listen, when you brought me home, did you see anyone else around?"

"No, who would be around at that time of the night? Frank, what's going on?"

He sighed. "When did you get home? Just a while ago?"

"I'm not at home," she said. "I'm in San Francisco. Like I told you, I called my machine for messages and when I heard yours I telephoned immediately because you said it was urgent. You still haven't explained why."

He cleared his throat. "Kay, Sam and Bert Aspeth found a dead girl by my dock this morning. No one knows how she died yet, but she was totally naked. A corpse turns up at my place and I have no memory of what happened last night. Are you beginning to see the problem?''

''My God,'' she said.

''My sentiments precisely.''

''Surely they don't think you killed her.''

''I can't even convince myself I had nothing to do with it, let alone the police. That's not to say I'm guilty, because I've never hurt anyone that way and can't imagine doing it. On the other hand, I was more or less out of my mind.''

''Oh, Frank…''

''Yeah, well, I was hoping you might be able to tell me something to put me at ease, if only that I was too far gone to rape anyone.''

There was no response from her for several moments, then Kay asked, ''Was she raped?''

Frank could see he was getting ahead of himself. ''It's possible. They're doing an autopsy.''

''You aren't a rapist, Frank Keegan. Drunk or sober. And certainly not a murderer. That, I'm sure of.''

''Thanks. It means a lot to me that you'd say that.''

''You can be an asshole at times,'' she quickly added, ''but not a criminal.''

He chuckled. ''I guess I spoke too soon.''

There was another lull, then she said, ''If you need me to vouch for you, Frank, I will.''

He appreciated the gesture, but at the moment the only testimony she could give that would truly serve him would be to say *she'd* slept with him. At least it would have put *his* mind at ease. ''I appreciate you calling,'' he said. ''And I'm glad you only consider me an asshole.''

Kay laughed. ''Don't worry,'' she said. ''You're a benign asshole.''

''Good night, Kay.''

''Good night.''

Frank hung up the phone, knowing he was no better off than before, except that he still had a friend...of sorts, somebody who believed in him...kind of. The other thing that was apparent was that if Kay had called from San Francisco, she was with Mort Anderson. He'd been deluding himself with the notion Kay might have gotten it on with him. Whoever he'd laid, it wasn't her. Now he had to pray it wasn't Jane Doe.

Sunday
February 16th

Watermark Slough

Frank Keegan had a bad night. He couldn't get Jane Doe out of his mind. Then, when he finally slept, he had restless dreams, some of them about his daughter. He woke up depressed, wondering what in the hell he'd done.

It was the neediest he'd felt in a long time. Since his divorce he'd become emotionally self-sufficient out of necessity. Kay had been a friend and confidant, as well as lover, but now she was out of the picture. He had drinking and fishing buddies, Chet foremost among them, but he didn't have what he considered a close male friend. That meant he was pretty much on his own.

It being Sunday, Frank flirted with the idea of going to mass, but on reflection he decided the cure was worse than the disease. He hadn't set foot in a Catholic church since before he and Arlene, who was Presbyterian, were married. That pretty well put him on the road to hell. Of course, Frank and religion had parted company long before his marriage. He used to say he was born lapsed, which meant, never having had the faith, he hadn't been in a position to lose it.

Were it not for his mother, he'd have had no association with the church at all. But she'd taken him to mass in her arms and taught him the rosary as he was learning to walk. The upshot was that Catholicism had attached itself to his genes like a congenital disease. Had his mother not died before he was old enough to attend Catholic school, he might be battling Catholic guilt to this day.

If there was anything he knew for sure, it was that wallowing in his own angst wouldn't do any good. So he did what most guys in emotional pain did—he tried to figure out how to fix it. The problem was there were so damned many unknowns.

After putting coffee on, he grabbed his jacket and went up to the road to get the paper, figuring he'd update himself on the facts of the case. The newspaper in hand, he crossed the pavement and peered down at the dock. There was nothing to indicate that tragedy had occurred there. The yellow police tape was gone. Even so, Frank knew he'd never be able to look at the spot again without seeing that child's naked body lying innocently on the rocks.

The Sunday edition of the *Sacramento Bee* was bloated like most Sunday papers, but the article he cared about was only a little piece on page three of the Metro section, maybe four or five inches in length. Dumping the rest of the paper on the floor, Frank plopped onto the sofa to read. The headline read Girl's Body Found in Delta Slough. The article went on to say:

The body of an unidentified teenager was found by two fishermen in Watermark Slough in Sacramento Delta Saturday morning.

According to Riverton police, the naked body of the victim was spotted on the bank by two men as they passed by in their boat at approximately 11:00 a.m. The girl, estimated to be between the age of twelve and fifteen, was believed to have drowned sometime during the night, but police say the circumstances of her death are unclear.

Police Chief Abby Hooper, of the Riverton Police Department, indicated that there were no clear signs of foul play, but that an investigation was being conducted and an autopsy was scheduled. According to Hooper, there have been no reports of missing persons fitting the description of the victim and police are asking for help from the public in making the identification.

The girl is described as white, slightly built, 5 feet 5 inches in height and weighing 106 pounds. She had shoulder-length light brown hair, blue eyes and no distinguishing marks. Anyone having information about the victim is asked to contact the Riverton Police Department at (916) 555–2100.

Frank put the paper aside. The description of the girl was chilling. It could have been Beth, though the photo he'd been shown did not remind him of his daughter, apart from her youthful innocence.

As he'd expected, the news report wasn't helpful. They rarely were. Abby had given the media only the essentials because her objective at this point was to identify the victim and signal potential witnesses to come forward. Frank, though, was more than a little curious about who Jane Doe was and what had happened to her.

Deciding there was no point in sitting around waiting, he called the police department's administrative line. Because it was Sunday, the dispatcher on duty answered the call.

"Hi, this is Frank Keegan," he said. "Is Chief Hooper in?"

"No, but she's expected later."

Frank decided to ask, anyway. "I'm curious, has there been an ID of the drowning victim, the Jane Doe?"

"Not to my knowledge, Frank," the dispatcher replied.

"We've had a few calls, people with questions, but nobody reporting anybody missing."

"Do you know when the autopsy's scheduled?"

"I heard today, but I'm not sure. Do you want me to have the chief call you?"

"Yeah, if she gets anything. Tell her I'd appreciate being informed."

"Will do."

Frank hung up, feeling no better than when he'd awakened. He went into the kitchen to have some coffee. It wasn't quite ready, so he sat at the table to wait.

He still couldn't believe he had harmed the girl. Small flashes of memory were coming back to him. He was almost certain he'd had sex with somebody. If it was with Jane Doe, where in the hell did she come from and how did she end up in the slough? Actually, that was the problem. She wasn't in the water when she was found, she was on the bank. The Aspeths told the police they hadn't touched the body. That meant if the girl drowned, somebody else had fished her out of the drink.

Frank didn't believe he'd done that. In fact, if it hadn't been for the evidence of sex in his bed and Kay saying she hadn't so much as come inside his front door, he'd have bet his life that the girl turning up by his dock was completely random.

It did occur to him that the girl might have been in his place with somebody else earlier, before he got home, but there had been no signs of forced entry and he was always careful to lock up before leaving. No one else had a key. And why had he awakened the next morning with his pants off?

No, chances were he'd been the one who'd gotten it on in his bed—and the prospect that it had been with Jane Doe made him sick. The results of the autopsy would probably confirm whether she'd had sex and, thanks to DNA technology, probably with whom. Frank was eager to know the outcome, but at the same time he was scared shitless.

The phone rang in the other room and he went to answer it.

"Frank, this is Dix."

The somberness of the sergeant's tone gave him pause.

"What's up, Dix?"

"Have you talked to Chet?"

"No, not since I saw you guys at the bowling alley yesterday afternoon. Why?"

"I don't know," Dix said. "I'm kind of worried about him."

"How so?"

"The hard-on he's got over Chief Hooper. He overdoes it, Frank."

"Yeah, I know. But between losing Sally and adjusting to retirement, he's struggling. The guy's proud. You know that."

"Yeah, but I wish he'd let go of the department."

"What do you mean? He's not meddling, is he?"

"No, but he always has to know what's going on. Like this Jane Doe thing. Chet and I went over to the Queen after we left the bowling alley. We were there when we heard about the girl being found. Chet immediately got kind of funny and he left. Just up and walked out. Didn't even finish his beer. I thought maybe he was going to your place. Then a couple hours later I got a call from him at home, and he said he wanted a briefing on the case. I told him I didn't know any more than he did because I hadn't been in to the station. So, Chet asks me to meet him down there so he could see the file."

"He asked to see the Jane Doe file?"

"Yeah. I told him there probably wasn't that much to see, but I couldn't talk him out of it. Even when I told him he was putting me in a spot with Chief Hooper he pressed. Anyway, I met him down at the office and we looked at the reports and the photos and everything.''

"And?"

"Well, he really got funny, Frank."

"What do you mean, funny?"

"Weird. I mean, he started pacing, mumbling to himself. Your name was in the reports, considering where the body was found. I figured that was what was bothering him. So I said, 'Chet, there's no point jumping to conclusions. Nobody's accusing Frank.'''

"Was there something in the file that pointed at me besides where the body was found?"

"That's nothing we ought to be discussing, Frank," Dix replied. "It's Chet I'm talking about. His reaction."

Frank was silent. He didn't want to point out he had a stake in the thing himself, but the fact seemed lost on Dix. But then the sergeant suddenly seemed to realize the implications.

"Not that there's anything for you to worry about, Frank. There's nothing in the file you don't already know, I'm sure."

Frank felt better, but he did share Dix's concern about Chet. "Well, I haven't talked to him. If he's agonizing for my sake, he hasn't said anything to me."

"Actually, I'd feel better if he had," Dix said. "I tried calling him this morning, but didn't get an answer."

"Chet's an early riser. He might have gone for a walk or a drive or fishing or something."

"Yeah, I know."

"If he calls, I'll ask what's troubling him," Frank said. "I might even swing by his place later. I was thinking about talking to him, anyway."

"Do that, Frank."

They said goodbye and Frank stared at the phone after he'd

hung up. Picking up the receiver, he dialed Chet Wilsey's number. There was no answer.

Riverton Civic Center

Abby sat at her desk, which had been Chet Wilsey's until a month ago, reviewing the missing-persons files. There was nothing promising. Sighing, she stared off through the window at the gray sky. It was a sad commentary, but she still didn't feel at home in the chief's office. More like an interloper. She hated that. Hated her self-doubts. Fortunately, though, she could put on a good show. Abby managed to inspire confidence because she was a battler. Still, it would be nice to get Chet behind her.

She glanced around—in her first week she'd transformed the office from the leather and wood of Chet's era to the plants and watercolors of her own incarnation, careful not to let the look get too frilly. Diplomas and commendations hung on the wall, fewer in number than those of her predecessor, but projecting the same clean, businesslike image. The point was the office still looked like it belonged to a law-enforcement professional, which was her intent.

Abby flipped open the file again and gazed at the Polaroid shots of Jane Doe. She had a bad feeling about the case, almost certain it would get really messy before it was over. They'd put the data on the girl into the system, but the only two inquiries in person did not look promising. It was a ninety-percent certainty the girl wasn't local. The best bet was that she was from Sacramento or the suburbs. The folks up there used the Delta to dispose of bodies with some regularity, and more than a fair share of those that showed up were kids. The trouble was, this didn't look like an ordinary body dump because the victim appeared to have drowned. Nor did it seem coincidental that it was Frank Keegan's place where the body was found. That bothered her more than anything.

Other than Frank's total lack of recall—the old Richard Nixon approach to the Fifth Amendment—he hadn't said or done anything to suggest guilt. In fact, he'd seemed as bewildered as everyone else. But that scratch on his face, which he couldn't explain, was troubling. It had gotten worse, though, after the crime-lab technicians had done their thing. One of them had pointed out flecks of rust and red paint chips in the victim's hair. Frank's truck, a Toyota pickup that Abby had seen in the drive, was red. It was old—an '84 or '85 model—and wasn't in the best shape. She hadn't inspected it, but it wouldn't have surprised her if there were some rusty spots in the bed.

Abby had spent the night second-guessing herself about whether she should have talked to the D.A. about a search warrant. But it hadn't yet been established that there had been a crime—or that Frank was connected. The autopsy would be critical, though Abby was aware that drownings were tricky from an evidentiary standpoint. The line between accidental death and homicide was fuzzy, and it usually took associated findings—like wounds that would indicate a struggle—to prove foul play.

That was where Abby's case was weakest. The technicians at the scene said they didn't see any sign of a struggle. Apart from the scrapes on Jane Doe's heels, the scratches were superficial, the sort that would have been sustained in moving the body. Also, indications were that the damage to the corpse had occurred postmortem.

The coroner's office said they might have some findings by early afternoon, so Abby decided to hang around until then. At eleven-thirty her intercom line buzzed and Carole, the dispatcher who doubled as departmental receptionist on weekends, told Abby she had a visitor. Before she said who, Carole had to take another call.

The station, located next to City Hall, was a small free-standing building, consisting of a reception and radio room, an interrogation room, a coffee room and a squad room for the beat officers, one corner of which contained a private cubicle for Dix Fowler. The administrative section was in a separate wing, housing the clerical staff, the chief's office and a small conference room. Abby made her way out to the reception area, where she found a tall, good-looking man in jeans and a fashionable leather jacket standing at the window, peering out through the Venetian blinds at the street. He turned and, despite the wraparound reflective sunglasses, the familiar smile, gleaming white teeth and tawny hair made him instantly recognizable. Darren Armstrong.

"Abby, Abby, Abby," he said, looking her over, his sensuous mouth the picture of delight. "Jesus, I expected gold braid and medals."

It took a couple of heartbeats for her to gather a response. "Only for funerals, Darren," she said dryly.

He grinned, still taking her in. Abby had put on slacks and a little cotton sweater to come into the office and had hardly bothered with her hair. No makeup. She didn't even think she'd taken a moment for lipstick, but couldn't remember.

"God," he said nodding, reverence in his tone, "you look great, you really do."

"Darren, is there a reason you're here?"

"I had to come, Abby. I think you understand that."

"No, I don't. I made it clear I had no desire to see you."

Darren took off his sunglasses so that she could see that her words had wounded. Only then did she remember they weren't alone. Glancing past the counter into the radio room, she noticed that Carole was listening with obvious curiosity, her jaw slack. Seeing Abby glance at her, she quickly turned her chair to face the console behind her. The byplay made Darren grin all the more.

Abby gave him a hard look, then held up her hand, showing two fingers. "Two minutes," she said under her breath. "I'll give you two minutes." Then she turned on her heel, assuming he'd follow, and headed for her office.

East Levee Road
Riverton

Frank pulled up in front of the River Queen and turned off the engine of his '84 Toyota pickup. He didn't get out right away. Instead, he slumped in the seat and stared at the light mist coming down. He wasn't even sure why he'd come, except that he knew he had to get out of his trailer.

Riverton's principal watering hole offered a panorama of the river that was especially pleasant on a summer day, when you could sit out on the deck and watch the river traffic going by—everything from large yachts to small pleasure boats—feeling like the parade was being put on just for you.

To a lot of folks the River Queen and Kay Ingram were synonymous, though it wasn't her creation. It had been a landmark in the Delta before she was even born. The owner for years and years had been a fellow named Smith, whose tenure went back to before Prohibition. He was dead now, but he'd told Kay the River Queen was already called that when he bought it. The old establishment was most likely named after a boat than a woman, but nobody seemed to know for sure. Even old Tong Lee up in the town of Locke, who claimed to be as old as the river, didn't know how the Queen came to be.

The place was welcoming. Countless feet, elbows or rear ends had worn grooves in the wood of the bar and floors. There were half-a-dozen ceiling fans that worked summers but rested in the winter. The huge mahogany bar had come around the Horn on a steamer a hundred years ago and was practically an historic marker itself. The furniture Kay had put in was in good shape but no longer new—like a middle-aged woman who still cared enough to mind her figure.

The walls, covered with pictures from Smith's era and before, helped date the place. The subject of each was connected to the river—a Model T Ford on a levee road, an old barge with dredging equipment circa 1900, Chinese workers in coolie clothes lined up on a dock, an aerial view of the river rushing through a levee break—that kind of stuff. The pictures and the walls under them, Kay liked to say, were the Queen's wrinkles.

The barroom's heartbeat was the unofficial town bulletin board, which hung near the front door. It was where you posted a notice to sell your boat or looked if you wanted to buy one. You could advertise a lost dog, find guitar lessons, tractor work or apricot jam.

A woman in town, a fortyish German immigrant named Frieda Benke, used to put up a card toward the end of each month before the rent was due, offering massages. Kay would take the card down around the second or third, after Frieda had made her rent money. Nobody in Riverton's establishment, Chet Wilsey foremost among them, wanted organized prostitution in town, but nobody wanted Frieda evicted, either. Frank wondered if the new police chief's attitude would be any different. Somehow he couldn't see Abby patting Frieda on the rump the way Chet had.

There was seldom trouble at the Queen, but there'd been a few occasions when Chet and his boys had put down a disturbance. More than once Frank had wondered what would happen if Abby's intervention was required.

Abby and Kay's problem seemed rather unimportant at the moment, however. Frank was suffering over the Jane Doe case. And it wasn't just because he was under suspicion. For the first time in his life he was facing a problem in a total haze. The sad fact remained that he didn't know who the fuck he really was.

He hated to admit it, but he missed Kay's friendship, her care, even her love. He regretted breaking things off now. What a woman did for a man, he'd come to realize, was give comfort, even while he played at being strong and self-sufficient. The really good ones could do it without letting a guy know how needy he was.

Kay Ingram understood male psychology as well as any woman. Frank considered it one of her great strengths. They'd been good for each other in many ways, but in the end, the relationship served his needs, but not hers. He either had to address that or get out. And so he'd walked away—not for himself, but for her.

Though Frank was sure that at some level Kay understood his motives, she had a lot of pride and didn't take kindly to being dumped. So she'd made him pay.

When she'd taken up with Mort Anderson, Frank had been arrogant enough to think she was trying to make him jealous. As time went on, though, it became apparent she was serious about her relationship with the guy and made damned sure Frank knew it.

If there had been revenge in her heart, Kay certainly knew how to get results. The best way to get his goat was to mention Mort Anderson's name. He suspected she didn't fully appreciate the depth of his animosity. "If what Mort did was so horrible, why didn't you sue him?" she'd once asked.

The answer was Frank was so embarrassed about allowing himself to be taken that he'd chosen to ignore it. Besides, it wasn't clear he had a good case. Mort had no scruples, but he knew how to walk the narrow line of the law.

Mort, a former member of the City Council, a Lions Club treasurer and at that time president of the Board of Realtors, had brokered the purchase of Frank's orchard. But it wasn't until after the close of escrow that Frank discovered it was virtually impossible to sell a crop of pears without a canning contract in hand, which of course he did not have. With his crop rotting on the trees, Frank had been forced to use all his reserve capital to stay afloat. Mort, already the wealthiest of Riverton's half-dozen certified millionaires, collected his real-estate commission, of course, never having lost a minute's sleep over it. A lawsuit wouldn't have bothered Mort, who'd had his share over the years, but a protracted legal battle probably would have sent Frank into bankruptcy.

That had been the crux of his differences with Mort, until Kay entered the picture, that is. Mort had had a thing for Kay for years—the general consensus was that he'd divorced his wife to marry Kay—and losing her to Frank had been the ultimate blow. Frank took satisfaction in that.

On the other hand, Kay, who always chose her enemies with care, had managed to stay on friendly terms with Mort, which was a constant source of irritation to Frank. But he realized that was the point. As long as he offered her little more than cribbage and a good time, it was to her advantage to keep Mort waiting in the wings. And as soon as he and Kay had split, she'd installed the long-suffering Mort in the catbird seat. Now it was Frank's turn to be on the outs.

So here he was at the River Queen, if anything needier than two nights ago when he'd gotten drunk and thrown himself at Kay. Ironically, he didn't even know if she'd be here. He had other reasons for coming to the Queen, though. At some point he needed to find out what people were thinking. By now word would have gotten around that he'd been too drunk to recall anything that would explain how the nude body of a girl had ended up by his dock. If the town was going to turn on him because of it, the Queen was the place to find out. Sighing, he pulled up the collar of his jacket, opened the door to his truck and ambled to the entrance.

The barroom, which Kay kept well lit, was not crowded. A dozen or so customers were spread among the tables, booths and along the antique bar that ran down one side of the room. He was relieved when he saw Kay. She was in one of her boob-showcasing sweaters, mixing a drink, her back to him. Her blond hair was twisted up, exposing her neck and inviting a kiss, even at a distance of twenty feet and after a year of separation. He had been conditioning himself not to think about her in those terms, though, so he forced himself to look at the other faces.

One by one, heads turned his way. He sensed curiosity in their eyes more than hostility or disapproval. The people nearest nodded or smiled. Frank judged that in the public mind, not having been found guilty, he was apparently still innocent. That came as a relief.

Then he spotted Mort Anderson at the near end of the bar. And he wasn't just smiling, he was grinning. Frank glared. Mort returned the favor.

The bastard was in his early fifties and, to be fair, rather good-looking and distinguished. He had a head of white hair, a strong jaw and a fairly trim build. His clothing was expensive, but the style dated. Mort was the classic big fish in a small pond.

"Well, if it isn't Frank Keegan," he said loudly enough to draw most of the patrons' attention. "Understand you had a rough weekend, sport."

There were a few snickers, though more in reaction to Mort's audaciousness than pleasure at Frank's discomfort. His cheap shot drew Kay's attention.

"Shut up, Mort," she said, her voice as loud as his. "Don't you have any dignity?"

That brought a grumble from Anderson and a few chuckles at his expense. It wasn't much consolation, though. Frank felt like the butt of a very bad joke.

Kay regarded him, but she didn't maintain eye contact. Frank moved along the bar, acknowledging mumbled greetings, getting a handshake from one or two folks who had as little use for Mort Anderson as he did. Even so, there was a smell of caution in the air. People clearly didn't know what to think. The irony was, Frank didn't, either. The truth, most likely, was being uncovered at a police lab in Sacramento perhaps at that very moment.

Feeling as though he had nothing to lose, Frank went to the booth at the rear where Kay normally held court and sat down. Several people noticed his bold move, including Kay and Mort. Frank figured it was a sure way to get a little attention, which, after all, was half the reason he'd come.

Kay paused only long enough to draw a tap beer, which she carried over to the booth, putting it in front of him. She didn't sit down. Instead, she stood with her hands on her hips, giving him an appraising look. Out of the corner of his eye, Frank saw Mort get up, take his raincoat from the hook near the door and stomp out. If Kay was aware, she gave no sign. She kept her eyes on Frank.

"So, did you finally remember what happened Friday night?" she asked.

He shook his head. "No."

Kay's brows rose. "No?"

"No," he said again.

"Then why did you sit in my booth?"

"I thought we could have a little more detailed conversation about Friday night."

Kay seemed annoyed. She glanced toward the front and, seeing Mort was gone, half rolled her eyes, then slid into the booth across from him.

"Don't make anything out of me dressing down Mort," she said. "Sometimes he's an ass. He treats me fine, but I don't like the way he treats other people—certain other people, that is."

"I appreciate you defending me."

Her eyes narrowed. "I didn't defend *you*, Frank. I would have done the same for any patron."

"Well, thanks anyway," he said.

She leaned toward him. "Are you really under suspicion in that girl's death?"

Frank was aware of her large breasts lying on the table. Kay, apparently sensing it, leaned back. He rubbed his chin. "They haven't determined that a crime has been committed, but if they do, I imagine I'll be the prime suspect."

"Suspected of doing what, exactly?"

He shrugged. "Depends on what they turn up. Homicide, rape, kidnapping, corrupting the morals of a minor, who knows?"

"When could you have done these things? Do they know when she died?"

He shook his head. "They think sometime during the night. They're doing an autopsy. It should tell more."

"You did not rape or kill anyone, Frank. That much I know."

"Are you saying that because of my impeccable character, or do you know something I don't?"

She blushed. He wasn't sure why.

"Once you got into your cups you were pretty feisty," she said.

"Could you be more specific?"

"You started acting like we were still on friendly terms," she replied, coloring again.

He was beginning to understand. He was also embarrassed to say he was enjoying her discomfort. "*Aren't* we on friendly terms, Kay?"

She gave him a look. "You know what I mean."

"Are you saying I propositioned you?"

She flushed even darker, anger in her eyes. "That's exactly what you did."

"But meaningless, because I was drunk." He watched her shift uneasily. "I assume others witnessed my shameful display."

"There were a few people here. Belinda, of course. She helped me get you to your truck so I could drive you home."

"What time was that, Kay?"

"After one."

"Which meant you didn't get me home until sometime around one-thirty in the morning."

"Something like that," she said.

"Did I seem in any kind of condition to go chasing some kid around, trying to get into her pants?"

Kay sat very still, staring at him.

"Well?" he said.

She shook her head. "No."

"Funny thing, though, I have sketchy recollections of…"

"Of what?"

He sighed. "Of getting laid," he said under his breath.

Kay seemed uncomfortable. It was hard to tell whether she shared his disgust over what he might have done to the girl or if she disapproved of him in principle.

"I have absolutely no recollection of doing it with some kid, though," he added.

"Who, then?"

"If I would have had to pick someone, I'd have said you." She did not look pleased.

"I'm sorry, Kay. I know how offensive that must be."

"They can't charge you with rape or murder just because you can't remember, can they?"

"No. Short of an eyewitness, there'd have to be physical evidence linking me to the crime. DNA match, fingerprints, hairs or fibers, that sort of thing. It's the uncertainty of what the hell happened that's getting to me."

"I'm sure it will all work out."

"Let's hope so." He looked at the beer, the mere sight of it turning his stomach.

Kay twiddled her fingers, obviously ill at ease. "Frank, can I ask a favor?"

The request surprised him. "Sure."

"Belinda is the only one besides you who knows I drove you home. I didn't say anything to Mort—not that I'm accountable to him. You know that's not my style."

"But... I know there's a 'but,' Kay."

"But I'd rather not make an issue of it, unless it's necessary. Mort's sensitive about our past. Not that he doesn't trust me, but it's a matter of pride. He cares what people think. You probably noticed that he walked out when I brought you the beer."

"Don't worry, I understand."

"I'm not sure you do. Things between me and Mort have gotten real serious, Frank."

"I know that. It surprised me when you came to my defense."

She lowered her head. "I hate it when he does things like that. Mort is really a very dear man, but he has a bad habit of gloating. And he jumps on people when they're down."

"Everybody has their faults," Frank said, studying her. This was the most they'd talked in months, the first opportunity he'd had to pick up on the unspoken vibrations between them. The subsonics were there, but something was different. Kay had made up her mind that Mort was the man, and Frank realized that anything she still felt for him was more in the realm of nostalgia. Life, she seemed to be saying, does go on.

Kay reached over and patted his hand. "Thanks for understanding. And for being a friend."

"I guess things haven't been that friendly between us lately, have they?"

Again she reacted with embarrassment, abruptly withdrawing her hand. Frank realized he must have said the wrong thing.

He was vaguely aware of somebody coming into the bar, but it didn't really hit him until a hush fell over the place.

Kay became aware about the same time. They both turned toward the door, where a slight figure in a Riverton P.D. rain slicker stood surveying the room. It was Abby. Kay shifted uneasily as her daughter walked toward them. Every head in the room followed her.

Kay started to get up, but Frank stopped her. "This day was going to come eventually," he said softly. "Might as well get it over with."

Kay eased back into her seat. Abby glanced at her briefly, but she focused her attention on him.

"Excuse me for interrupting, Frank," she said, "but I was told I'd probably find you here."

"Your informant was correct, Chief."

"I'd like to talk to you," she said, her tone businesslike. "Would you mind coming by the station before you go home?"

He sensed something ominous in her tone, and it was clear she wouldn't have come to the Queen if it wasn't important. Heavy as that was, he was still intrigued with the byplay between her and her mother. Although the air was crackling with awareness, neither had addressed the other. Frank decided to leave it there.

"Sure, I'd be glad to," he said.

Abby nodded.

"I take it it's a good sign you aren't slapping the cuffs on me."

She again darted Kay a glance. "I have additional information and we need to talk about it."

"Results of the autopsy?"

She drew a breath. "Yes. Preliminary results."

There was a difficult silence.

"Abby," Kay said, her voice surprisingly thin, "I can tell you right now this man did not do anything to that girl."

Abby looked at her squarely for the first time. "I appreciate your view, but all I'm interested in right now are the facts. Unless you have knowledge of—''

"I do, as a matter of fact," Kay said, cutting her off. "Friday night Frank was here at the River Queen until after one in the morning. Then, when—"

"I got loaded, Kay closed out my tab," Frank interjected. "She knew I was in no condition to drive, and while she was in back calling a taxi, I left. Walked right out of the bar—or maybe staggered out is more accurate."

"Frank, that's—"

"Please, Kay," he said, cutting her off again. "I'm sure the chief would agree you met *your* responsibilities. What happened after I left are *mine*."

"It wasn't very responsible of you to drive home in that condition," Abby said. "You could have killed yourself or somebody else."

"Guilty," he said. "But that's all the evil doing I'm admitting to."

Abby was not amused.

"Frank—" Kay said.

"Please, let me handle this, Kay. I know you're loyal to your regular customers, but there are limits." He slid out of the booth, dragging his jacket after him.

Abby looked at her mother, as did Frank. Kay appeared to be in pain. It was not clear for which of the many possible reasons.

"We may need to talk to you at some point," Abby said to her.

"You're welcome to talk to me anytime you want," Kay replied, her voice almost sad.

Abby shifted self-consciously, then turned to Frank. "See you at the station?"

"Yes, I'll be right over."

She headed toward the door, a dozen pairs of eyes following her until she was gone. Then heads swiveled toward the

back of the bar. Enough of the conversation had been overheard that the rest of Riverton would know all about it inside
of two days.

Kay slid from the booth as Frank put on his jacket.

"You shouldn't have done that," she said.

"Look," he replied, taking her hands, "it isn't going to
make a lick of difference to the police how I got home, but
it will to Mort. What they care about is what happened once
I got there. Unfortunately, that's where I'm at a disadvantage."

"Oh, Frank…" Her expression was virtually pleading.

He took it as compassion. He leaned over and gave her a
kiss on the forehead. "Thanks for being a pal when it really
counted," he said. "It means a lot to me, Kay." He turned
for the door, but not before noticing there were tears in her
eyes.

The faces of the other patrons were more somber now,
though they still weren't hostile. Several muttered goodbyes.
Pulling up the collar of his jacket, Frank went out into the
still-falling rain. Maybe he was about to discover just how
good or bad a human being he truly was.

Riverton Civic Center

Abby didn't bother going to her office. She waited in the
reception area, half listening to Carole bantering on the radio
with the patrol officers. Except maybe for her relationship
with Chet Wilsey, this business with Frank was the most
unpleasant thing she'd dealt with during her short tenure as
chief of police. And she hadn't particularly liked having to
go to the River Queen to find him, either.

After she hadn't been able to reach him at home, she'd
had Carole radio the patrol officers to be on the lookout for
him. Sandy Mendoza, who was investigating a break-in of
Elmer Potter's toolshed, radioed back that Frank was prob-

ably at the Queen and that he'd swing by there after he'd finished up at Elmer's, but it might be half an hour or so. Abby considered telephoning the bar, but she realized she was trying to avoid her mother. That was cowardly and she didn't like being a coward, so she decided she might as well go to the Queen herself. "Tell Sandy not to bother," she'd told Carole.

Now that it was over, Abby couldn't say she felt a whole lot better. Being in the same town with Kay Ingram and never seeing her—never *wanting* to see her—was the most troubling aspect of her return to Riverton. She couldn't remember exactly how long it had been since she'd seen Kay, though she did know that her mother had come to see her twice while she'd been living in Sacramento. The first time was soon after Kay's return to Northern California. Her third, much older husband, Harvey Ingram, had died of a heart attack down in San Diego, leaving her enough money to buy a business. Kay chose to make it the River Queen, the place where she'd worked as a barmaid years before, and the place, coincidentally, she'd met Abby's father, Ty Hooper.

The story was well-known. After five years of marriage and a child, Kay had run off to Arizona with a man she later married. For a few years she had returned to Riverton every few months to see her daughter, but Abby remembered the visits as being tense and unpleasant. Whether it was a product of her father's bitterness or actual fact, Abby had come to regard her mother as a fallen woman, immoral and corrupt. Eventually she'd learned to hate Kay as much as her father did.

From the time she was eight or nine, Abby only saw her mother sporadically. Occasional letters and gifts arrived, but Abby disregarded the overtures, once writing to Kay that she never wanted to see her again. It wasn't until Kay showed up at Abby's apartment in Sacramento that they'd really talked.

"I'm not the person Ty made me out to be," Kay had lamented.

"Don't disparage my father," Abby had shot back. "He was a good, decent man and the only parent I ever had!"

Things had gone downhill from there. Abby had angrily sent Kay away, the bitterness of the past too strong, the wounds too deep to overcome. Their other encounter came a few years later at the ceremony where Abby received her commendation. They only spoke for a few minutes and it was in public. Kay had tearfully told her she was proud of her and hoped that one day they could be friends. Abby had turned away with tears in her own eyes.

There was something about that day, brief as the encounter was, that had affected her. Maybe she'd finally seen her mother as an adult—flawed, perhaps, but not the monster she had imagined. And she also came to realize that even if she'd been wronged as a child and had cause to be resentful, the time might have come to put the past behind her. Still, old ways of thinking did not die easily.

Frank Keegan came in the door just then, his hair and eyelashes glistening with rain. His sudden appearance reminded her of the matter at hand—her work, Jane Doe.

She greeted him, smiling to be polite, but the fact was her heart ached. This was grim duty, especially hard because she liked Frank. "Come on back to my office," she said, leading the way.

Ironically, she'd made the same walk with Darren Armstrong only a few hours earlier, her emotions starkly different from what they were now. Darren was a ghost from the past. Frank represented what was real and immediate. And yet she hadn't been able to dismiss Darren as easily as she'd hoped. Their conversation had been brief.

"Abby," he'd said, "I can't tell you how hard it hit me when I heard I'd gotten you pregnant. Jesus…it devastated me."

"It wasn't very pleasant for me, either."

"Why didn't you tell me?"

Her blood pressure took an upward blip. Tears of anger threatened, but she fought them back. "Oh, I intended to, but it seems you'd already made other plans for your life. Wasn't her name Shelly?"

"But I had no idea you were pregnant. None."

"Of course not. It was my responsibility to keep problems like that from darkening your door. Your concerns began and ended with getting laid."

"That's not fair, Abby. You can't hold me responsible for ignoring something I didn't know about."

"Okay, you tell me, Darren. You come back from your sexy weekend with Shelly and find me sitting on your door-step, saying I'm pregnant. What would you have done? Asked me to marry you so the little tyke would have a mommy *and* a daddy? No, I'll tell you what you'd have done, cowboy—you'd have asked me to take care of the problem. Maybe you'd have offered to pay for it, but it would have stopped right there."

"Abby, that was then, this is now."

"That's right, Darren. This is now. We've both moved on. And there's no longer any reason for us to talk."

"But that's not fair. You've had years to deal with this. I've just found out. Maybe I need to talk about it, process it."

"You can think about it all you wish," she'd said.

"Would it hurt to talk about it?"

She'd looked at her watch. "I've got work to do, Darren. This is not the time."

"When *is* the time?"

She'd hated this. Her stomach had felt like she'd swallowed a rock. "Let me think about it," she'd said.

Darren, to his credit, hadn't argued. He'd dutifully left, making her wonder if she hadn't been a little too hard on him, too unfair. He was a shit, but he was right about one thing—he hadn't known about her pregnancy and therefore couldn't be held responsible as though he had. But it was also more his problem now than hers.

Abby went to her desk, dropping into her chair. Frank took the seat Darren had occupied. The incongruity struck her. They peered at each other as she searched for a place to begin. Frank, she noticed, seemed weary, though not nearly so much under the weather as the day before. He beat her to the punch.

"You look good, sitting in that chair," he said. "Chet has big shoes, but you fill them well."

"Surely you aren't trying to butter me up, Frank," she said, saying exactly what was on her mind. She preferred directness, and with some people it was easier than with others. Frank Keegan was one of the easy ones. She couldn't explain why.

"It may be my last chance, Chief," he said, sounding both amused and self-conscious. "But let's don't pussyfoot around. I can smell blood. What have you got?"

"We talked about a lawyer yesterday. Are you sure you don't want somebody? I'm going to be asking questions."

"You've informed me of my rights, Chief. Proceed."

Abby reached for the pad on which she'd written her notes from the phone conversation with the deputy coroner. "I can't tell you how bizarre this is shaping up," she said by way of introduction. "They've confirmed that the girl drowned. There was water in her lungs."

"Shit."

"Why, shit?"

Frank sighed, squeezing the bridge of his nose between his thumb and forefinger. "I've been trying to figure this thing out. I thought maybe the girl was drunk or drugged and fell in the water accidentally. Rather than drowning, I figured maybe she crawled out of the water, but passed out, then maybe died of exposure.''

''Sorry, Frank, that's not what the autopsy says.''

''So, she drowned, but it doesn't say how or why.''

''No, it doesn't. The deputy coroner did notice something strange, however.''

Frank managed to keep his composure, but she saw a twinge at the corners of his mouth. ''What's that?'' he asked.

''He'd previously done autopsies on drowning victims in the Delta. Once you get out of the main channels of the river, a lot of pesticides show up in the water, especially in the collateral sloughs.''

''So?''

''Well, there was no trace of anything like that in the girl's lungs.''

He thought about that for a moment. ''What are you saying, Chief—that she didn't drown in the slough?''

''The coroner thinks it's quite likely she didn't.''

''So where did she drown?''

Abby shrugged. ''Who knows? A bathtub, maybe?''

''Well, was the water in her lungs chlorinated?'' he asked.

''There's no way to tell. Chlorine dissipates almost immediately. It can't be measured.''

Frank's brows rose as if to say he was impressed.

''I asked,'' Abby explained.

''Well, at least we're thinking along the same lines.''

Abby couldn't see any advantage in that, but let the comment pass. ''Even if she drowned someplace else, like a bathtub, for example, they're pretty sure the victim did spend some time in the slough. There was sediment and debris in the outer portions of her mouth and nostrils.''

''But it would have gotten there after she'd died,'' he said.

''That's right.''

''So we're back to somebody pulling her out of the water.''

"Yes."

"Maybe in an attempt to save her."

"Possibly," Abby said. "There's so much about it that's strange. Say, for the moment, it was a homicide and it occurred somewhere else. If the intent was to make it look like an accident, you'd have thought they'd have dressed her and left her in the water."

He contemplated that for a moment. "Is there an estimate of time of death?"

"A broad one. Sometime between 8:00 p.m. Friday and 4:00 a.m. Saturday, based on the rigor mortis and lividity. The deputy coroner said the water complicates things, though. If it's relatively cool, it retards the depletion rate of the ATP in the muscle tissue. Without knowing how long she was in the drink, it's difficult to extrapolate. He felt the condition of the corneas narrowed the range somewhat, but you know as well as I time of death is mostly a crapshoot."

Frank had the look of a man who'd just gotten more detail than he cared to hear, but Abby saw no way around it. He was a professional and in a very difficult spot, and he needed to know what he was up against. Frank engaged her eyes with question.

"None of that implicates me, especially. You must have more."

Abby again consulted her notes. "Unfortunately, yes. The autopsy shows signs of a struggle we didn't notice at the crime scene."

"Like what?"

"There were traces of flesh under the victim's fingernails. The samples were badly degraded. They may not be able to do DNA testing, but they're going to give it a shot."

"But having seen this scratch on my face, you'd like specimens from me, just in case."

"If you're willing."

"You'll get them eventually, so let's not futz around."

"Okay, I'll advise the lab and they'll be in touch."

"What else you got, Abby?" he asked, indicating her notes with a subtle nod of his head.

"The girl had had sex before she died," she replied. "They found semen in her vagina, as well as lubricant. Petroleum jelly."

"The donor won't be too hard to identify," he said grimly.

"Probably not. *If* we can find him."

"Thanks for saying that."

"I'm a cop, which means keeping an open mind." She drew a long breath. "But there's something else, Frank. A rather sad, poignant detail. The girl was pregnant, too. In her first term, but definitely pregnant."

"Jesus."

"It just makes me ill," Abby said.

"I can guarantee you I had nothing to do with any pregnancy."

"I'd like for you to guarantee you had nothing to do with any of this."

"Believe me," he said, "so would I. But I'm not going to sit here and lie about what I did or didn't do, because I don't know. I have a hunch, though, that your technicians are going to tell us both how involved I was."

"Yes, I think they will."

"Are we through?" he asked.

"No. There's more. They found red paint chips and rust in the victim's hair."

"So?"

"So, your truck is red."

"Red is a lot of people's favorite color," he replied.

"Frank, when I went to the River Queen, your truck was parked out front. When I walked past it, I saw rust in the bed. And the paint looked chipped in places."

"It's an old truck, Abby."

"Paint samples can be tested."

"You'd like samples from my truck."

"You know I would. If there's a match it won't prove a crime, but you'd be further implicated. I'm sure I don't have to tell you that."

He rubbed his jaw. "Sounds to me that, claims of being open-minded notwithstanding, you're beginning to draw conclusions."

"I'm gathering evidence because it's my job."

"And you're doing it well."

She picked up the pad. Staring at the page, she drew another long breath. "What's your blood type?"

"A negative."

She closed her eyes involuntarily, the disappointment that great. She looked at him then. "Frank, the samples of blood they found on the rocks by the body…the blood type is A negative. The victim's blood type is O positive."

He seemed stunned. She could almost see the color draining from his face. He looked like he wanted to say something, but couldn't. She spoke for him.

"You obviously aren't the only person in the world with A negative blood."

"No, but it's one of the rarer types. Something like fifteen percent of the population. The odds of my innocence are getting longer."

If it was black humor, it fell flat. Still, she felt compassion for him. He seemed like a victim himself. It was her intuition that told her that, not the mounting evidence against him.

"Last question, Frank. Do you do cocaine?"

"Coke? No, Abby, margaritas are my drug of choice. After Friday night I'm not sure they're a whole lot better, though. Why? Was Jane a druggy?"

"Preliminary toxicology report indicated use—not enough to kill her, but she was high when she died."

"That opens up some possibilities, doesn't it? Could be a body dump, after all. The kid is horsing around, doing coke in her friend's pool while Mom and Dad are out of town. The kid drowns and the other kids panic. They put the body in the back of a rusty old red pickup—something like mine— drive down to the Delta and dump Jane in the slough.''

"All possible, I suppose," Abby said, "but why isn't somebody looking for her? Kids don't normally disappear without somebody noticing. Because this Jane Doe was a young girl, the case got pretty good publicity. No calls from frantic parents or family, no calls period."

"Have they run her prints through the state Department of Justice?"

"Yes. There was a note when I got back. No match."

"Nobody wants her and nobody knows her," he observed.

"At least not yet."

"It's still fairly early."

"This one's going to last awhile," she said. "I've got a hunch."

They exchanged looks.

"So, what are your plans?" he asked. "You can't make an arrest based on a blood-type match, a scratch on my face and a red truck. Not without the lab work that ties it all to me."

"True, which means I'm going to have to try to do just that."

"Yeah, I know. It's your job."

"I spoke with a deputy D.A. We're getting a search warrant. It should be on its way here as we speak. The lab guys are going directly to your place. They'll try to find evidence placing the victim there."

"I understand."

She could see by his demeanor he fully appreciated the gravity of the situation. "Don't you think it's time you find a lawyer?"

"You may have given up on me," he said, "but I haven't quite written myself off. You see, my old man wasn't the most wholesome character, but he taught me one thing that's served me well over the years. Ol' Dad said, 'Frank, if you're going to know somebody well, make it yourself.' I think I know the guy inside this skin of mine, Abby. Drunk or sober, he doesn't have sex with children. And he certainly doesn't drown them and dump their bodies in the slough.''

Abby tossed the pad aside and gave him a long, hard look. ''You'd make a hell of a witness, Frank.''

''Let's just hope it doesn't come to that.''

Watermark Slough

It took them more than three hours to go through his place. Early on the rain had stopped, so Frank had gone for a long walk. Most of the time, though, he spent sitting in one of the patrol cars, waiting. The lab guys didn't want him inside and wouldn't let him near their truck.

Abby and her people were a little more tolerant. They were local, they knew him, and every one of them—including Abby—was aware that, had a single council member voted the other way, he would have been chief of police. That didn't put him above the law, but it meant he was deserving of a little extra courtesy. Besides, all these people were his friends.

The guys from the crime lab offered to take tissue samples from him while they were there, to save a trip to the lab. Frank complied.

''Just make damn sure you don't get the labels mixed up with somebody else's,'' he said within earshot of Abby.

Sure, it was false bravado, but Frank was grasping at every straw he could. The day's revelations had been a blow. The worst part still was the fact that most of the evening was a blank. He could only hope it wasn't some kind of repressed-memory thing that would one day come pouring out.

Abby was the last to leave. Frank stood next to her car with her as dusk fell.

"Any surprises in there?" he asked, tilting his head toward his mobile home.

"A pair of women's panties hidden in the back corner of your closet," she said.

"Hidden?"

"I'm sorry, Frank. That's where they found them. That's what I should have said."

"They might have been in the back of the closet because some lady lost them years ago. I only do spring cleaning once a decade, you know."

Abby managed not to laugh. "Well, I must admit they looked a little large for Jane Doe. They were the panties of a woman, not a girl."

"One for the good guys," he said.

"Maybe."

"Anything else, Chief?"

"Sheets in the laundry basket."

"That bothered me, too."

"Why didn't you wash them, for crissakes?"

"What are you saying, Abby? That I should have destroyed evidence?"

She shook her head. "Are you nuts or just compulsively honest?"

"Maybe a little of both."

She stared off at the fading light of the sky. "Frank, maybe you aren't taking this seriously enough. I know a criminal defense lawyer in Sacramento who's really good. His name is Eric Ross. Why don't you give him a call?"

"I'll wait until the lab reports come back. If they connect me to the girl, indicating guilt, then it becomes a question of guilty of what? For that I *do* need a lawyer."

"I admire your confidence," she said.

"For the moment I'm putting my faith in dear ol' Dad."

Abby nodded. "Well, I've got to go."

"Thanks for…everything you've done."

"I haven't done anything but try to build a case. Unfortunately you've been caught in the middle of it."

"Due to no fault of yours. But I appreciate how considerate you've been."

She smiled. "I'm out of here. I don't want anyone thinking I'm fraternizing with a suspect. I've got to maintain an appearance of objectivity."

"Does that mean you're sympathetic?"

"Bye, Frank."

"Oh, Chief," he said, stopping her from getting in the car.

"Yeah?"

"If the lab tests come back giving me a clean bill of health, you owe me dinner."

"Oh? Why's that?"

He chuckled. "Because I'm cheap. And also because I know a good long-shot bet when I see one."

"If the lab tests implicate you, who buys *me* dinner?"

"The warden at San Quentin."

She gave him a look and got in the car. Frank watched her drive off. Then he went inside.

His home had been carefully turned upside down—not trashed, but thoroughly rumpled. He wasn't surprised. Without a maid on the team, things never got put back quite right. He took a look in his closet, wondering if the panties belonged to Kay. He sure as hell didn't hide them two nights ago. If they were Jane Doe's, somebody was working overtime to set him up. It was a possibility that had only begun to roll through his mind.

Frank was at work on the closet, taking the opportunity to straighten up the place a little, when the phone rang. He went to answer it.

"Frank, what happened?"

It was Kay.

"What do you mean, what happened?"

"Abby questioned you, didn't she? I want to know what happened. Do they think you did it?"

"Kill the girl, you mean?"

"Commit a crime."

"They're tightening the noose, Kay, but I'm not on the gallows quite yet."

"Frank, I want a straight answer. Are you in serious trouble?"

He sighed. "I'm at a big disadvantage because I don't know what happened. But I don't have to prove I'm innocent. The D.A. has to prove I'm guilty."

There was a very long silence.

"Kay?"

"I'm thinking."

He waited a while longer.

"Care to share your concern?" he said when she still didn't speak.

He heard a groan of anguish. "I swear to God, I hate you, Frank Keegan."

"Well, that's always good to hear. Mind telling me why? Have I killed somebody else I don't know about?"

"I didn't tell you everything about Friday night," she said curtly.

"Oh?"

"Honest to God, I wouldn't tell you this, but I can't bear to see you blamed for something you didn't do."

"Nobody's blaming me for anything, Kay. At least not yet."

"They will. You know it and I know it."

"Okay, fine. What happened Friday that you didn't tell me about?"

She hesitated. "I brought you home like I told you, but I didn't just drop you off, Frank. I went inside with you."

He waited, knowing that wasn't all. "And?"

"We…"

"Yes?"

"We had sex."

For an instant he was speechless. "We did?"

"Yes, damn it. I don't know why the hell I went to bed with you, but I did."

"Then I didn't *imagine* it was you," he said.

"No."

"Kay—"

"I don't want to hear it. Don't apologize. Don't ask me why. Don't ever mention this again."

"Okay, I won't."

"When you told me you didn't remember anything after leaving the Queen, I thought you were trying to spare me the embarrassment. Then, when they found that girl…well, I've been agonizing, waiting to see what was going to happen."

"I don't know if your confession will make any difference in the long run, but it certainly makes me feel better," he said. "I've been dying over the possibility I hurt that kid."

"I know you have. That's another reason I had to make this call. But there's more, Frank."

"Lord, this is turning into a soap opera."

"That scratch on your face came from me. When I was helping you into the house, you tripped and I grabbed for you, scratching you by accident."

"You didn't leave your panties behind by any chance, did you?"

"What?"

"Never mind," he said, "just a thought."

"Something else happened that Abby should know about," Kay said. "I didn't think much of it at the time, but now, knowing that girl died, I realize it could be important."

"I'm listening," he said, his curiosity really piqued.

"After we made love, you were out like a light. I fell

asleep, too, but I was awakened in the middle of the night by screaming. It sounded like a girl."

"You mean outside?"

"Yes. I tried to wake you, but you were dead to the world. I was concerned, so I went to the front door. By the time I got out onto the porch the screaming had stopped. But then I saw them, two people up on the levee road. The rain had ended and the moon was shining through the clouds, so I could see them real well. They were hurrying along, one of them limping. The other one kept saying, 'Come on, hurry. We've got to get out of here.' I watched them until they were gone."

"What time was this?"

"It must have been two-thirty or three."

"Could you describe them?"

"My impression was they were kids, Frank. Both quite thin. One a little bigger than the other. The little one was limping."

"You wouldn't be able to identify them?"

"No."

He thought for a moment. "That puts at least two other people at the scene of the crime."

"Yes," she said, "I know. That's the other reason I had to say something to you."

"But we've got Mort to worry about, don't we?"

She was silent.

"Making you a reluctant witness," he said.

"I'll do what I have to do," she said with a sigh. "Even if it means testifying I spent the night with you and I end up messing up my life."

"That may not be necessary, Kay."

"What do you mean?"

"If you're the one I had sex with, then there won't be any evidence tying me to the girl. Without that, they've got nothing."

"But you'll still have to suffer through the suspicion and gossip."

"I've endured worse."

"I still think I should say something. Abby can be discreet, can't she?"

The notion of Kay talking to Abby about them having sex gave him a jolt. Saving his butt was one thing, but saving his pride was another. "It doesn't quite work that way, Kay," he said.

"But they still have to find the person responsible, don't they? I'm a witness of sorts. I don't want to make any public announcements, but I can't pretend like nothing happened, can I?"

"Why not let me take care of it?" he said. "There are ways to point investigators in the right direction without naming names. Besides, what about Mort?"

"I suppose you know what you're doing," she said.

"You just relax and let me handle it."

"Okay."

"But listen, Kay, I really appreciate you making this call. I know it wasn't easy."

"The other night wasn't easy, either."

He heard a lilt in her voice. Ironically, it made him sad. "Pals?" he said.

"Pals."

Frank hung up, feeling better, but knowing he had a different ball to juggle. Best of all, he realized how truly wise his old man had been.

Monday
February 17th

Watermark Slough

Frank went to bed early, slept well for the first time in days and got up with the sun. He felt better knowing he wasn't a child molester, rapist and murderer, though now it seemed absurd he'd ever had doubts. Drink was the demon—as well as those niggling bits of evidence pointing at him—but Kay, bless her, had relieved his torment. At the same time, though, she'd sort of sneaked back into the forefront of his life, leaving him wondering. Sleeping with him was an odd slip on her part and especially confounding when he considered he could scarcely remember it.

Now he was able to turn his attention to the question of what had really happened to Jane Doe. First they had to figure out who she was. Since she was found by his dock, he felt more than a little responsibility for helping to bring her story to light. The cop in him knew that in solving a crime of this sort, the place to start was always with the victim's family and friends. When you were dealing with a Jane Doe, you were at an immediate disadvantage. But these things almost always worked out in time because few lives existed in total anonymity. Eventually somebody would start asking questions. Once the police knew who Jane Doe was, the circumstances of her death would likely follow.

Frank was glad to see that the weather had cleared. The morning sky was pale blue and nearly cloudless. February could be unpredictable in California. He'd seen almost summerlike weather some years with the temperature rising into the seventies or even eighties. This, he could tell, was not going to be a hot day, but there'd be some sun.

Grabbing his jacket, he decided to take a walk in his orchard for a close look at his pear trees. They were still dormant, of course, and had been since the pruning in December. This was the slow season. There wasn't much to do until spring when the codling moth showed up and the spraying began.

In Wayne Neely, Frank had the best pest-control adviser, or PCA, in the business. Fortunately Wayne had taken a liking to him and helped in extra ways, even though Frank was a relatively small-time operator. Maybe Wayne had felt a little sorry for him after the fiasco with Mort.

Frank had learned the pear business was a fine science, involving skill, luck and connections. Dumb cops usually weren't well connected and they were seldom lucky, but he kept plugging away, trying to make up with determination what he lacked in skill and knowledge. He pruned and took care of all the irrigating, even hand-shoveling the berms to move the water from check to check. The only work he hired out was the spraying and disking.

His eighteen acres barely qualified as a truck farm compared to the big operators like the Hays brothers over on Grand Island, but at certain times of the year it kept him pretty busy. He was enough of a realist to know the days of starting with nothing and becoming a millionaire farmer were over. If you didn't inherit a bunch of free-and-clear orchard land from your daddy, you could forget it.

So Frank had set his sights lower, hoping simply to

achieve economy of scale by enlarging his holdings. His neighbor, a widow named Constance Butterfield, had forty acres of trees, a nice old white clapboard house and no bank debt. When she was ready to throw in the towel, the obvious solution was to buy her out. Assuming he'd gathered sufficient capital.

Frank's security business paid most of the bills in the meantime. Winter was when he concentrated on that vocation, which by his choice tended more toward installing burglar alarms than mounting investigations. He did the latter on a pick-and-choose basis, mainly to avoid spousal problems, which he found messy and unrewarding. Even so, he'd get caught up in a case every once in a while, usually because he just couldn't turn his back on somebody in need. It had been that way when he was a cop, too. He'd get wrapped up in a case and the rest of his life would go to hell. He'd hear about it from Arlene, of course.

Ironically, divorce hadn't insulated him from her criticism. Early on, before she'd remarried, she'd knocked him for not living up to her expectations for financial assistance with Beth. "Maybe we could afford to send her to private school if you had the sense to work for people with money," she said during one angry confrontation. He was glad those days were behind him. Nowadays, if he felt bad about not busting his butt to rake in every available dime, at least the guilt was coming from within.

At the moment even his security business was slow. There wasn't much on his calendar for the next two weeks—a few maintenance jobs and that was it. Which meant he'd have some free time and, if Abby didn't object, he'd help with the Jane Doe case.

Because of the high water table, the ground stayed very wet after a rain, which meant Frank had to slog through mud when he walked about the orchard. The trees were mostly to one side of the trailer and behind it, spread out enough that it took him several minutes to walk from one boundary to the other. It was a ritual he performed periodically, the appeal, he assumed, was that it helped him feel connected to the land.

After his little tour of his estate, Frank headed back to the house, stimulated by the brisk morning air. As he drew near, he could hear the phone ringing. He jogged the last few yards, but the caller had hung up by the time he got inside, and there was no message on his machine because he'd forgotten to turn the damned thing on again. That reminded him he'd never gotten hold of Chet, so he dialed his friend's number, but still got no answer. He decided to phone Dix at the station to see if he'd heard from him.

Frank checked the time. It was still early, but Dix was often at work before the office crew. The sergeant was basically a paperwork guy and liked to do his desk work before the phones started ringing. Frank figured it wouldn't hurt to give him a call.

Dix was there. "Naw," he said, "haven't heard a peep from Chet. Could be he went up to his cabin."

"In February?"

Dix said, "You're right. Chet hasn't cross-country skied in years."

"Maybe I'll give that old gal who lives next door to him a jingle, the one who always worries after him. What's her name? Emma something."

"Winnans," Dix said.

"Yeah, that's it."

"Let me know what you turn up," the sergeant said.

Frank got out the Riverton phone book the Chamber of Commerce put out. He'd ripped off the back page because Mort Anderson had a big color ad on it, complete with a quarter-page photo of his grinning puss. There were some things about which Frank didn't mind being adolescent.

"Mr. Keegan," Emma said when he reached her, "how did you know I'd called?"

"Was that you, Mrs. Winnans? I ran to the phone but didn't quite make it in time."

"Chet said if there's ever a problem, I should contact you."

Frank was touched his friend held him in that kind of regard. Chet had never said anything to him along the lines of who to contact if there was an accident, where he kept his important papers and such. Once Sally died, the old boy was pretty much on his own. They'd never had children and Chet's only immediate family was a half sister in Missouri he hadn't seen in over thirty years. Frank could only assume Chet regarded him as an honorary cousin or the like.

"So, you think there's a problem?" he asked the woman.

"Well, I haven't seen him since Saturday morning and there are two papers on his porch. Chet never goes away without saying something to me because I feed Sally's cat, take in his papers and his mail when he's gone."

"It might have been a last-minute thing."

"Personally, I think there's something wrong, Mr. Keegan. Last night late I noticed a funny glow coming from Chet's front room, like the TV set was on. The shades are drawn so you can't see in, but I was able to look in his garage this morning. His car is there."

"I'd better come over," Frank said.

Riverton

Riverton was, in a sense, two towns. The Bottoms, on the east side of the river, contained the commercial district and the older neighborhoods. It dated to the nineteenth century. The residential portion was made up of rickety, old clapboard houses of that era, though a couple of blocks on Walnut and

Oak Streets had been fixed up some, and the yards behind the picket fences and climbing roses were tidy.

The Chinese section looked run-down on the outside, but the insides were neat, clean and modern. The Mexican and white sections met at St. Joseph's, the Catholic Church. The Baptist church was at the southern end of the Bottoms. Beyond it were three black families, a few more whites and then the orchards started. Frank's place was outside of town in that direction.

The Grove, located across the river, was the tony part of Riverton. Chet lived there, as did Kay, Mayor Joyner and most of the town's business owners. The really fat cats like Mort Anderson lived in big houses on the outskirts. Like everything else in Riverton, the Grove was below the levees so that only rooftops, treetops and church steeples were visible from the other side of the river. The area was four blocks by six blocks, set out in a perfect rectangle. It was bounded by the river and levee on one side, large pear orchards to the north and south, and open fields to the west. The steeples, by height, were the Presbyterians', Methodists' and Congregationalists'. The homes in the Grove were on quarter- to half-acre lots with two- or three-car garages. None of the houses in the Bottoms had more than a one-car garage, many had none. That may have been the most telling sociological fact of all.

Whenever Frank drove across the bridge into the Grove, he always felt like a pretender, though most of his friends were from that end of the socio-economic spectrum. He was never sure whether his plebeian leanings were because he didn't have money or because he had a man-of-the-people outlook. Be that as it may, he sort of liked being able to walk both sides of the street—or in this case, both sides of the river.

Unless the drawbridge was up, it didn't take five minutes to get from one side of Riverton to the other, so Frank found himself at the Grove in no time at all. He drove past the fire station, the Congregational Church, then turned onto Biscayne Avenue where Chet lived. Incongruously the streets in the Grove all had the names of bodies of water, whereas over in the Bottoms the streets were named after trees—a fact for which he'd never heard the explanation.

As he pulled up in front of Chet's place, Emma Winnans, in a heavy cardigan over a housedress, came out her front door before Frank made it to the sidewalk. He didn't really know the woman, but every time he saw her, she seemed to have her gray hair in rollers.

"I'm so glad you've come, Mr. Keegan," she said. "I'm sure there's something terribly wrong."

"I'll poke around," he replied.

Frank went onto the porch and rapped on the door loudly. He tried to peer in the windows, but the shades were carefully drawn. Next he made his way along the side of the house, Emma Winnans padding along behind him. Through a crack in the shade of one of the side windows, Frank was able to see what appeared to be the glow of a TV set coming from the dark interior. It was difficult to see inside, but he thought he could make out a figure in the recliner in front of the set. The first thought through his mind was that Chet had had a heart attack while watching TV.

"Mrs. Winnans," he said to her calmly, "why don't you give Dix Fowler a call at the police station and have him send somebody over."

"Oh, dear," she said ominously.

She scuttled off and Frank took a peek in the window of Chet's garage. The car was there, like the woman had said. Next he went to the back door. It was locked, but by breaking one of the panels of pained glass, he could get access. Deciding not to wait for Dix, Frank took a brick from the border of the flower bed and knocked out a panel of glass. Then he reached inside and unlocked the door.

The kitchen smelled of garbage, but as he moved toward the front of the house, he picked up another scent—the smell of gore and death. Even before he entered the front room he knew there'd be a body. Chet was in the recliner as Frank had expected. But he had not expected his head to be tilted grotesquely, a hole in the side of it and blood all over the front of his shirt. Chet's service revolver was in his hand.

No matter how often a person came upon such a scene, it was impossible not to feel a clench of squeamishness. Chet, being a friend, made it much worse. Frank swallowed hard, then out of habit glanced around the room. The TV set was on, but not tuned to a station. Rather the screen was blank, which struck him as curious until he realized the VCR was on. Chet appeared to have been watching a video.

His eyes becoming accustomed to the obscurity of the room, Frank noticed a container for a blank videocassette on the floor by Chet's chair. Frank didn't want to disturb the scene, though he was tempted to have a quick look at the tape. The remote control was on the table next to Chet, but Frank didn't touch it. Instead, he went to the VCR itself, pushing the rewind button. After half a minute an image came on the screen and he pushed the play button. It was a picture of a handwritten note, in block print, apparently taken by a video camera. The note said, "This is a copy. The original will cost you ten thousand dollars. I'll be in touch." After a few seconds the screen went blank again. Frank pushed the stop button, then rewind.

"Mr. Keegan!"

It was the neighbor at the back door. Frank went to the kitchen to find her standing in the doorway.

"What's that smell?" she asked, frowning.

"I'm afraid there's been an accident, Mrs. Winnans," he told her. "Chet's dead."

"Oh, dear God."

"Did you get Dix?"

"He was in a meeting with the police chief. I left a message."

"If you don't mind calling again, tell them to interrupt the meeting. They'll want to know. And tell them I think Chief Hooper might want to come, as well."

"Certainly, Mr. Keegan."

The woman went off and Frank returned to the front room. The tape was rewound. He pushed the play button on the VCR. The screen was blank for several moments, then an interior shot of a bedroom came on the screen. The picture was not clear, giving the impression it was heavily filtered, possibly taken from a hidden camera.

After several moments a man entered the room followed by a girl in a very short skirt. The man was Chet Wilsey. The identity of the girl wasn't quite so obvious, but when she turned and looked directly at the camera, Frank realized it was the same face as in the Polaroid shots taken of the drowning victim out at his place. It was Jane Doe.

Riverton Civic Center

They sat on opposite sides of the conference table watching the TV at the far end of the room. The last images of Chet Wilsey screwing the girl flickered across the screen. The creaking of the bed and Chet's groaning stopped at the same moment. Chet rolled off the girl, who lay motionless and silent until he told her to get up and get dressed. Gathering her clothes, Jane went off to the bathroom. Chet lay on his back in full view of the camera for maybe half a minute. Then he sat up, took something from the drawer in the bedside table. Moments later the girl reappeared, dressed.

"Should I go?" she asked him.

"The boy pay you?"

"Yes."

"Here's a little extra," he said, handing her a couple of bills. "Now go on, get out of here."

The girl moved out of camera range. The sound of a door opening and closing was heard. Chet, still sitting on the bed, lowered his head into his hands. The printed note came onto the screen then. When it disappeared, Abby pointed the remote control at the TV set and turned it off.

She glanced at Frank, her stomach in a knot. He appeared ill, having trouble looking her in the eye. Neither of them spoke for several moments.

"You as sick as I am?" he asked after a while.

"Yes."

"That child could have been his granddaughter."

Abby said, "I guess it goes to prove you can never know somebody completely."

"Is the human race that bad or am I more naive than I thought?"

She had no answer. There was no justifying anything they'd seen. She was as appalled as Frank, though she didn't take it quite so personally. Chet Wilsey might have been an adversary, but he was also an icon of the department she headed. She could not take pleasure in the fact he'd dishonored himself. To the contrary, she was embarrassed for him.

What wasn't clear was what this did to her case. Chet clearly had been involved with the girl, but did that also mean he'd been involved in her death? Common sense indicated there'd be a connection. But what? What circumstantial evidence she had pointed to Frank.

"How could the stupid bastard do that?" Frank muttered.

"I can understand him shooting himself," Abby said, "but why didn't he destroy that tape? He had to know people would be appalled."

Frank did not answer immediately. He sat rubbing his jaw. "Maybe it was his way of confessing," he said. "Chet didn't leave behind a family to be humiliated by it. There isn't anybody to care but me and a couple of his other friends.''

"What confuses me is if Chet was struggling at the end to do the honorable thing—to confess, in effect—why didn't he tell us who was blackmailing him? That might shed some light on Jane Doe's death. Surely Chet realized that.''

"I don't know,'' Frank said. "Nothing is making a lot of sense to me.''

She gave him a long look, wondering if his apparent confusion was intended to feed hers. She was coming to realize that she wanted him to be innocent, but at the same time she was afraid to think he was—afraid her compassion for him might blur her judgment. The very last thing she wanted was to allow herself to be made the fool. And yet, it was hard to make herself nail him.

"I wish you hadn't gone in his house alone,'' she said. "It would have been better if you'd waited for us.''

"Why?''

"Because then I wouldn't have to wonder what else might have turned up.''

"What are you suggesting? That I destroyed evidence—say, a suicide note somehow implicating me in the girl's death?''

"I'm not saying anything, Frank. But look at this from my point of view. You're a suspect, don't forget. My *only* suspect at the moment. I'd feel a lot better if one of my officers had entered Chet's place and secured the scene.''

"Well, maybe you're right, but I have the advantage of knowing I'm innocent,'' he replied.

"Need I remind you that you don't recall what happened that night?'' she said.

"True, but it turns out I've got a witness, an exculpatory witness.''

He'd managed to surprise her. "Since when?''

"Since last night.''

Abby sat upright, her interest piqued. "Is this something you plan to share?"

"Definitely," he said. "Just waiting for the right moment. There is one small problem. My witness is going to have to remain anonymous."

"Anonymous?"

"Yeah. You see the lady…well…let's say she stands to be embarrassed by the fact that she was at my place that evening. But she can vouch that I was with her all night."

Abby let her disgust show. "You expect me to accept that on faith? Come on, Frank, give me a break."

"It doesn't matter whether you believe me or not. I now know I'm innocent and that's the part that had me concerned—my own doubt."

"Frank, have you lost your mind? *I'm* the investigator. I'm making a case against you. My analysis and my opinion do matter. Your witness has to tell *me* what she saw and did."

"What I'm trying to tell you is that it doesn't matter because you don't have a case against me. The DNA testing is not going to show a match. The A negative blood on the rocks wasn't mine. I don't know who had sex with Jane Doe, but the semen samples will prove it wasn't me. I don't need an alibi witness because your evidence will implicate somebody else. That's the point."

"So, why did you bring it up, pray tell? To show how macho you are?" She couldn't help her annoyance bubbling over.

"No," he replied. "I'd rather have said nothing. To be honest, I'm embarrassed by what happened. But my witness had other things to say which bear on your investigation. *That's* why I'm speaking up."

"I'm listening."

Frank explained how his companion had been awakened by screaming and how subsequently she'd seen the two figures up on the levee, fleeing.

"If true, that's very significant," Abby said.

"It is true."

"Your witness may have convinced you, but before I go chasing after a couple of phantoms in the night, one of which was limping, she's going to have to convince *me*."

"You'll have to settle for my secondhand account," he said.

Abby went to the window and peered out at the sunny sky. She didn't like the way this was going. Not at all. She'd been tolerant, but she was beginning to see that was working against her. If she wasn't careful, Frank would make a fool of her.

Turning to face him, she said, "I've been awfully casual in the way I've handled this case, especially when it comes to communicating with you. I wonder if it isn't time to put our relationship on a more formal footing."

Frank looked annoyed. "Unless, of course, I'm willing to give you the name of my witness. Isn't that what you're saying?"

"In my shoes you'd take the same position."

"Look, how long before you get the DNA report back? Once I'm cleared, this all becomes a nonissue."

"Routinely these things take weeks, as you know. I've asked for rush status and I've been promised preliminary results in a week or so...if I'm lucky."

"So you're willing to let the trail go cold because you're convinced I'm your man."

"I'm not convinced of anything, Frank," she snapped. "And I'll pursue any viable lead. If there's a witness who's willing to step forward and say she spent the night with you and saw others up on the levee, I'll certainly listen and take action accordingly."

Frank shook his head, clearly displeased. Abby studied him, fighting her instinct to believe him because she was even more afraid of being wrong.

"What it comes down to is we're both in a bind," he said. "And I'm real sorry about that because it's getting in the way of solving this case. What I'd really like to do is help in the investigation."

"That's absurd, Frank, and you know it."

"The longer you focus on me, the colder the trail is going to get."

"Okay, if you really want to help, why don't you tell me how Chet's relationship with the girl might have figured into her death. Who killed Jane Doe? Chet?"

"After the surprises in this case, I hesitate to say no to anything, but I don't see that he'd have a motive. Unless she was the one blackmailing him."

Abby considered that. "If so, and Chet killed her because of it, why would he have killed himself? She was dead, and he had the tape. Or are you saying he killed himself out of guilt?"

"I think guilt was a factor, but not necessarily guilt about having killed her—seeing himself with her on the tape might have been enough. That, and knowing the kid was dead, maybe because of the life she led, being involved with people like him. Then, too, there's the probability that the girl had an accomplice. Did you catch his reference to a boy?"

"Yes."

"Well, there's something else we have to look at."

She found herself amused by his insistence on putting himself on the side of the law. Either Frank Keegan had chutzpah or he was truly innocent.

"Personally," he went on, "I think your top priority ought to be finding the people who were on the levee that night."

"On the basis of testimony by your mystery witness." There was sarcasm in her voice, but she couldn't help it. Abby paced back and forth, thinking. Finally she stopped. "I'd like to formalize things," she told him. "If and when you're ready to produce your witness, we'll talk. Otherwise,

I'm treating you like a suspect, not a member of the family. I'm going to advise my officers to do the same.''

"I'm a persona non grata, in other words."

"Get an attorney, Frank."

"Why would I kill that girl and leave her by my dock?"

"I have no comment."

"Yes, you do have a comment," he said angrily. "I want to hear a theory."

"Okay, Mr. Keegan," she snapped. "You want a theory? Here's a theory. Chet has this little hooker and he tells his buddy about her. She's waiting at your place when you get home drunk. You have sex with her. She climbs in your bathtub, then something goes wrong. Maybe it's an accident, or maybe you kill her in a drunken rage. You put the body in your truck, thinking you'll dump it someplace, but you're so drunk, you're lucky to make it up to the levee road. You decide to dump her in the slough. You're bleeding from the gash she gave you during your struggle. The blood gets on the rock. You stagger to your truck, retreat back down the drive and go to bed.''

"How does Jane get out of the water and onto the bank?" he asked.

"Maybe you had second thoughts and tried to drag her out, only getting her as far as the rocks before giving up. Or maybe you go back down to the slough in the morning. I don't know. You wanted a theory and I gave you a theory. The point is I have reason to treat you as a suspect."

"And Chet? What's your theory about him?"

"Chet kills himself because he's being blackmailed and he sees what his friend has done. He feels responsible. It's too much to bear.''

Frank slowly nodded. "Okay, Abby, fine. But I'm going to hold you to that dinner when the physical evidence shows I'm innocent."

"I hope I have to buy it for you."

"So do I."

He got up and went to the door, where he paused for a moment and gave her a long, appraising look. His expression wasn't cocksure, but neither was it cautious. The guy either knew he was innocent or he was one hell of an actor.

"So long, Chief," he finally said. Then he left.

After he had been gone for a minute or two, Abby rewound the tape and put it in the evidence bag. She didn't know what to think. All she knew for sure was that the possibilities seemed to be getting worse. She had yet another problem—contending with the fact that the former police chief and town hero was a child molester.

Frank had her completely baffled, which was probably his intent. That hurt worse than anything. Odd, but the deeper he seemed to sink into the quagmire, the more she regretted it. Shaking her head, she took the bag and headed for her office. What could possibly have made her think she wanted this job?

Tuesday
February 18th

At 9:00 a.m. Abby entered the conference room. The entire staff, except for the dispatcher on duty, was there. So was the mayor. She'd asked W. C. Joyner to come since he was her nominal boss. And like everyone else, W.C. had heard about Chet.

The mayor had not been one of Abby's fans. But this was one of those situations where everyone tended to pull together. W.C., the owner of a pesticide company and farm-implement dealership, had actually been rather gracious when she'd spoken to him on the phone the previous evening. "Of course, I'll be there, Chief Hooper," he'd said. "It's important that we close ranks in a time of crisis."

Abby did not know the man well. They'd interacted at council meetings and in her job interview, but she couldn't say she had any knowledge of him on a personal level. W.C.'s real name was Wendell Chauncy, but he'd fight anybody who called him that. He was sixtyish, heavyset and a cigar smoker, having been one long before it came back into style. W.C. got along with just about everyone, which made him an ideal small-town politician. Frank losing the vote for police chief had been one of the mayor's few setbacks. According to all indications, W.C. intended to use the present crisis to establish better relations with her, a development for which Abby was truly grateful.

Her primary reason for calling the meeting was to put people's minds at ease. She knew incidents like Chet's suicide could be a blow to a department's morale. So she made a brief speech designed to buck people up. Afterward, W.C. said a few words, assuring everyone of the city's support. Though primarily a businessman, W.C., for all his homespun tendencies, did have a way with words.

When he'd finished, Abby thanked him and asked if anyone else had anything to say. Nobody did, so she closed the meeting. W.C. lingered after the others had gone.

"Abby," he said, "I want you to know I'm pleased with the way you're handling this matter. You inspire confidence."

"Thank you, Mr. Mayor, I appreciate you saying that."

"Please, it's W.C." He took a cigar out of his pocket and toyed with it, rolling it between his fingers. "I know that police business falls into a special category, and that even in my capacity as mayor I don't have a right to get involved, but I'd like to know if you seriously suspect Frank of being responsible for that girl's death."

Abby took a moment to roll the question through her mind. "There is evidence that may link Frank to what may have been a crime. Beyond that I won't speculate."

"But Abby, honey, we're talking about a man who lost his own little girl through a drowning. There's no way he could have hurt that child."

Abby's brows rose with the term "honey," but she saw W.C. was being emphatic, not patronizing, and was probably unaware of what he'd said. She chose to deal with the substance of his remark. "W.C., I don't make judgments based on whether I like a person or not. I go strictly on the basis of the facts and the evidence. If reputation was all that mattered, I'd have to ignore that tape in Chet's VCR.''

"Is it as graphic as they say?''

"I'm afraid so.''

W.C. shook his head as he studied the cigar between his fingers. "I'd never have believed it. Never in a million years.''

"Since we're discussing it,'' Abby said, "do you have any reason to believe Frank might have been involved with the girl?''

"Involved?''

"The way Chet was,'' Abby replied, finding it difficult to speak directly.

"Frank Keegan? Never.'' He twisted his mouth uneasily. "Of course, I'd have said the same thing of Chet.''

"Chet and Frank were friends,'' she said. "Isn't it possible they had this little hobby in common?''

"I would have said no, but I've already been fooled. Seems to me there's a big difference between their situations, though. Chet recently lost his wife and he retired. Everybody knows he's been down in the dumps. Maybe he acted out of desperation, even mental illness. Frank on the other hand…well, he lost his kid, but that was several years ago. Frank's the type who will do things his own way, but he's sound as a dollar.''

"Do you have any reason to believe either of them were involved in drugs, did a little cocaine from time to time, that sort of thing?''

"Frank and Chet involved in drugs? No,'' W.C. said. "Never. Oh, they could both drink—to excess on occasion. I'm not saying they were choirboys, but illegal drugs, absolutely not. And that's the sort of thing a person can't hide. Not from people who know them well. Why do you ask?''

"The toxicology report indicates Jane Doe had used drugs before she died. That doesn't mean the person or persons responsible for her death were necessarily druggies, but he—they—may have supplied the girl with a little nose candy. Many hookers will take payment in drugs as readily as cash.''

"It wouldn't have been impossible for Chet or Frank to put their hands on some cocaine, I suppose, but that doesn't strike me as their style. I'd have believed they got her drunk before they'd have given her drugs. But then, without that tape, I wouldn't have believed any of this was possible.''

Abby had him talking in a reasonably candid fashion and decided to press him a little. "Since we're talking about vices and virtues, W.C., are you aware of a particular woman Frank might be keeping company with?''

Now it was the mayor who arched a brow. "No, I'm not.''

"He claims to have a witness who can vouch for him, but he won't reveal who she is. I'm wondering if it's a story he's made up.''

W.C. put his cigar back in his pocket. "If Frank says it, I'm inclined to believe it. It's in his character to spare the lady's honor.''

"It could also be a matter of convenience that he's so honorable,'' Abby said.

"Doesn't sound like the man I know.'' W.C. cleared his throat. "Yes, I'm aware I'd have said the same of Chet.''

"Who has Frank been involved with in the past?'' she asked.

W.C. wagged his finger at her. "Now you're getting into the area of gossip, young lady. I probably do my share, but not in the context of an official investigation. Sorry.''

"It's a small town. I can't imagine it's much of a secret.''

"True,'' W.C. said, "but even small towns can be discreet. Should it become necessary, I imagine the lady in question will step forward.''

"What makes you think so?''

"Because of the way Frank's regarded in this town, Abby.''

"Chet was considered a saint, too."

"Yes and no."

"What do you mean?"

"Those of us who knew Chet knew he had a randy side. I'm not going to speak ill of the dead, but I'll say this—Chet had his fun. The surprise this time is that it was with a young girl. And if you want my opinion, that's why he killed himself. Chet knew he'd done wrong and he couldn't live with the consequences." W.C. took out his cigar again. "Now, unless you have some more questions, I'll be on my way."

"No, I don't have any more questions. But thank you for sharing your thoughts."

"Anytime," he said. Then, patting her hand, he left the room.

Abby watched him go. She didn't like feeling paranoid, but again she wondered if the good old boys weren't closing ranks. If so, what did it mean? Could Frank have been blackmailing Chet?

The thought made her quail. She was the law, but she was the one who was beginning to feel isolated. It was almost as though she was on the outside looking in.

Galt

Frank had just sat down at a table in McDonald's with a cheeseburger and a cup of coffee when his beeper sounded. It was Kay's home number. Figuring it wasn't so urgent he couldn't finish his lunch first, he chomped down his burger, took a couple of gulps of coffee, then went to the phone.

"Oh, good," she said, hearing his voice, "your beeper worked. I tried to leave a message on your machine, but it never answered."

"I must have forgotten to put it on. Sorry."

"Frank, how are you ever going to operate a successful

business unless you learn the basics, like making yourself available?"

"*You* want me available, Kay?"

"I'm talking about your customers," she said.

"Oh."

"Where are you?"

"Over in Galt. One of my commercial accounts did some remodeling and I had to rewire part of the system. No big deal, but it got me out of the house for a few hours."

"I'm glad to see you aren't so depressed you can't function," she said.

"We're talking about Chet?"

"Yes, I couldn't believe it. Chet and a young girl."

"In fairness, she was a hooker. This was no innocent child."

"Frank, you're making excuses for him."

"I don't mean to," he replied.

"Nobody wants to put what happened in the worst light," Kay said, "but I'm still appalled."

"I think Chet was, too."

"No, he couldn't bear the humiliation. There's a difference."

"He left the evidence right there for everybody to see, Kay. I think he was making the punishment fit the crime."

"Only a man could look at it that way," she said, a tinge of disgust in her voice.

"Somehow I don't think you called me to talk about Chet. What's up?"

"I'm worried."

"About?"

"You."

"Regarding?"

"Oh, Frank, don't be obtuse. That girl, Jane Doe. The word around town is Abby means to hang you."

"Kay, she can't even bring charges without evidence. And

she'll have nothing to use against me because I was otherwise occupied when the girl died.'' He paused, his heart doing a little flip. "Unless you're recanting your testimony."

"No, but I'm thinking it may be best if I talked to Abby. Why should I make you go through this?"

"Because of Mort," he said hastily, perhaps too hastily.

"I appreciate your concern and I'd rather people—Mort especially—not know I spent the night with you, but we can only hide the truth for so long. Do you know how many reporters were in town this afternoon? At least two from the *Bee.* And somebody said they counted four mobile TV crews. This has turned into a big story, Frank."

He didn't care about the press. Nor was Mort the issue. Frank didn't want Abby to know he and Kay had had an affair. It was bad enough that they had been lovers in the past, but the fact that they'd been together as recently as last Friday would cook things with Abby for sure. She'd be turned off, if not revolted. Not that he had any realistic hope of becoming involved with her, but he had his fantasies and he liked clinging to them.

"Look, Kay," he said, determined not to give up on his dream just yet, "I'm the one hanging. If it's okay with me, it should be okay with you. Besides, the lab results should be back in a week and it'll all be academic at that point."

"Actually, you aren't the only one I'm concerned about, Frank. Belinda knows I drove you home. I can't ask her to lie to the police or ignore what she saw."

"She doesn't know we slept together." As he said the words an elderly woman passed him on her way to the ladies' room. She gave him a look of disgust.

"No," Kay replied, "but I won't ask her to lie. Dix already called this morning to make arrangements to interview everybody here. Toad will have to say he brought your truck back the next morning, for example."

"That's consistent with me being driven home by my lady

companion. It doesn't have to be you. Seems to me Belinda's the only one we've got to keep from Dix. Can't you arrange for her to be unavailable for at least a week?''

''Frank, why are you so eager to protect me? I would have thought you'd be happy to throw this in Mort's face.''

''All right, I admit I don't give a shit about Mort,'' he replied. ''You're decent enough not to want to see an innocent man go to the gallows. I'd like to be decent enough to preserve a lady's honor. Anyway, your happiness is important to me. We *are* still friends, Kay. At least I think we are.''

''Is that what this is, Frank? Friendship?''

''What else?''

She hesitated. ''I don't know what else, but something.''

Frank felt like a heel. It wasn't that he didn't care about Kay, because he did. But he was attracted to Abby. ''Look,'' he said disingenuously, ''how about this—I wouldn't mind you owing me one.''

''Now *that* I can buy.''

''I say we relax and let this one play itself out.''

''Okay,'' she said, ''unless and until things get off track.''

''That's fair enough.''

''Promise you aren't pulling a fast one on me,'' she warned.

''Scouts' honor.''

Tyler Island

Tristan was waiting for her at the gate, oblivious to the rain, ready to tear the wheels off her Bronco, his eyes gleaming in the headlights, his teeth bared, his hoarse baritone inviting combat. But when Abby got out to open the gate, calling to him, her fierce German shepherd was instantly transformed from Tristan-the-dragon-slayer to a whimpering, tail-wagging, slobbering guardian-of-the-hearth.

She'd only had the dog for three months, but they'd bonded almost immediately. Tristan had flunked out of the Sheriff's Department canine course and was looking for a new home when Abby heard about him. He had the qualities she wanted in a guard dog—loyalty to her and antipathy for everyone else.

"Did you miss me, Tristan?" she asked, taking his head in her hands and bending to reward him with air kisses.

Tristan responded with a spirited bark and blast of dog breath in her face. Abby gave his thigh-high haunch a couple of sturdy slaps and ordered him to move back from the gate. Tristan complied, sitting at the edge of the drive in Foo dog fashion, his chest puffed with pride as Abby drove into the compound. Once she'd secured the gate, the dog romped toward the huge, old turn-of-the-century Victorian with its cupola, spires and gables rising into the night sky.

Once inside, Abby kicked off her shoes and tossed her coat on a chair. She would have gone upstairs to change, but she didn't have time before the early news came on, and she wanted to see the interview she'd done with Channel 31 that afternoon. There was time to pour a glass of wine, so she turned on the TV set, then went to the kitchen to do so.

As she returned to the front room, the news was coming on. Lowering herself into her favorite chair, she watched the teasers. Their little soap opera in Riverton wasn't one of the leads, which came as a relief.

Abby hadn't had a lot of experience dealing with the media, but she was well enough informed to know they had a talent for distorting words. How they would paint her, using her own words and images, was anybody's guess. Not that she believed they had bad intentions, but as the media liaison in the Sheriff's Department once told her, the press had one objective—to tell the most interesting story they could put together, not necessarily the most accurate story. The result was that sometimes they played footloose with the truth.

After the hooks came the commercials. Abby, a little glassy-eyed from fatigue, sipped her way through those. The first few stories weren't worth the pomp and circumstance. One was about a group of neighbors who were trying to get a registered child molester thrown out of their neighborhood. Naturally that made her think about Jane Doe. As a child prostitute, the odds were the girl was a runaway, which meant her family, if she had one, could be quite far away. And it might be a very long time before they traced her identity.

On the TV, the news anchor read another teaser before going to commercial. "Coming up, more trouble in Riverton as the town's former police chief is found dead in his home, the victim of an apparent suicide…"

Abby took another sip of wine, knowing her interview was coming up. She was curious to see if the reporter would try to connect Chet's suicide with the Jane Doe case. The question had been asked, but Abby hadn't revealed that they had a tape showing Chet having sex with the girl.

In her conversation with Frank, they'd touched on the possibility that Chet had killed the girl. With that in mind, Abby had checked Chet's personnel records to see what his blood type was. Digging through his file, she'd hoped it would be A negative, but it was O positive. Her disappointment had been almost palpable.

Abby wondered about her reaction. Did she want Chet to have been responsible for Jane Doe's death so the case could be brought to a tidy end? Or was it because she didn't want Frank to be responsible?

Complications did seem to be popping up with regularity. That afternoon, just before quitting time, Mae Brown had come to Abby's office.

"Chief," she said, "I'm not one to go bad-mouthing people, but there's somethin' that's been rollin' through my head that I think you ought to know about."

"What's that, Mae?" Abby had said.

"Years ago, when I was new in the department, Maxine Shear complained about the way Chet handled a case. Maxine was loyal to Chet, but that time she really grumbled."

"Who's Maxine Shear?"

"Oh, I forgot, honey, you're the new kid on the block. Maxine ran the office for twenty years. When she retired, I got her job. She's living in a mobile-home park down in Stockton these days. We see each other occasionally, exchange Christmas cards, stuff like that."

"So what about this case made Maxine grumble?"

"Well, as best I can recall, she thought Chet showed some favoritism. The guy involved was a friend or relative of Chet's. I don't remember exactly who."

"Do you recall what the case was about?"

"That's the thing," Mae had said, lowering her voice. "It was child molesting. That's the reason Maxine was so disgusted."

"Child molesting, huh?" Abby had said, raising her brows.

"And this is the funny part," Mae had continued. "I spent an hour after our meeting this morning looking for the file. It's not there. Everything else from that period is still on file, but nothing involving child molesting, child prostitution or corrupting the morals of a minor. Nothing. Couldn't even find a reference to it in the log."

While probably not bearing on the case at hand, Abby still found what Mae told her to be interesting. "Could you get Maxine's address for me, Mae?" she'd asked. "I think it might be worth me paying her a visit."

Mae had gotten the woman's address and phone number, and Abby had gone to her office to telephone her. There was no answer, not even a machine.

The commercial ended, but instead of going to the Riverton story directly, they went to one about a controversial bridge-widening project that had people up in arms. Annoyed, Abby took another gulp of wine. About then Tristan started raising a ruckus. She hoped he'd taken exception to a stray cat outside the fence or had let a jackrabbit get his dander up, but when the barking persisted, Abby decided she'd better investigate.

She went to the front door and flipped the switch to turn on the yard light. Then, looking out, she saw a red Corvette beyond the gate. Tristan was barking frantically at a rather unhappy-looking Darren Armstrong.

Popeye's Marina

Frank sat on a bar stool at Popeye's, watching the news on the big TV behind the bar, though he was hardly paying attention. He was still thinking about Abby. Her interview had been on when he'd arrived. His first reaction to seeing her on the tube had been surprise; then, as he watched the performance, admiration set in. Even so, he chafed at the fact they were at odds. Crueller still was the reality that his alibi put him in a bad light.

He hadn't wanted to go to the River Queen because he figured the talk would be about Chet, and he wasn't in the mood for that. Popeye's seemed like a good alternative. It was on the south fork of the Mokelumne River near the eastern edge of the Delta and on the road back from Galt, which made it a convenient place to stop. The Riverton crowd didn't drive over much, but the place had a friendly ambience and the food wasn't bad. A suitable place to pass the evening.

The marina was a large complex serving a variety of pleasure craft owned mostly by people from out of the area. There was also a large restaurant and bar. Popeye's was one of those woody, rustic places built on multi-levels with lots of potted plants and waitresses in short skirts—not in every case to good effect, unfortunately.

He'd ordered a beer, venturing back into the world of

booze for the first time since Friday night. Sipping it slowly seemed to work all right. The bartender was a buxom gal with platinum hair and dark roots. She'd worked at the Queen for a couple of months a few years back, but he couldn't remember her name. When things went into a lull, she moseyed over to where Frank sat.

"You're from Riverton, aren't you?" she said. "The ex-cop?"

"You've got the memory of a bartender," he said.

"Now I wonder why that is."

"Frank Keegan," he said.

"That's right. It was on the tip of my tongue." She leaned her elbows on the bar, letting her tits bulge out of her scoop-neck sweater. "I'm Joy."

Between her breasts and the name, Frank immediately recalled why Kay had gotten rid of her—Joy liked to hit on customers. He had a vague recollection of some incident involving Mort. Some bar owners liked the help to flirt a little, but Kay wasn't one. Friendly but chaste, that was the philosophy at the Queen. And it definitely hadn't helped Joy's standing that she'd picked Mort, of all people, to play games with.

"Weren't you in the running for police chief?" Joy asked.

"Yep, I was the also-ran."

"I'd have voted for you," she said flirtatiously.

"I'm flattered," he said, drawing on his beer.

Joy was looking past him toward the door. "Speaking of which, isn't that the woman who beat you out?"

Frank turned around and his jaw went slack when he saw Abby. She was in the company of a handsome young stud.

"God, who's the hunk?" Joy said.

"Damned if I know."

"Don't look like a Delta boy to me."

To that Frank had to agree. He watched Abby glance around as her companion conferred with the hostess. She spotted him. Even at that distance Frank picked up a flicker of alarm on her face. Without acknowledging him, she turned away. Then, as he watched, the hostess led them off. A surge of jealousy went through him, especially when he saw the guy put his arm around Abby's waist. They descended the steps and were eventually seated at a table on the lower level, partially shielded from his view by some plants.

Frank turned back to his beer and the barkeep, his face red. She had a knowing look in her eye. "You don't look too happy, Frank. Don't tell me you got a thing for the new chief."

"You like to ask questions, don't you?"

"I don't mean any harm. Hell, it gives me something to talk about. There's an advantage to being a woman bartender. Guys discuss the damnedest things. I've even had them telling me about sex with their wives."

"I won't be troubling you with that one," Frank said.

"No, but it could be you have the hots for the new police chief. I saw that glint in your eye just now. But hey, no crime in that. She's cute."

"I never discuss my personal life with a bartender," he said, "so the discussion ends here, okay?"

Joy shrugged. "You're the customer."

Glancing through the ferns at Abby, Frank considered how strange it seemed to have status, even if the recognition only came from a bartender.

Now that she'd seen Frank, Abby was positive it had been a mistake to go to dinner with Darren. She hadn't wanted to let him in her house, but he had managed to make her feel sorry for him because she'd kept him in the dark about her pregnancy and abortion. Not that what she'd done wasn't within her rights, but she decided maybe she owed him the courtesy of a conversation about it. If she gave him that, he might let go. More than anything, that was what she wanted.

So far he hadn't said much about her pregnancy. He'd been trying to charm her, instead. But Abby knew his tricks and had kept him at arm's length. Darren was still Darren, of course. Good-looking to a fault. Handsome, even features, great hair, styled to perfection—too perfect. If he'd changed at all, it was that he was even more polished and confident for the years he'd spent in Southern California. His suave manner almost struck her as plastic. He'd lost what boyish innocence he had.

Darren studied her, his fingers steepled, his index fingers pressed thoughtfully to his chin. "If I'd known about the baby, there'd have been no Shelly. You know that, don't you?"

"Please, Darren," she replied, "don't insult my intelligence."

"It's true."

Abby closed her eyes, trying hard not to get angry. "If you want to know the truth, I'm glad things worked out as they did. I'd rather have found out about Shelly before I did something stupid like marry you. Better than putting up with your womanizing after it was too late."

He sighed wearily. "I know I was an asshole. I deserve it. But even though I've been living a full life in L.A., my feelings for you haven't changed."

"Look, I'm going to give it to you straight," she said. "You and I have had our fifteen minutes together and they're over, done, kaput. So do me a favor and don't try to ingratiate yourself. I'd really rather you stay out of my life."

"Then why did you come with me?"

"To be polite, to give us each an opportunity to say any final things that need saying before we close the chapter."

He looked somber.

"If you misunderstood my intentions," she said, "I'm sorry. You seemed to want to say something and I haven't given you a chance until now. This is your chance."

Darren took several moments to gather his thoughts before launching into his speech. "First off, I gotta know that you're all right, Abby. Crystal said there hasn't been anyone since me."

"Well, Crystal doesn't know everything," she said, hating this more by the moment. "But I don't want to talk about it."

The waitress arrived. Darren told her to bring a bottle of their most expensive wine. "A special wine for a special occasion." Abby groaned, seeing he just wasn't getting it. Either that, or he was too stubborn to take no for an answer.

The wine arrived promptly. Darren filled both their glasses. "To what might have, should have, been," he said, touching his glass to hers.

"No, Darren," she said. "To letting bygones be bygones and going our separate ways."

"You can't forgive me, can you?"

"Of course I can. You're forgiven. I don't hold what happened against you and I hope you can do the same. But forgiveness and acceptance are two different things."

He drank down half his wine. His eyes shimmered and it was hard to tell if it was from the sting of alcohol or from emotion. "I'll never forget you or what you meant to me," he said.

"Past tense, Darren. In your mind, think past tense."

"Let me ask you something," he said, brushing her comment aside. "Are you bitter because deep down you care about me, or is it because of the life and the child we didn't have?"

The remark made her so angry it was all she could do to keep from leaving. As it was, she was embarrassed to be having this conversation in public. What had possessed her to come with him?

His eyes continued to shimmer as he stared at her. She couldn't imagine what he was really thinking. Nor what he hoped to gain. Surely he didn't think that bagging her now was the ultimate challenge, a conquest he couldn't pass up. She knew he was selfish, but just how evil, she didn't know.

"I don't blame you for hating me," Darren said, refilling his glass. "I deserve it. But this conversation has proved one thing. I still love you. If winning your love is no longer possible, then so be it. I can live with myself now, though, because I've told you what's in my heart."

Abby glanced around uncomfortably. He was talking too loudly, but at least he was beginning to sound like he accepted her decision. She looked up toward the bar, seeing Frank through the ferns.

Darren craned his neck to see what she was looking at. Abby turned her attention to him. "I'm glad for that, Darren," she said. "The important thing for both of us is to move on."

He drank a lot more wine, filling his glass again. Abby began to worry. When the waitress came to take their orders, Darren asked for more wine.

"Don't you think we've had enough?" Abby said softly.

"No, I don't!" he snapped. "What's it to you? You don't give a shit about me, anyway."

He was very loud and heads turned in their direction. Abby felt like she could die. Darren seemed to have realized what he'd done, though, and apologized. "Jeez, I'm sorry," he said. "It's just that I hate it being this way between us." He finished what was left of the first wine bottle. Then, putting his glass down, he said, "Tell me the truth, didn't it hurt just a little when you got rid of my baby?"

She knew the color drained right out of her face. "Of course it did," she whispered, her tone emphatic. "You think that was easy for me? Lord, you left me alone and pregnant. What would you have expected me to do?"

"Call me," he said much too loudly. "I'd have expected

you to call me before you killed it. It was *my* baby, too, for crissakes.''

Abby heard a gasp. She saw a roomful of heads turn her way. She couldn't bear it any longer. She grabbed her purse and coat and headed for the exit. As she climbed the stairs, she heard footsteps behind her.

''Jesus Christ, Abby,'' Darren said, ''give me a break, will you?''

She ignored him, continuing to the top of the stairs. But he wouldn't give up. Grabbing her arm, he stopped her, making her turn around.

''Look,'' he said, his tone contrite, ''I'm frustrated because you're not understanding my feelings. I had a little too much to drink and I mouthed off. You can't hold that against me.''

''Darren,'' she said through her teeth, ''let go of my arm.''

''I will if you promise to come back to the table with me.''

''I said, let go of my arm!'' She knew everyone was staring at them, but she didn't care. She wouldn't pull a cop routine because it was a personal matter, but neither was she going to allow herself to be bullied.

Darren, fool that he was, tried pulling her back toward the stairs. Abby resisted.

''Is there a problem here?'' came a voice from behind her. She glanced over her shoulder. It was Frank.

''There's no problem,'' Darren said to him, ''so butt out.''

''Looks to me like the lady is taking exception to your bullying, mister. I suggest you let go of her arm.''

Darren did let go of her, but not so much in compliance as to prepare himself for combat. The adrenaline and testosterone crackled in the air. Abby knew she had to stop this. She moved between them.

''Okay, this ends right here,'' she said. ''No playground antics.''

''Who does this bastard think he is?'' Darren snarled. ''Nobody tells me what to do.''

"Frank happens to be a friend of mine, Darren. If anybody's out of line, it's you. Now I suggest you go back to the table, have your dinner and some coffee and then go home."

"If you're leaving, I'm taking you."

"No, you're not." She glanced at Frank. "You wouldn't be going back to Riverton, would you?"

"As a matter of fact, I was just leaving."

"Could I get a lift?"

"Sure."

Darren was stunned, confused by the speed with which things were moving. "Hey," he said, "you can't just leave."

"I not only can, I am." With that she glanced at Frank. "Shall we go?"

They went off, leaving Darren Armstrong sputtering. Frank opened the door for her, and Abby stepped into the cool night air and the strong boggy smell of the river. She went along the wooden walk for a few steps, then stopped under a light and turned to face him.

"Thanks for helping, Frank. I appreciate it."

"The guy must really be bad news if you have to turn to an accused child molester and killer to get rid of him."

"You're not accused."

"Suspected."

Abby could see he was teasing her more than he was giving her a hard time. "The lesser of two evils."

He chuckled.

They moved along the walk toward the parking lot.

"What was with that guy, anyway?"

Abby didn't want to talk about Darren, but given the circumstances, she could hardly avoid it. "We dated years ago when I was with the Sheriff's Department. He recently came back to Sacramento and wanted to renew our friendship. I made the mistake of going out to dinner with him. Misguided compassion."

"You must be softhearted."

"The story's a bit more complicated than it seems. His sister also happens to be my best friend."

"Judging by his reaction, you weren't doing him any favors."

"Hey, whose side are you on?"

Frank had a big grin on his face. "The one who's trying to nail me on a felony conviction, obviously."

She stopped again. "You're right, this is crazy. What am I doing asking *you,* of all people, for a ride?"

"Could be that deep in your heart you know I'm innocent," he said, amused.

Abby glanced back at the restaurant, half expecting Darren to come storming out. Normally he wasn't the type who posed a physical danger, but he could get testy when he'd been drinking. She could go back inside and call somebody from the department to come and get her, but that made walking out with Frank in the first place look even more inane. How did she get herself into these situations, anyway? She engaged his eyes.

"Would it be a problem for you to give me a ride as far as Tyler Island?"

"Of course not."

When they got to his truck, Abby glanced at the rusty bed. What irony that she should be rescued in this vehicle, the one she suspected had transported Jane Doe's body. Frank climbed into the driver's side and started the engine. He put his arm on the seat back behind her to reverse out of the parking space. They went through the lot to the road, bumping over the potholes as they went.

Once they were on the highway, they purred along the dark stretch of road. She was at a loss for what to say, so she said nothing. Frank, too, seemed to be searching for a topic of conversation. He finally fell back on the predictable. "Guess you haven't turned up anything on Jane Doe's identity."

"Not yet. I have a feeling it's going to be a long time before we do. Unless somebody comes forward."

"There might be some clues on the videotape that'll help you track down its origins," Frank suggested.

"The lab is working on that."

"Good."

There was another lull in the conversation, then Abby said, "The road leading to my house is just up ahead."

"How far down is your place?"

"A couple of miles."

"I'll drive you."

"It's not necessary, Frank. A little night air will do me good."

"Your friend, Darren, might have decided to follow," he said, slowing. "I'd hate to have him catch up with you on a lonely road."

"Darren's a boor, not a psychopath."

"I'd feel better taking you to your door," Frank said, pulling onto the shoulder of the pavement. They were opposite the point where the road intersected with the highway.

The prospect of him taking her home wasn't frightening because Frank had never seemed dangerous to her, but it seemed inappropriate, hypocritical even. "I really can take care of myself," she told him.

"I guess my chivalry is misplaced."

"Not misplaced. Unnecessary." She opened the passenger door.

"It'll only take two minutes to run you home."

"Thanks, but I really would enjoy the walk."

"Suit yourself."

"Good night, Frank."

Abby slammed the door shut, walked in front of the vehicle and across the highway. The side road was paved, but lightly traveled. There was a good chance she'd make it home without encountering a vehicle. She noticed that Frank didn't drive on immediately. He waited until she'd gone twenty or thirty yards down the side road before putting the truck in gear and heading toward Riverton.

Alone on the deserted road, she was enveloped by the silence of the night. There was no wind, but the air had a chill. The sky was a carpet of stars. She felt the melancholy of her lonely existence. In her desperation Abby had allowed Darren to stick his foot in her door and she'd paid the price of embarrassment. Though she'd kidded Frank about it, she was right when she'd said that he was the lesser of evils. And he'd said something else she now realized was true—in her heart she did know he was innocent. At least, she truly wanted to believe he was. That right there said an awful lot.

Watermark Slough

From the levee road, Frank could see the lights of a vehicle illuminating the front of his house. Turning down the drive, he pulled up behind the car, a large, late-model Cadillac. A man Frank had never seen before was at the front door. The man, who was wearing a sport coat and tie, came toward him. He had to be in his late sixties, walking stiffly, even limping a bit. His white hair was reminiscent of Chet's. Frank got out of his truck. The man squinted into the glare of the lights.

"Mr. Keegan?" he called.

"Yes, I'm Frank Keegan." He moved around to the front of the Cadillac where the guy had stopped. "What can I do for you?"

"My name is Witherspoon, Lloyd Witherspoon," the man said, extending his hand. "I'm sorry to drop in on you like this, but I took a chance I'd find you in."

"You almost didn't," Frank said, taking the man's clammy hand.

"So I see."

"You don't look like an encyclopedia salesman."

Witherspoon grinned. "No, I wanted to talk to you about Chet Wilsey."

The comment was unexpected. "Regarding?"

The man's expression turned somber. "Would you care to sit in my car with me to chat?"

"We can go in the house," Frank said.

"No, I don't wish to impose on your hospitality. But I would appreciate a few minutes of your time."

Witherspoon was well-dressed and drove a nice car. He seemed respectable enough. Frank saw no reason for alarm.

"Sure," he said, "we can talk."

Witherspoon motioned toward the car and Frank went around to the passenger side. They both got in. Witherspoon turned off the headlights, plunging Frank's yard into darkness. The interior of the Caddy smelled of cigarettes. Witherspoon reached for the pack of Camels on the dash.

"Smoke?"

"No, thanks."

"Mind if I do?"

"To be honest, Mr. Witherspoon, tobacco smoke irritates the hell out of my sinuses. We can stand outside, though, if you want to smoke."

"No," the other man said, tossing the pack back onto the dash. "It's a rotten habit. I shouldn't be doing it, anyway."

"So, what about Chet did you want to discuss?"

Witherspoon stroked his chin as he stared at Frank's mobile home. "I understand you were Chet's closest friend," he began. "I thought maybe you could bring me up to speed on what happened."

"It would help if I knew what your connection was to Chet and why, exactly, you'd like to know."

"Of course," Witherspoon said, shifting uncomfortably. "I thought maybe Chet had mentioned me."

Frank shook his head. "Afraid not. At least, that I recall."

"Well, I'm a relative of his. A distant cousin, actually. Friends would be the best way to describe our relationship. We saw each other a bit more after Sally died. No big deal," he said, nervously drumming his fingers on the steering wheel. "I mean, it was nothing special. But since we go way back, Chet's passing did upset me."

"I understand."

Witherspoon caught himself and stopped the drumming. "I found out about it when I saw an article in the *San Francisco Chronicle.* Former Police Chief Found Dead was the way the headline read, I believe."

"How'd you know about me? Did Chet mention my name?"

"No. It was Chet's attorney down in Stockton, Fred Parker. I've known Fred as long as I've known Chet. He's a cousin, too. Third or fourth, something like that."

Frank knew Judge Parker from his own days on the Stockton police force. Parker in his time had been a law-and-order maverick, an outspoken Ronald Reagan Republican and a heavy drinker. He was an old man now, probably in his eighties. After retiring, he practiced law part-time. Frank recalled Chet mentioning he'd had the judge draw up a new will for him after Sally died. He was also aware the judge was a distant relative of Chet's, but it had been years since Frank had seen him.

"I'm surprised the judge remembers me," he said.

"My impression is, it was more the fact that Chet mentioned you frequently."

"So, Judge Parker told you to ask me about Chet."

"Yes. I was down in Stockton this afternoon visiting Fred. We got to talking and discovered that neither of us knew what actually happened. The reports in the papers are quite vague."

"Why didn't you talk to the police? When it's a relative asking, they tend to be a little more forthcoming."

"Well," Witherspoon said, drumming his fingers again, "I didn't want to make an official inquiry. What I'm really after is the inside scoop, so to speak."

"And you think I would have it?"

"It's a small town. You're his best friend."

Frank looked for a pitfall. The guy claimed to be a distant relative of Chet's, but who could be sure? Frank didn't smell cop or reporter or insurance investigator. He was dealing with a nervous man, that much he knew. It occurred to him there was more to be gained than lost, so he proceeded to inch further into the conversation.

"Chet's been depressed since he lost Sally."

"Yes, I know," Witherspoon said, the furrow in his brow deepening. "Did he really kill himself?"

"That's the way it appears."

"Was there a suicide note?"

Frank noticed apprehension in his tone. "No."

"Then there was no indication why he did it?"

"It was possible he was being blackmailed," Frank said. Witherspoon's brow rose. "Blackmailed? By whom?"

"We don't know."

"But you must have some idea why he was being blackmailed."

"Do *you* have any idea, Mr. Witherspoon?"

The man's head turned abruptly toward Frank. "No, most certainly not."

"It wasn't an accusation, it was a question."

"I have no idea," Witherspoon said, his voice more controlled, less defensive.

Frank considered how to proceed. "Chet may have been involved with a prostitute," he said.

"Oh?"

Witherspoon was definitely on his guard. Frank wondered if he'd found out what he'd come for. "From what you know of Chet, does that ring true?" he asked.

"No, it doesn't," Witherspoon replied vaguely. "How about to you?"

"That's a side of Chet I didn't know."

"Me, neither."

They both considered the night in silence.

"Mind if I ask what you expected to learn in coming here?" Frank said.

"Nothing in particular. The truth, I guess. When something happens to someone you think you know that doesn't make a lot of sense, you wonder."

"Yeah," Frank said, "I know the feeling."

"Well, I've taken a lot of your time, Mr. Keegan. I appreciate your candor."

Frank was surprised by how eager the guy was to leave. He'd been given his cue to get out of the car. If he had to guess, it was what Witherspoon *hadn't* heard, not what he *had* heard, that was important.

"You're obviously concerned," Frank said. "Should I hear anything interesting in the coming weeks, do you want me to let you know?"

Lloyd Witherspoon considered that—longer than the question would seem to merit. "Sure, why not?"

"Have a card?"

"I believe so." Witherspoon checked his coat pockets, finally coming up with a business card. "You?"

"I should have one." Frank got out his wallet and found one of his cards. It was bent and a little worse for wear.

Witherspoon slipped it in his pocket. Frank opened the door. He put one foot out, then stopped. "By the way, you wouldn't be into teenage hookers, child porn, that sort of thing, would you?"

Even in the dark Frank could see the man's eyes flash.

"Absolutely not! And how disrespectful of you to ask like that!"

"We've come to discover that Chet had fetishes along

those lines, Lloyd,'' Frank said. ''I thought maybe it was in the genes.''

Witherspoon responded with a glare so hostile it almost burned through the darkness. Then, ''Goodbye, Mr. Keegan.''

Frank got out and closed the door. The engine of the Caddy started immediately. As he watched, Witherspoon made a hurried U-turn, then drove quickly up the drive, his tires kicking up gravel. Frank made a mental note of the license number. When he got inside the house, he jotted it on the back of Witherspoon's business card, which contained only his name and a phone number with a San Francisco area code.

Wednesday
February 19th

Riverton

Abby turned the corner and was relieved to see Wally Benson's patrol car parked in the middle of the block. She pulled up behind it and got out. It was ten o'clock in the morning, another bright sunny day. The temperature was pleasantly warm, but even so, she wore a department windbreaker over a dark wool pantsuit. Like most chiefs and sheriffs, Abby mostly wore business attire on the job. She had a uniform, but it was only for ceremonial occasions.

Wally had radioed he had a domestic dispute on his hands that could have implications for the Jane Doe case. Abby had no idea what kind of people the Millers on Elm Street were, though she was aware that Chet would have known everything about the family right down to the kinds of fireworks they bought for the Fourth of July.

Wally, a big cuddly guy who was equally good at inspiring trust and maintaining order, came out the front door of the old white clapboard house. Abby waited for him at the foot of the stairs.

"What's going on?" she asked.

"I've got everybody calmed down inside, Chief," he said, "but you're definitely going to want to talk to Ella."

"I don't know the Millers. Who are we dealing with?"

Wally scratched his head, a nervous habit. "Ella's a single mother with two kids," he replied. "Tiffany's home—she's a freshman in high school, Andy, the son, is at school. He's in junior high."

"No man in the picture?"

"Tom's long gone, Chief. Him and Ella had kids late. It kinda screwed up their marriage. Ella's been having a rough time with the girl."

"So, the mother and daughter were fighting?"

"A real screaming brawl, apparently. We got a call from a neighbor who was sure they were coming to blows. Ella broke her foot a few weeks back and it's in a cast, so she's a little hobbled."

"But they've quieted down now?"

"Ella's in the front room. I got Tiffany back in her bedroom."

"What's this about the Jane Doe case?" Abby asked.

Wally scratched his head again. "Ella thinks Tiffany knows something. I didn't get a lot more than that. I figured it's best if you talked to her."

Abby nodded. "Fine, let's go."

Wally led the way up the steps. He rapped on the door, then opened it, stepping aside for Abby to enter. She found a woman in a housedress and fuzzy cardigan lying on the couch of the cramped front room, her injured foot elevated on a stack of pillows. Ella was in her late forties, thin, with tinted brown hair and sunken eyes. Seeing Abby, she tried to scoot upright, but Abby told her to stay comfortable.

"I'm Abby Hooper, Chief of Police," she said, sitting on the badly worn easy chair nearby. "I understand there's been a little emotion in the family this morning."

"God, I wish that's all it was."

"These things happen to everybody, Ella. We're here to help."

"I can't tell you how embarrassed I am," the woman said, wiping her eyes with the sleeves of her sweater. "I know I should be able to control that girl, but sometimes she's just impossible."

"It's not easy being a teen, or the parent of a teen," Abby said. "Why don't you tell me what happened?"

Ella Miller drew a ragged breath. "Well, half the problem's her boyfriend, Paul Ottmeyer. Ever since she took up with him she's been getting into trouble."

"That's a lie, Mom!" came a disembodied voice from the back of the house.

Ella rolled her eyes. Abby tossed her head, indicating to Wally to go speak to the girl.

"Go ahead," Abby said to the woman.

"I tried to keep her from going with just one boy, to date in groups, but it was no use. She'd sneak off with Paul, anyway. I had the doctor talk to her about birth control, knowing that's what she was doing. I try to get her to be home at a decent hour. Sometimes she does and sometimes she doesn't." Ella shook her head. "What can I do?"

"I take it there was an incident that set off this latest argument."

"Incident? Lord, I wish that's all it was. It happened Valentine's Day—night, I should say. Tiffany went out with Paul. Well, she didn't come home. By two in the morning I was ready to call the police. But finally she comes dragging in, all bloody and limping and soaked to the bone. She looked like she'd been in an accident or raped or something. I asked what happened and she refused to talk to me. Just refused."

"She didn't give you any explanation at all?"

"No. She stayed in the bathroom for the longest time, cleaning herself up. Then she went to bed. I figured I was lucky she was in one piece and that the best thing to do was let it rest until morning. The trouble was, she didn't stick her nose out of her room until almost dinnertime on Saturday."

"You said she was bloody and limping. Did you see her injuries? Were her clothes torn?"

"She was soaked to the bone, like I said, but her clothes weren't torn. She had a cut on her hand. I think that's where most of the blood came from. When I finally got a look at it, I could see it wasn't serious. She also bruised her knee and twisted it pretty badly."

"So, did you talk to her the next day?"

"I tried, but she was real closemouthed. All she'd say was that she'd fallen. She refused to tell me where she'd been or what she'd been doing. She claimed it wasn't Paul's fault. If she said that once, she said it ten times."

"But she wouldn't say what happened."

Ella Miller sat upright, easing her broken foot to the floor. Then, leaning toward Abby, she said in a low voice, "I thought sure she'd been sexually assaulted, but she insisted she hadn't. She kept saying she'd fallen, that was all. That it was no big deal. I got worried, though, when she didn't want to go to school on Monday, saying she didn't feel well.

"I called Paul's mother then, and we talked. She said Paul was acting strange, too. He'd become obsessed with listening to the news on TV and even reading the newspaper. Both Mrs. Ottmeyer and I wondered if it could have anything to do with that girl who drowned." Ella looked beseechingly into Abby's eyes. Her fear was apparent. "I love my child," she said, "but if she had anything to do with somebody dying, the truth's got to come out, no matter what."

With her last words, Ella's voice cracked. Tears filled her eyes. Abby reached over and took her hands.

"Don't worry," she said. "You're doing the right thing. Do you mind if I talk to her now?"

"No, please do," Ella replied tearfully. "Maybe you can reason with her. I can't."

Abby got up and headed toward the back of the house.

She found Wally standing in the hallway, next to a closed door.

"She's inside," he said.

"Why don't you go keep Mrs. Miller company. And, if you don't mind, take this with you, Wally," she said, removing her windbreaker.

Wally went off and Abby rapped lightly on the door. There was no answer, so she opened the door a crack. She saw a girl lying on her stomach on a narrow bed against the wall, her face buried in a pillow.

"Tiffany," Abby said softly, "can I talk to you a minute?"

The girl lifted her head and looked back at her.

"I'm Abby Hooper," she said, entering the room. "Your mom told me about your accident. I thought maybe we could talk about it."

Tiffany sat up on the bed. She was in an oversize sweatshirt and pants, her feet bare. She was about the same age as Jane Doe, similar in appearance, except that she was blond. Her eyes were red. She'd been crying.

"You're the police chief," the girl murmured.

"The new police chief, which sort of makes me a freshman, too."

The girl half smiled and moved back against the wall, sitting cross-legged on the bed, eyeing Abby warily.

Abby glanced around the room. It was the typical room of an adolescent girl with elements of both childhood and teen years. The walls were pink, the curtains white. The stuffed animals remained, but there were also posters of the Spice Girls and Leonardo DiCaprio above a shelf of soccer trophies. In the corner there was a pile of magazines and a cardboard box filled with cassettes. Shoes spilled out of the closet.

"Okay if I sit down?" Abby asked.

Tiffany nodded.

Abby sat at the foot of the bed next to a badly worn teddy bear, which she picked up and held on her lap. "I had a bear when I was a teenager," she said. "I even took him to college with me. His name was Brownie. Does this guy have a name?"

"Not really."

Abby gave the bear a casual hug. "I guess you've had a rough couple of days," she said.

"Sort of."

"Did you hurt yourself very badly?"

"Not too badly."

"Fall?"

The girl nodded.

"It was out at Watermark Slough, wasn't it?"

Tiffany's lower lip sagged open. "How did you know?"

"Somebody out there saw you and Paul on the levee. Afterward, when you were running away."

"We didn't do anything," the girl implored. "I swear we didn't do anything. We were only trying to help. We didn't know. I swear…" Then her face crumpled and she began to cry into her hands.

Abby reached over and patted the girl's knee. "It's all right, honey. No need to worry. But I've got to know exactly what happened. It's very important you tell me."

Tiffany looked up, her face streaked with tears. "We didn't hurt anyone. We were scared. That's why we ran away."

"I know you were scared. And you're scared now. But there's no reason to be. Not if you tell me exactly what happened."

"Do you promise Paul won't get in trouble? You won't make him go to juvi hall? Do you promise?"

"That's not up to me, Tiffany. It all depends on what happened that night."

"But nothing happened," the girl lamented. "We didn't

do anything. We were just fooling around. We didn't know.''
Again she began to sob.

Abby went over to the dresser and took some tissues from
the box sitting on top. She brought them back to Tiffany,
handing them to the girl. Tiffany wiped her eyes and blew
her nose, then looked up at Abby through wet lashes. ''If
you don't hurt anybody and you don't steal anything, you
can't be punished, can you?''

''Probably not, Tiffany, but what I need from you is the
truth—everything that happened from the time you left home
until you got back. Everything. Understand?''

Tiffany slowly nodded. Abby let her wrestle with her conscience for a moment.

It seemed dealing with teenagers had become a big part of
her job of late. Monday morning before they'd gotten the call
about Chet she'd spoken with the boys involved in the bowling-alley brawl. She considered it an important part of her
job to instill in people a respect for the law, particularly
young people whose values were being formed. Parents were
the key, of course, but it *did* take a village to raise a kid these
days. All responsible adults had a role to play in socializing
young people and turning them into conscientious citizens.
And when the Ella Millers of the world had their hands full,
people like Abby had to step in and fill the breach. It was
not only her job, but her moral obligation as a member of
the community.

Tiffany Miller blew her nose again and said in a small
voice, ''What if Paul hates me?''

''I don't know Paul,'' Abby replied, ''but if he'd ask you
to lie, he's not the kind of friend you want. My guess is he
wants to tell the truth as much as you do.''

The girl nodded. ''Okay.''

''What happened Friday night? Start at the beginning,
honey.''

''I met Paul at the bowling alley. Some of our other friends were there, but it was like really boring. Paul was in a bad mood because he'd had this big fight with his father. So we decided to go for a drive. We went out by Watermark Slough because it's...well, like a good place to park and...you know. Anyway, Paul had a little bit of weed in the car because somebody had left it. I don't know who. Paul didn't buy it or anything. We don't do marijuana much," she said, lowering her voice. "And there was only enough for one joint. So we smoked it and Paul said he wished he could leave home. He told me as soon as he turns eighteen he's going to join the navy because he really likes boats.

"Anyway, we both got a little high and Paul said we ought to go boating. I asked him like how can we go boating without a boat. And he said there were boats all over the Delta. We wouldn't have to steal one or anything. We could just borrow it for a while, take a ride and bring it back.

"Anyway, what we did was leave the car and went looking for some boat we could take. Paul said if we drove somebody might hear us. So we found this dock about a quarter of a mile from where we parked. We had to climb down some steps on the levee to get to the boat. It was really dark and I was scared, but Paul wasn't, so I didn't say anything.

"So I'm standing on the dock, shivering because it had started raining. Paul was mad because the outboard motor and boat were chained to the dock. He started swearing. That was when I looked in the water and saw a face staring at me. I was so scared I started screaming and screaming. I couldn't help it.

"Paul was scared, too, but he made me shut up. He looked at the body and said it was a girl without any clothes and maybe she wasn't dead yet. He said we should pull her out of the water. She was right by the shore on this rock, which kept her from sinking, I guess. I didn't want to touch her, so Paul pulled her out onto the shore next to the dock."

Tiffany stopped her account, wiping her eyes with the tissue.

"Then what happened?" Abby asked.

"Well, we could tell she was like...dead," Tiffany said, sniffling. "Then we thought she was naked because maybe somebody had killed her. Paul got real scared because he knew his fingerprints were all over her body. I guess we kind of panicked. Paul was afraid somebody had heard me screaming and had already called the police. We decided we had to get the hell out of there. It was so dark I tripped on the steps and cut my hand. Then halfway up the levee, I fell and twisted my knee. Paul pulled me the rest of the way and I limped back to the car. We hurried to town and promised each other we'd never tell." She bit her lip. "Now I've broken my promise."

"Sometimes promises are made for bad reasons, Tiffany. You and Paul made a mistake. You should have gone to the police."

"We didn't want to get in trouble." The girl sniffled.

"You won't get in trouble for cooperating. But I have a few questions. What time was it you found the body?"

"I don't know."

"Try to figure it out. When did you leave the bowling alley?"

"I guess about midnight."

"How long did you drive around?"

"Maybe half an hour," the girl replied.

"And you parked and smoked dope for how much longer?"

"About an hour, I guess. We didn't have sex or anything. Like, we mostly talked."

"So, you probably left the car around one-thirty and it was maybe two o'clock by the time you found the girl in the water."

"I guess."

"I want you to think about the minutes just before and after you saw the body. Did you see anyone around, hear any noises, see anything else in the water or on the shore? Clothing, maybe? Anything?"

Tiffany shook her head. "It started raining real hard, I remember that. The rocks were real slippery. That's why I fell."

"Honey, do you know your blood type?"

"No, but maybe Mom does."

Abby reached over and patted the girl's hand. "I know this has been hard for you, but you've done the right thing."

"Paul won't get in trouble, will he?"

"If he tells me the truth and it's the same as you've told me, I don't see any reason why either of you will be in trouble. But don't get any more ideas about going for joy rides in other people's boats. And stay away from dope."

Tiffany hung her head. "I won't do it again."

"Let's hope not."

"Who was that dead girl, anyway?" Tiffany asked.

"We don't know yet, but we're trying to find out."

"I'm sorry for what we did. And thanks for not being mean about it," Tiffany said.

"Want to know something? Your mother and I both care about you. Talk to her about your problems and help her with hers, Tiffany. It'll be a lot more pleasant around here if you do." Abby handed the girl the teddy bear. "If you think of something you haven't told me, have your mom give me a call."

The girl nodded.

"See you, then," Abby said, rising. She went to the door. Looking back, she saw the girl hugging the bear, recalling a hundred moments like that of her own.

Returning to the front room, she found Ella Miller talking to Wally Benson. The woman looked at her expectantly.

Abby told Ella the gist of the conversation, emphasizing

the positive where she could. As she finished, she said, "I do have one more question before I leave. Do you know Tiffany's blood type?"

"Yes, A negative. She was a preemie and had all kinds of medical problems as an infant. If I heard it once I heard them mention it fifty times."

The response put a zing in Abby's heart. She nodded. "Thanks, Ella." Turning to her officer, she said, "I think we can go, Wally."

"Right, Chief."

They left the house. At the foot of the stairs Wally Benson spoke. "So, did you get anything useful in the Jane Doe case?" he asked.

"A couple of things. I know how the body got from the drink onto shore and when. And I may have lost a suspect and regained a friend."

"Frank Keegan?" Wally said as they headed for their vehicles.

"Yeah."

"I never thought for a minute Frank could have done anything."

"He's not completely out of the woods, but it's looking better for him." Abby wagged her finger at him. "That's not for public consumption."

"No, no. I understand."

Abby looked at her watch. "Well, we've both got work to do."

"Right Chief."

They each went to their cars. Abby was putting on her seat belt as Wally drove off. She figured in two or three hours' time, the town would know, and wondered if she should give Frank a call. But that somehow seemed overeager. Better she proceed in a businesslike fashion. Still, it probably wouldn't hurt if she gave him a buzz that evening. She might have her pride, but the man was also entitled to his peace of mind.

Stockton

"You're late, dear, and I'm not about to miss my bingo because of it." Maxine Shear, gaunt and slightly stooped, opened the screen door, keeping it from closing with her cane. She stepped onto the tiny porch of her mobile home, turned to close the main door behind her and carefully locked it. Once again she faced Abby. The pasty skin of her face was masked by sunglasses. The brim of her hat was so broad it extended nearly to her shoulders.

Abby couldn't say the face was familiar because she couldn't see enough of it to be sure, but there was something about the jaw line and mouth that suggested they'd met before—undoubtedly during Abby's childhood, perhaps at Aspeth Drugstore or the supermarket or while walking down Riverton's main drag.

"I don't mean to sound hard," Maxine said, explaining herself, "but Wednesday afternoon is bingo at the Palms. It's the highlight of my week."

"I'm terribly sorry to be late, Mrs. Shear," Abby said, "but I had a break in the Jane Doe case. Two witnesses turned up. I had to interview them."

"No need to apologize, Miss Hooper. I understand police work. You were doing your duty. But I'm retired and *my* duty is to enjoy my leisure while I can. Who knows, I may not live to see another Wednesday."

Maxine Shear gingerly stepped down off the porch, then inched along her walk to the roadway. Abby followed.

"Perhaps if you let me drive you to bingo, we can talk on the way."

"That will hardly do," the woman replied, "I *walk* to bingo. It's in the park clubhouse out back. Walking there is my exercise."

"May I accompany you then?"

"Of course you can. As long as you know the talking stops when we get there."

"Certainly."

Maxine, despite the sunshine, her sombrero and glasses, wore a raincoat, which was buttoned to the neck. Considering the speed at which the old lady crept, Abby figured she wanted to be prepared for not only a change in the weather, but perhaps a change in the season, as well.

They made a slow right turn into the roadway. Abby took Maxine's arm, prompting a glance in her direction.

"If you're wondering why I seem so decrepit for my age, it's because of crippling arthritis. There are women living here older than me who play tennis and golf. But the good Lord, in His wisdom, has seen fit to make me a bingo player, instead of an athlete. I still have my mind, however. I expect that's what you're interested in."

"I do have some questions about Chet."

"What a terrible, terrible shame that was. It really was suicide, was it?"

"Yes, Mrs. Shear. I got a copy of the coroner's certificate today."

"When's the funeral?"

"Tentatively, it's set for Saturday."

"I'll try to attend," Maxine said. "It'll all depend on whether I can get a ride, of course. With these hips, I don't drive."

Maxine had steered a course into the middle of the roadway, moving like a lumbering ocean liner leaving port. Abby knew she had to take control of the conversation.

"In the course of our investigation we've turned up some possible links between Chet's death and the Jane Doe case," she said. "And we've also discovered some old files that could shed light on the matter are missing. I thought you might be able to help me get to the bottom of things."

"My, but aren't you the diplomat? You want dirt on Chet. Isn't that what this is about?"

A car came around the corner but Maxine didn't falter. She continued ahead as though she were a semi-truck in the passing lane. The car was obliged to swerve around them.

"I wouldn't put it that way, Mrs. Shear."

"Never mind what we call it. Ask me your question, dear."

"Mae Brown told me Chet's handling of a child-molestation case some years ago had upset you. She couldn't remember the details and when she searched for the file, it was missing. Do you have any recollection of the case, and would you be willing to fill me in on what you know about it?"

"Your Jane Doe was molested, was she?" Maxine said grimly.

"Worse, in a way. We believe she was a child prostitute."

"Oh, dear."

They took a dozen careful steps, Maxine Shear obviously processing what she'd heard. Abby wondered if the woman's loyalty to Chet would survive his death. Rather than press her, she decided to let Maxine respond at her own pace.

"Mae was referring to the Dougherty case," Maxine announced in good time. "Cindy Dougherty was the child's name, as I recall. There's no file because I destroyed it. At Chet's direction."

They'd come to the corner and Maxine made another right turn onto the main thoroughfare. The clubhouse was dead ahead, but a good hundred yards away. Given the time it would take to get there, Abby knew she could let Maxine tell her story at her own pace.

"You're wondering why Chet would want the file destroyed, of course," she said, "but I'm not sure I can give you a complete answer. I can tell you what I know, however. One day...let's see, it has to be twelve or fifteen years ago...Ed Dougherty came to see Chet, all upset. According to the file, which I read before destroying, Mr. Dougherty claimed his eleven-year-old daughter, Cindy, had been molested by a neighbor. Chet went to talk to the guy, who at first admitted everything, then denied it. Exactly what transpired next I'm not sure. But this much I know—inside a month Ed Dougherty, his wife and child left Riverton for someplace in Southern California. They practically disappeared overnight.''

''So, you don't know why or what happened?''

''There was no explanation in the file. But I had a friend who worked at Henke's Hardware, the same place Ed Dougherty was employed as a warehouseman. She told me Ed had come into half a million dollars and that he was going to start his own hardware business down in Southern California where his wife was from. The source of the money was a big secret—no hitting the jackpot in Reno or rich uncle dying that anybody knew about.

''When there was no arrest in the molestation case and no charges brought, I put two and two together. My theory was that Chet brokered a deal between the guy and Cindy's parents. I can picture Chet saying something like, 'The harm's already done. This way the family comes away with something to build a life on. If there was a prosecution, the girl and her parents would have had the hardship of a criminal trial, then a civil suit, if they hoped to collect damages.' Chet must have figured letting the guy buy them out was the clean and simple way to resolve the matter.''

''Yes,'' Abby said, ''but meanwhile a child molester goes free.''

''That's what upset me. But the guy left Riverton a few months after the Doughertys. And there were mitigating circumstances, which made me understand Chet's thinking a little better.''

''Like what, for heaven's sake?''

"The child molester was a relative of Chet's. Not a close relative, but about the only one he had, as I understand it."

"Who was he?" Abby asked.

Maxine Shear took a few more steps, her thin lips pressed together. "His name was Lloyd Witherspoon. I hardly knew him. He had a big house on the edge of town and traveled a lot. People hardly ever saw him around."

"Where did he go?" Abby asked. "Do you have any idea?"

A pickup truck came up behind them and swung around to pass on the left. Maxine Shear didn't miss a beat.

"None at all," she replied to Abby's question. "Witherspoon disappeared in the night much like the Doughertys. All that was left behind was the file, and Chet had me shred it. Beyond that, I don't know a thing."

"You never talked to Chet about the case?"

"Not until I retired. The day I left I told him working for him was one of the proudest experiences of my life—with one exception. The Cindy Dougherty case."

"And what did Chet say?"

"He told me that Cindy went on to become a cheerleader in high school and to attend UCLA. He also said that Lloyd Witherspoon had straightened out his life and never harmed another child."

"Was that true?"

"I have no idea. But if Chet lied to me, Miss Hooper, it was the first and only time, so far as I know. He may not have been perfect, but he was a good man."

Abby saw no point in telling what she'd seen on that tape. Why spoil a perfectly good bingo game? Like Maxine said, you never know which one is going to be your last.

Watermark Slough

As he soaped himself down, Frank sang in the shower for the first time in ages. When he'd gotten home from his boating expedition, there was a message on his machine from Dix Fowler. "Good news, Frank. Call me." That was it.

They'd traded phone calls, Frank missing Dix's second when he'd taken his garbage can up to the road for the next day's pickup. When Frank called back, Dix had left for the day. Forty-five minutes later, Dix phoned him from home with the news about the Miller girl and her boyfriend, Paul Ottmeyer. "The girl having A negative blood was the kicker," Dix told him.

"So what did Chief Hooper say?" Frank asked.

"Haven't talked to her personally," Dix replied. "She went down to Stockton to talk to somebody."

"Probably my old watch captain."

"No," Dix said, "it had something to do with Chet."

"Suppose I'll be hearing from her?"

"I don't know, Frank. That's why I called—to make sure you know. On the Q.T., of course. I don't want my ass chewed for going behind her back."

"I understand. And I appreciate the consideration."

"Figured you'd sleep a little better."

"I haven't been worried, Dix, but it's nice that other people know I'm not a child molester."

"Nobody believed it for a minute."

Frank smiled. He knew how that one went. But Dix's call had given him a lift—mainly because Abby now knew he wasn't a total liar. It remained to be seen how much she'd hold back. Professionalism dictated she reserve judgment to a certain degree, but he figured that even with her he was probably over the hump.

He had other problems with Abby, though. Mort Anderson, of all people, had found a way to spit in the soup.

As he climbed out of the shower, he thought about his encounter with Mort that morning. Frank had taken his boat out for a spin, going up where the slough intersected with the Sacramento River. Just as he was swinging the skiff in an arc across the wide stretch of water toward the Grand Island shore, he saw a big inboard speeding upriver, its black hull gleaming in the sun. Frank moved closer to the far shore to avoid the wake, but the boat veered to port, as well, squeezing him closer to the bank. It was almost as though the bastard was trying to swamp him. Then, when it was about twenty-five or thirty yards away, the guy cut his engine and the speedboat dropped out of warp, settling in the water like a fat goose on a pond. It was then that Frank saw it was Mort.

The outboard putted up to where Frank had stopped. Mort had on a yachting cap and his supercilious grin. "Well, if it isn't Don Juan," he said.

"What's the matter, Mort? You got penis envy again?"

"That's funny, Frank, coming from a guy who's only worldly goods are in his pants. And I'm not referring to your wallet."

"We both know you've got inadequacy problems, so if you've stopped to gloat about your checkbook, save your breath for somebody who'll be impressed."

"Actually, I stopped to do you a favor."

"Yeah?"

"Here's some friendly advice, Keegan. Keep your pecker in your pants. Kay's a nice person. She takes pity on the indigent. Don't try to take advantage of her compassion, because I'm not nearly so tolerant. In fact, I'm easily pissed off by scumbags like you."

"Am I mistaken, Mort, or did you just make one of your adolescent attempts to threaten me?"

The two boats had drifted close enough that they were almost touching. Mort glared.

"Let me put it this way, Frank," he said. "A little bird told me you've got the hots for Abby Hooper and you're trying your damnedest to get into her pants. Now I admit I don't know whether it's because you really fancy her ass or because you figure you can sidetrack her investigation in the Jane Doe case. But either way, lusting after a mother and a daughter at the same time is not going to win you the Riverton popularity contest. Kay wouldn't appreciate it and neither would Abby. So stay away from Kay, my friend, or I'll make sure they both end up hating your guts.''

''You know what, Mort? Manhood is a terrible thing to waste. You're lucky you don't have very much of it to lose.''

''Say what you want,'' Anderson said. ''Just stay away from Kay. And if you think you can boff Abby and keep your past with Kay a secret, have at it. Frankly, I don't give a shit. But if you want my cooperation, you'll have to dance to my tune, Frankie boy.'' He grinned like the fat cat he was. ''A word to the wise, old buddy.''

With that Mort thrust the throttle of his boat forward and swung the wheel to port. The speedboat lifted like a waterfowl taking flight. In the process, it kicked up a wave that lapped over the gunwale of Frank's skiff. Ignoring the water at his feet, Frank stared after Mort, wondering where the bastard had gotten his intelligence about Abby. Was it a lucky guess, or did his tentacles extend all the way to the far reaches of the Delta, to places like Popeye's, for example?

The thing about Mort was, he could be unpredictable. Frank figured his motive was to shore up his position with Kay, but at some level, Mort had to realize he was playing with fire. The bastard could be vindictive enough to hurt him, but in doing so, he also ran the risk of shooting himself in the foot. Regardless of how the gambit played out, the day had been more good than bad. Dix's news had come as a big relief.

Frank was standing buck naked before the bathroom mirror, combing his hair, when he heard a vehicle descending the drive. Checking his watch, he wondered who the hell would be showing up at this hour. It was nearly eight.

Slipping on his robe, he went to the front room. Through the window he saw a woman climbing from an old beat-up compact. The light wasn't good enough to see her features. She was tall and broad-shouldered with thin legs protruding from a miniskirt. She had a sack in her hand. The woman tiptoed precariously across the gravel parking area on what must have been four-inch heels. She was blond with cork-screw curls and, as she drew near the porch light, Frank could see her face. It was Frieda Benke, Riverton's semiprofessional lady of the evening.

"What the hell?" he muttered. He knew the woman, of course, but they hadn't spoken more than a dozen words in all the years he'd lived in Riverton.

As Frieda stepped onto the porch, Frank cinched the belt of his robe tighter and went to the door, opening it just after she knocked. She greeted him with a grin.

"Hi, Frank. How's it going?" she said in her deep contralto, still bearing echos of her German heritage. She had on a waist-length mohair sweater jacket with big shoulder pads that must have been in her closet for twenty or twenty-five years.

"Frieda," he said. "To what do I owe this surprise visit?"

She pursed her red-painted lips, then smiled. "I thought maybe we could party." She lifted the sack, grasping what was obviously a bottle by the neck. "French champagne, *ja?*"

He chuckled nervously. "A nice thought, Frieda, but not the way I was planning to spend my evening. Are you under the impression... I...I mean, do you have me confused with some other—"

"Frank," she said, putting her hand on her hip, "the evening's paid for. I'm not going to ask you for money."

"Paid for?"

"*Ja,*" she said. "Paid for. No charge. It's a free party."

He scratched his head, completely confused. He smelled a

setup, but Frieda's countenance was so guileless it belied perfidy.

"Zo, Frank, are you going to make me stand here in the cold, or are you going to let me come in?"

He stepped back to admit her. "Sorry. Come in, Frieda. But I think there's been a mistake. Or somebody's putting you on."

As she moved past him her perfume was so strong it practically made his eyes water. He closed the door. Frieda looked around like somebody making sure she knew where the fire exits were. Then she faced him, throwing one leg out to the side in the exaggerated pose of a fashion model. "Zo, what's the problem? You don't look like you're ready to party. Or is it me? You don't want me, just say so, Frank, okay?"

"Look, Frieda," he said, embarrassed, "I'm kinda confused. Who sent you?"

She pursed her lips again. "I'm not supposed to tell," she said. "I promised."

The list of possibilities was short. Mort Anderson was at the top of it, though Frank couldn't see an obvious motive. There was no question that Mort had influence with Frieda, being her longtime landlord. The rumor was that Mort used to ball Frieda in lieu of rent money. That was back in the days when he was still married and couldn't be seen with respectable women like Kay.

"Frieda, it was Mort, wasn't it?" Frank said. "He sent you."

"Look," she said, losing patience, "do you want to fuck or don't you?"

He could feel his soft heart starting to get in the way of his better judgment. Hookers weren't supposed to be hurt by rejection, but Frank regarded Frieda Benke as a lost soul more than a true prostitute.

"Sit down," he said, pointing to the chair.

Frieda took off her jacket. She wore nothing under it but a knit tank top. Her breasts were not huge, but braless, nipples erect, her chest was an attraction. She sat, crossing her long legs very pointedly. She didn't have on any panties and wanted him to know. For the briefest of moments, Frank considered taking Frieda into the other room and screwing her, but he reminded himself that everything that was too good to be true probably was. And besides, he was old enough to know that there was no such thing as a free lunch. He sat on the arm of the sofa, careful to make sure his robe covered his thighs.

"What are you afraid of, Frank?" she asked, seemingly aware of his internal struggle. "You're a strong man. I know I don't scare you."

"No, you don't scare me," he said.

"You want that I open the champagne? You want that I put my hand under your robe? Tell me what you want."

In his forty-six years he'd learned that sometimes the only thing worse than taking advantage of a woman was not taking advantage of her when she wanted you to. The question was, how needy was he? And which did he need most—to say yes or to say no?

As he toyed with the question, he heard the sound of another vehicle outside.

"Christ, what now?" he muttered, not knowing what to expect as he went to the window.

He nearly died when he looked out and saw Abby Hooper coming around her Bronco, earnest and righteous and painfully adorable—all that was good in his soul about to come face-to-face with all that was evil.

"Shit," he said, glancing down at himself.

"Who is it?" Frieda asked, sounding worried.

"The law."

"The law?"

"The police chief."

Frieda gasped about the same time Abby rapped on the door. There was no hiding, he realized, maybe no explaining. He'd been caught again, this time with his pants literally down and the town hooker on his sofa with a bottle of champagne in her hand. That horrible sound in his head was Mort Anderson's evil laughter, there was no mistaking it. The bait had been set, he'd taken it and now the trap had been sprung. Frank quickly opened the door, wanting to get it over with.

Abby stood on his stoop, smiling and expectant, her cheeks rosy, her eyes full of merriment. Then when she saw his bare legs beneath his robe and his bare chest, her expectation turned to uncertainty.

"Looks like I caught you at a bad time," she mumbled.

"Not half as bad as you know, Chief."

Abby looked past him, if not actually seeing Frieda, sensing her presence. "Oh, gee, I'm sorry, Frank, I should have called before coming over. I was in Stockton today and just got back to town." She edged back off the porch, ready to make a getaway.

"No, no, no," he said, stepping out and taking her by the arm. "Don't leave. Come in."

She peered around him very pointedly, this time most certainly seeing Frieda.

"You've got company, Frank. I'll give you a call in the morning."

"Actually, my company was about to leave, Abby. I insist you come in."

She gave him a most unappreciative look. There may have been a little anger in it. Frank didn't care. The situation had only one way to go and that was up. It was one of those full-speed-ahead-damn-the-torpedoes circumstances. Balls to the wall.

"Really, Frank," Abby said, resisting.

"Look," he said, looking straight into her eyes, "Frieda's

about to leave and I need to talk to you. About Jane Doe,'' he added.

She was clearly annoyed, but relented, stepping into his mobile home. After the fresh air, Frieda's perfume was strong enough to make even a nonasthmatic gag. Abby looked at the woman. Frieda had gotten to her feet and was tugging at her miniskirt as though she could add six inches to the hem if only she tried hard enough.

"Hi," she said, a shit-eating grin on her face.

As Frieda squirmed, Frank was aware of her tits swinging under the tank top. Abby couldn't have missed them, either. Thank God, she was standing and not displaying her panty-less crotch. Abby's presence had changed Frieda's countenance completely. No more innocent child in a harsh, real world—it was strictly the accused before the judge and jury.

"Abby," Frank said, "this is Frieda Benke. Some of the boys sent her to deliver a bottle of champagne."

Frieda grinned. "*Ja*, like Frank says, to deliver some champagne." Seeing the bottle on the sofa, she went to pick it up. In bending over, Frieda showed more ass cheek than probably was legal, even though she contorted her body, her knees going one way, her butt the other, in a futile attempt to avoid the display. Grabbing her mohair jacket at the same time, she pranced over in her heels, little-girl like, thrusting the bottle into his hands. "*Zo*, that's it, then, Frank. Enjoy your wine and have a nice evening." Pulling her jacket on, she made her way to the door. "*Gute Nacht!*" she cried, not able to get outside fast enough.

He stared at the door for a moment, imagining her scampering to her car like a scared rabbit pursued by hounds. The absurdity of the situation almost made him laugh. But he maintained his aplomb, removing the bottle from the paper sack.

"Ah, how about that?" he said, examining the label. "Perrier Jouët champagne. The real McCoy. The boys outdid themselves.''

''I'm not enjoying this, Frank,'' Abby said. ''If you are, that's another matter. I really think I should go.''

''Why? Because you're embarrassed…or embarrassed for me?''

''A little of both, I think.''

He rubbed his chin. ''You're voting guilty before the defense has put on its case.''

''This is not a trial,'' Abby said firmly. ''You're not accountable to me and I have no idea why you want me to stay when you're clearly as embarrassed as I am.''

''What did you see, pray tell?''

''Huh?''

''What did you see when I opened the door?''

''Frank…'' she said, sounding more annoyed than disgusted.

''No, it's a serious question. You're a detective. You must have drawn some conclusions. I mean, a man opens the door, he's in his bathrobe. There's a painted lady standing in his living room with more perfume on than's available in most perfume shops. She's armed with champagne and a willing expression. Isn't the conclusion inescapable?''

She put her hands on her hips. ''What's your point?''

''It's called salvaging one's pride.''

''There's no need,'' she said.

''Oh, I beg to differ.''

''What makes you think I care?''

''You don't, but I do. That's my point.''

''All right, so say what you've got to say.''

''Sit down and make yourself at home,'' he said, pointing to the sofa. ''Can I take your jacket?''

''No, thanks, I'll only be staying a minute.''

''Suit yourself,'' Frank said, sitting in the armchair as she dropped onto the edge of the sofa. He crossed his legs, covering his bare knee with the flap of the robe. "Okay," he began, "defendant's just finishing his shower when there's a knock at the door. He opens it to find a good-time girl standing there, indicating she's come for a party. Defendant inquires as to reason, determining through cross-examination that good-time girl was sent by an erstwhile friend with a bad sense of humor. As defendant and accomplice discuss the relative morality of the situation, the cops arrive, drawing obvious, but erroneous, conclusions. Discretion being the better part of valor, painted lady makes a hasty retreat, leaving defendant to explain to skeptical police chief."

Abby tried not to smile, but couldn't help herself. "All right, fine."

"So, what are the chief's conclusions?"

"That's there's insufficient evidence to press charges."

"In other words, innocent as far as the justice system is concerned, but guilty in your heart."

"Frank, you act like it matters what I think."

"It does."

She gave a big sigh, shaking her head in a disapproving manner.

"With the state of my moral character in limbo, maybe we would profit from a change of subject," he said. "Jane Doe?"

Abby appeared to relax some. "Good idea."

"I've got news," he said.

"So do I."

"You first, then."

"Have you heard about the kids confessing they pulled Jane Doe from the slough?"

"Yeah."

"I figured you would."

Frank shrugged. "It's a small town and I've been here long enough to have made a few friends."

"Friends with expensive taste," Abby said, indicating the bottle, which he still had in his hands.

"Different set of friends."

"The point is, the testimony of your mystery witness has been corroborated, assuming, of course, she exists."

"Meaning?"

"Meaning you could have been the one who heard the screaming, seen the kids and made up the story about a lady friend. Though after tonight, it's not inconceivable someone was here with you. Was it Frieda Benke, Frank?"

"Nope."

"She doesn't strike me as someone who'd hold up under questioning."

"Have at it, Abby, if you must. Question her."

She appeared to consider that. Frank was not getting the positive response he expected. What he couldn't determine was whether Abby's reaction was from conviction or pique. What's more, he couldn't decide which one was better.

"You're still a skeptic," he observed.

"About your innocence? No, things are starting to fall in your direction. Tiffany Miller's blood type is A negative and she admits to cutting her hand when she fell on the steps. I also got a call from the county crime lab. The pubic hairs on your bed sheets were not Jane Doe's. And the tests on the paint and rust in her hair indicate they did not come from your truck."

"So, my truck is innocent, too."

"Let's put it this way—I'm beginning to understand the basis for your cocksure manner."

"Abby, I think that's the nicest thing you've said about me yet."

She laughed. "Frank, you're a nut."

"Not a killer, not a child molester, not even a man of low moral character. Just a nut."

"Criminal indictments are not issued for being weird. Consider yourself fortunate, Frank. But before you go opening that bottle of champagne, I still want to see the results of the DNA testing.''

He grinned, shaking his head. ''You won't allow me the satisfaction of a victory, will you? Is it because you want to wriggle out of that dinner you owe me?''

''Dinner?''

''Remember, if I turned out to be innocent, you have to buy me dinner.''

''That's right. And if you were guilty, it was going to be the warden at San Quentin who bought me dinner.''

''But you lost,'' he said.

''Or so it seems.''

''Any more news?''

Abby took off her windbreaker and set it beside her. ''Actually, yes,'' she said, leaning back on the sofa. She told him about her conversation with Maxine Shear. ''She didn't want to tell me the molester's name,'' she said, ''but I finally coaxed it out of her.''

''Lloyd Witherspoon,'' Frank said.

Her brows rose in surprise. ''You know him?''

''Met him last night for the first time. Lloyd came by to stick his toe in the water.'' Frank related the gist of the conversation.

''Witherspoon's somehow involved in the Jane Doe case,'' Abby said, scooting up to the edge of the cushion again, her policewoman instincts coming to the fore.

''Considering he's a child molester, it's a reasonable assumption. And he was clearly troubled by the *circumstances* of Chet's suicide, more I'd say, than by Chet's death itself.''

''We've got to talk to Mr. Witherspoon,'' Abby said.

He arched a brow. ''Was that a royal 'we'?''

She chuckled. ''Yes, I guess so.''

''I'd like to be involved,'' Frank said.

"Hey, you've only got one foot out of the penalty box, Mr. Keegan. Isn't that jumping the gun a little?"

"You've known I'm innocent all along, Abby. Admit it."

"I was resisting what the evidence was telling me," she confessed.

"Then it's time to give me a vote of confidence. I want in. Seriously."

"Let me think about it," she said. "First, I've got to find Witherspoon."

"I've got his license-plate number," Frank said.

She eyed him. "And I imagine you're willing to share it with me in exchange for the right to be involved in the case."

"Not a bad idea."

She shook her head. "Frank, you're really too much."

He liked the tone in her voice, liked it a whole lot better than the one she'd had at the beginning of the conversation. They exchanged long looks. He felt the vibrations. She did, too, he could tell, and was still fighting them, but not as hard as before.

"So, give me the license number and I'll run it down," she said.

Frank went to the kitchen and transcribed the number of Lloyd Witherspoon's vehicle tag from the business card onto a slip of paper. He took it back to the front room and handed it to Abby. She glanced at it and stuffed it into a pocket.

"Are we partners, then?" he asked.

"Like I said, I'll think about it."

He again contemplated her. "In any case, I'd say we've got cause for celebration. How about some champagne?"

She laughed, shaking her head. "Thanks for the kind offer, but that's more in Frieda's line of work than mine."

"I'll get dressed first," he said, poking his tongue in his cheek.

"I've got to go. Really."

"I won't let you leave without setting our dinner date."

"You're serious about that, aren't you?"

"Damned right."

"Why?"

He took a moment. "The politically correct answer is I'd rather we be friends than enemies. The politically incorrect answer is I like you."

Abby lowered her eyes, but she appeared more flattered than offended.

"What do you say, Abby?"

She looked up at him for a long moment. "Are you a fight fan?"

"Fight, as in boxing?"

"Yeah."

"Well, I fought some as a youth. Police-league kind of thing. They figured it was a good way to knock a little vinegar out of me. And it worked. But to answer your question, I don't keep up with it much. The fight game sort of ended with Ali as far as I'm concerned. Why do you ask?"

"My best friend is fighting in Sacramento tomorrow night. Thought you might like to go. We can have dinner before. On me."

"You want to take me to a prizefight?"

"You gotta admit, it's novel as far as first dates go."

Frank smiled. Abby smiled. He liked the way things were going a whole lot. "Time and place?"

"How about if I pick you up at five?" she said. "That should give us time to grab a bite before the first bout."

"Great. By the way, who's your best friend?"

"Crystal Armstrong. Darren's sister. I mentioned her the other night."

"Oh, yeah. But you didn't say she was a prizefighter."

"This is her first bout. And, to be honest, I hope her last."

"I'm honored you've invited me."

"Don't make too much of it, Frank. I owe you a dinner,

and a boxing match is not someplace I want to go to alone. I'm killing two birds with one stone.''

"What the right hand giveth, the left hand taketh away."

"You're a biblical scholar, too?"

"A loose paraphrase."

Abby grabbed her jacket and stood. Frank got up, too.

"I'm glad you came by," he said.

"I think I had something to do with Frieda Benke's eagerness to leave."

"I am but made of mortal flesh," he replied. "Like any man I can be sorely tempted. But the moral fiber is strong. In the end I usually do the right thing."

"You're full of it, too," she said with a laugh.

She put on her jacket. Frank went with her to the door. She stepped onto the porch. Then, turning to face him, she said, "I'm glad your story is checking out. I didn't like thinking you were in any way responsible for what happened to Jane Doe."

"I didn't like it very much, either."

"Now all I have to do is figure out who your mystery lady friend is." Giving him a rather endearing smile, she headed off to her vehicle and he watched her go.

Frank was perfectly aware how disastrous it would be if Abby found out about Kay. Until he figured out a way to get out of this mess, he could only hope her police skills came up a little short.

Thursday
February 20th

Riverton Civic Center

It was early, but Abby was ready for her third cup of coffee. Getting up from her desk, she headed for the coffee room with her mug, yawning. She'd been awakened before dawn by a call from Frank and hadn't been able to go back to sleep.

"A thousand pardons for the earliness of the hour," he'd said, "but I got a call late last night from a contractor I know in Roseville. Granite Bay, actually. He wants me to wire a couple of new homes by Saturday. The guy he had for the job flaked out and the drywallers are coming in. It's got to be done like now."

"So you can't go to the fight tonight."

"Not exactly. The bad news is I've got to leave in a few minutes and I'll be gone two days. The good news is that since I'll be in the Sacramento area, anyway, I can meet you someplace and we can go to dinner and the fight from there. I just won't be able to ride up with you."

"That'd work," Abby said, brightening.

"Six okay to meet?"

"That should give us time."

"Where?"

"Let's meet at Lufta's. That's where I've made reservations."

"Hey, I'm honored," Frank said. "That's a pretty swank place."

"Considering the hard time I gave you, I figured it was the least I could do."

"Maybe I should consider becoming a suspect more often."

"You don't have to go to those lengths, Frank, honest."

They'd ended their conversation and Abby had lain in bed pondering their growing friendship. The night before she'd fallen asleep thinking about him and maybe dreamed about him, as well. What was happening? Was she developing a thing for Frank Keegan?

When she thought about it, he was an unlikely candidate for romance. First there was the age difference. And second he grew pears and installed burglar alarms. Not that she looked down on people of modest income and life-style. She didn't have pretensions. But there was something about Frank. He had virtue of a different sort—maybe his humanity. He was also down-to-earth and real. She sensed a goodness and depth in him, a kindred spirit. Plus the guy had whimsy in his soul and a sexiness about him. All that couldn't be ignored.

Dix Fowler was in the coffee room when she got there. He was stuffing the last of a sugary doughnut in his mouth and licking his fingers. "Morning, Chief," he mumbled. "You're in early."

"I was awake, so I figured why sit at home enjoying myself?"

Dix grinned. "Chet was the same. Must be something about the job."

Abby hated to think being police chief of Riverton, California, was all there was to life, but aside from her abortive dinner with Darren the other evening, she hadn't been on a proper date in six months. And even longer since she'd gotten laid. Maybe that, too, would help explain her interest in Frank Keegan.

"Anything new on the Jane Doe case?" Dix asked as he dumped a third teaspoon of sugar in his coffee.

"Yesterday I contacted the San Francisco and Sacramento departments to see if the child-prostitution angle might ring any bells. The state Department of Justice had nothing on her, but I thought somebody who knew the streets might recognize her. If Chet found her that way, odds are it was either in Sacto or S.F."

"Good thinking, Chief."

"Haven't heard anything yet, but I'm hoping." Abby filled her mug with coffee. "There are a couple of other things I wanted to discuss, if you have a minute. Want to come to my office?"

"Sure."

They made their way through the building to her office. Dix settled his corpulent frame into one of the two visitors' chairs. Abby sipped her coffee and put the mug down on the coaster.

"Tell me what you know about Lloyd Witherspoon," she said.

There was a flicker of surprise on Dix's face. "Lloyd Witherspoon. Boy, it's been a while since I've heard that name." His brow furrowed thoughtfully. "I didn't know the guy or much about him. Lloyd was a distant relative of Chet's, from the moneyed side of the family, as Chet put it. Years ago Lloyd had a house outside of town, but he wasn't around a whole lot. I don't know where he spent his time, but he didn't mix much with the locals. It must have been ten years ago or so that he moved away. I've never heard anything about him since."

"Chet didn't talk about him?"

"Not to me."

"Dix, were you aware of any investigation concerning Witherspoon?"

"Here in the department?"

"Yes."

Dix Fowler shook his head. "Nothing I know of. Why?"

"I have reason to believe Witherspoon was involved in a child-molestation incident here in Riverton that Chet personally investigated. The file's been destroyed, so I can't look into it. I thought maybe you recalled something."

"Not a thing, Chief. Do you think there's a connection with Jane Doe?"

"Related subject matter," she replied.

Dix nodded.

"There's something else I've been wondering about," Abby said. "What can you tell me about Frieda Benke?"

He shifted uncomfortably. "Uh...well, she's a lady of, let's say, easy virtue."

"That's what I gather."

"She's never been a problem. I mean she doesn't serve the general public, attract undesirable elements, that sort of thing. She has a few regulars and pretty much confines her business to them." His brow furrowed again. "Are you thinking of making her an issue?"

"My philosophy is vigorous enforcement of the law," Abby replied. "But I also try to be pragmatic."

"Chet adopted a policy of live and let live as far as Frieda was concerned and it worked pretty good," Dix said.

"Yes, but I don't want people hiding behind that, either."

"What do you mean?"

"Well, using Frieda as an alibi, for example, because she's supposedly untouchable."

"I still don't get you," Dix said.

Abby took another sip of coffee. "Let me be direct. Is Frank Keegan one of Frieda's regulars?"

"Frank?" he said, grinning. "No, not Frank. Frieda's not his style."

"Why do you say that?"

"Frank doesn't need to… Well, some guys are willing to pay for it, others aren't."

"I thought maybe Frieda was his mystery witness, Dix."

"It'd surprise me, Chief."

"Well, do you know who else it might be? Frank seems to be quite the man about town—at least according to his buddies—but nobody'll say who his girlfriends are."

Dix shrugged.

Abby became annoyed. "What is this, Dix? Are the boys sticking together out of loyalty to protect his phantom lover, or is the whole thing bullshit?"

"That's all bachelor stuff, Chief. I don't get into it much. I'm a married man."

Abby gave him a look, knowing he was lying—or being loyal to Frank, which was a more generous way to put it. There wasn't much point in being insistent because, for the moment, anyway, it no longer mattered to the investigation.

"So tell me then," she said, "do you think I should question Frieda?"

Dix scarcely hesitated. "If it's important to the case, I guess you've got to do what you've got to do."

The words weren't said with much conviction. Abby saw she was up against ancient loyalties. When it came to things like their private lives and the town hooker, the boys stuck together like peanut butter and bread. And it was a cinch nobody over at the River Queen was going to slap *her* on the back and say, "Well, Chief, I think I'll swing by Frieda's and knock off a piece."

She gave Dix a level look. "Guess I'll have to take the matter under advisement." She fiddled with her coffee mug. "By the way, how did your questioning over at the River Queen go?"

"Didn't turn up anything of interest, Chief. As a matter of fact, I was working on my report this morning. Memo to the file. Want me to bring it over when I'm through?"

"Yes, but give me a quick rundown now. Did you find out who took Frank home Friday night?"

"No. He apparently left the Queen under his own power and got a ride, but nobody knows who gave it to him. Kay took his keys from him and Toad returned Frank's truck the next morning at her instruction. She'd gone to San Francisco with Mort."

"Mort Anderson."

"Yes," Dix said, shifting uneasily.

Abby was aware that her mother was keeping company with the town's richest citizen, a fact that struck her as eminently predictable. But Abby had bent over backward to keep her personal feelings about her mother from coloring the investigation. That was the main reason she'd sent Dix over to the River Queen in the first place.

"Who did you say returned Frank's truck?" Abby asked.

"Toad."

"Who's he?"

"Bartender at the Queen. His real name is Juan Lopez."

"Did Mr. Lopez have anything to say about Frank's condition when he saw him the next morning?"

"Only that he had a terrible hangover. Frank drove Toad back into town and that was it."

"Surely somebody at the bar that night saw something."

Dix shook his head. "Kay said it was late and the place was pretty empty. She couldn't recall who was still around. 'One night blends into the next,' was the way she put it."

Abby couldn't help wondering if her mother wasn't protecting her customer and his lady friend. As the proprietor of the River Queen, she was practically a member of the old boys' club. But since Frank's innocence or guilt was no longer at issue, there was no need to press the matter.

"Frank's mystery lady may or may not become an issue. We'll have to see how the investigation goes," Abby said. In saying that to Dix, she was, in effect, announcing it to the town. "I know you've got things to do, but I'd like you to do something for me, if you don't mind."

"Sure, Chief."

Abby gave him the license-plate number she'd gotten from Frank and asked him to run down an address for Lloyd Witherspoon. She also wanted him to check to see if he had an arrest record.

"You must think Lloyd's involved in this," Dix said.

"Well, he's the only lead I've got at the moment." She watched the sergeant take a gulp of coffee. "By the way, Dix, have you heard whether arrangements have been set for Chet's funeral?"

"Saturday at ten. His lawyer, Judge Parker, is handling things. Fred told me there'd be no service. Just the internment and it'll be open to the public."

"Sounds like I won't need to prepare a eulogy."

"Fred said Chet's instructions were that there was to be no pomp and circumstance."

"I'm sure people in the department will want to go to the internment, though. Will you make sure everybody's notified? And if whoever's on duty wants to be there badly, see if you can juggle the schedule to accommodate them, okay?"

"Right, Chief."

Dix went off and Abby pondered her situation. Compared to the typical life of a small-town police chief, her first month certainly hadn't been boring. The hell of it was, she was in danger of coming up empty on her first big case.

She'd been thinking about Frank's request to be involved in the investigation. At first blush, it seemed like a bad idea. But the more she thought about it, the more positives she saw. There could be political benefits—the victor and the vanquished joining forces to solve the crime of the decade.

She'd give W.C. a call and run the idea past him. Already she'd learned how important it was to cover your bases politically.

For lunch Abby had had an egg-salad sandwich at Thelma's. She'd ended up bringing half of it back to the office in a doggy bag, mostly because she'd lost her appetite when her mother had shown up at the diner.

Apart from her visit to the River Queen, it was the first time Abby had encountered Kay Ingram in public. Judging by her mother's reaction, it was purely a chance occurrence. Kay didn't seem any happier to see her than she was to see Kay, at least initially.

Abby had been alone, reading the *Bee* at a table in back, when the little bell over the door jangled and a hush fell over the crowded establishment. She'd looked up and there was her mother, her blond hair swept up, looking rather elegant in a knit suit and pearls. Abby had always felt a certain prejudice against Kay because of her sexiness and beauty. Ty Hooper had repeatedly characterized his former wife as a trollop and a Jezebel, and Abby had been conditioned by that, reacting negatively to everything coquettish and alluring, not only in Kay, but in women generally.

Abby was attractive in her way, but her appearance had never been central to her identity. Maybe that explained her feminist proclivities and the constant battle between her desires and her convictions. She was both independent and strong, and she wanted to be appreciated for it. Men, it seemed, didn't find that a turn-on.

Her first serious love affair—with Darren—had been disillusioning, casting doubt on both her feelings about men and about herself. The humiliation of having let herself be used was the worst. So when Darren left town, she'd taken refuge in her work. Yet the alienation bothered her. It was one of those "damned if you do, damned if you don't" situations.

For a while after she arrived at the Riverton Café, Kay had sat at the counter chatting with Thelma, while people looked back and forth between mother and daughter, wondering what would happen next. Finally Kay had picked up her cup of coffee and walked toward the rear of the café as several dozen eyes watched, the only sounds in the place Kay's heels on the linoleum and the rattle of dishes in the kitchen. When she stopped at the table, Abby glanced up.

"Mind if I join you?" Kay asked.

Abby hesitated, but only momentarily. "Suit yourself."

Her mother sat in the chair opposite her. Their eyes met.

"There are a couple of items of business I'd like to discuss with you, if that's okay," Kay said.

"I try to make myself available to every citizen," Abby replied.

Kay ignored the snide innuendo. "I've heard the rumors that Frank Keegan is off the hook," she said. "If it's all right, I wanted to confirm it's true."

"I normally don't discuss cases under investigation with the general public," Abby replied, "but since I already talked to him in your presence, I'll give you an update. Frank's story, his alibi, if you will, seems to be holding up. The preliminary lab reports also seem to confirm his version of the facts. At this time I don't consider him a suspect in any possible criminal activity connected with Jane Doe."

"At this time?"

"The situation could change if other incriminating evidence should come to light, but I don't expect that to happen."

Kay had stared at her then, an odd look of disbelief in her eyes.

"What's the matter?" Abby said.

"My child, my grown-up daughter, a police chief, sounding so official. I know there's nothing remarkable about that, but I still struggle with it."

"I'd like to think I sound like the person I am," Abby said.

Kay smiled painfully. "I'm sorry, Abby, I know you don't want to hear this. I'm only human. I do get sentimental."

Abby had become very uncomfortable. She didn't want to talk about their relationship—or lack thereof. She decided to use the opportunity for purposes of her own. "Since we're discussing Frank Keegan," she said, "mind if I ask a few questions?"

"What do you want to know?"

"How familiar are you with his private life?" Abby asked.

Kay seemed wary. "What, for example?"

"He has a lady friend, his mysterious alibi witness, who seems as much a fiction as reality. Have any idea who it might be?"

Kay stared at her.

After several moments Abby shook her head. "Nobody wants to talk about it. What's with this conspiracy of silence? Don't people in this town care that a serious crime was committed?"

"You're asking a rather personal question."

"There's a dead girl in the morgue who was abused and either killed or left to die," Abby snapped. "I consider that rather personal, too."

"You're right, but what does that have to do with Frank's sex life?"

"I thought the woman he was with might be Frieda Benke," Abby said, ignoring the question, "but I can't get confirmation. What do you think? Frieda or somebody else?"

Kay drank from her mug and put it carefully down on the table. "You don't like to discuss your cases with the public and I don't like to discuss my customers' private lives with the police," she said. "I don't mean that snidely or to be difficult—it just happens to be a fact."

"This town is gossip-hungry unless it's the police chief

asking. It's funny how suddenly everybody's lips are sealed.''

"Maybe that comes with the territory, Abby. This is a close-knit community and people know what's harmful and what isn't. They also know who the good guys and the bad guys are.''

"Good guys? You mean like Chet Wilsey?''

Kay fiddled with her coffee mug. "None of us are angels. Chet obviously had serious problems. I feel sorry for the man, if you want to know the truth.''

"I feel sorry for the child he raped,'' Abby rejoined.

"I do, too, of course. That was a horrible tragedy. There's not a soul in town who doesn't think that, including Chet's best friends.''

Abby was silent and so was Kay.

"But we aren't really arguing about Chet, are we?'' Kay said after a while. "The anger you feel is really directed at me. I represent everything that's bad in this town and maybe everything that's bad in your life, don't I?''

Neither of them had been speaking loudly, and though the rest of the clientele in the café were aware of what was going on at the back table, the conversation was, for the most part, discreet. Yet Abby felt like they were onstage. It was the most she'd interacted with her mother in years, and the emotion she felt was surprisingly strong. Resentment for having been abandoned burned in her heart, resentment she'd carried inside her since childhood. But there was another feeling, as well—confusion, the confusion that comes when the need to love is stifled by hatred.

"To be honest, I don't care to discuss my feelings about you,'' Abby said, unable to hide her bitterness. "And playing a blame game doesn't interest me, either.''

"There's not a lot I can do about that,'' Kay said. "If you're ever going to forgive me, it will have to come from your heart. I just want you to know I'm willing to discuss it whenever you are.''

Only then did Abby realize how unprepared she'd been for this conversation. Her mother had made overtures in the past, but she'd assumed that Kay understood she had no desire for a personal conversation, let alone a relationship. She was so befuddled it made her angry.

''Look,'' Kay said, ''I can see I've put you on the spot and that wasn't my intent. I really wanted to discuss Jane Doe.''

''What about her?''

''I don't know if you realize how deeply her death has affected the community. It's all people have been talking about for days. They want to do something constructive, Abby, but they're at a loss.''

Abby wanted to say they could cooperate rather than clam up, but there was nothing to be gained by slinging another arrow.

''I had an idea I wanted to run past you,'' Kay went on. ''This town could use a boost. I thought maybe raising money for abused children would give people something to get excited about. Say we have a fund-raiser, a charity event, maybe a dance. The proceeds would go to an organization devoted to helping girls like Jane Doe.''

''It's a good idea,'' Abby said, not expecting something like this to come from her mother. ''I'd certainly support it.''

''And I thought any publicity that was generated might also bring attention to the case and perhaps help you to identify the poor child.''

''It couldn't hurt.''

Kay seemed pleased. ''I'll be happy to organize the event. It would be nice to have your support.''

''You've got it.''

''W.C. will want to be involved. Either or both of you

could give a little speech, maybe. I assume that would be all right.''

"Sure.''

Kay smiled. ''I'll get to work on it, talk to other merchants, the Chamber of Commerce. And I'll keep you informed.''

"Fine.''

Kay looked down at her coffee mug, obviously wrestling with her thoughts. "I don't want to press you, Abby, but I wish you'd keep an open mind to the possibility of us sitting down sometime for a long talk. I know your feelings about the past, but there is a future, too. I'd like to think there's something in it for us, however small it might be.''

Abby nodded, but she couldn't quite bring herself to say, Sure, great, let's do that. Her heart simply wasn't there.

Kay had gotten up from the table and gone back up front, where she'd chatted briefly with Thelma before leaving. Abby had watched her, reminding herself that was her mother, the woman responsible for the years of grief and resentment, the woman Abby hadn't allowed herself to love, though in truth she'd dearly wanted to. Now, ironically, they'd been brought together by the tragic death of a young girl. She was not one to say that bad things happened for good reasons, but even the smallest of events had unpredictable consequences.

Back in her office, Abby continued to ponder her encounter. The softening she felt in her heart was a little frightening—especially since she'd spent years building a wall around her feelings. But that afternoon Kay had succeeded in making her doubt, if not who her mother really was, then whether turning a cold shoulder to her was the right thing to do.

Soon the phones started ringing. First she got a call from a detective in Missing Persons in the LAPD. A short conversation verified that Jane Doe was not his girl. Then she got a return call from an officer in the Sexual Assaults and

Child Abuse section of the Sacramento department, a woman she'd interfaced with on a rape case a couple of years earlier. "Showed your Jane Doe's picture to everybody in the section," she said. "Didn't set off any bells. Sorry."

Abby thanked her and hung up. This was going to be one of those cases where nothing came easily. If there was to be a break, she had a hunch it was going to be with Lloyd Witherspoon. Dix had reported back that Witherspoon had a clean record except for a single arrest for solicitation three years ago. The charges had been dropped, but it was another little mark against him. The key had been his visit with Frank. That discreet inquiry made her believe that there was some kind of a connection between Witherspoon and Jane Doe. The question was how to uncover it.

W. C. Joyner was the next to return her call. "Bringing Frank in as a contract investigator is a wonderful idea," he said. "The department's simply not staffed for an extensive investigation. If the funds aren't in the budget, I'll find them somewhere."

W.C. was almost too enthusiastic, making Abby wonder if W.C.'s reaction was more a reflection of a lack of confidence in her than a recognition of the need for additional resources. "My plan would be to use him whenever I didn't have the manpower available for a critical assignment," she said. "I'll be in charge, though. That won't change."

"How you handle it, Abby, is completely up to you."

That made her feel better. Abby admonished herself for her insecurity.

No sooner had she finished with the mayor when Crystal called. "Are you coming tonight, Abby?" They were the first words out of her mouth.

"I plan to, yes."

"Oh, good. I think."

"What's the matter?"

"Well, for starters, I'm scared shitless," Crystal replied.

"I've already thrown up twice. But then, my manager said I'm supposed to be nervous."

"It's not your nerves that concern me, it's your health—mental, as well as physical."

"Listen, Abby, if you're going to be squeamish, maybe you shouldn't come tonight. It could be bloody."

"Well, I am coming, regardless. I've got a date."

There was a silence on the line, then Crystal said, "A date? A man?"

"Yes, a man."

Another silence.

"Is there a problem with that?" Abby asked.

"Darren will be crushed."

Abby began to wonder if this was more than just a commiseration call. "Is that what this is about, Crystal? Are you Darren's stalking-horse?"

"No, but he's been despondent ever since he saw you the other night."

"Well, damn it, he deserves to be despondent. Your brother was an ass."

"I'm sure he was. In fact, that's what he said himself. But I've never seen him like this, Abby. Ever since I made that slip about you getting pregnant, he's been obsessed. It's like you're all he talks about."

"He certainly has a funny way of being obsessed."

"I think it's desperation, if you want to know the truth. He was hoping to see you tonight."

"If he's at the fight and I'm at the fight, we may be seeing each other, but I'll be with my date."

"Darren will be upset."

"Darren's problem is he's just not used to being blown off."

"Well, to hear him tell it, he's still desperately in love with you."

"Still?"

"That's what he says."

"It's a little late," Abby said. "He's gotten more from me than he deserves. But let's not talk about your brother. You've got more important things on your mind—like keeping that pretty face of yours pretty."

"Guess I'll have to knock Mulroney out in the first round, then."

"Do it, girl."

Crystal sighed. "Jeez, I love you. You're the best ever, I swear. Will you come to my dressing room after the fight? Win or lose, I want to see you, okay?"

"I'll be there, Crystal," Abby said, "cheering my head off. Kick some butt for me, too, huh?"

"Thanks for being my friend."

Abby hung up, a little misty-eyed. Crystal was amazing, if only because she never ceased to amaze. But the business with Darren was odd. Crystal used to be indifferent toward him, hostile even. Now she was practically pimping for the guy. Why did this feel wrong?

Sacramento

Frank decided to check into a motel in Sacramento, rather than stay in Roseville. It would mean a long drive in the morning, but it would be against rush-hour traffic. He found a modest place on Sixteenth, not far from Memorial Auditorium where the fight was being held. It wasn't exactly a hot-sheet establishment, but it had probably seen its share of nooners over the years. With all the politicians in town, there was sure to be plenty of sport fucking.

Lufta's was elegant by the standards of the valley, so Frank had brought a sport coat and tie. He'd be overdressed for the fight, but that was okay—what he cared about was being with Abby. He still couldn't get over her inviting him. She had to be feeling some of the same things as he was.

The restaurant was in Midtown, an older residential section east of downtown, with yuppified commercial islands—a sort of Greenwich Village stuck in the middle of California's Great Central Valley. Scattered among the old Victorians were coffeehouses, restaurants, bookstores and art galleries.

Lufta's was on J Street about ten blocks from his motel. Frank would have walked except that his butt was dragging from climbing in the rafters and stringing wire all day. He found a place to park and arrived at the restaurant before Abby. For a guy who tended to run fifteen minutes late everywhere, it was quite an accomplishment.

Sacramento was a laid-back town and the life-style casual—L.A. without the smug pretension of being "with it." The summers were so damned hot people couldn't dress and winters were rain and more rain. Restaurants and bars ran to informal. Lufta's was one of the few special-occasion places where men were expected to be in ties and women in skirts.

He'd only been waiting in the reception five minutes when Abby arrived. Frank had to stare. She looked incredible in a long black coat and heels with her dark hair up. And she was wearing makeup. Her eyes especially looked nice—big and alluring.

"Hi, Frank."

"Wow, don't you look gorgeous!" he said.

Abby smiled with embarrassment. He felt brazen enough to lean over and kiss her cheek, which, surprisingly, she didn't seem to mind.

"Mmm, and you smell good, too."

"Now you're embarrassing me," she said under her breath, though there wasn't anyone around at the moment, the maître d' having taken a couple to their table.

Frank could tell she was pleased by the compliment, though. He helped her off with her coat. Abby was in a black gaberdine suit, but under the V of the neckline was a low-cut little black lacy thing rather than a blouse. Chet's remark about Abby dressing like a lesbian came to mind, and Frank had to chuckle to himself. If the old boy could have seen her now…

"So how did your work go today?" she asked, taking her coat from him and draping it over her arm.

"Nearly half-done. I may have to work a little longer tomorrow, but I should make it okay."

"That's good."

"It's a nice chunk of change for relatively little time."

"Glad you were able to make our date."

"Wouldn't have missed it for the world, Abby."

She gave him a shy, self-conscious glance.

The maître d' returned. "Ah, the lady has arrived, I see," he said, a public-relations smile on his lips. "I can seat you now if you like."

They followed him into the candlelit dining room with its dark walls, white tablecloths and gold chandeliers. Frank noticed the hem of Abby's skirt was short. She had great legs—firm and slender.

The other diners were mostly silver-haired with a few elegant younger women scattered about—second wives or mistresses, he surmised. There was one thirty-something stud at a table of four with a pretty girl and an older couple. The guy was vaguely reminiscent of Abby's former boyfriend. Frank wondered if she noticed the similarity, especially when they ended up being seated at a nearby table.

The maître d' helped Abby with her chair. Frank took the other one at her left elbow. He picked up his napkin as the host set a menu and the wine list in front of him. God knows he rarely ate in places like this, but Arlene, who'd been raised with social graces, had given him an education over the course of their marriage. It was perhaps her most beneficial legacy.

Abby seemed to know what to do. Frank had heard her father, Ty Hooper, had had quite a bit of money at one time and he'd probably schooled her. The story Chet told was that Ty had lost a substantial portion of his wealth in the decade before his death, which prevented Abby from becoming an heiress. The Hooper family home and some land was the extent of her inheritance, though nobody was completely sure how much it amounted to.

Frank studied her in the candlelight.

"You act like you've never seen a woman with mascara on before," she said.

"Am I gawking?"

"Yes."

"You really do look lovely."

"And the rest of the time I'm chopped liver, right?"

She said it with a smile, and he knew she was more flattered than offended, but he sensed something underneath. "So which is you?" he said, venturing into the subject a bit further.

"Both. But you can be sure I don't spend a lot of time in expensive restaurants. So maybe the cop me, the pizza and beer, is more natural."

"I like both, to be honest."

"What a diplomat."

He smiled.

"You look spiffy yourself. How long has it been since you've had on a tie?"

"You've got a detective's eye, Abby. I was trying to figure that out myself as I was getting dressed."

"Then this is a little pretend for both of us."

"Living out our fantasies, maybe."

"Whoa," she said, giving him a look. "I'm paying off a bet."

"Is that all?"

Abby studied him. "No, that's not all, but I don't think we need to talk about that just yet." She picked up her menu.

Frank was pleased. They were sparring and that was almost always a good sign. He surmised Abby wasn't really sure how she felt about him, but there was interest—or at least curiosity.

"I've got some business to discuss with you, too," she said.

"Well, then, let's take care of it sooner rather than later so we can enjoy the evening."

His comment seemed to amuse her and he wondered if she could be thinking what he was thinking. On reflection, he decided she couldn't be that far along. Women rarely moved quickly because they were process-oriented. Guys were more bottom line.

Kay had taught him most of what he knew about female sexuality. "Forget where you're going and concentrate on how you're getting there," she'd once said. "Most women care more about being appreciated than fulfilled, anyway."

Frank had no illusions that things would be going very far, very fast with Abby. They would get where they were going because it was inevitable, not because of any brilliant engineering on his part. That was another thing he'd learned from Kay—"Make everything you do seem like God intended it, not you. It's much easier for a woman to submit to a deity," she'd said.

Abby said, "How about if we order before talking shop?"

"Okay. But I've been thinking. Why don't we split the tab tonight? You take me to dinner and I'll take you."

"No, this is my treat."

"I'm at least getting the wine," he said. "That's nonnegotiable."

"All right. If you insist."

They concentrated on the menu and then ordered. Abby chose sea bass in a wine sauce, Frank the rabbit. It was disguised by several fancy French words, but it was rabbit. For starters they both wanted lobster bisque. The wine he picked was a twenty-eight-dollar bottle of Chardonnay.

The waiter brought the wine right away. Frank watched him open it, thinking that it was only a week ago that he'd drowned his Valentine sorrows in a bucket of margaritas at the Queen, all the while ogling Kay. Man, he'd come a very long way in a very short time—from a melancholy visit to the past with the mother, to a fantasy-filled evening with the daughter. And never the twain shall meet.

"Shall we drink to your friend's success in the ring tonight?" he asked, picking up his glass.

"To her survival, for sure."

"What's her name again?"

"Crystal."

"To Crystal, then. And to you, Abby, for being brave enough to bring a tired old pear farmer to your friend's big night."

They sipped their wine.

"Are you tired and old, Frank?"

"Well," he said, poking his tongue in his cheek, "I like to keep people's expectations low."

"Expectations for what?"

He grinned. "You have a nasty streak in you, don't you?" Abby smiled.

"Expectations for the quality of the company," he said.

They looked into each other's eyes for an unusually long time.

"Mind if we talk a little business now?" Abby said, spinning the stem of her wineglass between her fingers.

"It's your party."

"Okay, I've been busy today. Among other things, I checked out Lloyd Witherspoon."

"Ah, now there's a delightful subject. And what did your crystal ball say about Lloyd?"

"He's managed to stay clear of the law except for one little incident, an arrest for solicitation. An adult hooker, apparently. He wasn't prosecuted. But this afternoon I talked to a sergeant in the S.F. Vice Crimes unit. Witherspoon is known. They were taking a close look at him when they busted up a child-prostitution ring a year and a half ago. They couldn't get the goods on him, but had strong grounds for suspicion that he was a regular customer."

"Abusing professionals, instead of neighborhood kids, in other words. What a sweetheart."

"My sentiments precisely."

"Still want to talk to him, Abby?"

"That was my next point," she said, pausing to sip her wine. "W.C. and I had a chat." She told him about her idea of bringing him in as a contract investigator. "You won't get rich, but a week or two of your time could make a big difference to us, especially since the trail is getting cold."

"I'm flattered," he said.

"There's political capital in it for me, so don't go organizing a fan club," she chided.

"Your sarcasm is nearly as endearing as your candor, Abby."

She grinned.

"This is my slow time of the year," he said, stroking his chin. "Finding the time shouldn't be a problem."

"Will you do it, then?"

"Sweetheart, I'd be honored."

"Great." She took her glass and reached over, touching it to his.

Frank felt wonderful, just wonderful. "So, when do we see Witherspoon?"

"I was thinking it would be nice to go tomorrow, but you've got another day of work here, don't you?"

"Unfortunately."

"Monday then, I guess," Abby said. "Chet's funeral is Saturday."

"That's what I heard. We could leave right afterward,

though, couldn't we? Doesn't Witherspoon live in the West Bay?''

"Yes. San Francisco. St. Francis Wood. The bastard owns an auto dealership down in Burlingame."

"Caddy?"

"Yes."

"Have his home address?" he asked.

"Sure do."

"Let's grab him Saturday afternoon, then, Abby, before he goes prowling."

"I suppose we could," she said.

Their soup came and they agreed not to discuss business again. But even their conversation about Witherspoon had been all right as far as Frank was concerned. He hadn't been able to take his eyes off her. That lace thing under her suit and the bit of cleavage showing got him to thinking. She had to know how sexy she looked. Frank found himself hoping her thoughts were moving in tandem with his.

Leaving Lufta's, they decided Frank would drive his truck back to his motel. Abby would follow and he'd ride with her to the auditorium. As she followed Frank's pickup down I Street, Abby thought how much she'd enjoyed dinner. In a way they'd both been playacting, engaged in a sort of adult game of dress-up. And she liked it that he wasn't any more at ease in the role than she.

For Abby, dating had always been hell. Even her first few dates with Darren had been torture—lots of excitement, but not much comfort. Darren, she now realized, was somebody to give your virginity to. Frank was somebody to savor, or so it seemed at this early stage.

It was odd she should feel that way, considering the age difference. That made her wonder if there was some kind of daddy thing involved. There was nothing about Frank that reminded her of her father, nor did she feel like a girl around him. To the contrary, he made her feel womanly, desirable. There was a lot of mutuality, as well, and she liked that.

They found a parking spot on N Street, right next to Capitol Park. As they headed back to Memorial Auditorium, Frank took her arm.

"So, what was your wife like when she was married to you?" she asked. "Before she got the doctor and the big house in San Francisco?"

"She was aspiring to live in a big house and be married to a doctor," he said with a laugh. "She knew what she wanted and went for it doggedly until she got it."

"That's a formula for success," Abby observed.

"If success is important."

"You say that like it isn't."

Frank said, "For me the question always was—at what price? Maybe I'm lazy or maybe I'm scared, but I never wanted to spend what it looked like it took to be a big shot—at anything."

They waited at the light at East Capitol Avenue and Sixteenth. "So what *is* important to you?" she asked.

She saw a trace of pain in his eyes.

"When my daughter died, all kinds of things came into question," he replied. "It's terrible that it takes something like that to make you examine your life."

"You're right. But at least you've done it. Look how many people continue to stumble along selfishly, grabbing at things until their last breath."

"And grabbing at people."

"Yes, and at people," she agreed.

The light changed and they started across the street.

"How about you, Abby? What's important to you?"

She thought for a moment. "Doing my job well, I guess."

"You have aspirations, though."

"The older I get, the more I lower my sights," Abby replied. "Getting burned by Darren may have had something to do with that."

"He was really a big deal at one time, wasn't he?"

"*Was* being the operative word," she said. "But Darren is not one of my favorite topics. I shouldn't have brought him up."

They walked along for a while, not speaking.

Then Abby said, "One nice thing about getting older, you begin to realize that your own petty little problems really aren't at the center of the universe."

"What's somebody like you talking about getting older for?" he chided. "You've scarcely cracked thirty."

"I'm thirty-three."

"I remember when I was thirty-three, but just barely," he added.

"You're not old, Frank."

He glanced at her. "If you want to know the truth, Abby, I think what makes people smart in their old age isn't so much the things they learn as the fact they kind of get used to the rules of the game. Basically, there are two directions you can go—you either get bitter and resentful, or you learn to accept things and chill out."

She took his arm as they walked along, knowing why she liked the guy so much. How many people could you have a conversation like this with? At least, how many under thirty-five?

There were more and more people in the streets as they neared the auditorium. Most were men. Quite a few had congregated on the steps of the old building. Some were smoking, others talking and laughing with friends. She drew more appreciative looks than usual. Maybe it was the heels and the makeup. Though it wasn't like her to be self-conscious about the attentions of men, she was glad she was with Frank.

The crowd, Abby could see, was heavily Hispanic. No surprise, since the fight card was more than half Latino. Abby didn't know any of them. Her sole interest in the event was that it was Crystal's debut bout.

They entered the lobby. Abby felt the electricity in the air, the anticipation. The line at the will-call window where Crystal had left the tickets was shorter than the others. Abby went to retrieve them while Frank picked up a program. He was studying the fight card when she got to the door leading to the arena.

"Your friend's in the third bout, just before the final prelim," he said.

"Is that good or bad?"

Frank smiled. "Neither, particularly. A change of pace for the crowd before a couple of heavyweights go at it. The main event is two welterweight contenders. Donny 'The Bomber' Cervantes versus Felix Juarez. Ten rounds."

"You ever heard of them, Frank?"

"I remember seeing Cervantes's name in the sports pages. He's from Modesto, which sort of makes him a local boy. I don't know anything about him, though."

They went into the arena. The ring, bathed in light, sat in the middle of the auditorium floor amid an air of expectation—like a turkey on the Thanksgiving table. The surrounding seats were partially populated. Frank found theirs in the fifth row.

"Not bad," he said. "Close enough to see the grimaces, but not enough to get spattered with blood."

"Did you have to say that, Frank?"

"This is a blood sport, my dear."

She gave him a look. "I'd rather not think about that in connection with my best friend."

"Sorry."

She'd told him she'd be seeing Crystal after the fight and that it may or may not be all right for him to come along. They'd have to wait and see.

Abby glanced around at the gathering crowd, as more and

more people began streaming down the aisles. There were other women, but the crowd was predominantly male. Guys who brought dates brought them for display like trophies—at least that was the way it appeared from the body language and gestures.

She searched the faces moving in their general direction, half expecting to see Darren. The prospect of running into him had been in the back of her mind ever since she'd spoken to Crystal. There'd been real worry in her friend's voice. Still, the thought of Darren being obsessed with her seemed so strange. When they'd gone together, he'd always been laid-back, not the jealous type at all—much of the time, anyway. One night they'd gone to a bikers' bar on a lark and a huge tattooed dude with a beard and twenty-four-inch biceps asked her to dance. Darren had been jealous then. Mostly, though, he was so confident of his charm that he wore Abby like an ornament, far more aware of the girls flirting with him than the men ogling her.

Men, she'd found, put a lot of stock in being in control. Maybe the transformation in Darren was no more complicated than the fact that she was no longer marching to the beat of his drum—that, and maybe her abortion. He'd really fastened on it.

"Isn't that your old beau across the ring?" Frank said.

Abby looked and sure enough it was Darren. He was in a black turtleneck and brown jacket, his hair Hollywood perfect. And he was glowering at them. She engaged his eyes for a moment, then glanced down at the program. "Yes, that's Darren," she said.

"He doesn't look too happy."

"No, he doesn't."

"Jealous, maybe?"

"Darren's not accustomed to losing." Having said it, she wasn't sure how Frank would take the remark. She didn't mean to imply that he had won at Darren's expense; she simply meant Darren Armstrong was no longer the golden boy in her life.

"What does the guy do, anyway?" Frank asked.

"I'm not sure what he does at the moment. The impression he gave was that he was back from L.A. for a visit." She snuck a peek and found Darren still staring at them.

"Is he an out-of-work actor?"

Abby could see how someone might get that impression. Darren looked the part, though he didn't have any particular talent. At least not that type of talent.

"I think he did some work as a stuntman," Abby said in answer to Frank's question. "When I met him he was a medivac helicopter pilot, skier and all around fitness fanatic. But Darren has trouble with authority and was constantly in and out of hot water. He lost his job about the same time we split."

"Which was why? If that's not too personal a question."

Abby glanced across the ring, but Darren was gone. "He dumped me for another woman, to be perfectly honest."

"A singular lapse of judgment," Frank said.

Abby appreciated the remark. "Shelly was a babe. He didn't trade down, I assure you. In fact, she was the one with the Hollywood connections. Anyway, they went to Southern California to live the Hollywood fairy tale."

"And got bitten by reality?"

"I don't know what happened."

"Well, the man's a fool," Frank said. "And that's not just flattery. I can't imagine what he was thinking if he dumped you."

"Like a lot of men, Darren thinks with his gonads and he's a slave to his ego. I'm sure Shelly did more for him on both scores."

"But you're not bitter about it, right?"

Abby chuckled. "I guess I sound it, don't I?"

"Do you still have a thing for him?"

"No."

"Seriously, no?"

"Seriously no. I really did learn my lesson."

Frank didn't say anything and she couldn't tell whether he believed her. She meant what she said. But maybe she meant it a little too much, and Frank picked up on that. She already knew the guy was perceptive.

"You're divorced," she said. "Are you bitter toward your ex?"

"I guess I got rejected and that's never easy. But I'm good at rationalizing. I figure Arlene never knew me. It doesn't really matter, though. I've moved on."

"Moved on to being Riverton's man-about-town."

Frank chuckled. "What gives you that idea?"

"That's what I hear."

"Now *that* I don't believe."

"I've been checking up on you, Frank."

"And that's what people are telling you?" There was genuine disbelief in his voice. "I think somebody's been putting you on."

"It's your own fault," she said. "That mystery woman of yours."

"I'll tell you how mysterious she is, Abby. I don't remember a damned thing about that night. It's all a fog. So she's a mystery to me, too."

"But you do know who she is."

"Yeah," he said reluctantly.

"I rest my case."

Abby saw him grimace and figured he was struggling with this more than he wanted her to know. The irony was, it made her all the more curious.

There was some commotion in the ring as a referee in a white shirt and bow tie climbed through the ropes to scattered applause. The man had to be sixty, but he was small and wiry with wavy, gray, plastered-down hair that looked like it came right out of the forties.

"Here we go," Frank said.

Most of the ringside seats had filled. There was a murmur as a fighter in the opening bout came down the aisle from the dressing rooms. Abby thought of Crystal, wondering if she was heaving up her guts or sitting backstage in a daze.

The second fighter arrived and the two men, lightweights, took their places along with their handlers. The ritual glaring had begun. Abby wondered why Crystal would want to emulate this.

The ceremonial introductions were made, followed by the meeting in the center of the ring. The interest of the crowd welled with anticipation. Modern sensibilities and state law being what they were, there was no cloud of cigar and cigarette smoke hanging over the ring, but the testosterone and the smell of body odor, spiced with cologne and booze, was definitely in the air.

The bell sounded. The referee, his face a mask, brought the two small but sinewy fighters to the center of the ring. They kissed gloves and the dancing began. The first blows thrown were more gestures of salutation than aggression. Within moments the hurtful punches began to fly. The smack of leather on flesh seemed more immediate than on TV. Abby could taste and smell the sting of each blow, and she winced. She'd been hit and taken punches, so she knew the feeling. But this was different.

Mercifully the round ended with no noticeable effect on either fighter but a sheen of sweat on their caramel skin. Abby could hear the handler of the fighter in the nearest corner spitting out emphatic instructions in Spanish. This was not a brawl, after all, but controlled combat with tactical objectives and strategy.

The next few rounds went by with only marginal wear on the fighters. Enough punches found the mark that the pace slowed and there wasn't as much spring in either boxer's legs. Whistles and shouts greeted the more remarkable blows or flurries. When the fighter named Garcia was staggered by an overhand right, a cheer went up. Abby felt more compassion than exhilaration, particularly when the young man's look of determination turned to dismay.

Garcia, who appeared to be getting the worst of it, had a pretty good mouse on his eyes by the middle of the last round. He fought valiantly until the final bell, then waited in his corner while the judges pondered his fate. It turned out Garcia lost by a unanimous decision, but the scoring was close on all the judges' cards. Half-a-dozen punches going the other way could have changed the outcome of the fight, Frank said.

The next bout was between a couple of lethargic middleweights. It was the pro debut of a baby-faced black kid named Jermal Wilson, who looked to Abby like he didn't want to be there. Neither fighter was skillful. At the end of four rounds Frank said he had no idea who won. The judges seemed just as confused. The black kid won, it turned out, on a split decision. "Must have been his footwork," Frank said.

Crystal's bout was next. The interest of the crowd lifted when the first boxer appeared. Ann Mulroney was pug-faced with brown curly hair that made her look like a boy in a wig. Crystal, her face a mask of grim determination, had pulled her hair back in a stubby ponytail. Her entrance to the ring brought a few whistles, which Abby was sure must have annoyed her.

Crystal's handlers helped her off with her robe, resulting in a catcall or two, but mostly the crowd was respectful. Mulroney did a little shadow boxing in her corner, evoking a few chuckles from the more knowledgeable boxing aficionados. Abby noticed the poor thing had piano legs. She wasn't as toned as Crystal, but she had a stout, pugnacious appearance that made her seem dangerous.

The women met in the middle of the ring with the referee, who put a hand on each of their shoulders as he went over the rules of engagement. Abby watched Crystal's face as she glared into Mulroney's eyes, the mouthpiece distorting the shape of her mouth. She appeared in a mood to kill.

The two fighters went to their corners and awaited the opening bell. Abby dug her nails into her palms as she watched. Her mind drifted back to the lazy afternoon at McKinley Park, musing with Crystal about the vagaries of life. It had only been a few years ago that they'd met, but they'd quickly bonded. Abby had been on leave from the Sheriff's Department at the time, rehabilitating her wounded leg, and Crystal had been fighting her own demons—those that had been haunting her following a particularly brutal rape on the bike trail down by the American River.

"Do you think it's worse for a lesbian to be raped by a man than a straight chick?" Crystal had asked that day as they lay side by side on the grass, staring up at the summer sky. "I mean just because a woman fucks guys out of choice doesn't mean she's going to like it any better than, say, me when she's forced, right?"

"Seems to me violence is violence," Abby said. "Rape doesn't have anything to do with sex, you know."

"True, but from my standpoint, there's no such thing as a good screw with a guy. Does that make sense?"

Abby had never discussed lesbian sex before, and Crystal was more willing to share details than Abby preferred, but in the process she'd discovered that people of different sexual orientations had more in common than they realized. If their friendship had accomplished anything special, it taught them how they could transcend their differences and share their common humanity. "I wonder," Abby had once said to Crystal, "if I'll ever find a man I can love for the person he is and not just for what he does for my fantasy life and my body.''

How ironic that here, under the bright lights of Memorial Auditorium, Crystal Armstrong, that wounded young woman who found her bliss in her sisters, should be pawing at the dirt like a bull, nostrils flaring, ready to do combat with a fellow member of the fairer sex. And how ironic, also, that this blood dance should be performed under the eyes of a mob of cheering men.

The bell sounded and Crystal moved forward, her shoulders rounded and her body turned slightly to the side in a defensive pose, weighing her gloved fists as she readied to thrust them at her opponent. Crystal feigned first right, then left, unleashing a crisp jab that landed in the middle of Ann Mulroney's brow, jolting her head back. Mulroney seemed unfazed.

Thirty seconds of feeling each other out followed, then they traded a combination of more serious blows. Crystal's dancing, shuffling style, reminiscent of Ali's, seemed effective. Every time she landed a punch, the crowd whooped. Not much damage was being done by either fighter, but the spectators were really into the bout.

In the second round there was a bit more punching, but the technique of both fighters deteriorated. Toward the end of the round Mulroney threw a roundhouse right that staggered Crystal, who managed to keep her feet, immediately coming back at Mulroney with two sharp jabs.

During the break before the third and final round, Frank said he thought Crystal was well ahead. ''Neither can hit very hard, but Crystal knows how to box.''

''For a girl, you mean?''

''For anybody.''

Abby gave him a coy, bemused smile.

The bell sounded for the final round. Mulroney came out swinging, but landed no telling blows. The aggression may have been a mistake because her hands began to drop. Crystal zeroed in on her like a killer bee. A straight right followed by a left hook dropped Mulroney on her butt. The punches weren't lethal enough to knock her out. Mulroney didn't even look groggy. She was more shocked than anything. Sitting in the middle of the ring like a little girl in a sandbox, her eyes round, she was apparently so flabbergasted she almost forgot to get up, but finally did when she realized the referee was standing over her, counting.

Pawing at the mat from a neutral corner, Crystal charged forward. Mulroney began backpedaling before the first punch was thrown. Abby could see the poor thing's spirit had been broken. During the final seconds of the round all she could do was hold out her hands to deflect Crystal's blows. By the time the bell sounded, both fighters' hands were hanging at their sides. The crowd went wild.

Unlike Mulroney, Crystal didn't sit on her stool, waiting for the judge's decision. She stood in her corner, taking water, rocking back and forth on her feet as she peered through the lights and into the crowd. A couple of times she looked Abby's way, but it wasn't clear whether she saw her.

After Crystal's victory was official, she and her defeated opponent hugged. Then, as Crystal climbed out of the ring, she looked in Abby's direction again, this time seeing her. She smiled and waved. The crowd, not knowing who was being acknowledged, whistled and cheered. Abby sat back in her seat, drained, relieved, happy. And afraid Crystal might have liked the experience a little too much.

She turned to Frank. "I'm going back to her dressing room. Want to come or wait here?"

"Whatever you prefer."

Abby looked across the ring, but didn't see Darren. "Why don't you come with me," she said, "and if Crystal wants privacy, you can always wait outside."

"Okay."

They got up and made their way up the aisle in the direction of the dressing rooms. Abby saw no sign of Darren, though she half expected him to confront her. There were a couple of security guards in the hallway outside the dressing rooms.

"Are you Abby?" one said, seeing her approach.

"Yes."

"Crystal's expecting you. Go on inside," he said, jerking his thumb to indicate which door.

She glanced at Frank and he nodded, indicating he knew she wanted him to wait. Then she rapped lightly on the door before opening it. Inside, Crystal was lying on a training table, staring at the ceiling. She was alone. Lifting her head, she saw Abby in the doorway and sat up, swinging her legs off the table.

"Abby," she said, beaming, "you made it!"

"Congratulations!" Abby said, entering. "You won, kiddo!"

Crystal got to her feet, taking the towel from around her neck and wiping her sweaty face and chest before giving Abby a quick hug. "I don't want to mess you up," she said, looking her over. "Hey, man, but aren't you all dolled up!"

"Went to dinner before the fight."

"That's where I'm headed after I shower." Again Crystal beamed. "So, what did you think?"

"I'm no expert, but you looked pretty good from where I was sitting."

"When I remembered to box," Crystal said with an embarrassed smile.

Abby studied her friend. Crystal's upper lip was swollen and she had a small mouse under her left eye. No cuts. Again she mopped her face with the towel.

"You think I look bad, you ought to see Ann. She's going to have a shiner for a week."

"And that's all right with her?"

Crystal retreated to the training table and sat on a corner of it. "She'd rather have knocked me on my butt, of course. I didn't really hurt her, Abby. And she's taking a grand home for her trouble. I got two thousand. Not exactly like winning the lottery, but hey. Next fight it'll be five and who knows after that…assuming I keep winning, of course."

"You intend to keep at this?"

"If it's no worse than tonight, why not? Maybe I got it in me to be a champ."

They exchanged smiles.

"So, where's your date?" Crystal asked. "Outside?"

"Yep. I figured you wouldn't want to meet him when you were fresh out of the ring."

"*I* wouldn't want that or *you* wouldn't want that?"

"I brought him to see you fight, didn't I?"

Crystal contemplated her. "So, is it serious? I mean, it doesn't exactly sound like your normal casual date."

"Frank's a friend."

"A *good* friend?"

Abby shrugged. "Not yet, but who knows, down the line maybe he will be."

Crystal shook her head. "Darren's worst fears realized."

"What's with you and Darren, anyway? All of a sudden you're promoting him like crazy."

"It's not that. There's nothing going on," she said, lowering her eyes.

"Crystal…"

Crystal sighed. "Okay. A while back I borrowed a little from Darren. Quite a little, actually. He was flush and I was hurting. It saved my butt. Now I owe him a big favor and he kind of decided the favor was a little help with you."

Abby's face dropped.

"Yeah, I know, that makes me a shit," Crystal said, "but I knew you weren't going to do anything you didn't want to do. I mean, it's not like I sold you into white slavery or anything.''

"That's why I got invited to the fight, wasn't it? This was all designed to get us back together.''

Crystal refused to look up at her.

"And then I messed things up by bringing a date.''

"I don't really care what guy you're with," Crystal said, "but my little brother's not too happy about you getting involved with someone else.''

"That's too damned bad.''

Crystal shrugged.

Abby studied her. "Is there anything else I need to know? Like what's gotten into Darren, for example?''

"Give me a break, Abby. You're a cop. You expect me to sell the little shit down the river?" She shook her head in disgust. "Just forget I said anything, okay?''

"I'm not going to press you, Crystal, but is there something I should know?''

"Definitely not.''

"'Definitely not' sounds like 'definitely yes' to me," Abby said.

"Look, kiddo, just forget it. Please. And be careful.''

"Crystal…''

"Okay, I'll say this and that's all. Darren is not the same as before and there's a good reason. I mean, haven't you wondered why he's not working, but he's still flush?''

"I get it," Abby said. "He's dealing drugs. And he's on something, too.''

Crystal pointed a finger at her. "You didn't hear that from me.''

"Maybe you need to get him some help.''

"Yeah, well, good luck.''

Abby moved closer to her, taking her hand. "Crystal, I'm so sorry.''

"The stupid little bastard will pay in the end. I tried to tell him. But, hey, who am I to talk? I borrowed some of his dirty money."

"Get uninvolved as quickly as you can," Abby told her. "Seriously. Do you need to borrow a little to get yourself out from under?"

Crystal shook her head. "No, I sold you out, Abby, so I'm square with my brother. And don't you bet that makes me feel great?" There were tears in her eyes. "Damn it to hell."

Abby pushed her friend's wet hair back off her swollen cheek. "Our friendship will survive. But I really should go now. Why don't you get in the shower and put some ice on your face. We'll talk later."

"Abby, you aren't going to have Darren arrested, are you?"

"Of course not."

Abby gave her a kiss on the cheek, then went out the door. The first thing she heard was the sound of angry voices. At the end of the hall she saw Frank and Darren squaring off, two security guards trying to keep them apart. Just then, another guard arrived and helped restrain Darren, who was the more aggressive. Abby headed toward them. Seeing her coming, Darren turned his attention to her.

"Abby, what the hell's going on? You really came with this clown? He's old enough to be *my* father, let alone yours."

"You're certainly immature enough to be his son, Darren. Why are you suddenly acting like a twelve-year-old? You didn't used to be this way."

Her presence calmed him and the security guards relaxed. Frank seemed more annoyed than upset. She turned her attention to Darren, whom she saw through different eyes now.

"I don't like the way you're treating me, Abby. No matter what I do, you give me a hard time."

"You're your own worst enemy," she told him. "The sooner you realize that, the better."

Darren glared at Frank, who was amazingly serene. Then to Abby he said, "I just want a straight answer. Does this sonovabitch mean anything to you?"

"Frank's my very good friend," she said. "And your disrespect is not helping your cause."

"Don't do this," Darren said, bristling.

A security guard took each arm. "Look, buddy," one said, "I think you'd better go back out into the arena. And if you don't calm down, we'll have no choice but to throw you out."

Darren jerked his arms free, but he'd gotten the message. "Fine," he said. "I'll go. But you, pal," he said, pointing at Frank, "if I were you, I'd watch my back. You don't belong with her any more than the man in the moon." With that he strode off, glancing back angrily over his shoulder.

Abby turned to Frank. "I'm sorry," she said. "You didn't deserve that."

"It's not your fault. Mr. Armstrong seems to be the type who isn't happy unless he's fighting. He should probably be in the ring, instead of his sister."

"Boy, you've got that right," said one of the security guards.

Frank nodded at him and his cohorts. "Thank you, gentleman. If it weren't for you, we might have had the main bout here in the hall."

"The match is in progress," the guard said. "One of us can escort you to your seats, if you like."

Abby and Frank exchanged looks.

"You know," she said, "I think I've seen enough for one night. Want to go?"

"You were reading my mind," Frank said with a smile.

Frank could tell something was bothering her—he assumed it was his confrontation with Darren Armstrong. What he couldn't be sure of was the basis of her concern. Was it for Darren or for him?

They'd walked a block without speaking. Frank decided not to press her. She'd let him know her feelings in good time. Capitol Park was ahead, the illuminated dome of the Capitol building glowing above the treetops. The air was chilly. He wanted to put his arm around her, but it was too soon. When the time was right, he'd know.

"It's a nice evening," he said. "Feel like a stroll in the park?"

"Sure, why not?"

Capitol Park occupied an area as large as several city blocks on the east side of the Capitol Building. It was filled with huge trees and shrubs, many of which were rather exotic. Paths meandered about the grounds, which by day and in the good weather were well populated. The police had enough of a presence that the park was fairly safe, even at night.

Near the northeast corner of the park a Vietnam Memorial had been erected with the names of California's war casualties inscribed on its marble walls. Frank had visited the memorial soon after it was built and found the names of a couple of buddies he'd served with. The emotion the visit had evoked surprised him. Most of the Vietnam vets he knew had repressed their experiences, some treating their tour as a lost year of their lives—no different, say, than a term served in juvenile hall as a wild-assed kid. But having seen the names of his friends, Frank had been reminded that Vietnam was a lot more than a bad dream.

They entered the park at the corner nearest the memorial and strolled toward it. The marble slabs, shining in the moonlight, encircled a large statue of several soldiers and were somewhat reminiscent of Stonehenge.

"You were in Vietnam, weren't you?" Abby said as they neared the memorial.

"Yeah."

"Was it terrible?"

"It was war, so sure. A lot of quiet and boredom punctuated by flurries of activity. The only clear objective was to survive. I was there right at the end, which I guess was the most confusing time of all."

"Ever dream about it?"

"Not much anymore. I did for a while."

"I was just a little kid at the time and don't really remember it, but I think I would have hated being there," she said.

"Supposedly we were playing a policeman role. You ought to be able to relate to that, Abby."

"Is that the way you felt—like a cop?"

"Not really. The whole thing struck me as stupid. For better or worse, though, I didn't talk much about it—before I went, while I was there or when I got back. And the funny thing was, nobody at home had any interest in talking about it, either. You're probably the first person to ask me about my war experience in twenty years."

Abby glanced up at him, taking his arm. "I guess I'm just curious."

"About what happened over there?"

"About you."

That made him feel good. It was flattering for someone to be curious about the things that were in your heart. Kay had done that some, but not in quite such an intimate way. Maybe Abby cared about him more than he thought.

Once they were inside the memorial, Abby put her hand on the bronze statue. Frank peered at the engraved names, the semidarkness summoning up recollections of nights spent on the perimeter of their compound on the Mekong. All that was missing was the soupy air and the rich smells of the river.

Perhaps sensing his nostalgia, Abby came over to where he stood, slipping her arm about his waist. He put his arm around her shoulders and pulled her gently against him. It was a nice moment and it seemed headed in a direction he longed to go. But then, everything unwound in the passing of a second.

The men seemed to appear simultaneously at every gap in the circle of stones, like VC commandos, bareheaded, armed with clubs and knives. Six of them, none very tall, dressed in dark clothes. But they weren't black pajamas and these weren't Viet Cong soldiers. Abby gasped at the sight of them and Frank instinctively moved in front of her, backing her against the wall.

Without a word the guys moved in on them from all sides. One hit Frank on the shoulder with a short club like a sawed-off baseball bat. The blow knocked him to the side. He tried to recover, but he was hit from the other side, then grabbed by two or three of them. Frank went on the attack, getting in a couple of kicks. He hit one guy in the head with his elbow before they knocked him to the ground.

He couldn't see Abby because of the flailing legs and bodies around him as his attackers kicked and clubbed him, but he heard her cry out angrily, followed by a man screaming, "Fucking bitch!"

The men's attention was drawn to her, and Frank lifted his head to see Abby beating one of the men with some sort of shiny object, knocking him to the ground. A couple of the guys rushed toward her, but stopped when she pulled her service revolver from her purse and brandished it.

"Freeze! Police!" she shouted.

They split in a panic, disappearing though the gaps in the walls as quickly as they'd come. At least one, the guy Abby had knocked down, was limping badly. She didn't fire on them, rushing over to Frank, instead.

"You all right?"

He was dazed and blood was running down the side of his face. The sharp pain in his side told him he might have a cracked rib. "I'm alive," he said with a groan. "I guess that's something."

He managed to sit up and get a handkerchief from his pocket. He pressed it against the cut on his forehead.

"Do you want me to call an ambulance?" she asked.

"No, I think I'm going to be all right."

Frank got to one knee, then stood. He felt woozy, but apart from some bumps and bruises and a cut over his eye, he was okay. The rib was more likely bruised than broken, he decided, judging by the way he was able to move and breathe.

"How about you, Abby?"

"I'm fine. All they did was grab hold of my arms."

Frank rubbed his sore shoulder. "What the hell do you suppose that was about?"

"Lord, I don't know."

"Did they try to grab your purse?"

"No."

"They didn't demand money or my watch. I don't think the motive was robbery. If I didn't know better, I'd say the whole intent was to beat the shit out of me."

"Did you recognize any of them?" she asked.

"No. You?"

She shook her head.

"Mostly Mexican, I'd say."

"Yeah," she said, "that was my impression."

"Maybe a gang prank. Five points for beating the shit out of some guy with a pretty girl."

"A flatterer even in pain," she observed. She pulled the hand with the handkerchief away from his head and took a close look at his eye. "I wonder if you should get that checked at the emergency room. Maybe you could use a stitch or two."

Frank rolled his aching shoulder. "I think I'll just go to the motel and wash it off. If it looks like I can't tape it shut, then I'll go somewhere."

"I left my damned phone in my car or I'd call the police," Abby said. "I should probably report the incident."

"Suit yourself. All I want right now is an aspirin."

"Let's go to my car and I'll drive you to your motel."

About five minutes ago he would have liked the sound of those words an awful lot. At the moment, however, he was lucky to be able to walk. They moved toward the exit.

"I guess I owe you my limbs, if not my life," he said, moving gingerly. "What did you hit that guy with, anyway?"

"Handcuffs," she replied, lifting them from her jacket pocket. "At Chet's suggestion. Remember?"

"Never can tell when a little piece of advice might come in handy, huh?"

"They gave me time to go for my gun."

They walked toward the corner, Frank wondering if he was going to be able to get out of bed in the morning. The thought of a hard day of work ahead was less than appealing.

Abby had her arm around his waist. He leaned over and inhaled the scent of her hair, relishing a pleasant sensation in contrast to the pain. This was nothing compared to the time in 'Nam when he'd taken shrapnel in the gut. The guy in front of him had tripped a grenade booby trap hidden under water as their platoon was fording a stream. His buddy took the brunt of the blast and was so badly wounded he was evacuated to the States. Frank got two weeks in a field hospital near Saigon and a return ticket to his unit. One of the nurses was kind of cute, as he recalled. Abby was much better.

Fortunately it wasn't far to Abby's car. She helped him into the passenger side and drove him to the motel. From his room she called the police and helped him clean his cut and put a Band-Aid on it. It wasn't as serious as the bleeding indicated. Frank lay down on his bed while Abby met the officers in the parking lot. They came inside for a minute to confirm her story and ask some questions. He wasn't able to add much to the descriptions Abby had already given them.

When the officers had gone, Abby sat on the bed beside him. "I wonder if Darren could be behind this," she said.

"The thought crossed my mind," he admitted, "but he would have had to organize the boys pretty damned quick."

"This morning I told Crystal I was bringing you. Darren would have known in advance."

"It might have been a gang thing, though the guys seemed a little old."

"The cops said there haven't been any reports of this sort of attack elsewhere. When it's strangers, it's almost always robbery or rape."

"Then I guess we've got a mystery on our hands."

Abby scooted closer to him and, reaching out, brushed his hair back off his forehead. There was intimacy in the gesture. She smiled self-consciously. "I have to go, Frank. There's a long drive ahead and I have an early morning."

He took her hand, rubbing her fingers between his thumb and forefinger. "Yeah, I've got an early one, too."

"Are you going to try to work tomorrow?"

"I have to. Anyway, aspirin works wonders."

She put her hand on his cheek and looked down into his eyes. "I'm really sorry about tonight."

"I wouldn't have missed it for the world. Fabulous dinner."

"And I enjoyed the wine."

There was warmth and caring in her expression. The well of emotion he felt impelled him to pull her hand to his lips and kiss her fingers. "You like beer and chili?" he asked.

"Sure. Why?"

"I make great chili and I always have beer on hand. Why don't you come over for dinner to let me thank you for the nursing?"

"I'd like that."

"Maybe next week," he said.

"Okay."

He wanted very badly to take her face in his hands and pull her mouth down so he could kiss it. Maybe Abby read his desire because she said, "I was sort of hoping you'd kiss me before I left."

Her directness surprised him. "Well, it's not too late."

She leaned down and lightly kissed his lips. He touched her cheek and they kissed more deeply. But not for long. She pulled her face away.

"Good night, Frank."

"Good night," he said.

She got up from the bed and went to the door. "Call me when you get back in Riverton and we'll talk about going to see Lloyd Witherspoon," she said.

"And chili at my place."

"And chili at your place."

Friday
February 21st

Granite Bay

Frank had spent the morning wiring the last house, every bend, twist and step a painful experience. He knew he should have stayed in bed, but the job had to be finished. He got through it by pretending a godawful hangover, rather than a godawful beating, was the cause of his misery.

In the middle of the night he realized he probably had a mild concussion. If he'd been smart, he'd have gone to the hospital, but being smart wasn't the only issue. He didn't have medical insurance—not when the only decent coverage available cost double your average car payment. On his income he couldn't even afford the car payment.

Breaking for lunch, Frank hopped in his truck and headed for the sandwich shop at the intersection of Auburn-Folsom Road and Douglas Boulevard. The morning had started out clear and sunny, but as the day wore on, clouds came in from the coast—thin, high ones at first, then by noon the sky was completely overcast. Even so, it was a pretty area with gorgeous homes everywhere.

Granite Bay, the tony suburb in the rolling hills surrounding Folsom Lake, was made up of swank subdivisions studded with oaks and artificial lakes. The streets curved about houses that were, in size, only a few rooms shy of your average Motel 6. Frank felt no resentment for the folks who lived in these posh mansions, nor did he envy them. His idea of gracious living was trading up from a mobile home and eighteen acres of pears to, say, a setup like his neighbor, Constance Butterfield, had, with her forty acres of trees, a nice old white clapboard house and a few dollars in the bank. The Mercedes and the Lexus he could live without.

Which, as he pulled up in front of the sandwich shop, made him think about Abby for the millionth time that day. Thanks to her father, Abby had a house and land, which meant she was at least comfortable. He sensed she didn't have aspirations beyond that, but he didn't know her well enough to be sure. If he was to guess, though, he'd say she, like him, cared more about people and the land than about acquiring things.

Despite their more obvious differences, Frank was beginning to think they were on the same wavelength. That was exciting. She was the first woman he'd truly clicked with in a long time, and that was huge.

As he stood at the counter waiting to order, Frank gazed up at the menu board and pondered the problematical side of his relationship with Abby—the ticking bomb that wouldn't go away. Kay would become a factor in this before it was over. The unknown was whether he'd be able to finesse it. Unfortunately, finesse was not his long suit.

The psychology of relationships could be a confounding thing. One of his army buddies, a guy from Orange County named Steve Garrison, had fancied himself a real Don Juan. They'd lie in their bunks at night, listening to the outgoing artillery, and kibitz about the girls they'd known. If half the exploits Steve had claimed were true, he would have been an absolute phenomenon. "Rule number one," Steve would say, "is to always keep them wanting—emotionally, sexually, psychologically, materially. A woman is best when she's on edge and crazy with desire. When they can't get enough of you, you've got 'em. Never forget that, Frankie, and you'll have all the pussy you could ever want.''

Over the years Frank kept Steve's notion about women in the back of his mind, and while he saw evidence of truth in it, he couldn't help thinking it was a good way to win the battle and lose the war. Playing games could get you laid, give you power if you were skilled, but Frank could never quite convince himself that having a sexual slave should be a man's highest goal. And the older he got, the more he realized that at twenty-five Steve Garrison couldn't have understood what mattered in a mature relationship between a man and a woman.

The irony was Frank hadn't been very successful at defining what was important, either. The only meaningful relationship he'd had since his marriage—with Kay—had given more credence to Steve's approach than any alternative. Of course, for various reasons, his relationship with Kay had involved a lot of game playing, the tug-of-war that comes when lust, loneliness and the need to be loved are in competition.

What Frank thought he wanted was a woman who saw the world like *he* saw it, a woman who understood him profoundly and could share his life and give him space with equal facility. That had seemed an impossible dream—until he'd met Abby Hooper.

Frank knew he could be deluding himself, but the better he got to know her, the higher his hopes rose. Maybe he'd find a greater truth than Steve Garrison espoused. Sadly Steve himself would never know whether the incubus of life had vindicated him or proved him a false prophet. The poor bastard's name was one of the thousands engraved on the wall of that memorial in Capitol Park. A month before their tour of duty was to end, he took a round from an AK-47 right between the eyes.

Frank ordered a corned beef on rye with a side of coleslaw and gingerly sat at one of the tables along the wall to eat. He was edging toward calling Abby—just to touch base with her—but knew overeagerness could turn her off. Playing games was only bad, he decided, if the intent was to manipulate. But still, his ego made him wonder if she might have tried to reach him. If so, there would probably be a message on his machine.

After lunch Frank used the pay phone outside the nearby supermarket to call home. There was a message all right, but it was from Chet's cousin, Judge Fred Parker. Thinking he might as well find out what was on the judge's mind, Frank dialed the number in Stockton.

"Frank, thank you so much for returning my call," the old man said. "You're aware I'm handling Chet's affairs, I assume."

"Yes, Judge, I heard."

"As a courtesy I wanted to inform you about the content of Chet's will. I'll be probating it in due course, and you'll be receiving formal notification, but you may be pleased to know you're the primary beneficiary. There are a number of bequests to charity and a substantial one to Chet's half sister, but you are to receive the residuary estate."

"What does that mean?"

"You get what's left after the other beneficiaries have been satisfied. I expect it to be in the order of several tens of thousands of dollars."

"Me, Judge?"

"That's right, Frank. The contingent beneficiary is Lloyd Witherspoon. I believe you know Lloyd."

"We've met. But what is a contingent beneficiary?"

"He stands in your shoes in the event you're deceased before the property in the probated estate is distributed."

"If I'm dead, he collects, in other words."

"That's right. Chet wanted Lloyd to take precedence over

your heirs, but he felt you had a greater need than Lloyd, who has a substantial estate of his own.''

''The need part is definitely right, but I'm still shocked, Judge. Chet never said a word.''

''He played his cards close to his vest when it came to personal matters,'' Fred Parker said. ''Which brings me to my next point. Among Chet's personal papers was a sealed envelope. It was addressed to you in Chet's handwriting with instructions that it was to be opened by you and only by you in the event of his death or disability. In the event you were deceased, it was to be destroyed unopened by his executor, namely me.''

''You're the executor, Judge? I thought if you drew up the will you couldn't be the executor.''

''That's correct. But I didn't actually draw up the will. We discussed it. The work was done by a colleague so that I could be Chet's personal representative, which was what he cared about.''

''I see.''

''In any case, I believe you should have a look at this envelope. I have no idea what's in it, but the date on the outside suggests it was prepared only last weekend. I'm concerned that it may have bearing on the circumstances of Chet's death.''

''You mean, like a suicide note?''

''That's possible. I haven't mentioned this to the police under the theory you will make them aware of anything they need to know. In other words, I'm relying on your good judgment, and I'd like that to remain in confidence, Frank.''

''Sure, Judge.''

''The question is, when will you be able to pick up the envelope?''

''Are you coming up for the burial tomorrow?''

''That's my plan.''

''Why don't we meet then?'' Frank said.

"Good idea. See you tomorrow."

"Count on it."

Frank hung up the phone as a light rain began to fall. He glanced up at the dark gray sky, then, rolling his stiff, bruised shoulder, he headed for his truck, wondering what little surprise Chet had in store for him this time.

Riverton Civic Center

Abby spent the morning dealing with paperwork. She checked the wires, the postings on the Internet, returned a couple of Jane Doe-related calls, but mostly she agonized about what had happened last night. Her concern was both professional and personal. She had a hunch Frank was the innocent victim of conflicts in her personal life, which made her somewhat responsible. She also was concerned about the crime that had been committed. Sure it was a simple assault, but it could have ended as a homicide. What confounded her—and she believed what confounded Frank, too—was what was behind it. The whole thing screamed Darren Armstrong, but she didn't want to think he was that far gone.

It wasn't her problem, legally speaking. Fortunately it was in the hands of the Sacramento police, and they were taking the incident seriously. After she got back from lunch, she had a call from Jones, a detective in the Gang unit.

"We had a close look at the memorial this morning," he said. "There was a trail of blood leading out the walk to the south. Are you sure you went out the other direction?"

"Positive."

"Could any of your assailants been so badly wounded that he'd have left a trail of blood? We're not talking a few drops, Chief Hooper. There was quite a bit."

"Well," Abby said, "it was dark, but the guy I hit with my cuffs could have had a serious scalp wound I didn't see, and those can bleed. Frank got one guy in the face with his elbow. I saw him fall back and grab his nose. I suppose he could have bled, as well.''

"It does give us a little physical evidence,'' Jones said.

"Right. Anybody show up at a local hospital to be treated last night for a wound that might correspond?''

"Nothing's turned up yet.''

"Any theories what this was about?'' Abby asked.

"I don't think it was gang-related,'' the detective said. "Doesn't have that feel.''

"I had the same thought, but then, I'm no expert on your local situation.''

"Right now things are fairly quiet on the gang front. Most of what's going on is neighborhood specific. Capitol Park is an odd place for an incident like this.''

"I thought so, too.''

"In the report there was nothing about the possibility you were followed from the auditorium. Do you have any reason to think you were?''

"We didn't notice anything, but it was a social occasion and we weren't as observant as we probably should have been.''

"I know how that is. How about Mr. Keegan? Might he have anything to add to what's in the report?''

"Not to my knowledge, but I haven't talked to Frank today. He's on a job up in Roseville and I don't know how to reach him.''

"Well, if anything should come to your attention, give me a jingle, will you?'' Jones said. "I'll keep you updated from my end.''

"Thanks.''

Abby hung up. The call hadn't helped to clarify matters. About all she could say for sure was that the entire incident was bizarre.

Mae Brown came in with the operations report and some

files Abby had requested. They were chatting when Abby got a call from out front.

"Kay Ingram is here to see you, Chief."

It was a simple enough statement, but it bore the icy chill of the announcements her father had made over the years. "Your mother has written and wants you to visit her in San Diego, honey. What do you think? Is that something you'd like?" The question had been pro forma. Ty Hooper had known Abby's feelings. He'd been their author.

"Tell her I'll be right out," Abby said.

Watermark Slough

Frank soaked in the tub until the water turned tepid. It had been a challenging day, but he was home now and the aches and pains were manageable. His stomach burned from the aspirin he'd been eating, but he could live with that.

He was rapidly coming to the conclusion that old age was hell. Twenty years ago he'd have bounced right up. Hell, ten years ago he'd have shrugged off that beating. But now that he was in midlife he paused before stepping off a ladder, let alone mixing it up with a gang of toughs.

Putting on his robe, he went to his bedroom and stretched out on the bed. He hadn't had dinner, but he wasn't sure it was worth the trouble to fix something—the mattress and cool sheets felt so good. But before he could decide between food and sleep he heard a vehicle coming down the drive. Frank checked the alarm clock on the bedside table. It was nearly nine, an odd time for a visitor. As he dragged his body to the front room, there was a light, ladylike rap on his front door. His first thought was Abby.

Opening the door he found Kay, looking all business. The belt of her trench coat was cinched tight at her waist, and her hair sparkled with water droplets from the misty rain. She wasn't smiling.

"Frank," she said without ceremony, "we've got to talk."

His stomach dropped at her tone. "We do?"

Kay did not wait to be invited in. She moved past him, unfastening the belt of her coat and removing it. She draped the coat over the back of a chair and sat on the sofa. Frank sat in another chair. Kay paid no attention to the way he was dressed, which also gave him pause.

"So what's up?" he said.

Kay was in a baby-blue cashmere sweater, a navy wool skirt and navy heels. Her hair was up and there was lots of gold jewelry on her—bracelets, necklace, earrings. She stared off vacantly for a moment, fiddling with her necklace. Then she met his eyes.

"I dropped by the police station this afternoon to see Abby."

His stomach dropped another foot. "And?"

"Frank, are you romantically involved with her?"

"No. Why do you ask?"

Kay took a long, slow breath. "I went to give her a check for ten thousand dollars to start a reward fund for anyone who can help in the identification of Jane Doe. I did it for the town and I did it for Abby. I didn't put it that way, but I think she understood my motives. Incidentally, I made the donation anonymously, so don't go spreading it around."

"I won't, but what's with this question about being romantically involved?"

"Well, I've been doing what I could to establish a relationship with Abby. We've talked a couple of times and I think I've managed to break the ice."

"Kay," he said, trying to stifle his annoyance, "will you get to the point?"

"We chatted briefly about my relationship with Mort," Kay went on, obviously determined to do this at her own pace. "Then your name came up."

"My name."

"Yes, it was just a passing comment, but I heard something in her voice, something that told me you weren't just a former suspect. What gives, Frank?"

He hesitated, unsure how candid he dared to be. It mattered a lot which way this went. "In what capacity are you asking? As a mother? As my friend? My former lover? Concerned citizen? What?"

"Okay, so maybe it's none of my business, but I want you to know I'm not going to cover for you anymore. Abby didn't say anything direct about you, and I sure as hell didn't ask. Maybe it was nothing, but I'm a woman and I read the lilt in her voice. And you aren't doing anything to dispel my suspicion."

"Wait a minute, Kay. You're making it sound like I'm on trial here. I'm not. The fact of the matter is W.C. has made additional funds available to the department so that I can be hired as a contract investigator to help in the Jane Doe case. Abby and I will be working together on it."

"So you're saying there's nothing going on?"

"Hey, I like the woman. I won't deny it. But are we an item? No."

Kay crossed her legs. "Well, maybe it's more her than you. In any case, I wasn't going to say, 'Yeah, Frank's a nice guy and did you know we used to be lovers?' It would have been easy to get into it, but I didn't—out of respect for you and because I thought you ought to know the score before I opened my mouth."

"I appreciate your consideration," he said. "I really do."

"But be warned, Frank. I have an interest in that girl. She's my only child and I'd like to have a relationship with her. To be honest, I'm surprised she hasn't heard about us already. There are enough people around town who know."

"People are aware you and Abby have been estranged. The average person tends to be sensitive to things like that."

"Yeah, well, it will come out eventually. I won't go out

of my way to announce it to her, but neither am I going to run from it. Fond as I am of you, Frank, my relationship with Abby comes first. That's why I came over here—to let you know."

"Again, I thank you."

Kay studied him. After a while she shook her head. "Frank, you're a dirty old man. Of course to me, you were a dirty young man, but that's neither here nor there. I've met any obligation I have."

Frank weighed his response, deciding to let things lie. "And you don't have anything to worry about—unless it's Mort."

"Mort isn't going to give me any trouble. Abby's a completely different matter. But you know my feelings now. Enough said."

Kay got up and put on her coat. She cinched the belt, then looked him dead in the eye. "I never thought I'd be saying these words to you, not in a thousand years. But here goes. Don't hurt her, Frank. That's all I've got to say. Just don't hurt her."

His silence was his answer, and it seemed to satisfy Kay. After she'd gone out the door, he stood pondering what had been said. He'd have to talk to Abby. The question was, when? Too early and he might nip their relationship in the bud. Too late and she might hate him forever.

Saturday
February 22nd

East Levee Road
Riverton

Predictably, it rained all morning. A perfect day for a funeral. Frank had had his second cup of coffee watching the rain fall outside his kitchen window. Then he'd driven to the River Queen, where the mourners were to gather before the drive up to Franklin for the interment. Considering that most of the Delta was at or below sea level, people weren't buried there. The available cemeteries were on higher ground to the east.

It had become a semi-tradition that Riverton's unchurched would get their farewell send-off at the Queen. Once the body was in the ground, it wasn't uncommon for the mourners to reassemble at the Queen to remember the dearly departed over a glass of whiskey or beer, be the deceased churched or unchurched. The teetotalers were the exceptions, of course, but there were few of them in Riverton—at least, few who mattered. Chet, being about as secular as you could get, was going to get the before and after treatment.

The funeral was early enough that only the hardcore were drinking. Most people were having coffee, which Kay served for free. Frank sat at the bar with Wayne Neely on one side of him and W. C. Joyner on the other. Kay, in a black suit, pearl gray blouse and black hose and pumps, was dispensing the coffee from behind the bar. When she wasn't pouring, she was at the front of the bar, talking to Mort.

Frank ignored them, partly because the last thing he needed was to piss Mort off and have him dropping poison-pen notes to Abby, and partly because Kay herself was a ticking bomb. If his relationship with Abby was going to get anywhere, Frank knew it had to happen quickly.

"Jesus," W.C. mumbled between sips of coffee, "I never thought I'd be burying Chet Wilsey. I was sure the sonova-bitch would outlive me by a decade."

Everybody nodded. Nobody had mentioned Jane Doe or Chet's connection with the girl, though the details were now common knowledge. Funny how the dead had, by the act of dying, earned forgiveness. Maybe people wanted to know that in death they'd find respite from their own catalog of sins.

The other thing the dead could no longer do was pay. They were either burning in hell or they no longer existed, de-pending on your theological orientation. In a word, it was over. But the consequences of their lives were never over. Chet, in taking his life, had set all kinds of wheels in motion. One that Frank felt could be of real consequence was that envelope Judge Parker was bringing.

Every once in a while he'd take a peek out the front win-dow to see if the judge had arrived. It had been some years since Frank had seen the old boy, but he knew he'd have no trouble recognizing him. Fred Parker was more in the spirit of Herbert Hoover than Bill Clinton, whom he must have considered a flag-burning, draft-dodging hippy who just hap-pened to make it to the White House.

During his tenure on the bench, Judge Parker had been notoriously hard on criminals. Back in the sixties, when he was operating his right-wing inquisition down in Stockton, he'd had more than one longhair shorn before they were allowed in his courtroom. Frank had always been fairly liberal as cops went, but in Fred Parker's eyes he was still a cop who put his life on the line so the citizenry could sleep at night, and that made him a stand-up guy. And the purple heart he'd earned in Vietnam practically made him a saint.

"You expecting somebody?" Wayne asked after Frank took another look out front.

"Yeah. Judge Parker."

"Oh, I talked to the judge this morning," W.C. said, overhearing.

"Did he know we're meeting here to form the funeral procession?" Frank asked.

"Sure thing."

Kay made another pass along the bar with her coffeepot and W.C. told her she looked beautiful in black. "And even prettier in white, I bet," he added with a wink.

"I left white behind a long time ago, W.C.," she said. "Not that I won't someday be the *mother* of the bride." As she said it, she gave Frank a look.

He felt himself color. Kay, a half smirk on her lips, moved along. Frank could see he was in a hell of a spot, with painfully little wiggle room. Kay might turn out to be a loose cannon. Her attitude would probably depend on Abby's feelings, and Abby's feelings could be affected by a whole slew of things—what Kay said or didn't say among them.

"I heard Kay and Abby have talked recently," W.C. said under his breath, "but was she dispensing news or talking through her hat just now?"

"Talking through her hat, I think," Frank said.

"Maybe Abby's got a fella," Wayne said.

Frank took a big gulp of hot coffee, burning his throat in the process. He checked outside again. Mercifully the conversation turned back to Chet. Somebody told a fishing story about him and somebody else a golf story. Frank half listened, half contemplated Kay, wondering if she'd find a way to make his life miserable. If she cared about Abby as much as she said, then he couldn't imagine her doing anything to upset his applecart—except to protect her own interests.

Amid the laughter following another story about Chet, the front door opened and Judge Fred Parker entered, a black fedora on his head and a dripping umbrella in his hand. The judge, no slave to fad, was in a three-piece navy pin-striped suit with a gold watch chain draped across his round little belly. Out of sight, but almost certainly present, would be a pair of long johns and braces. The spats and detachable collars he'd probably abandoned, if only because they were no longer made.

The Queen fell into a silence, prompted undoubtedly by the judge's stern demeanor. He had the face of a man used to hearing "All rise!" when he entered a room.

"Is Frank Keegan here?" he stated in a clear voice that rose over the murmur in the back of the barroom.

"Yes," a couple of voices replied.

"I'm here, Judge," Frank said, getting to his feet.

Fred Parker squinted through his wire-rim spectacles. "Oh, good. Could you step out to my automobile for a moment, Frank? I have some business to discuss with you."

"Sure, Judge."

Everybody watched as Frank made his way to the front of the bar. He shook hands with Parker, then took his raincoat from one of the hooks. At the door, the judge opened his umbrella and they went out to the big black Lincoln parked in the handicapped space.

"Perfectly legal," the judge said, pointing to his license plate with the handicapped insignia. "I have a heart condition."

"I wouldn't doubt it for a moment."

"Door's open," Parker said, motioning to the passenger side.

He lowered his umbrella and got in about as gingerly as Frank. The judge's excuse was probably arthritis. It wasn't raining hard, but they were both flecked with a sheen of droplets. The judge brushed off his shoulders with his bony hands.

Removing his hat, Parker turned stiffly toward Frank, rotating his torso as much as his head. "So, how are you, Frank? It's been a while."

"Yes, it has, Judge. I'm fine, thank you."

"I understand they selected a woman over you for police chief."

"Yes. Abby Hooper."

"Sign of the times," Parker said, slowly nodding. "Miss police work, do you, Frank?"

"Sometimes."

"That's work a man can do for only so long. Not like being a lawyer. As long as a man has his wits and can still sit in the saddle, he can lawyer. I had to give up the bench, however. Caseload was such that I could no longer carry my weight. A man has to put his responsibilities before his pride. And that's not always an easy thing to do," Parker said, waving an arthritic finger in Frank's direction.

"No, it's certainly not."

"Well, so much for the chitchat," the judge said. "The envelope is in the glove box. Go ahead and take it."

Frank opened the compartment. He saw a fat, oversize brown envelope, which he removed. Under it was a gun.

"Perfectly legal," the judge said, indicating the weapon. "I've got a permit."

Frank closed the glove-box door and studied the writing on the front of the envelope. Frank recognized it as Chet's.

"Open it now or later as you see fit," Parker said. "The decision is yours."

Frank decided to open it. Wedging his finger under the back flap, he forced it open and peered inside. He was amazed to see a thick wad of bills, secured by a rubber band. Without removing them, he riffled through the stack. They were all hundreds, several thousand dollars in all. There was also a two-page letter in the envelope, which Frank removed, then unfolded. He read:

Frank,

By the time you get this you'll know of my connection with the girl they found in the slough at your place. I want to assure you, I had nothing to do with her death. Nor do I know how it happened or who is responsible. I want you to track down the son of a bitch and see that he's brought to justice. The money is to cover your expenses. The only condition is that your investigation be discreet. Don't tell Abby Hooper any more than you have to. I don't see any need to mention either the money or the fact that your investigation is at my request.

Unfortunately, I can't be of much help. I don't even know the girl's name. The only time I ever saw her was in San Francisco, the time the film was made. I don't know who's responsible for the blackmail, but my guess is it's her pimp. I'm reluctant to tell you how I found her, but I see no other way, so here goes.

My cousin, Lloyd Witherspoon, heard about her through a bar owner he knows. That's the extent of my knowledge. Please do everything in your power to see that Lloyd is kept out of it and spared any humiliation. He was innocently trying to help a guy who was really down. I take full responsibility for what happened. You have my permission to show Lloyd this letter if he is reluctant to cooperate. (This is why I'd prefer you keep Hooper out of it. She wouldn't understand.) If you'd rather not be involved, then please destroy this letter. Frank, that's my dying request. I beg you to honor it.

Whatever you decide to do, there's one final favor I'd like to ask. Please give a thousand dollars of the money to Frieda Benke. Tell her it's from me and say I said thanks for being there for me. (I wish to hell I'd gone to see her that night instead of the girl. God, am I sorry.)

I know you must not think much of me about now, Frank, and believe me, I can't blame you. I feel like the sorriest son of a bitch who ever walked the earth. Nothing will ever make up for my mistake, but I'm doing all I can see to do. You got to give me that.

Chet

Frank glanced over at Fred Parker. The judge was staring straight ahead, sober-faced. He didn't so much as blink.

"There's nothing here we need to discuss," Frank said, cramming the envelope into his coat pocket. "But since we're alone, I do have a few questions for you, if you don't mind. As you know, I've spoken to Lloyd Witherspoon, but he didn't reveal much of himself. What can you tell me about him?"

The judge cleared his throat and pursed his lips thoughtfully. "Lloyd was born with a silver spoon in his mouth and it ruined his life. Always thought the world owed him. Cared too little about responsibility. Never married—I think because he was too damned selfish. That said, Lloyd has had the good sense to consult me in recent years, so he gets a few marks for improved judgment. But there's a dark side. It's not common knowledge—and I tell you this in confidence, Frank—but Lloyd's had financial problems of late, serious financial problems. I did not learn about that in my capacity as an attorney, so there's no breach of ethics in passing that bit of information along. If you're wondering why I'm telling you, it's because I'm convinced Lloyd played some role in Chet's demise. What sort of role and how direct his involvement, I have no idea."

"What makes you think so?"

Fred Parker pressed the tips of his fingers together as though grasping an invisible grapefruit. "As you know, I was the one who sent Lloyd to see you. The reason was he'd come to me emotionally distraught over Chet's death—not the fact that he'd died, but rather the circumstances of his death and the implications. He was also very interested to know what was in it for him. And he wasn't at all pleased when I told him he was a contingent beneficiary."

"Lloyd must be pretty desperate because Chet was not a wealthy man."

"There's more in the estate than you might think, but yes, we're not talking about a great deal of money. I attributed Lloyd's interest to a simple lapse of character. Personally, I was more interested in his questions about what was behind Chet's suicide. He wanted me to speak to the police on his behalf, but I declined, saying he'd find out more talking to you. My thought was you'd detect the smoke, if there was fire."

"I was immediately suspicious," Frank said.

Judge Parker nodded. "I thought you would be."

"At the moment all I have is suspicion. But I intend to investigate."

"Good. I'm prepared to live with the outcome, whatever it may be."

"I must confess," Frank said, "Lloyd is a mystery to me. You said he never married. What's the story of his personal life, do you know?"

"I don't believe he's a homosexual, if that's what you're asking, Frank. He has an interest in women. The question in my mind was always whether it was a *healthy* interest. But I have nothing specific to base that on. Merely an impression gleaned over the years."

"You aren't aware of any criminal behavior, for example?"

Parker again rotated his torso toward Frank. "Are you suggesting there has been some?" he asked. "Of record, I mean?"

"No convictions. One arrest for solicitation."

"I'm not surprised. But I am embarrassed to call him a relative," the judge said, smirking.

Frank fell silent, reflecting. Judge Parker hadn't given him much, and he was pretty sure that was because he didn't have anything but his own suspicions. What Chet had said about Lloyd in his letter was even more disappointing. Chet was clearly being protective of his cousin. He characterized Witherspoon as a go-between, an accessory. If that was the extent of his involvement, it didn't amount to a hill of beans. But Chet had recognized that Lloyd was the key to finding the person or persons responsible for Jane Doe's death. Even if he didn't know the girl's identity, then he probably knew who did. That made a trip to San Francisco all the more important.

The patrons of the River Queen started spilling out the front door. Frank looked through the rear window of the Lincoln and, sure enough, the hearse had pulled up. A Riverton police car was in front of it, lights flashing. Sandy Mendoza was driving. Frank could see Abby in the passenger seat, riding shotgun. Sandy's wife was in the back seat, along with Mae Brown and an elderly woman Frank didn't recognize. There was a second patrol car filled with officers and departmental employees.

"It appears the procession is about to get under way," Judge Parker said.

"Looks that way," Frank replied as the mourners went to their respective cars.

"I'd invite you to ride with me," the judge said, "but I'll be returning directly to Stockton on I-5."

"No problem, Judge. I'll drive or catch a ride."

Parker extended his hand and Frank took it, the old man's

parchmentlike skin as cold as a tombstone. His eyes were sharp and lively, though, his expression as steely as ever. "Do the right thing, Frank," he said.

"Count on it, Judge."

Franklin

The funeral procession had followed the Sacramento River north to Twin Cities Road, then east out of the Delta and across I-5 to Franklin Boulevard, essentially a farm road that ran parallel to the freeway all the way to the city. There were twenty or twenty-five vehicles in all. Judge Parker was the sole blood relative in the entourage. Chet's half sister in Missouri, somebody said, had surgery recently, but nobody would have expected her to come, anyway, much less Chet. Lloyd Witherspoon wasn't there. Under the circumstances, Frank wasn't surprised.

He ended up riding with Wayne Neely in his new Ford pickup. The two of them talked pears a little, but there were long silences. Frank was distracted and Wayne must have been able to tell. Rain fell steadily during the entire drive; predictably it started coming down heavier as they were getting out of their vehicles at the cemetery.

Umbrellas popped up like tulips in a time-lapse photography loop. The women, who were fewer in number than the men, grumbled about their shoes or hair getting wet. Frank and Wayne trooped along toward the rear of the covey of mourners. Mort, holding an umbrella over Kay as if she were an Egyptian queen, ushered her to one end of the grave site, front row. Abby, Judge Parker, W. C. Joyner and the elderly woman—who, Frank learned, was Maxine Shear, the retired department mom—occupied the places of honor where the widow and children would have stood. This being a secular affair and no clergyman present, Caesar's man, W.C., was to officiate.

Frank stood directly opposite the semiofficial coterie, in the second row. He had a good view of Abby, decked out in her police chief's uniform and service raincoat, her officers arrayed behind her. She looked terribly official in her brimmed uniform hat with braid, suitably somber and cute as a bug. Funeral or not, Chet wouldn't have minded him checking out Abby's figure, especially as he would have been doing the same. Frank thought about that kiss she'd given him in the motel in Sacramento. He also wondered when he'd have a shot at a repeat performance.

After the last stragglers found places to stand, W.C. took half a step forward. "We have come to this place," he said, his voice modulated, but carrying over the gathered throng, "to lay our brother to rest. Chester Arlo Wilsey was the chief of police of Riverton for nearly eighteen years. A civil servant who served his community with dedication and distinction, Chief Wilsey was a tough cop and a fair cop. He put the welfare of the citizenry he served above all else. Riverton was fortunate to have Chief Wilsey watching over its neighborhoods and businesses.

"Chet will be remembered not only as an officer of the law, but also as a husband and a friend. There was no better golfing partner or fishing buddy in Riverton than Chet Wilsey. I'll never forget the day I was first elected mayor and Chet came to me and said, 'W.C., now you've got to be on good behavior. The people of this town won't tolerate corruption in high places and neither will I.'

"That comment may strike you as ironic, considering the events of the past few weeks. In the end, Chet chose not to run from the truth and neither should we. Like us all, he was human, he had his failings and his flaws. The mistakes of his life, as tragic and hurtful as they may have been, cannot undo the good he did, nor the legacy he left behind. A man should not be judged by one side of his soul alone, either the good or the bad. A whole human being is, in the end, human. Chet,

I'm sure, would be the first to tell you that he'd have chosen differently a second time, given the chance. But for better or worse, we are judged by the life we lived. On behalf of Chet I ask you to look at the whole man, the whole life, and forgive him his mistakes.

"Now it is time to say goodbye, goodbye to our brother, Chester Arlo Wilsey. May you rest in peace, Chet. May you rest in peace."

W.C. bowed his head and there was a silence. Frank could hear sniffles and an isolated sob or two.

After several moments W.C. looked up and said, "Now, good people, as Chet would say, it's time for a drink. See you at the River Queen!"

"First round," Kay piped up, "is on the house."

A general murmur of approval was heard and the mourners began filing back to their cars. Abby embraced W.C. and some of her staff, then looked over to where Frank stood. There was nobody between them. She gave him a tentative smile. He checked, but Kay and Mort had already headed for their car. Abby turned away.

Frank moved around the casket, stepping carefully across the soggy ground to where Abby was talking to Wally Benson and a red-eyed Dix Fowler. When she turned, she found him waiting.

"Hello, Frank."

"You going to the Queen, Chief Hooper?" he asked.

"No, I don't think so," she said.

He was glad, but didn't say so. "Still want to go see Lloyd Witherspoon this afternoon?"

"Definitely."

"Good. I've got some information that makes it all the more important we talk to him."

"What's that, Frank?"

He glanced at the others, waiting for them to move off. Nobody had been listening, but he didn't want to risk being overheard. Once the others were gone, Frank moved to her side. "Chet wrote me a letter the day before he shot himself. I just got it this morning. We need to discuss it."

Abby looked at him from under the brim of her hat. A drop of water had gathered on the tip of her nose. Unable to help himself, he wiped it away with his thumb. First she blushed, then she glanced toward the retreating crowd, glad, it seemed, his gesture hadn't been seen. At that moment Frank didn't care. If he'd kissed her, he almost wouldn't have cared about that, either.

"Why don't you come by the station?" she said. "I have to ride back with the others."

"Okay."

They began walking toward the waiting vehicles.

"So, how are the aches and pains?" she asked.

"This old body's making sure I don't easily forget what I did to it."

"I've felt terrible, because it's really my fault."

"Don't, Abby. You're not to blame. Not by any stretch of the imagination."

"What a thing to have happen, though. Ask a guy out on a date only to have him beat up before your very eyes."

"You saved my butt, sweetheart. That's what I remember."

Abby seemed a bit ill at ease with his familiarity, but at the same time showed signs of liking it. "I keep thinking Darren was somehow involved."

"It could have been anybody or nobody. Who knows, maybe even Lloyd Witherspoon."

"Why do you say him? Was there something in the letter?"

Frank only shrugged. They'd reached the roadway, and most of the people were in their vehicles and headed for the gate. Just as they stepped off the path and onto the pavement, Mort Anderson's Mercedes glided by. Kay looked at them and so did Mort. His window rolled partway down, Mort said, "Don't you two get wet now."

Abby didn't seem to attribute any special significance to the remark, though she had a questioning look on her face. Frank again wondered when and how he'd ever be able to tell her about Kay. What words could he use? "Oh, and by the way, Abby, once or twice a week your mother and I would get loaded on margaritas and screw our brains out." The thought of having to broach the subject at all sickened him.

Frank glanced up the roadway and saw Wayne sitting in his truck, waiting. The patrol car, with Sandy Mendoza at the wheel, pulled up in front of them. Sandy lowered his window.

"Ready, Chief?"

"Yes, Sandy."

Abby, somewhat incongruously, extended her hand and Frank took it, glad for the opportunity to touch her. "See you at the station," she said.

"Right."

She went around to the passenger side of the cruiser and got in. The car proceeded on toward the gate. Once again the rain began to fall harder. Frank watched her go, his heart heavy with dread about the future. It was a difficult day, though not because of Chet—that goodbye was complete. Frank felt the weight of the burden he was carrying and he hated it. Of all the women in the world for him to have a thing for, why did it have to be Kay Ingram's daughter?

Riverton Civic Center

Abby reread the last lines of the letter before glancing up at Frank. "You're right, we've got to talk to Witherspoon as soon as possible. But if you don't mind me asking, why are you willing to share this with me, knowing Chet's feelings?"

"He said not to tell you any more than I had to. In my judgment I have to tell you everything. Chet had problems with you, it's true, but for all the wrong reasons, mostly that you weren't his choice for police chief and maybe that you're a woman. Personally, that's the thing I like best about you—it makes it a little easier to live with the fact that I'm attracted to you."

She gave him a look. "Maybe that's a subject best left for after hours," she said.

"Right, Chief."

Abby repressed a smile. She liked what he'd said, but could hardly admit it.

"I take it as a vote of confidence that you're willing to share," she said.

"You should."

"So, how do you read this, Frank?" she said, tapping the letter. "What really happened? Have a theory?"

"I take it pretty much at face value. I don't think a man in Chet's situation lies or distorts the truth much. Maybe he tries to put the best light on things for Witherspoon's sake, but he also knows that the only way to find out who Jane Doe is and what happened to her is through the old codger. It's possible Witherspoon was more deeply or even more criminally involved than Chet realized, but I doubt it. Chet was no fool and he wasn't a bad cop."

"And the trail grows cold."

"Even as we speak."

"I've got to change out of this uniform," Abby said, the urgency of the situation gripping her.

Frank nodded, his blue eyes full of messages, messages that gave her a funny, yet pleasant feeling.

"I don't mean to be presumptuous," he said, "but what do you think of taking an overnight bag? If we do turn up something, we might want to stay over to save ourselves another trip back to the Bay Area."

A twinge went through her, a reaction to the promise in his words, but also to her own fear. "I was thinking the same thing," she said cautiously.

"I should grab my shaving kit and a change of clothes, too."

"Let's take my vehicle," she said. "It'll be more reliable."

"That's an understatement," he said, his eyes twinkling. "So, where shall we meet? Would back here cause any problems for you?"

"You're an investigator and part of the team, Frank. If people have trouble with us going off on assignment together, that's too damned bad."

He grinned. "I like your attitude, Chief."

Abby folded the letter and handed it to him. She had trouble dealing with Frank because her feelings toward him were so garbled. Her instincts pointed in one direction, her better judgment in another. She did have a strong desire to understand him, though. "I know it's none of my business, but are you going to give anything to Frieda?"

"Sure. That's what Chet wanted, so that's what I'm going to do. Right away, before it's spent."

"That's honorable," she said, "but Chet also asked you to keep me out of it. How do you square that departure with giving a prostitute conscience money?"

"Duty. My duty to you and the justice system and the people of Riverton is higher than honoring Chet's prejudices. But the money for Frieda is as much hers as whatever he's giving to the police youth league or me. Whatever else Frieda was to Chet, she was his friend."

"I'm astonished by the reverence that woman commands," Abby said. "And I never cease to be amazed at men's ability to rationalize what hookers do."

"Well, you work on my morals and I'll do what I can to lighten you up."

"That sounds fair," she said, enjoying the banter. Still, she had to be careful. She looked at her watch. "Being a woman, it's going to take me a while to get ready. I'd better go."

Frank got to his feet. "See you back here in what? An hour?"

"Will that give you time to see Frieda?"

"I guess I'll just have to be quick, Chief."

She motioned him toward the door. "See you in an hour."

San Francisco

As they passed through the tunnel on Yerba Buena Island, midway across the San Francisco-Oakland Bay Bridge, she glanced over—catching him watching the play of lights and shadows on her face. But he didn't mind. Abby fascinated him and she affected him in ways that were outside his normal realm of experience. Maybe because he'd guarded against this sort of thing in the past—even with Kay.

Abby had been all business from the moment they'd left Riverton, perhaps thinking they'd gotten too friendly too fast. Their conversation had been mostly about Jane Doe. The most personal it had gotten was when they'd chatted about college and his marriage.

"How did your wife feel about you wanting to be a cop?"

"Arlene wasn't thrilled. For a while, though, she grimly endured my dreams. I think because she saw them as part of my post-traumatic stress disorder and felt it was her patriotic duty to endure them. What she didn't understand was that she wasn't doing me any favors. It was easier for her to project onto me rather than take responsibility for her feelings. That way she didn't have to look inside herself."

"You seem to have her pretty well figured out. Was it because of counseling?"

"No, pure defense mechanism, Abby. It's always easier to

paint the other person with the problem. She did the same with me.''

Abby hadn't shown much interest in talking about her personal life and he didn't press her. He half expected her to bring up Frieda again, but she didn't. He would have told her what happened when he went by, how Frieda had cried when he'd handed her the ten one-hundred-dollar bills. ''I really liked the old bastard,'' Frieda said, wiping her eyes. ''He had a good heart, Frank. In spite of everything, he had a good heart.''

Frank couldn't decide if the tears were for Chet or for the money. Abby would probably be able to tell him, but he figured the less discussion he had with her about women, the better.

''Pretty sight, isn't it?'' Abby said, indicating the San Francisco skyline.

Frank gazed over at the sparkling columns of steel, cement and glass, the most prominent the Transamerica Pyramid, because of its shape, and the Bank of America building, because of its height. ''Yeah.''

He couldn't look at that skyline without feeling a stab of nostalgia. For years he'd driven to the city to see Beth, following this same route. He'd taken her to the Carnelian Room at the top of the B of A Building for her eighth-grade graduation—just the two of them—only weeks before she'd died. That was one of his most vivid recollections of her—his daughter, edging toward adulthood, schooling him on the proper choice of flatware, thanks to her mother's instruction. Beth glowing, one part embarrassed for him, two parts proud of being so grown-up.

''Middle lanes?'' Abby said.

''Yeah. Follow the signs for 101 and San José. Then take the 280 cutoff.''

Once off the bridge, they were on an elevated freeway bypassing the downtown, but giving a good view of it. After

the isolation and quiet of the Delta, the vibrancy and soul-
lessness of the city seemed forbidding. But it had an appeal,
too. The energy could be as tempting and seductive as the
lure of drink or sex. Yet a guy couldn't be drunk all the time.
How did people live in the city, without the respite of a dewy
morning or the sight of a slowly circling hawk?

"My dad used to take me to San Francisco every December to Christmas shop," Abby told him. "We'd visit a mu-
seum and see either *The Nutcracker* or *A Christmas Carol.*
That way I got my culture, my taste of the city life and Santa
Claus all in one fell swoop."

"Did you like it?"

"Yes and no. It was different and exciting, I guess. But I
was always afraid we'd run into my mother. I don't think
Kay ever lived in San Francisco, but it was the place I
thought of as 'being away from home' and it was always
forbidding. I never admitted that to my father, but if I had,
I'd probably have spared myself some grief."

Frank wanted to ask about her feelings for Kay, but it was
a dangerous subject. He let the opportunity pass.

The traffic backed up soon after they got off the bridge.
The stop-and-go gave her more of an opportunity to look at
him, which she did. Frank found himself wanting to touch
her. Being alone with Abby in the car in the big bad city, far
from everything and everybody they knew, was a turn-on.
He wondered if she was feeling the same thing.

"I suppose we should talk about our strategy with Witherspoon," she said, probably picking up on the vibrations
coming from him.

"Good cop, bad cop?"

"If it feels right."

"Have a preference which?" he asked.

"I should probably use my gender to advantage," she replied. "It's amazing how guys will sometimes open up because you're a woman."

"Haven't they extended the Miranda rule to cover that yet?" Frank quipped.

"You mean like, 'You have the right to remain silent and to be interrogated by a male officer'?"

He chuckled. "Something like that."

"Since Lloyd already knows you're cheeky, you might as well play the hard-ass," she said.

"Okay, as long as you recognize I'm being cast against type."

"Duly noted."

They reached the 280 interchange and made the ascent up the hill. At the Geneva-Ocean Avenue exit they got off the freeway. Frank, consulting his map, had her turn off a few blocks before they reached Junipero Serra Boulevard. St. Francis Wood wasn't the most exclusive neighborhood in the city, but it was in the top tier. Following the curvy, hilly street, they finally reached Lloyd Witherspoon's place and pulled over. The houses were large, freestanding and had garages, which meant parking on the street wasn't at the same premium as in most of the city.

Frank took in the dark two-story stucco house, tightly ensconced in large shrubs. "Looks like we may have struck out, Chief," he said. "Unless Lloyd's in the basement watching kiddy-porn movies."

"Let's give it a try."

They went up to the front door, but there was no answer when they rang the bell.

"We can hope Lloyd's out to dinner and not in Mexico or someplace," Frank said.

"Right."

Abby was clearly disappointed, but they'd known they were taking a risk dropping by unannounced. On the other hand, they hadn't wanted to warn Witherspoon they were coming.

"Speaking of dinner," Frank said, "are you hungry?"

She gave a shrug as if she hadn't given it any thought. "It's still kind of early."

"What say we go over to Stonestown and kill some time? Then we can eat and swing back here again afterward. Maybe we'll be lucky."

Abby agreed and they drove to Stonestown Galleria over on Nineteenth Avenue, the only suburban-style shopping mall in San Francisco. It was near St. Francis Wood and also Lowell High School, the highly acclaimed special-admissions public school Beth would have attended if she hadn't died. There were memories everywhere, it seemed. The incongruity for Frank was in reliving them with Abby Hooper at his side.

They parked the Bronco and walked through the mall, populated primarily by teenagers—gum-chewing girls with teased hair and short skirts, boys in baggy pants and funny haircuts. They were all cruising, the name of the game to see and be seen. The kids came in all sizes, shapes, races and colors. This, after all, was San Francisco, the great melting pot on the eastern rim of the Pacific. There were fifteen-year-old Filipino girls dressed and coiffed like the Spice Girls, Latinas with a look reminiscent of Madonna in an earlier incarnation. Boys with earrings and nose rings, Michael Jordan shoes and Dennis Rodman tattoos. Whites almost seemed an alien species in this part of the city, except, of course, for their culture, which was everywhere—coming through the headphones and in the McDonald's sacks, courtesy of Madison Avenue and Montgomery Street.

Abby glanced at him, seemingly bemused, or suffering sensory overload, it was difficult to tell which. Urban America. It was enough to make you throw up or want to dance. And it wasn't always easy to tell which urge was the stronger. The magic was in the narrowness of the line separating the two, Frank surmised.

They looked in shop windows. Abby lingered in front of

a jewelry store. They went into See's Candy and Abby bought a couple of truffles for later—one for each of them. Frank didn't mention he'd taken to watching his waistline the past few years.

He put his arm around her shoulders, an act of friendliness she didn't seem to mind. "Ever had Vietnamese food?" he asked.

"I've had Thai."

"Vietnamese is different. Unless it's closed, I know a place not far from here. Run by a former ARVN colonel."

"You're the expert. I'm game."

They found the restaurant, but the owner wasn't in. Beth had been a classmate of the guy's daughter, Cali. On a visit to see Beth some years ago, Frank had accompanied her to meet Cali's father because Mr. Nguyen had wanted to size up an old comrade-in-arms and swap war stories. Their girls had been singularly bored by the conversation. Vietnam, after all, was ancient history, sort of like World War I or the Spanish-American conflict.

Now Frank had returned with Abby, another few years removed from Southeast Asia and still carrying the vivid memories. The smells, above all else, did it for him, especially the pungent aroma of *nuóc mắm*, the first whiff of which carried him instantly back to the early seventies and the steamy Mekong Delta.

He shared his recollections with her as they ate beef-and-noodle soup, shark fin with bamboo shoots and roast duck. They ate with chopsticks. He'd perfected his technique in 'Nam, she in college. They had coconut ice cream for dessert, using plain old spoons.

After they'd finished, Frank checked his watch. "Maybe we should go see Lloyd, so I can be a hard-ass."

"Right," Abby said, "and I'll try not to overdo the sweet routine."

Frank boxed her chin playfully and called for the check.

* * *

When they got to Lloyd Witherspoon's house, there still weren't any lights on.

"Damn," Abby said. "I hope this doesn't turn out to be a long ride just to have some Vietnamese food."

"The company hasn't been bad—at least not from my perspective."

"Mine, either," she said, reaching over and touching his hand.

His awareness made her withdraw her hand. Frank realized he couldn't take her willingness to connect for granted. Abby wasn't a woman to be rushed. She peered into the rearview mirror.

"Well, what do you think we should do?" she said, drumming her fingers on the steering wheel.

Frank thought of how Witherspoon had done the same thing when they'd sat in his Caddy talking that night. "I suppose we can wait around for a while. He might yet show up."

Abby glanced across the street. "We could ask the neighbors if they've seen him around."

"I guess."

Frank wasn't eager to poll the neighborhood, but if that was what she wanted to do, he'd do it. Abby showed no intention of getting out, though, sitting motionlessly instead.

"You all right?" he asked, reaching over and brushing her cheek with the back of his fingers.

Abby allowed the affection for a moment, then gently took his hand. She didn't let go. "Frank, we have to be careful."

"Of?"

"Getting sidetracked."

There was equivocation in both her words and her tone.

"All work and no play makes Jane a dull girl," he said.

"Yeah, well, that's one way to look at it, I guess."

Not exactly a rebuke. He took heart. Cautiously.

"Is it wrong for a person to go with their feelings?" he asked.

Abby stared straight ahead. She didn't reply. She seemed torn, stuck on top the fence, not inclined to topple either way. He let her think about it. The silence lasted a long time. Finally she said, "Don't you think it would be a bad idea for us to…get involved?"

It was a bid for reassurance. "Not if it's honest."

"Honesty doesn't have anything to do with it. We've got a job to do, Frank. A professional relationship to maintain."

"I don't see that as a problem."

"No, I don't suppose you would."

There was a touch of sarcasm in her tone. Not a good sign.

Just then a car came up the street from behind them and turned into Witherspoon's drive. It was the Caddy Chet's cousin had driven to Frank's place.

"Looks like fate has chosen duty," Abby said, sounding relieved.

Frank was not pleased. But he could hardly argue with the facts.

Abby was energized by Witherspoon's arrival. She reached for the door handle like she couldn't get out of the vehicle fast enough. Sighing, Frank went along. They met Witherspoon in the drive. He eyed them warily as they approached.

"Mr. Witherspoon," she said, "I'm Abby Hooper of the Riverton Police Department. Could we please have a word with you?"

Witherspoon still hadn't closed his mouth. Then he seemed to recognize Frank.

"Evening, Mr. Witherspoon," Frank said. "We meet again."

"What is it you want?" he demanded.

"We have a few questions we'd like to ask," Abby said.

"Concerning?"

"Chet Wilsey."

"There's no doubt it was suicide, is there?" Witherspoon asked. "I mean, what's there to talk about?"

"Why don't we go inside?" Frank said. "Or would you rather have the neighbors listening in?"

"Am I under arrest?" He spoke in a very low voice.

"No," Frank said, "but if you'd prefer that, it can be arranged."

Witherspoon appeared uncertain what to do.

"Mr. Witherspoon," Abby said, "we only have a few questions. It won't take long."

The man relented. "All right. Come in. But I know my rights. If I ask you to leave, then you will."

"Certainly," she said.

Witherspoon led the way to the front door. After unlocking it, he showed them inside, turning on the hall light. The front room was just off the entry. It was large, the furniture mostly leather, masculine. Brass lamps, dark woods, earth-tone pillows set the mood. Pleasant but unspectacular landscapes hung on the walls. The stale air reeked of tobacco smoke.

Frank and Abby sat on one of the two sofas. Witherspoon seemed reluctant to sit at first, but, taking a pack of Camels and a lighter from his coat pocket, he dropped into a wingback armchair.

"What do you want to know?" he asked, taking a cigarette from the pack.

"We've got a Jane Doe that washed up naked in a slough over in the Delta," Frank began. "A child prostitute. Chet was one of her johns. He left us a note. Seems you procured for him, Lloyd. We want the particulars."

"That's not true!" Witherspoon said, getting to his feet and removing the unlit cigarette from his mouth. "I didn't procure a prostitute for Chet or anybody else. And I won't have you sitting in my house saying such a thing. You'll have to leave."

"Would you like to read a copy of Chet's letter?" Frank

asked, taking some folded sheets of paper from his inside coat pocket.

Witherspoon glared. He did not take the papers or ask to see them. His face was contorted with fear and anguish. He seemed uncertain what to do.

"Mr. Witherspoon," Abby said, "our objective is very simple. We want to identify that girl and learn the circumstances of her death. She must have family somewhere, and they need to know what's happened to her. Your help may be essential."

Witherspoon sat again, but he didn't settle back in the chair, staying, instead, on the edge of the cushion. He lit his cigarette, blowing smoke toward the ceiling. "I swear I know nothing about that girl."

"But you did find her for Chet. Through a bar owner you know."

"Oh, God," Lloyd said, lowering his face into his hands. "Chet told you that?"

"All we need from you is the specifics."

After what seemed like at least a minute, he looked up, squinting through a ribbon of cigarette smoke. "You can't make me answer your questions."

"You might as well know money's not going to get you through this one, Lloyd," Frank told him. "There's no one to pay off."

Witherspoon blinked. "What are you talking about?"

"I'm talking about Cindy Dougherty. Remember her? Innocent little girl back in Riverton gets molested by the Big Bad Wolf. Big Bad Wolf would've gone to jail, too, except his cousin happened to be the police chief, and the wolf had enough cash to buy off Cindy's parents. Kinda odd how cases like that just won't die. You think it's over, long forgotten by the world, then bam, somebody remembers."

Lloyd Witherspoon's eyes narrowed. "Are you blackmailing me, Keegan?"

"Blackmail? No, Lloyd. I'm just reflecting on the kind of guy I'm dealing with here."

Witherspoon's gaunt face looked like a storm ready to break. "Doing somebody a favor, introducing people, is not a crime," he said. "I know it looks bad on the surface, but what I did was innocent. I had no idea what would happen."

"What are you saying, Lloyd, that procuring a child prostitute is just an act of friendship?" Frank chided.

"No, I'm not saying that at all!" Witherspoon shot back. "I didn't procure anybody. I told Chet who to talk to, that's all."

"The bar owner."

"Yes."

"Who is he?" Abby asked.

"Isn't there another way?" Witherspoon lamented. He took a deep drag on his cigarette, holding the smoke in his lungs before letting it trail out his nostrils. "This is a bad time for me. I've got problems with my business. I don't need this on top of everything else."

"Come on, Lloyd," Frank snapped. "Quit stalling. Give the lady the information she wants."

"It's for the best, Mr. Witherspoon," Abby assured him.

Witherspoon took a deep breath and, coughing slightly, said, "All right, but I want your word there won't be any publicity, no stories in the press. I want to know that what I tell you will be kept in confidence."

"Our investigations are confidential," she replied. "Unless the district attorney chooses to bring charges, what you tell us won't be made public."

Again Witherspoon drew on his smoke. "Okay. Several weeks ago I got a call from Chet. I hadn't heard from him in a while. We usually see each other a couple of times a year. Whenever he's in the city and I'm in town we have a drink together—that kind of thing."

"You said this happened several weeks ago," Abby said. "Can you be more specific?"

"Let me see. It was early February, right after I got back from L.A. That was on the third, so that means it must have been the fifth. Chet called the day before, so yes, it was on February 5th."

Abby had taken a notepad from her purse and jotted down something. "I'm sorry I interrupted you, Mr. Witherspoon. Go on with your story."

"All right. So, anyway, Chet came by the house. We sat here in this room. He was depressed as hell. I told him he needed a party, to find a young piece and have a good time. Chet questioned whether any young piece would want to party with an old fart like him. And I told him there were plenty of girls around, though sometimes they needed a little extra incentive. Chet said if I was talking about a street-walker, he wasn't interested."

Witherspoon stopped talking. He sat back in the chair, drumming his fingers on the arm.

"Then what happened?" Abby asked. "You put him in touch with this bar owner?"

Witherspoon seemed reluctant, but he continued. "I told Chet about this friend of mine who happens to own a night-club. And he knew people who knew people. He didn't get involved himself. By that I mean he didn't have a financial interest. He could tell people who to call if they had a special...let's say, interest."

"Like children, Lloyd?" Frank said.

"No, not like children. I told you, I have no knowledge of that girl. I have no idea who she was. Chet got the name from...my friend."

"Who's your friend?"

Witherspoon took a quick drag of his cigarette. "Is this really necessary?" he asked, turning to Abby.

"If your friend was the one who introduced Chet to the

girl, Mr. Witherspoon, then it *is* necessary. It's the only way we'll be able to piece together what happened. Please.''

Witherspoon lowered his head. "His name is Biff Roberts. He owns a place in the South of Market called 'Biff's.'''

Abby continued to take notes.

"We're not close friends,'' Lloyd went on, "but we've done each other favors over the years. Biff's not a criminal. And for God's sake, please don't tell him you got his name from me.''

"We won't say any more than is absolutely necessary,'' Abby said. "But tell us exactly what transpired. Did you introduce Chet to Mr. Roberts?''

"Chet and I went down to the club. Biff was there. We talked. I explained that my cousin needed a lift, some sweet young thing to liven his spirits.''

"Did he understand you to mean a child prostitute?'' Abby asked. "A young girl?''

"No, no. At least that wasn't what *I* meant. I was speaking figuratively.''

"So did Biff give Chet a name?''

"I wasn't there. I introduced them, then I went to the rest room. By the time I got back, they'd exchanged information and Biff was off talking to someone else. Chet told me he got a phone number and I encouraged him to call. He went to the pay phone, came back and told me he had a date. Then he left.''

"When was the next time you saw him?'' Abby asked.

"That night. I was at my place and the doorbell rang. It was Chet and he was all upset. He said he'd done a terrible thing. The girl turned out to be young, really young. He figured she'd be maybe sixteen, eighteen, but she was quite a bit younger than that.''

"He had no idea when he left the bar?''

"I don't think so. Either that or his conscience started bothering him afterward.''

Abby said, "Did Chet describe his experience to you, Mr. Witherspoon?"

"Not in detail. He was very upset. Mostly with himself. He felt awful. Over and over he said, 'She was just a kid, Lloyd, a kid. How could I have screwed a kid?'"

"Did he tell you where he went? Who was present, anything like that?"

Witherspoon took a final drag on his cigarette and stamped it out in an ashtray. "He said he went to a nice apartment on Russian Hill. The pimp was waiting outside."

"Did Chet describe him?"

"Chet said it was a boy, a few years older than the girl. Chet paid him two hundred dollars. The boy let him into the building, punched the elevator button and let him go up on his own."

"No names?"

"No names," Witherspoon said.

"Is that all Chet told you?"

"That's it."

"So Chet felt guilty. What happened next?"

"Well, I tried to comfort him. I told him she wasn't some virgin and it wasn't like he stole her innocence. Basically, I encouraged him to forget it."

"But he never mentioned a name."

"No. My impression was he had no idea what it was. All he talked about was how young she was. It really had him going. After a while he left."

"Did you speak to him again?"

"Once," Witherspoon replied. "I was kind of worried about him, so a few days later I called to see how he was doing. He said he was all right, but he couldn't get the incident out of his mind. He wanted me to check up on her, to talk to Biff, but I told him that would be unwise. The last thing he needed to do was get involved. He agreed finally.

We ended the conversation and that was the last time I spoke to him."

"Chet didn't tell you he was being blackmailed?" Frank asked.

"He was being blackmailed? By the girl?"

"We don't know who," Abby replied. "But you weren't aware of it?"

Witherspoon shook his head. "Not till now."

"What can you tell us about Biff Roberts beside the fact that he owns a nightclub?" Abby asked.

Lloyd shifted uncomfortably. "He's well-known around town. Can't tell you much about his background. Real friendly, outgoing guy. Young. By that I mean a lot younger than me. I'd say forty or forty-five. His name gets in the society columns, but he can be down-to-earth. Not at all pretentious. Originally from Texas, if I'm not mistaken. He's engaged to some society woman and that gets lots of press. I forget her name. That's not my thing—opera, balls and all that." Witherspoon shook his head. "I sell cars."

Frank and Abby exchanged looks.

"Is there anything else you can tell us, Mr. Witherspoon?" she asked.

"No, that's everything. More than I ever wanted to say."

Abby glanced at Frank. "Any more questions?"

He shook his head. She took out a business card and handed it to him. "If anything else should come to mind, give me a call, will you?"

"Sure," he said, sticking the card in his pocket.

They all stood. Abby headed for the door. Frank followed. She said goodbye to Witherspoon as Frank opened the door. Neither of them shook Witherspoon's hand. Once they were both in the Bronco, Abby put the key in the ignition, but didn't start the engine.

"What do you think?" she asked.

"I think the man's a skunk."

"But is he a liar?" she asked.

"I don't know. My guess is he knew that he was getting Chet a child prostitute. Probably has had a few himself, maybe even Jane Doe. Seems to me Biff Roberts is the guy to talk to."

"Yes, I can hardly wait."

The cocktail waitress placed a beer in front of each of them. Abby looked uncomfortable, even though she'd agreed to have a drink. Frank was surprised because he didn't think she would once they learned that Biff Roberts wasn't in. The manager claimed Roberts was away on vacation and wasn't expected back for a while, though he wasn't sure when.

Frank suggested they stay, anyway, to check the place out. Biff's was a nineties version of a fern bar—all wood and brass. The crowd was well-dressed and mostly professional. In the adjoining room there was a small dance floor and a jazz group. Frank and Abby had stayed in the bar, mainly because that was the only place they could be seated. The place was lush with colognes of every description.

Abby was staring at her beer. "Damn," she said. "I had a feeling Biff wasn't going to be easy to find. Do you suppose Witherspoon tipped him off?"

"Who knows? But it is odd for a businessman to leave without telling his staff where he's going or when he'll be back."

"I thought the same."

"So what do we do, Abby?" Frank asked.

She pondered his question as she drummed her fingers on the table. It had been a long day and she looked tired, but she also struck him as especially pretty. Again he had the desire to touch her.

"As a minimum we can poke around town and find out what we can," she said. "I know some people in the SFPD.

There'll be stories about Mr. Roberts. That's a virtual certainty."

"Which means staying over."

"Right. If you don't mind."

"Where?"

"Someplace modest," she said. "The budget's tight."

"How about we stay someplace nice? On Chet. The donation of a concerned citizen."

"What did you have in mind?" she asked.

"I've always liked the St. Francis."

"You think that's how Chet wanted his money spent?"

"I think Chet was concerned about only one thing—the result. But the man understood the importance of morale, and he always wanted his troops in the best possible frame of mind to do their job. I'm sure he would approve."

She looked down at her beer again, keeping her eyes on the glass. "Why am I tempted?"

Frank liked the way she put it. "Maybe because you know I'm right."

Abby sighed, lifting her gaze toward the ceiling, exposing her slender neck. He sensed he needed to do something to relax her.

"Come on, Chief," he said, "you're too damned conscientious for your own good. The boss has to know when to kick back, too. Do you like to dance?"

Abby wasn't as surprised by his question as he expected. "The Chet Wilsey method of personnel management?"

"No, this is coming from me. I want to dance with you."

She studied him for a moment, then got up. They made their way through the crowd to the dance floor. Frank checked out her figure. She'd changed into a skirt and sweater. Most of the day she'd had on a jacket, but now that it was off, the lines of her body were more evident and he liked them very much.

There was a little space in the near corner of the floor. The saxophonist was playing a solo. "Moon River." Abby turned to face him, moving right into his arms, her slender body coming up against him. She let him hold her close and she didn't feel nearly as rigid as he'd expected.

They danced like lovers, close and intimate. Neither of them spoke. He savored the feel of her, the scent of her hair. It had been a long, long time since he'd experienced this sort of awareness of a woman. It went beyond sex, which said quite a lot since sex was the only standard he related to anymore. The tune ended. Another slow piece began. She looked up into his eyes.

"How many rooms were you planning on renting?" she asked.

Frank shrugged. "As few as the chief will allow."

"One?"

"Nice number," he said, kissing her temple.

"Can we dance again?" she asked.

"We can dance all night if you want."

"No," Abby said, "once more is enough."

Frank had the TV on and was watching an all-sports channel. He wanted to appear as nonchalant as he could to put her at ease, assuming she ever came out of the bathroom. Abby had been in there for what seemed like a very long time. She'd run a bath, but the splashing had stopped and he'd heard the water draining some time ago. Maybe she'd changed her mind.

He certainly hoped not. On the ride up in the elevator they'd kissed. Just as they had in the Bronco after leaving Biff's. He'd gotten hot and bothered even before they'd danced. In fact, all day long he'd been focused on Abby, the woman. Chet and Jane Doe and Witherspoon were all there, too. But mostly this day had been about Abby. And him.

The titillation had been intense, but he was still struck by the fact that sex per se seemed secondary. He wanted to make love with her, though, because the intimacy was important, the necessary step between thought and reality, expectation and satisfaction.

The bathroom door finally opened and Abby appeared. She was in an oversize T-shirt that came to midthigh. She looked young and pretty and vulnerable. No more badge or gun. No more cop. She was all woman.

"Bathroom's yours," she said, climbing onto the bed where she knelt, sitting on her heels.

Suddenly he felt very old and ashamed of loving her. Maybe he was deluding himself; maybe her willingness spoke more to her need than his virtue. It was no time for self-doubt, however. This was what he'd been telling himself he wanted.

He offered Abby the remote control, but she shook her head. He turned off the TV and got up. Moving to the edge of the bed, he leaned over and kissed her cheek. "You look beautiful," he whispered in her ear. She smiled, but she seemed nervous.

It was then that he noticed a deep purple scar on her thigh. He touched it with his finger. "What happened here?"

"When I was young and green, I took a bullet."

"Looks nasty."

"You should have seen it at the time."

"Want to see my war wound?" he said, showing her the scarring on his stomach.

"Shrapnel?"

"Yeah."

"I think I'd rather take a bullet, even if this isn't exactly a beauty mark."

"Your legs look great to me," he said.

"But it's a good thing I didn't get shot in the butt, huh, Frank?"

"Yeah," he said wryly. "I might not have been able to handle that."

She rolled her eyes and Frank, grinning, went into the bathroom.

He'd decided on a shave and a quick shower. Predictably, he cut himself on the chin and had a hell of a time stopping the bleeding. With the cut over his brow from the fight the other night, he looked more like a boxer than a lover. He had his shower, but was at a loss as what to wear. Not having brought pajamas or a robe, it was either a towel or nothing. He opted for the towel.

He'd brought condoms with him, but not wanting to admit it, he'd bought more in the hotel shop. Better this seem spontaneous from his point of view, as well. He left the bathroom.

Abby had turned off all but a single lamp in the corner, which cast a warm glow over the room. She was under the sheet and looked frightened. He didn't get under there with her, instead, lay on his stomach on top of the sheet. It was obvious she needed reassurance.

"I read somewhere that men like the first time best and women like it least," he said. "It always struck me as a shame."

"Why?"

"Doesn't seem very mutual."

"Sex isn't very mutual," she said.

"You don't think so?"

"Not without practice."

He caressed her cheek with his finger. "You know, I was attracted to you the first time I saw you—how much and in what way was in doubt, but I was definitely attracted."

"I didn't think about you in those terms at all."

"No?"

"Don't take that as an insult. My mind doesn't work that way."

"That's the difference between women and men," he said. "It was your kindness and your manner I found attractive," she said. "But to realize that, I had to get to know you."

"See, that's women."

"All you noticed was what? My body?"

"Your butt especially."

"God, that's really flattering, Frank."

"There are lots of butts. Abby-the-person is why I'm here."

"That's a little better," she said.

He kissed her deeply, Abby putting her arms around his neck and kissing him back. He moved partway on top of her, getting his hand under the sheet and running it down her side to the bottom of her T-shirt. He stroked her thigh.

She came up for air. "I've got to tell you something," she said.

He eased back to give her space. "What?"

"It's been a while since I've been with anyone. I don't know how I'll... I might..."

Frank kissed the tip of her nose. "Don't worry, sweetheart."

He pushed away the towel that was already half-off and got under the covers. Abby was tentative, grasping his hand and holding it tightly. He kissed her fingers, then her mouth. Reaching under her T-shirt, he found her naked. She seemed so small, her skin so smooth. When he touched her between the legs, she gave a little gasp. He was gentle. She slowly relaxed and opened her legs.

Frank pulled up her shirt and kissed her stomach and her breasts. She'd tense, then relax, seeming to appreciate the slowness of his rhythm, his care. When he'd gotten her excited she said, "Make love to me."

He put on the condom and she watched, caressing herself, the T-shirt up above her breasts, her eyes glassy-wild, and when they kissed, she bit his lip and dug her nails into his flesh. As he prepared to enter her, she tensed again, only to soften as he gently slipped inside her. Then the fire returned, her fears evaporating. Incredibly, she came first, quickly followed by him. Afterward she held him with his full weight on her. He kissed her neck and withdrew from her. Abby pulled down her shirt and lay staring at the ceiling. He wondered if she was thinking of someone else.

He reached over and caressed her chin. "You okay?"

She rolled her head toward him and gave him a distancing smile. "I'm fine. You?"

"Couldn't be better."

They were silent for a while. He held her hand.

"I thought you might be good," she said, "but you were better than I expected."

"I'm not sure how to take that."

"It was a compliment." She lapsed into another silence. Then she said, "Now I know all those stories about you being the town lover are true."

The thought of Kay hit his gut like a heavy boot. "I'd like to say it's natural talent, but it's not," he said. "Sex is learned behavior."

"I guess I can't claim to be a near virgin either, then."

He took her hand. "You were wonderful, Abby."

"Maybe we shouldn't talk," she said.

He knew she was right. They were explaining themselves out of fear. Sometimes truth was a monster. Maybe she understood that, too, and sensed it was waiting to pounce. Or maybe she had a truth of her own, one he knew nothing about.

Sunday
February 23rd

Downtown San Francisco

Abby slept terribly, woke up early and went off to shower while Frank continued to snore. Men were surprisingly unattractive when they slept, she thought. Women probably were, too, but she had no experience with that.

Abby had known that sleeping with Frank would complicate things, but it had somehow seemed necessary. There would be a price, of course. Everything changed between a man and a woman once they had sex—usually for the worse, though not always because of who they were. The circumstances could be the problem, and these were not good circumstances.

After drying her hair, she put on lipstick and eyeliner. She dressed, wearing the same suit as the day before, but a different sweater. When she came out of the bath, Frank was reading the morning paper, the towel around his waist. Seeing her, he put down the paper.

"Good morning, sunshine."

She smiled. "Bathroom's all yours. Sorry to take so long."

"No problem. I usually don't sleep in, so you were lucky to beat me. You look terrific, by the way."

"In the same suit?"

"Yes, in the same suit."

"You don't have to flatter me, Frank."

"No, and I don't have to appreciate you, either. But I do."

He was making an effort and it pleased her. "You a breakfast eater?" she asked.

"Most important meal of the day, according to my mom."

Abby sat on the bed. He was trying to be chipper and put her at ease. She appreciated that. "Morning after" conversation was always tough.

"Why don't you give room service a call while I get cleaned up," he said.

"It'd be quicker to eat in the coffee shop."

"Is time of the essence?"

"My guess is we have a full day ahead of us."

"I'll be quick, then," he said.

Frank gathered his clothes and, on his way past her, stopped and kissed the top of her head. It was sort of a fatherly gesture, doubtless also designed to allay her fears. Frank Keegan was a good guy.

While he got ready, she read the paper. As he promised, Frank was quick. She had only read the front section by the time he returned, wearing the same jacket and pants as the day before, but with a fresh shirt. He had his case in his hand.

"I'd like to come back to the room after breakfast," she said.

He put down his case. "Okay, we can check out later."

"What happened to your chin?" she asked, noticing the cut.

"I did that last night shaving." He grinned. "Nervous, I guess."

"I didn't even notice."

"Maybe you were nervous, too."

"I was."

Frank stepped closer and took her in his arms. Abby gratefully hugged him back. They silently commiserated, then he said, "You're a special person, in addition to being a hell of a police chief, Abby. I want you to know that."

"Thanks. Thanks for being kind."

"You make it easy," he said, pressing his cheek against her forehead.

It was odd to feel friendship and attraction to a man at the same time, but that was what was happening. That didn't mean there weren't potential problems, though. "Come on," she said. "I need a cup of coffee bad."

They went to a nearby coffee shop. Frank had hotcakes. Abby settled for juice and a muffin. They both drank lots of coffee.

"So, what's the plan for today, Chief?"

She looked at her watch. "It's late enough that I can call my friend in the SFPD. I'll do that back in the room. If I can get Biff Roberts's home address, I think we should drop by, see if the manager at the club was telling the truth about him being out of town. Besides that, maybe play it by ear."

"Sounds like a plan."

Abby sipped her coffee, weighing whether she needed to say anything about last night. Often in these situations, the less said, the better, but she wanted to get some things out in the open.

"Frank, can we talk about last night for a minute?"

"Sure."

"I'm not going to pretend it was an anomaly. I wanted to sleep with you."

"I agree."

"But I'm a little worried about the future, about us working together."

"There's nothing to worry about, Abby. What happened last night was special. It was something between you, the woman, and me, the man. I can separate that from our work.

You're the chief. I don't have any more of a problem with that now than I did before."

"I'm not concerned about my authority," she said.

"No?"

"Appearances. What happens from here on out."

"I'm very discreet."

"I know you're a gentleman. It's not that, either."

"Then what?"

She realized she was having trouble expressing her concern. Maybe all she needed to know was that things wouldn't be any different. He'd already given her assurances in that regard. But it seemed there was more. "Maybe I'm concerned about expectations," she said.

"Mine?"

"Both of ours."

"Hey," he said, taking her hand, "you're putting pressure on yourself. Whatever happens in the future will happen because we want it to. Come on, just relax."

"Easier said than done."

"You're borrowing trouble."

She sighed. "Maybe I am." And maybe, she decided, she was worried over nothing.

Russian Hill

With the help of the SFPD, they found Biff Roberts's condominium without any difficulty, but had a hell of a time finding a place to park. Finally they located a spot a couple of blocks from his building and walked back. It was an overcast day, the wind biting. Abby had on her raincoat for warmth. Frank made do with his sport coat.

He chatted amiably—still in his putting-her-at-ease mode—while she reflected on the future. Having gone to bed with someone in San Francisco was a far cry from having a lover in Riverton. If they were to become an item, it would soon be the talk of the town. She wasn't sure how she felt about that, but it was a topic for another day. Now was the time to focus on Jane Doe.

Abby's conversation with her friend in the San Francisco Police Department had not only garnered Biff Roberts's address, but also some background on him. Biff, it seemed, was a good deal more interesting than Lloyd Witherspoon had made him out to be. He'd kept his nose pretty clean since coming to San Francisco eight years earlier, but in a former life in L.A. he had a criminal record—misdemeanor convictions for solicitation for prostitution and pandering pornography. He'd done six months of jail time. Going further back, there'd been a drunk-and-disorderly and minor assault convictions in Texas, but he'd been quite young at the time. Biff, it seemed, had a past.

Abby was eager to see the guy by the time they reached Biff's building and found his name on the directory. She rang his bell, but there was no answer. She buzzed the manager. A woman's voice came over the crackling intercom.

"I'll be right out," she said when Abby identified herself as a police officer.

The woman, Mrs. Ungar, came to the door wearing a jogging suit, an apron and a wary expression. Her short gray hair looked windblown. She was about sixty.

"Mr. Roberts doesn't spend much time here now," she said in answer to Abby's question about his whereabouts. "Mostly, he's in Marin with his fiancée. She has a big fancy house, I understand."

"Would you know her name, maybe have an address?" Abby asked.

"In my apartment. Would you like to come in?"

They went to her ground-level apartment, waiting in a living room crammed with knickknacks. Abby had seen collectable stores with less stuff. Mrs. Ungar came back from the other room. She'd written out everything on a piece of paper—Katerina Kreski, an address in Ross and a phone number.

"You say Biff isn't here much," Frank said. "Does the place just sit empty?"

"Sometimes friends or relatives of Mr. Roberts stay for a night or two. Longer occasionally. His niece and her boyfriend were here for a few weeks recently. Is there a problem? The owner's not responsible for anything that goes on there we're not aware of, you know. We've never had any trouble."

Abby and Frank exchanged looks.

"When, exactly, was the niece here?" Abby asked.

"I don't know, maybe from the end of January until two weeks ago."

"What did she look like?"

"Pretty girl. But there was something sad about her. I thought she looked sick. Painfully thin. Tall, brown hair, blue eyes. Her name was Sarah."

"Sarah what, Mrs. Ungar?"

The woman squinted, trying to recall. "I don't know that I ever heard. The boy's name was Rance. I remember that because it was such an unusual name. They were an odd pair. She seemed terribly young to me to be off on her own, but Mr. Roberts said she was older than she looked. Finished high school already, he said, but you wouldn't think it to look at her. I would have said she was no more than thirteen or fourteen, but kids aren't the same now as they used to be."

Abby reached into her purse and took out one of the Jane Doe flyers she'd prepared. She showed it to the woman. "Could this be Sarah?"

Mrs. Ungar studied the drawing. "It could be. Looks a lot like her. But what is this? Is she wanted for something?"

"The drawing is of an unidentified drowning victim," Abby replied. "A Jane Doe."

"She's dead?"

"Yes. She died the night of the fourteenth."

"Sarah and Rance were gone by then. For several days."

"Do you know where they were headed?"

"I have no idea. I hardly spoke to either of them. Once Sarah forgot her key and I had to let her in. Another time they were arguing in the entry. Had a terrible screaming fight. I went out to quiet them down and they left the building."

"Do you know what they were arguing about?" Frank asked.

"I don't know. I heard words of anger. That's about all I can say."

"Mrs. Ungar, did Sarah and Rance have many visitors?" he asked.

"You mean other kids?"

"Anyone. Men, maybe?"

The woman looked uncomfortable. "I can't say that I noticed anything in particular, but one of the tenants complained that there was quite a bit of traffic. I did call Mr. Roberts to discuss the matter. I spoke to his fiancée, Miss Kreski, actually. A few days after that Sarah and Rance left."

"How about drugs?" Frank said. "Any evidence they might have been doing drugs in the apartment?"

Mrs. Ungar frowned. "I wasn't aware of anything. But I suppose they could have. Like I said, Sarah didn't seem well to me. Maybe she was an addict. But I have no proof one way or the other."

"Has anyone been in the apartment since Sarah and her boyfriend left?" Abby asked.

The woman thought. "Mr. Roberts may have spent a night or two. I don't always know. But there haven't been any other guests to my knowledge."

"Would it be possible to see the place?" Frank asked. "I'm thinking maybe Sarah left an address or something behind."

"I normally don't go into tenants' apartments without advance notice unless there's an emergency."

"I'm sure Mr. Roberts would want to know if his niece has been in an accident," Frank said, "not to mention the rest of her family."

Abby gave Frank a look. Like most cops, she was willing to go right up to the line, but she was reluctant to cross it. Maybe Frank didn't share her sense of propriety. The problem, of course, would be tainting any evidence of a crime they might find due to an illegal search. Then again, maybe the snooping would help them identify Jane Doe.

"Let me get my passkey," Mrs. Ungar said.

Abby considered stopping her, but didn't. "What if Biff's our man and we lose our best evidence against him?" she said under her breath.

"I don't know about you, but I'm just trying to identify a drowning victim. She stayed here, didn't she?"

"Maybe."

"I'm no lawyer, but seems to me that's good enough."

"We need probable cause," she whispered.

"I say let the Supreme Court decide about that."

Frank's mild manner was deceptive. He had fire in his gut. Abby wondered if his passion had anything to do with his daughter.

Mrs. Ungar returned and the three of them went up to Biff Roberts's condominium on the eighth floor. The decor was contemporary, more masculine than not, yet with the unmistakable touch of a decorator. There several large oils on the walls, all geometric, the palette bright. The place was clean and tidy.

"Mr. Roberts has a cleaning lady who usually comes on Thursdays. She's probably straightened up once or twice since Sarah was here."

That was not good news. Abby and Mrs. Ungar headed for the kitchen. Frank went off toward the bedroom. There were two pieces of notepaper by the kitchen phone. One was a grocery list. Abby pointed it out to Mrs. Ungar.

"Do you recognized the writing?"

"I'm not real sure, but it could be Mr. Roberts's."

Abby allowed that it did seem more a masculine hand. The boyfriend, Rance, was another possibility.

A telephone number was written on the second slip of paper. There was no other notation. Feeling brazen, Abby picked up the phone and dialed the number. She got a travel agency.

"Is Sarah there, please?" she said.

"I'm sorry," the woman on the other end replied, "there's nobody by that name here."

"I must have the wrong number. Sorry." She hung up.

They went next to a small den off the front room. There was a desk and it appeared Roberts used the space as an office. With Mrs. Ungar standing over her, Abby was reluctant to go through the drawers, but she did glance at the items on the desktop. One was a utility bill. That gave Abby an idea. Roberts's phone bill for the past month might prove interesting. She made a mental note.

Nothing else was visible that might provide evidence either to Sarah's identity or to what might have happened to her. Abby and the manager left the room just as Frank called to her.

"Chief, come look at this."

Abby found him in the closet of a second bedroom. He was peering through what was evidently a one-way mirror into the master bedroom. The scene was familiar. It was the room she'd seen on the videotape of Chet Wilsey having sex with Jane Doe.

"The plot thickens," Frank said.

"We've got to find Biff Roberts," she replied in a low voice. "And maybe get a warrant to take this place apart— if we haven't already screwed that up."

"If we hadn't come in, we wouldn't know this was here."

"Is there a problem?" Mrs. Ungar asked from the room behind them.

"No," Abby told her. "No problem."

She and Frank stepped out of the closet, closing the door behind them.

"There's no need to trouble you any longer," Abby said to the woman. "We'll go now and let you get back to your duties."

They all went back downstairs. Abby gave Mrs. Ungar her card, asking her to phone if she saw or heard from Biff. The woman promised she would. Abby and Frank left the building and headed for the Bronco.

"Hey," he said, "you in a hurry?"

Abby realized she'd gotten a few steps ahead of him and slowed down. "Sorry, but I want to get to a phone."

"Biff has evaded the law this long. Another couple of minutes won't matter. Anyway, I'm a little gimpy. War wounds, remember?"

"I'm the one who got shot in the leg, Keegan. Come on, get the lead out."

"So to speak?"

She laughed. "So to speak."

Town of Ross
Marin County

Ross was the butterfat in the Marin County cream, probably richer than a couple of Central American countries, Frank could hardly conjure up the extent of the wealth to be found there. And though he couldn't claim to know a soul, he knew the type who inhabited the place, or thought he did. The guys—and some of the gals, for that matter—drove their Mercedes or Lexus over the Golden Gate each morning to spend their days in big corner offices in the high-rise jewel boxes on Montgomery Street. Or maybe, if they felt like slumming it, they took the Larkspur ferry to the city. It being Sunday, the good people of Ross were either out on the bay in their sailboat, or up at Silverado in the Wine Country, trying to squeeze in some golf or tennis, February weather be damned.

Katerina Kreski, apparently, was in the latter group. Her maid told Abby on the phone that Ms. Kreski and her companion weren't expected back from Silverado until midafternoon at the earliest. Abby hadn't asked if the companion in question was Biff Roberts because she didn't want to tip them off. "With any luck, it'll be him," she said to Frank.

"Could be the lady has a guy on the side," he replied.

"A society woman? I doubt it."

"Maybe she's on to Biff, same as us."

"If she isn't, she should be," Abby said dryly. "At the moment, though, I hope she's completely oblivious."

"Who did you tell the maid you were?"

"I said I was a friend in the Junior League. But I'm not sure it registered. The poor dear hardly spoke English."

"The help available these days is a disgrace."

Abby gave him a playful whack on the arm. She seemed to have gotten past the tension of the morning. Frank was glad. But he was still anguishing over Kay. The thought of telling Abby about them was getting more onerous with each passing hour. Now he regretted he hadn't confessed his secret up front. Of course, he might not be with her now if he had.

"How much farther before I have to turn?" Abby asked.

Frank again consulted his map. Katerina Kreski's street was just off Sir Francis Drake Boulevard. "It's coming up soon," he said.

Reaching the corner, they made the turn, then moments later, another. It was a street of large homes and huge shade trees. The newer, more modern homes were up in the hills. Katerina's neighborhood was older and more established. It had character and probably lots of old money. The Kreski estate, they discovered, was protected by a wrought-iron fence and large shrubs. The house, made of stone, was multi-storied and had a distinctive Eastern feel. Seeing it made Frank think of Arlene. She used to buy *Architectural Digest* and sit by the hour drooling over pictures of homes like this. Maybe his defensiveness was traceable back to that. Abby parked the Bronco and turned off the engine.

She looked past him to the front of the house. "Nice."

"Biff seems to have gotten himself a live one. Not bad for an ex-con."

"He must be pretty damned charming."

"I hope we find out," he said.

"Yeah. Me, too. Frontal assault?"

"I'll be right behind you, Chief."

They got out, went through the gate and walked up to the house. Frank rang the bell. It took a while for the maid to answer. Her little round face peered out through the narrow crack in the doorway. Filipina, Frank thought.

"Is Ms. Kreski home?" Abby asked.

"No, gone today."

"But you expect her soon, right?"

The woman shrugged.

Abby took her badge from her purse. "Police," she said. "We need to speak with Ms. Kreski or Mr. Roberts."

"You wait, please. She come soon." With that, the woman closed the door.

Frank and Abby looked at each other.

"Must be a cultural thing," he said.

"Either that or she thought we'd be more comfortable in the car."

"I guess I could break down the door."

"With *your* shoulder?"

"Good point."

They retreated along the walk to the street. Just as they

reached the Bronco, a woman in a large BMW pulled into the drive of the house across the street. It was on the uphill side and sat on a higher elevation than the Kreski place. They saw the woman get out of her car, open her trunk and remove a sack of groceries.

"Must be the poor folk of the neighborhood," he said. "Buys her own groceries."

The woman peered down the drive at them, perhaps wondering what someone in such a plebeian vehicle was doing there.

"Do you think the neighbors have any juicy gossip about Biff?" Abby asked.

"He seems like the type of guy who could provide the material."

"Let's see if the fish are biting."

They crossed the street and mounted the drive. The woman had gone inside and was returning for another sack when they reached her car. She was a tall, slender brunette of about his age, though she looked in better shape, maybe having had some repair work done. Judging by her condition, Frank figured there was a personal trainer in the picture, as well.

"Afternoon," Abby said. "I'm Chief Hooper of the Riverton Police. This is Special Investigator Keegan. Do you have a moment to answer some questions?"

She gave them a wary look. "Do you have identification?"

Abby took out her badge and showed it to the woman, who nodded. "You can never be too careful these days."

"That's for sure."

"I'm Suzanne Broussard, by the way. What can I do for you?"

"We're investigating a possible homicide, Ms. Broussard. A young woman who at the moment is unidentified, a Jane Doe."

"And you've come all the way from Riverside?"

"No, Riverton," Frank said. "Over in the Delta."

"Oh."

"It's on the Sacramento River. Lots of boats."

"Yes," Suzanne Broussard said. "My husband and I have sailed up that way."

Frank nodded knowingly.

"We're hoping to speak with Katerina Kreski's fiancé, Biff Roberts," Abby explained. "We understand he spends a lot of time at the Kreski home. Are you acquainted with him by any chance?"

The woman rolled her eyes. "Biff Roberts. A walking scandal."

"Would you mind explaining?"

Suzanne glanced at the sack of groceries in the trunk. "You want all the dirt, don't you?"

"Mr. Roberts is a possible witness…"

"Okay, I'll give you the whole Kreski-Roberts saga, but let me put my frozen food in the freezer first, will you? I'd invite you in, but we're in the middle of redecorating."

"No problem," Abby said, "we can wait here."

"I'll only be a minute."

Once she was gone Abby and Frank exchanged smiles.

"Do you get the feeling Mrs. Broussard is going to enjoy this?" he asked.

"You're very perceptive, Frank. Or do you just understand women?"

He gave her a quirky grin. Suzanne Broussard was back in just a minute. "Thank you," she said, leaning against her BMW. She folded her arms across her velour-covered chest. Frank wondered if she might have had a little work done there, too.

"The fact that Katerina is going to marry Biff is an absolute scandal," Suzanne began. "Even her friends, of which I'm not especially one, have turned their backs on her. I don't condone boorish behavior, mind you, but Biff is an embarrassment. Owns a nightclub. He's reputed to have unsavory friends, though I don't know that from personal experience."

"What's Ms. Kreski's story?" Abby asked.

"Katerina is the daughter of Werner Kreski," Suzanne said. "You've undoubtedly heard the name. Real-estate mogul, made a fortune in the boom years of SoMa when they were doing all that redevelopment. I only met Werner once, though my husband, Norman, knew him pretty well through the Bohemian Club. You know the Bohemians."

Frank and Abby nodded.

"Anyway, Werner was quite a dashing figure. Pilot, flew his own plane like my husband. In fact, they flew together a few times. Werner was a little more into flying than Norman. He had a couple of planes. Katerina sold the Learjet, I believe, when she took over. Werner left his empire to her when he died several years ago, as you probably know. Biff, being no fool, moved right in. The man is charming as hell, I have to admit. And Katerina's certainly not the first to fall under his spell. He's not the Casanova type, as you might expect. Actually, he's more a teddy bear, affable, down-to-earth, life of the party. Biff's one of those classless people who oozes savoir faire, if you know what I mean."

"They plan to marry?" Abby asked.

"'Plan' being the operative word. Katerina adores him, but the relationship is not without its problems. I'm not privy to the details, but you hear things."

"For example?"

"They've had screaming fights in restaurants. More than once she's thrown him out of the house. It's a real love-hate relationship."

"Do you know why she's thrown Biff out of the house?" Abby asked.

"I think a lot of it has to do with women," Suzanne said, lowering her voice. "I mean, he *is* a man." She glanced at Frank. "No offense."

"I'm a neutral observer, ma'am."

She smiled, half-consciously checking him out.

"I don't suppose you've ever heard mention of Biff's niece, Sarah, have you?" Abby asked.

"Biff has an niece? Lord, I was under the impression he didn't have family. The story I heard was that he was an orphan or a foundling or something."

Abby took a Jane Doe flyer from her purse and handed it to the woman. Suzanne studied it for a moment. "This girl is Biff's niece?"

"We're investigating the possibility."

Suzanne shook her head. "It's certainly news to me."

"The girl look familiar at all?" Frank asked.

"No, I can't say she does." Suzanne started to hand it back.

Abby said, "Keep it. Perhaps one of the other neighbors might have seen her."

"Yeah," Frank added, "circulate it at the next neighborhood picnic."

The woman arched a brow. "Joke, right?"

He grinned. "I'm prone to do that from time to time."

She chuckled. "So, any more questions?"

Abby had another. "You said Katerina inherited her father's empire. What does she do—manage investments?"

"Katerina's a shrewd businesswoman. Norman says she may even be sharper than her father. Since taking over, she's increased the value of the holdings by fifty percent. When it comes to business, she's absolutely ruthless. That's why it's so odd that she's allowed herself to be taken in by this good-time Joe who offers nothing, really, but a few laughs."

"Love is blind," Frank said.

"Yes, and a fool and her money are soon parted."

"Happiness is what you make of it," he rejoined.

Suzanne smiled. "Are you a romantic, officer?"

"No, just a guy."

"And guys stick together, right?" She turned to Abby. "Well, I've given you all the dirt that's fit to print. If you'll excuse me, I've got things to do. The carpet man is due soon."

"Certainly Mrs. Broussard," Abby said. "We appreciate the help."

"Well, look. There's the happy couple now," Suzanne said, pointing across the street.

Frank and Abby turned to see the electronic gate across the street open and a big Mercedes drive through. They thanked the woman and headed back down the drive.

"Of course, you didn't hear a breath of scandal from me," Suzanne called after them.

"Our lips are sealed," Frank called back.

Abby glanced at him out of the corner of her eye. "I swear, Frank, you have a gift with the ladies."

"Her? She was looking down her nose at me, Abby," he replied.

"She thought you were cute."

"You think so?"

"Yeah, I do."

Frank put an arm around her shoulders and squeezed. "Let's just hope you're projecting."

By the time they got to the Kreski house, the garage door was closed and the couple was inside. Frank pushed the doorbell again. Once more they were greeted by the maid.

"She home now. One minute, please."

The door closed in their faces. Frank gave Abby an amused look.

"Maybe we'd be better off trying the servants' entrance."

"You've been reading too many English murder mysteries, Frank."

"Right you are, Holmes."

They waited for what seemed like a very long time. Frank

was about to push the bell again when the door opened. A slender blond woman with her hair pulled back in a sleek chignon appeared. She wore a gray cashmere sweater and dark gray wool slacks, gold watch, diamond stud earrings. She was in her mid-thirties, not pretty—handsome at best— her drawn face narrow, her expression severe, impatient.

"I'm Katerina Kreski," she said without smiling. "May I help you?"

Abby again took the lead, introducing them and showing Katerina her badge.

"What do you want?" she asked.

"We'd like to speak with Biff Roberts, please."

"I'm afraid Biff is indisposed. Perhaps I can help you."

"We'd really like to speak with him."

"That's not possible, I'm afraid. I'm Biff's fiancée. I can speak for him."

The woman was tough and uncompromising. And very self-assured. Frank hadn't known any society types firsthand, but this one seemed to hold the world in contempt. If he had to guess, being haughty and condescending was her natural condition.

"It's quite personal, I'm afraid," Abby persisted, her tone patient, in its way as unyielding as Katerina's.

The woman eyed them. "It's about Sarah, isn't it?"

"You know her?"

"I know of her. Biff and I have no secrets."

Abby glanced at Frank, then at Katerina. "If Mr. Roberts is unavailable, perhaps you'd tell us about Sarah, then. May we come in?"

Katerina glanced at her watch. "For a few minutes, but I'm really quite busy. This is a bad time. We'll have to make it quick."

She led the way into the house. All Frank could think was it looked like something on TV, the Carrington house on _Dynasty,_ maybe. There was a marble hall table, with flowers in a huge crystal vase, an antique occasional chair, an enormous grandfather clock, a big crystal chandelier—and they were still in the entry. They went down a step to the front room, which, conservatively, was the size of his mobile home. A grand piano in a specially built window alcove, an acre of sofas, chairs, tables and enough flowers to fill a florist shop. The room was dominated by a huge portrait in oil over the mantel, a man with that "captain of industry" look. Frank assumed it was Daddy Kreski.

Katerina took them to the nearest seating group. She sat down on a chair and crossed her legs in one fluid motion. Frank was impressed by the setup—not intimidated, but truly impressed. It wasn't often a guy saw how the other half lived this close up. Arlene and her doctor husband had money, but they were petit bourgeois compared to this.

"So," Katerina said, "there's no point in beating around the bush. Biff knew Sarah briefly. The last time he saw her was a week or so before she died. Her death is a tragedy, of course. We know nothing about it, other than what we read in the paper. I'm sure we've been remiss in not going to the police, if only to contribute what little we know, but quite frankly, we were hoping it would all blow over and be forgotten."

"Ms. Kreski," Abby said pointedly, "the girl is dead, quite possibly the victim of foul play. I assure you, we are not going to let this 'blow over.'"

"I realize you have to do your job. What I meant was, blow over with respect to us. Our knowledge of the girl is quite limited and we have so much to lose."

Frank saw the smirk on Abby's face and he could tell there was a real possibility for animosity here. Katerina Kreski was a haughty bitch. He saw it. Abby definitely saw it.

"I'm cooperating with you," Katerina said. "I'd like the courtesy of discretion in return. You see, Biff and I are engaged. The last thing I need is scandal. I grant you he was incredibly stupid to have gotten involved with the girl, and he compounded the problem by playing right into her hands. Sarah's dead and that's unfortunate, but Biff is the real victim here, Ms. Hooper.''

Frank saw Abby flinch and her jaw tighten. He knew there'd be fireworks before this was over.

''Maybe if we stick to what happened, Ms. Kreski,'' Abby said. ''How does Mr. Roberts know Sarah?''

''A month or so ago she wandered off the street late one night into Biff's club. It was raining and the girl was soaked to the bone. The staff started to run her out, as she was obviously underage, but Biff, bighearted soul that he is, had one of the women take her in back to dry her off. They fed her, and Biff, who's one of those people who can't see a stray cat without taking it in, talked to her. She was a runaway. His inclination was to take her to the police, which God knows is what he should have done—for his sake, as well as hers. But he didn't. To make a long story short, he took her to his place and let her stay there. It was incredibly stupid, but that's what he did.''

''So Sarah stayed with Mr. Roberts. For how long?''

''He didn't stay *with* her. He's been living here with me. The point is, he let the girl stay for several days in his condominium. He told the building manager she was his niece.''

''And that's it?''

Frank could tell Abby was getting ready to pounce and was kind of enjoying watching her set Katerina up. The Kreski woman recrossed her legs, glancing impatiently at her watch.

''You know it's not,'' Katerina said dryly. ''There's no point in playing games. The little bitch was a prostitute. In Biff she had a fat goose and she was going to take him for all she could. Of course, she had a pimp and he was on the scene immediately. The bottom line is the two of them black-mailed Biff. They threatened to expose him for rape, molestation, you name it. Biff was terrified. All he could think of was what this would do to me, to us, our future. So instead of going to the police, he tried to placate the pair. He gave them money, he let them stay in his apartment, he even allowed them to use his place for prostitution. Men were brought there and, yes, they even coerced Biff into sending a few customers their way. The situation was out of control.''

"And Biff was the innocent victim in all this," Frank said, unable to mask his sarcasm.

Katerina gave him a withering look. "That's right, Mr. Keegan. Oh, I'm sure there are some minor crimes you can pin on him, if you choose. You can even try to make more of his involvement than was actually the case. Yes, he was guilty, guilty of being too kindhearted, guilty of wanting to spare me at any cost. I guess technically he procured for the girl, but he did it under duress. The pimp was dangerous. He threatened Biff. Terrorized him. That's what actually happened." Katerina again consulted her watch. "You want to know the outcome, I'm sure. So I may as well tell you, even if it means implicating myself. I first found out about Sarah after getting a phone call from the manager of Biff's building. She complained about the johns going to Biff's condo. I confronted him and he tearfully broke down, telling me everything. Naturally I took steps to resolve the matter."

"What did you do?" Frank asked.

"I threw Sarah and the boy out."

"Rance?"

Frank saw Katerina's eyes widen slightly that Abby knew the boy's name, but she immediately got control. She was cagey and tough as nails.

"Yes, Rance."

"What was his last name?" Abby asked.

"I have no idea."

"How about Sarah? What was her family name?"

"I don't know that, either."

"Do you have any idea where she was from, who she might be?"

"None whatsoever."

"What about Biff?" Frank interjected. "He spent time with her. Didn't he learn anything about her?"

"We discussed that," Katerina said carefully. "All Biff knew was that she was not local and hadn't been in San Francisco long. The same with the boy. That's as specific as their conversations ever got. They were purposely obscure, Biff told me."

Frank and Abby regarded each other briefly. Then Abby turned back to Katerina.

"So, you went to the apartment and confronted Rance," Abby said. "Then what happened?"

"I gave him a substantial amount of money and ordered them to leave. I told them if either Biff or I heard from them again, I'd have them killed."

"Killed?"

"I didn't mean it, of course, but I made sure they thought I did."

"When was this, exactly?" Frank asked.

Katerina thought for a moment. "Let's see, it would have been about a week or so before we read in the paper about the drowning. The end of the first week in February. That would have made it around the eighth or ninth of the month."

"Did they leave?"

"Yes, I made sure of it."

"And that was the last time either you or Biff saw the pair?" Abby said.

"Correct. You see now what I meant when I said we hoped it would all blow over. I realize it was an idle wish. I suppose it was inevitable that their trail would eventually be traced to Biff. Perhaps it was wishful thinking and foolish on my part to hope it wouldn't." She lowered her head, showing humility. "Biff and I love each other so much, and we want so badly to avoid scandal—needless scandal, I might add. I'd like to think that now that the story's been told we might…well, be spared.''

"We'll have to talk to Mr. Roberts, of course," Abby said. "Most of what you've told us comes secondhand."

Katerina contemplated them both. Frank could tell something momentous was coming.

"You have to do what you have to do, I suppose," she said. "And yet I'm sure you can do it discreetly, sensitively." She hesitated. "My relationship with Biff, our marriage, is very, very important to me. Anything you could do to minimize the impact on us, on our lives, would be most appreciated. And—" again she hesitated "—and naturally I'd be happy to…shall we say, make your effort worthwhile.''

Abby's brows rose. Frank knew what was coming.

"Ms. Kreski," Abby said, "you aren't trying to bribe us, are you?"

"Bribe?" Katerina said, returning once more to her haughty demeanor. "Of course not. I would expect that you conduct your investigation honestly. For the sake of justice, I'd insist on it. But I know you have control over whether the information you gather is released. If you chose, this can be kept very quiet."

"Ms. Kreski," Abby said, "you don't understand how this works. We collect evidence and turn it over to the district attorney. We don't conduct our investigations under the eyes of the press or anybody else."

Katerina Kreski came right back at her. "I'm no fool, Ms. Hooper," she said. "Let's be honest. You can do pretty much what you want to do, including recognizing the fact that Biff Roberts, while foolish and softhearted, was essentially a victim. His name doesn't need to be brought into this. Unless, of course, you intend to be spiteful."

Abby bristled. "I intend to do my job. And that includes

talking to Mr. Roberts. The sooner that happens, the better—for him.''

Frank cleared his throat, deciding it was time to intervene. "Look," he said to Katerina, "if Biff hides behind your skirts, it makes it look worse. If he's as innocent as you claim, then he has nothing to hide.''

Katerina got to her feet. "How dare you speak to me that way! I'm going to ask you to leave. I thought perhaps by reasoning with you we might get this matter resolved for all our sakes, but apparently you aren't that wise.''

Abby stood. "We don't take bribes.''

"That's *your* word," Katerina shot back. "I was merely hoping to dissuade you from giving in to the entreaties of the media and the gossip factory.''

"Katerina.''

The voice came from behind them. They all turned. The man standing at the entrance to the room was large, but not imposing. He wore a white dress shirt, slacks and loafers. He looked soft, his body spongy without being fat, a teddy bear, as Suzanne Broussard, the neighbor, had described him.

Biff Roberts descended the step. "Honey," he said, "in trying to save me, you're only getting yourself in trouble. Don't. Really.''

"Biff, go upstairs!" Katerina commanded. "We agreed on how we'd handle this.''

"No, babe," he said, coming toward them, "I can't stand seeing you doing this to yourself for me.''

"Damn it, Biff," she pleaded. "Go upstairs immediately. Please!''

He shook his head. "No, I've got to talk to them. It's best.''

Katerina stepped forward, grabbing his arm. She tried to drag him away. "Biff, you don't know what you're doing!''

He resisted. "Yes, I do.''

"Don't say anything to them! I'm begging you. If only for me, Biff. For God's sake, don't!"

He shrugged her off, and Katerina, in tears now, went running from the room. Frank glanced at Abby, who'd been taking this all in with the same incredulity as he. Biff, having watched his fiancée leave, turned to face them. He looked tired, sallow, with dark circles under his pale blue eyes.

"I'm sorry for the trouble, folks," he said. "Please forgive Katerina. She's very emotional about this. It's all my fault—you can't blame her. I'd appreciate it if you just ignore everything she said. She was trying to protect me."

"What does she have to protect you from?" Frank asked.

"One of the sadder chapters in my life," Biff said miserably. He gestured toward the sofa where they'd been sitting. "Please sit down, folks."

There was still a bit of Texas drawl in Biff Roberts's voice, but not a lot. He sat in the chair where Katerina had been, perching on the edge of the cushion. He did not lean back. He rubbed his hands together and looked quite distressed.

"I overheard what Katerina told you," he began. "It was mostly true. She left out a few things, though. Things that put me in a bad light."

"We're listening," Abby said.

"Sarah did come to my place of business one rainy night like Katerina said. But she wasn't a hooker, she was a runaway. And she'd come to San Francisco looking for her boyfriend."

"Rance?"

"Yes. Rance Tully's his name. He was the problem. A selfish little son of a bitch, to be blunt. He used Sarah something awful, mistreated her." Biff lowered his head. "Not that my hands are clean."

"Please explain," Abby said.

"Sarah—her last name was Gibbs—and the boy were from some kind of religious cult in a little town in Southern Utah.

They wanted to marry, but couldn't for some reason—I never got the details—and the boy left, coming to San Francisco. This was last fall. Anyway, Sarah was terribly unhappy and she took off, too, making her way to San Francisco. Along the way she was used and abused by men, but she made it here, desperate and at her wits' end, when she stumbled into my place.''

Abby, who'd gotten out her notebook earlier, had Biff repeat Rance's and Sarah's names. Frank watched her write "Gibbs" in block letters, underlining it twice. "Go ahead, Mr. Roberts,'' she said. "I interrupted you.''

"I took her home, got her fed and cleaned up. The poor thing was terribly grateful. She stayed with me a day or two. I was there with her. Katerina was away on business and I often stay in the city when she's out of town. Anyway, I did play the role of Good Samaritan. At least, that's the way it started. Then Sarah began begging me to help her find Rance. I had no idea how to find a kid like that and I told the girl so. She thought I needed encouragement, I guess, and…well, she seduced me. You probably don't care to hear the details, but…let me put it this way—for a fourteen-year-old, she really knew her way around the bedroom. She was no innocent.''

Abby shifted uncomfortably. "You had sex with her.''

"Yes.''

"You're saying it was consensual,'' Frank said. "You didn't coerce her or pay her?''

"No, she wanted to find Rance and would do anything to accomplish her goal. I mean, the kid was driven.''

"And?''

"Well, I dropped a few bucks around town and I managed to locate him for her. The two of them left and, with Katerina coming back from her trip, I was ready to end things, figuring…hoping, I'd never see either one of them again. But it didn't work out that way. After they'd been gone a few days, the two of them showed up at my club. The long and the short of it was that they intended to blackmail me. And they did. Or Rance did. Sarah was uncomfortable with it right from the first, I could tell. But he had her completely under his control. What the kid had, I don't know, but this girl was ready to die for him.''

"Seems like maybe she did," Frank said.

Biff sighed. "That I don't know."

"They were blackmailing you," Abby said, taking him back to his story.

"Yeah. I gave them money, turned my condo over to them. Anything to keep Katerina from finding out. Meanwhile, Rance, the little shit, figured in Sarah he had a cottage industry, I guess. He turned my apartment into a whorehouse. But it wasn't to make a few bucks with Sarah turning tricks. Later I found out he was videotaping Sarah having sex with the johns, then turning around and blackmailing them, if you can believe it."

"How old was the kid?"

"I don't know, seventeen, eighteen. But he had his act together. The little bastard was a one-man crime wave, and I was caught in the middle. I sent a couple of guys to them, out-of-towners, people I didn't know. Believe me, I was really feeling the pressure. By accident Katerina found out what was going on. She was livid—mad at me for getting caught up in the mess, of course—but really pissed at what Rance was pulling. She took matters into her own hands, though. Ran the little sonovabitch off."

"The guys you sent," Frank said. "Was one of them Chet Wilsey?"

"Yeah. Friend of an old turkey I know named Witherspoon, the classic dirty old man—not that I'm in any position to throw stones." Biff shook his head with disgust. "I think there was maybe one guy I sent before that. Businessman from Houston, as I recall. Can't even tell you his name. Conventioneer. Never heard from him again.''

"But it sounds like Rance had other sources for finding his pigeons," Frank said.

"Yeah, he was running guys through there pretty regularly, I gather. How many of them he blackmailed, I don't know. He was only in business for a couple of weeks, max, so my guess is he only nailed a handful. I'm sure the victims have been keeping their heads down."

"Can you give us any names?"

"No, most of what I know about the men coming and going the building manager told me."

Frank recalled the manager gingerly stepping around the issue. Biff's account was fitting the facts they had. And it had the ring of truth. The amendments and corrections he'd made to Katerina's story added credibility to his version. But Frank also knew that might not be an accident.

"How did you know about Rance's blackmailing scam?" Abby asked.

"Rance told me. He came by my club one day the second week, asking me to send him customers. Like I say, I sent a few. But when I heard about the blackmail, I stopped cooperating. Frankly, when I first heard about Sarah drowning, I figured one of her johns must have done her in. I expected to hear about Rance's body turning up, as well. When it didn't, then I wondered if maybe he'd done it." Again Biff lowered his head. "To be honest, though, I was a hell of a lot more worried about my part in this than I was about them. I just prayed that once Sarah was dead, it'd all go away.

"Don't think my conscience wasn't eating at me, though, folks. I knew if it wasn't for me, none of this would have happened. That makes me responsible for Sarah's death in the moral, if not legal, sense.''

"When was the last time you saw her, Mr. Roberts?" Abby asked.

He cleared his throat. "I guess a week before her death was reported in the paper."

"You knew Jane Doe was Sarah because of the drawing?"

"That and the fact she was found in the Delta. I figured it must be connected with Wilsey. I mean, if not, it's a hell of a coincidence, right?"

"Yeah, right," Abby said, her brow furrowed pensively. She was consulting her notes.

Frank decided to satisfy his curiosity. "Biff, why do you have a one-way mirror in your apartment?"

Roberts drew a long, slow breath. "I could say it was there when I moved in, but the truth is, I get off on watching myself have sex. When a girlfriend stayed the night, I video-taped it. It sounds horrible, I know, but nobody was ever hurt by it. Once Katerina came into my life I destroyed my entire tape library."

"Did she know about it?" Abby asked, her disgust unmistakable.

"Like Katerina said, we have no secrets. I don't have to tell you how terribly forgiving the woman is."

"You're lucky," Abby said. "Incredibly lucky."

Biff nodded. "I know."

Abby glanced at Frank. "Any more questions?"

"Not for now."

She flipped her notebook closed. "We'll undoubtedly be talking to you again, Mr. Roberts, probably to make a more formal statement. I appreciate your cooperation. And I'd like you to search your memory and see if you can come up with any information on other men who might have been involved with Sarah while she was at your apartment."

"Okay."

Abby got to her feet. Frank did, as well. Biff didn't rise immediately.

"I know you've got enough to prosecute me for my involvement with Sarah," he said. "Having sex with her was criminal. And sending over the guys. May I ask what you intend to do about it?''

Abby contemplated him, not answering immediately. When she finally did speak, it was with caution. ''I'll have to think about it, but your cooperation has certainly been a positive. You've given us an explanation as to why Sarah might have died, but nothing that would help us understand what happened the night of her death.''

''That's because I was out of the picture by then.''

He glanced nervously back and forth between them. Frank decided on another zinger.

''Do you do drugs, Biff?'' he asked.

Roberts kind of flinched. ''Well…'' he stammered, ''I have on a recreational basis, like most people.''

''Ever do drugs with Sarah?''

He swallowed hard. ''Uh, no, not really.''

''Seems to me you either did or you didn't.''

Biff's expression hardened. ''I didn't.''

''Did she do drugs?''

Biff shrugged. ''How would I know?''

''You did spend a lot of time with her.''

''Yes, but not that way.'' His voice had grown thin.

''You were just screwing her, is that what you mean?''

''Look,'' Biff said, standing, ''I've tried hard to be co-operative at great risk to myself. Why are you hassling me?''

''I'm just asking you questions, Biff. You see, Jane Doe—Sarah—had been doing drugs, cocaine to be specific, the night she died. I just thought that might ring a bell.''

''I'm afraid it doesn't.''

Roberts made signs like he wanted them to leave. Abby didn't move, though.

''Mr. Roberts,'' she said, ''did Sarah happen to mention to you that she was pregnant?''

He blinked, no doubt weighing his answer like a man who wanted to be sure of the implications. ''Yes. When I first met her. I assumed that was why she was so eager to find Rance—because she was carrying his child.''

"But you never talked about it?"

"Not in detail. I did say something to Rance once—the time he came to talk to me at the club. I asked him why he didn't get her medical care. God knows he had plenty of money by then."

"What did he say?"

"He was shocked, asked if I was sure she was pregnant. I guess he didn't know about it, because it seemed to upset him. But then he left. That was the last time I ever saw him." He looked toward the doorway. "Look, folks, I've got to go talk to Katerina now. God only knows what she's thinking, whether she's going to kill me."

Frank followed Abby to the door. Passing through the entry hall, they saw the maid in back. Biff opened the door, clearly eager for them to leave. Abby handed him a business card she'd taken from her purse.

"We'll be in touch, Mr. Roberts," she said. "Give me a call if you remember something important before you hear from me."

"Sure," Biff said, stuffing the card in his pocket.

They went outside, the door closing quickly behind him. They made their way along the brick walk, headed for the pedestrian gate.

"I don't know about you," Abby said, "but I think the first order of business is to find Rance. And I also want to get hold of the authorities in Utah. It's time the folks at home find out about our poor little Jane Doe. Assuming we've got good information."

"Yeah, I agree." Frank opened the gate for her and Abby went through.

"So was Biff lying or telling the truth?" Abby asked.

"A little of both, I think," Frank replied. "I was with him

pretty much until right at the end. My question about the drugs seemed to unsettle him."

"Yeah, I noticed that, too. I wonder why."

She climbed into the driver's side of the Bronco, Frank the passenger side. Frank looked at the gray sky through the trees. There were speckles of mist on the windshield.

"Couldn't be fear of prosecution for possession," he said in response to her comment. "I mean, he gave us enough without any prodding to hang a couple of convictions on him. Admittedly it was pretty small stuff."

"He was almost a little too eager to be candid with us," Abby said. "I know he was trying to save Katerina from having to lie for him, but I got the feeling that… I don't quite know how to put it."

"Like he was giving us a bone?"

"Yeah," she said, "that's exactly right."

"Makes me wonder if what ol' Biff is covering up isn't big."

Abby started the engine. They headed up the street.

"Do you think Katerina's performance was part of the act?" she asked.

"The thought did cross my mind."

"She lies, then Biff comes in and spills his guts to us, making us think it's the truth."

"Right. And I think a lot of it was the truth," Frank said. "But some of it wasn't."

"When did you think he started veering from the truth?" she asked.

"You first," Frank said.

Abby thought for a moment. Suddenly she pulled over, stopped the Bronco and turned to him. "I'd say when I asked him when was the last time he saw Sarah."

"Yeah, he said it was a week before she drowned."

"I don't believe it," Abby said. "I'd bet you a week's pay that wasn't the last time he saw her."

"I have a hunch you're right."

"The question is, did he see her the night she died? And if so, how do we prove it?"

Frank pondered the comment, watching the rain hit on the windshield. Abby contemplated the rain, too. His thoughts turned from Biff Roberts to Abby. He'd enjoyed seeing her at work. He liked her style and her manner. She was disarming, but clever. Not a woman to lie to, that was clear.

That notion sent a twinge through him. For all of Biff's burdens and secrets, Frank couldn't forget the fact he had one of his own. At the moment Kay Ingram was probably the farthest person from Abby's mind, but she was right smack in the middle of his concerns. And she would be in Abby's, too, once he broached the subject. Good old Biff had come clean with Katerina and had survived. Could Frank be half so lucky with Abby?

"Hey, did you see who that was?" Abby said, pointing to the Mercedes that had just passed by.

"No, didn't notice."

"It was the maid, driving Katerina's car."

"Probably on the way to the supermarket," Frank said.

"Let's follow her!"

"Why?"

"Don't you think it would be interesting to find out what she can tell us about what really goes on in that house?"

Abby put the Bronco in gear and they took off up the street in pursuit of the Mercedes.

"I hope your Tagalog is better than mine, sweetheart."

"My what?"

"Tagalog. The main language of the Philippines."

"My, but aren't you a man of the world? Or is it because you've had a Filipina girlfriend?"

He shook his head. "Abby, when are you going to realize I'm just an unassuming, mild-mannered, small-town boy, not this big Casanova you make me out to be?"

Abby laughed. "Frank, your nose is going to grow."

He wasn't quite sure how serious she was. Was it teasing or was there more to it? "Hey," he said, pointing at the side street, "your girl turned there."

The tires squealing, Abby made a sharp turn. The Mercedes was already at the next corner. She goosed the accelerator, flipping on the windshield wiper at the same time.

They sailed along, racing past the big homes, in hot pursuit. Abby's blood was up. Frank decided it was too bad the maid had come along when she had. He'd been about to ask Abby where she wanted to spend the night.

San Francisco

Frank lay on the bed, listening to Abby brushing her teeth in the bathroom. They were in a modest motel on Lombard Street, waiting for Dix Fowler to return her call. Abby had decided to get Dix working on tracking down Rance Tully and locating Sarah Gibbs's family, and so she'd called him at home before they'd gone to dinner. Dix's wife, Cookie, had said he was off with a friend to look at a boat in Rio Vista but wouldn't be back too late. Now they had to wait and it was Abby who had to answer the phone.

She appeared at the bathroom door, dabbing her face with a hand towel. "In all the cases you've worked, Frank, have you ever seen everything turn on a coincidence?"

He thought about her question. "No, can't say that I have. I've had cases solved by pure chance, but that's different."

Abby came over and sat on the edge of the bed. "Yes, that is different."

"Can't get that maid out of your mind, can you?"

"You have to admit it's strange that Katerina would let a woman who'd worked for her for years go on the very weekend Sarah died."

"And the fact that the maid left the country immediately," he added.

"I'm sure Biff's responsible for Sarah's death, Frank. I feel it in my bones."

Frank didn't have to look hard to see Abby's passion for her work. She'd practically come running out of the supermarket after talking to Katerina's maid, Nedi. They'd decided Abby would go into the store alone, under the theory the two of them might overwhelm the poor woman. The strategy worked. Nedi had spoken freely to Abby. Unfortunately she'd only been on the job a week, so her knowledge was limited, but she had given a critical and, from Abby's standpoint, damning bit of information—the previous incumbent, a Filipina named Evelinda DeLeon, had not only left Katerina's employ suddenly, but within hours of leaving Marin, had left the country, as well. Coincidence? They'd talked about it all through dinner.

"I hope this man, Father Caratay, can help us track down Evelinda," Abby said, folding the towel neatly and laying it across her knee. She'd changed into her T-shirt.

Frank reached over and took her hand. "We'll find out tomorrow," he said.

Father Caratay was the priest, himself a Filipino, who'd gotten both Nedi and Evelinda their jobs working for Katerina Kreski. Like her father before her, Katerina was a major contributor to Catholic charities, which was how she met Caratay in the first place.

Abby said Nedi's English was so bad that she hadn't followed the story clearly, but several points had gotten through. Evelinda had left her job suddenly, returning to the Philippines. Nedi didn't know why, but she insisted that Father Caratay would know how to reach Evelinda as he was the shepherd of the Filipino community in Daly City where both women had lived.

Abby glanced at Frank, a touch embarrassed. "I know I

sound like a kid in a candy store," she said. "But I want very badly to solve this case."

"Your job doesn't turn on it, sweetheart. Or your reputation, either. I don't think there's a person in Riverton who doubts your competence. Even Chet had grudging respect for you."

"Really?"

"He didn't like to say nice things about you, but I could tell what he was really thinking. His only regret was that you weren't a man."

"That doesn't surprise me."

Frank pulled her down on the bed beside him. "I can't say that I share his view," he said, gently nuzzling her.

Abby put her arms around him. They were quiet for a minute, then she spoke again. "You know one of the people I want most to impress?"

"Who?"

"My mother." She drew a long breath. "I hadn't realized it before. I've repressed it, I think, but she might even have been a major reason I wanted to return to Riverton."

Kay again. Frank had this awful feeling, like his guts were being sucked right out of him. There would be no peace, he realized, until he got his former relationship with Kay out in the open. It was right, it was inevitable, but he was a coward. He could say something now, right now, but it didn't seem the time to do it. There was always a right moment or an inevitable moment for things like this, but in this instance, he was having a hard time finding it.

"This case really has nothing to do with Kay," he said.

"Not directly, of course. But she's involved in it emotionally. The whole town is. You and your situation at the beginning were the reason she and I first spoke. In an odd sort of way, Jane Doe brought us together—all of us, when you think about it."

He had a terrible sick feeling. Maybe now was the time to

speak. He searched for the courage. But then the phone rang. Saved by the bell. Or damned by it. Abby rolled over, reaching for the phone on the bedside table.

"Yes?... Oh, hi, Dix," she said. "We think we've got a name for Jane Doe. And a couple of suspects... Yeah, once we got on the trail things started falling into place. But listen, the reason I'm calling is I'd like you to check with the authorities in Utah and get the ball rolling on identifying this girl. And I want to put out an APB on her boyfriend."

As Frank listened, Abby gave Dix the particulars so that when he arrived at the station in the morning he could get to work on it first thing.

"I'll give you a call mid to late morning," she told Dix. "You can let me know if you've turned up anything."

Finishing her call, Abby hung up, almost gleeful. She rolled back over against him and gave him a peck on the corner of his mouth. Frank put his hand on her hip. Only then did he realize she didn't have anything on under the T-shirt. The effect on him was electric, almost instantaneous.

"How'd you like to have a party?" he murmured.

"Isn't that why we got one room with one bed?" she asked.

"I hate to be presumptuous."

Abby ran her hand down between them, pressing it against his genitals. "Bullshit," she said. "You've been thinking about getting laid all afternoon."

He pulled his head back. "Now what makes you so sure?"

"Frank, you're a man."

"Guilty as charged."

Abby kissed him then, rolled on top, her sweet, soft body pressing down on him. When the kiss ended, he turned his head and saw their reflection in the dresser mirror. Her T-shirt had hiked up and he was able to see the smooth curve of her ass. He put his hand on her haunch and caressed it, watching in the mirror. A surge of excitement went through him and Frank knew there'd be no conversation about Kay Ingram this night.

Monday
February 24th

San Francisco

The rain stopped as they walked back to the motel from the coffee shop where they'd had breakfast. Abby had been in good spirits all morning. She felt great. Frank, she surmised, while not in a funk, was a little more reflective. A couple of times she'd almost asked if something was wrong, but she didn't want to put pressure on him. Once a guy had his conquest, he could become skittish. Though her experience wasn't vast, she'd learned that it behooved a woman not to get too possessive.

But she did take his arm, hoping he might open up about whatever it was on his mind. Having given it some thought, she decided to take the initiative and move the conversation in the direction of their relationship.

"Was last night okay for you?" she asked.

"Abby, it couldn't have been better. You're fabulous. What's not to like?"

If he was saying he enjoyed the sex, there was no surprise there. Most men did. Thankfully, Frank was a considerate lover. But like most guys, he had this dark little corner he wanted to retreat into after sex, whereas she, like most women, wanted to explore the emotional ramifications of what had just happened. If the relationship continued, it would be something for them to talk about. Seeing he wasn't eager to open up, she decided to change the subject.

"So, how are we going to nail Biff?" she asked.

Frank laughed. "From sex with me to nailing Biff. I'd like to be privy to that thought sequence."

"No sequence, just a change of subject," she said. "But I wasn't drawing comparisons, if that was what you're worried about."

"I'm relieved because I don't think Biff will ever be one of my heros."

They were standing at the corner, waiting for the light to change so they could cross Lombard Street. Abby let go of his arm. Maybe it was time for a little distance, she decided. You couldn't let a guy get too complacent.

Frank glanced down at her. She gave him a smile. The light changed and they stepped off the curb.

They were maybe three steps into the street when the roar of an engine in combination with the screech of tires made them look back. A car, making the turn from the side street, came hurtling toward them. They leaped back at the same time, the car narrowly missing them. But the right front fender did catch her purse and, as she spun through the air, the bumper hit her left foot, throwing her into Frank. They tumbled to the ground, landing in a heap on the pavement. Frank was under her.

"Jesus Christ!" he exclaimed as the vehicle, an old Chevy, went careening on up Lombard, giving no sign whatsoever it intended to stop.

At the next corner the car went through a changing light, nearly hitting a panel truck coming from the side street. Abby and Frank both watched the vehicle disappear from sight.

"Are you all right?" he asked.

They got to their feet. Gingerly.

Abby's foot hurt a little, but she'd taken most of the impact on the side and sole of her shoe. Her purse had been ripped from her hand and knocked farther up the street, its contents spread out on the asphalt. "Yeah, I'm all right," she said, even as her heart raced wildly from the adrenaline rush. "How about you?"

"Fine for somebody who just took a header in the street."

He brushed himself off. Abby checked the traffic before heading for her purse. The light had changed, but most of the drivers had seen what happened and proceeded past them cautiously. A guy in the middle lane rolled down his window and hollered at them.

"You people okay?"

Frank told him they were and followed Abby to where her purse had landed. He stood behind her, watching the traffic as she scooped her things back into her purse. Then she limped with him to the curb, her foot starting to ache a little.

"Did you get a license number?" she asked, taking a deep breath, hoping to quiet her pounding heart.

"No rear plate."

"Driver?"

"Didn't see him," he replied.

"Me, neither, though I had the impression there was more than one person in the car."

"Could be a stolen vehicle, kids on a joyride," Frank said.

Abby looked down at her shaking hands. "Somehow I don't think it was an accident." She noticed that Frank's hands were scraped where he'd landed on the pavement, and there was a tear in his pants. "We've made a few enemies recently. The question is, which one of them is behind this?"

Frank wiped off his hands with his handkerchief. "We didn't know Biff when we got jumped at the Vietnam Memorial," he said, "but it could be we're on more than one hit list. Either that, or someone is being pretty damned persistent."

"Then there's our old friend, coincidence," she said, testing her foot. "We might just be unlucky."

"Unlucky in crime, but lucky in love."

She gave him a look, then flexed her knee.

"Leg hurting you?" he asked.

"The car bumped my foot. Mostly hit my shoe. It was a glancing blow. I'm okay."

"I say we don't bother calling the police, because it'll cost us time and there's nothing to be accomplished," he said.

"It's people like you who make the criminal's job easier, Frank."

He gave her cheek a pinch. "Save that for when you're up against me for re-election."

"Plan to oppose me, do you?"

"I *am* responsible for all the critical breaks in the case, aren't I?"

Abby was ready to pounce, but then she realized he was kidding her. She whacked his stomach with the back of her hand. "You can be replaced, Keegan."

"But if I'm gone, who would keep a smile on the chief's face?"

"Before you get too cocky, there's only two of us who know what's happened the last couple of nights. I'll deny any rumors you start."

"How are you going to explain expensing only one hotel room?"

Abby considered his comment. "Oh, shit. I never thought about that."

Frank chuckled, taking her arm as the light changed again. "Maybe you can get the hotel to print up a phony receipt."

They checked the traffic carefully before starting across the street.

"I swear, Frank Keegan, you're living proof that the line between cops and robbers is a very thin one."

He laughed and squeezed her arm.

As they made their way back to the motel, her foot tight-ened up, but the pain wasn't bad. It was swelling, but she didn't think it was serious. The incident concerned her, though. Joking aside, they could easily have been killed. It was obviously time to watch their back a bit more carefully.

Abby lay on the bed, her foot propped on a pillow. Wrapped around it was a makeshift ice pack Frank had made from a plastic bag and ice from the motel machine. She was on the phone, trying to track down Father Caratay, the priest. The second parish church she called in Daly City was the winner, but the good father wasn't in. She made an appoint-ment for two o'clock that afternoon.

"So, what are we going to do to kill time?" Frank asked, his mouth twisted into a wry grin.

"You have a suggestion?"

"Well…I thought since you're already laid up in bed with that foot…"

"Yeah, I bet you were, Frank. But as Chief of Police of Riverton, I have a responsibility to the taxpayers. I don't think they'd appreciate my having trysts in San Francisco with the town dandy while on duty."

"Town dandy?"

She laughed to herself, realizing her teasing was starting to get to him. Of course, he was probably secretly pleased because men loved being admired for their libido. Frank, though, truly was worthy of admiration. She was becoming quite fond of him. And the better she got to know him, the more natural their relationship felt. For the first time she was beginning to imagine a future for them.

"More importantly," she said, "we've got work to do. I told Dix I'd check in with him and see how he's doing with Sarah and Rance."

"Okay, but you gotta eat. How about if I take you some-place nice for lunch? My treat."

"That's sweet, but at this rate you're going to blow all the money Chet gave you in one weekend."

"It's been worth every minute."

He was standing at the foot of the bed. Abby held out her hand and he stepped to her side, taking her fingers. She looked up at him, feeling a clutch of emotion, and said, "You know, for all the adversity we've faced and all the roadblocks, we've managed to get along fairly well, haven't we?"

"From my perspective that's putting it mildly, Abby. I've gotten pretty damned fond of you."

"I've gotten pretty damned fond of you, too."

The expression on his face was less joyful than she would have expected, maybe even pained. Sometimes he surprised her. The man was more complex than he appeared. But he was a wonderful lover—not the sort of attribute you'd normally associate with a retired cop and pear farmer. Or were her feelings more a reflection of her own need?

Abby gave his hand a final squeeze, then reached for the phone. She called her office.

"Good news and bad," Dix Fowler said, coming on the line.

"Let's have it," she said.

"I tracked down the town the kids are from in Utah. Morgan Springs, in Franklin County. I'm expecting a call back from the sheriff, a guy named Pierce Holland. From what his secretary said, there's quite a story behind those kids, Chief."

"You don't know what it is?"

"She wanted me to talk to him. Should be calling any minute."

"What's the bad news, Dix?"

"You won't be talking to the boy, Rance Tully. He's dead."

The words surprised her. Dead? Shit. Abby had been counting on Rance Tully filling in all the blanks in the case. "Damn," she muttered.

"Hold on, Chief," Dix said. "I've got a call coming in. It might be the sheriff. Let me put you on hold."

Abby looked sadly at Frank. "Rance is dead."

"How?"

"I don't know. Dix was about explain when he got a call. It must be something that happened in—"

"Chief," the sergeant said, coming back on the line. "It's him. Want me to patch the call through?"

"Sure. Might as well talk to him directly."

After a few moments Abby heard a gravelly voice.

"Hello?"

"Hello, Sheriff Holland? This is Abby Hooper, Riverton Chief of Police."

"Morning, Chief Hooper. Understand I'm speaking to you in Frisco."

"Yes, we've traced Sarah Gibbs here and think she may be the Jane Doe who turned up dead in Sacramento County about ten days ago."

"So I understand," Holland said. "Your deputy faxed us a lot of information early this morning and we've spent a couple of hours trying to sort things out on our end. I'm embarrassed to say this, but it wasn't until a day or two ago that we were even aware Sarah was missing. Her mother came to see me."

"And her boyfriend, Rance Tully. I understand he's dead."

"Right."

"Could you fill me in, Sheriff? We suspect foul play and it would be helpful to have a little background."

"Both Sarah and Rance were members of a bizarre religious sect called the Disciples of God's Shepherd. The Disciples got started maybe fifteen or twenty years ago when a small group of breakaway Mormons founded a commune on a ranch outside Morgan Springs. They were a secretive bunch, kept the outside world at bay and were rumored to be practicing all kinds of crazy rituals. Recent events have brought some of their beliefs and practices to light. Believe me, Chief Hooper, some of it defies the imagination.''

''Is there anything that would help explain Sarah's death?'' Abby asked.

''It certainly explains what she was doing in Frisco.''

''Go ahead.''

''Well, we've confirmed that the Disciples, that is, the elders, the men in charge, were exploiting their women and children something terrible. These fellows set things up so they had total control of the women, trading wives and daughters with each other, taking young girls as wives—sex slaves might be more accurate. These old boys began by controlling the wealth of the sect. Young men either had to buy their way in, if they had the means, or they got run out once they came of age.

''What we learned from Sarah's mother was that the girl and Rance fell in love and wanted to be together. Since the boy didn't have money, he wasn't eligible to have his own woman. Sometime last summer the elders, including the boy's father, Ezra Tully, ran Rance out. Meanwhile, they decided it was time for Sarah to marry, and Elroy Gibbs, her father, gave her to Ezra.''

''Sarah's father gave her to her boyfriend's father?'' Abby said incredulously.

''This is a crazy bunch, Chief Hooper.''

''That's putting it mildly.''

''It gets worse.''

Abby wasn't sure anything would surprise her at this point. ''Go on, Sheriff.''

''Evidently Sarah resisted violently and Ezra decided she needed to be collared. Their practice, we've learned, was to lock up and isolate the young brides from the other women until they got pregnant. Only then were they allowed back into the community.''

"My God."

"We in government have been suspicious that abuse of this kind was going on, but the Disciples successfully fought legal challenges from the county, including the right to educate their children at the commune. The women and young people were never allowed to leave the ranch. Only the men ever came to town."

"I can see why. Their little setup sounds like something out of the Dark Ages," Abby said. "It's barbaric."

"It certainly is. People do incredible things in the name of religion. But to get back to my story. The information given me by Alice Gibbs, Sarah's mother, was that once the girl was pregnant and freed from confinement, she immediately ran away. The first female ever to defy the elders, successfully, anyway."

In light of what had happened to the girl, Abby would have questioned the term "successfully," but she didn't comment. Frank, who was unable to hear, waited quietly, but she knew he could tell from what he heard on her end of the conversation that the story wasn't a pretty one.

"Obviously Sarah made it to San Francisco," Abby said. "We know part of what happened once she got here, but what's with Rance? How did he die?"

"We had our own little Valentine's Day massacre down here, Chief Hooper. A week ago last Friday, Rance Tully showed up here in Barton, the county seat. He bought himself a rifle, a couple of handguns and some ammunition and he drove to Morgan Springs. The accounts vary from that point, but our best guess is that Rance entered the Disciples compound and confronted the elders. Flashing rolls of money, he demanded to be made a full member in the club. I don't know if he robbed a bank or where he got his cash, but he was determined to become a player."

"He robbed what was left of Sarah's virtue, Sheriff," Abby said. "That's where he got his money." Adding a few words of explanation concerning Rance's blackmail scheme, she then asked Pierce Holland to continue.

"Things turned nasty at that point," Holland said. "There were words and tempers flared. Eventually gunfire broke out. Rance and Elroy Gibbs were killed outright, but not before Ezra Tully and three other men were wounded, Ezra seriously. He's still clinging to life in the hospital here, but the prospects aren't good. For a couple of days after the gun battle the sect was in shock, then people started leaving the compound. As the women and children began to surface and their stories were heard, all of Franklin County went into shock."

"Has Sarah's mother been told we have a Jane Doe who may be her daughter?" Abby asked.

"Yes. This morning I called the shelter where she and the younger children are staying. I guess she'd been expecting the worst. All she'd say was that dying in the water must have been God's plan."

"What did she mean by that?"

"This is arid country here in Suthern Utah, Chief Hooper. Water's at a premium. The Disciples of God's Shepherd believed it should be used only for drinking, bathing and baptizing. Needless to say, there were no swimming pools in the compound. Our information is that none of the children were taught to swim, by design. The idea was to enter the rite of baptism in fear of your life."

"And people call California the Land of Fruits and Nuts," Abby said.

"There are crazies everywhere, I'll grant you that."

"You've been generous with your time, Sheriff Holland," she said. "If there are dental records or anything that might help us make a positive identification of Sarah, we'd appreciate you sending them along."

"As I understand it, my people have already heard from your coroner's office."

"Good. Then it's in the hands of the technicians."

"I don't know if my information has helped with your case," Holland said, "but if there's anything else we can do, give us a holler."

"Thank you, Sheriff."

Abby hung up the phone and turned to Frank. "I couldn't begin to make up what I'm about to tell you," she said.

"What's the bottom line?"

"It's looking certain that Jane Doe is Sarah Gibbs."

"But Rance is dead."

"Yes," Abby said. "We've lost him not only as a witness, but as a suspect, too. He was in Utah, getting killed in a gun battle while Sarah was being drugged, raped and drowned here in California."

"Which means that Biff is still at the top of our list of suspects."

"My list, anyway."

"What's next?" Frank asked. "Genetic testing?"

"Maybe. As soon as we get back to Riverton, I'm giving the D.A. a call."

"First we've got lunch and the priest."

"What a way to spend an afternoon," she said with a laugh.

He arched a brow. "We can always stay here."

Abby swung her legs off the bed. "Come on, Keegan, we've got work to do."

Ocean Beach

The air was cold and damp, the gray sky so opaque that water, land and sky blended into one gauzy continuum. Abby limped along beside Frank, who kept staring out at the roiling white surf. They hadn't spoken much since leaving the Cliff House where they'd had lunch among the tourists, watching the sea lions cavorting on seal rock.

"I thought in winter it wouldn't be so touristy," Frank had said by way of apology.

"We aren't that different from the tourists," she'd assured him. "Not when you stop to think about it. In fact, my dad brought me to the Cliff House a couple of times when I was a kid. I loved watching the seals."

And she'd enjoyed seeing them again as an adult. There were hundreds of seagulls, as well, soaring poetically above the cliffs, but they hadn't stuck in her mind the way the seals had—or for that matter the bread sticks and the vanilla ice cream. San Francisco carried with it more nostalgic memories than she realized.

After they'd finished lunch Frank asked her if she wanted to visit the zoo, since they were already on the nostalgia trail, but she'd said that might be overdoing it. They were on tax-payers' time, after all. "But I wouldn't mind walking on the beach for a few minutes."

Abby and her father had done that, as well. It was at Ocean Beach that she'd seen the sea for the first time, and she recalled how gray, cold and frightening it had seemed, especially for a summer day when over in the Delta, a mere seventy-five miles away, it was a hundred degrees and water-skiers and speedboat jockeys were cavorting in the blazing sun.

"Sure you're up to walking on that foot?" Frank had asked.

"I think a little exercise would be good for it," she'd replied. "I don't want it to stiffen up."

They hadn't gone far from the parking lot, but walking in sand was not easy on the legs. At low tide, especially, there was plenty of it to cross to get to water's edge. They were maybe thirty yards from a man surf fishing when she stopped because her foot started to throb.

"You okay?" Frank asked.

"Maybe if I rest for a minute."

She dropped into the sand. Before Frank sat beside her, he turned to scan the beach in the direction of the parking lot. He hadn't said anything, but she'd noticed he was being extra vigilant. Nearly getting run down by that old Chevy had been a wake-up call. Abby also realized that a lone fisherman and a passing jogger notwithstanding, Ocean Beach on a foggy day in the dead of winter wasn't a bad place for a hit or even an act of violence designed to intimidate. The question was, who would want to hurt them and for what reason? If it was Biff Roberts, surely he didn't think he could dissuade them from their investigation.

Abby glanced over at Frank, who was staring out to sea. For a while she watched little balls of foam tumble across the wet sand. The briny wind stung her eyes, making them water. Frank's eyes were shimmering, too. He seemed terribly sad.

"You all right?" she asked.

Frank turned toward her, his eyes so liquid that she decided there was more than the biting wind at play. He wiped his eyes with his sleeve. "Sorry, feeling a little sentimental."

She gave him a questioning look.

"This is where my daughter drowned," he explained.

"Oh, Frank, I'm so sorry." She put her arm around him. "Why didn't you say something? We didn't have to come out here."

"I've been avoiding visiting the place because I knew I'd get all choked up, and I am. But it's something I was going to have to do eventually. I'm glad I could do it with you."

Abby was touched. Pulling him closer, she put her head on his shoulder. Frank patted her hand, obviously appreciative of her concern and emotional support.

Thinking about it, she did recall that he'd told her his daughter had drowned at Ocean Beach. But she'd been so wrapped up in the case and her own petty concerns that she'd forgotten.

"Does it hurt a lot?" she asked.

"More than I expected," he replied, his voice cracking. He tried to smile. "I don't know if a loss like this is worse than any other, but it's especially painful for me knowing that I was only a part-time father. I could never see Beth without my problems with her mother getting in the way. San Francisco was Beth's home, and I was just the father who lived over in the Delta in a trailer. But despite all that, I guess my biggest single disappointment is knowing I'll never being able to see my child as an adult."

Abby took his hand and kissed it, her heart going out to him. She'd had similar feelings of compassion when she'd thought about Alice Gibbs, Sarah's mother, and how she must be suffering now. Maybe the woman had contributed to her daughter's demise. Or maybe she had been so thoroughly victimized herself that there was nothing she could possibly do. Either way, Abby imagined the woman in terrible anguish. And how much more difficult it must be knowing the horror Sarah endured in the final months and weeks of her life. It was almost unbearable to think of one's own child suffering through those atrocities, the inhumanity and depravity she had to bear.

Abby understood more clearly Frank's passion about the Jane Doe case and how hard it must have been for him to have been a suspect. He was a quiet man, not given to displays of emotion, but she'd never doubted his humanity. It was his seeming decency that made it so hard for her to believe he'd been involved.

They'd covered a lot of ground since Sarah Gibbs had been Jane Doe. Abby knew Frank much better—not just as a lover, but as a man. Events had affected her in important ways. She'd reassessed a number of long-standing issues in her life. She'd broken the emotional hold Darren had on her, and she'd lowered some of the barriers between herself and her mother.

When she thought about it, that was one of the more ironic byproducts of the Jane Doe tragedy. Not surprisingly, Alice Gibbs's and Frank's suffering gave her new feelings of compassion for Kay. Parents were only human, and it was a mistake, perhaps, for a child to take a mother or father's failings personally.

Frank, who wasn't dressed for the biting wind, shivered and pulled his collar up. Abby rubbed his back.

"Let's go back to the car," she said. "No sense you getting sick on top of everything else."

He didn't object, helping her to her feet. Her bruised foot throbbed when she put weight on it, but the pain wasn't too bad. Again, Frank surveyed the scene before they began walking toward the parking lot. Abby checked her watch. They still had plenty of time before they had to be in Daly City, which bordered San Francisco on the south. All they had to do was follow the highway along the ocean, past the zoo and Lake Merced, and they'd be in Daly City. There'd be little traffic. In twenty minutes they'd be at Father Caratay's church.

When they reached the Bronco, Frank let her in the passenger side. Because of her foot, Abby had asked him to drive. He went around and got in, putting the key in the ignition without starting the engine. Then he just sat there, gripping the wheel. She knew something was wrong. But before she could ask, he spoke.

"Abby, we need to talk about something."

His ominous tone gave her pause. "What, Frank?"

"I've been agonizing over something for days and I realize I can't keep it inside any longer. There's something about me you need to know."

She waited, his tone having scared her.

"It concerns the mystery woman," he said. "The one who was with me the night Sarah died."

Dread came over her. She knew from his demeanor she

wasn't going to like what he had to say. Tense, she took a calming breath. "And?"

"Abby, it was your mom." He hesitated. "Kay was with me that night."

The words were so unexpected that for a long moment they didn't fully register. "My mother?"

"Yes. Kay and I had a relationship. It ended more than a year ago. Before she and Mort became an item."

"You're saying you and my mother had an affair."

"Yes."

Abby was stunned. How could she not have known this? For the past two nights she'd slept with a man who'd been her mother's lover. She thought of the conversations she'd had with her mother, the way she'd protected Frank. And Abby thought of the conversations she'd had with Frank, and the way he'd protected Kay. The two of them, playing her for a fool.

Abby flushed. Frank reached over to take her hand. She jerked it away.

"Why didn't you tell me?" she demanded.

"I've been trying to, but I just couldn't find the right moment."

"What was wrong with the very beginning, when the issue first came up?" she snapped.

"I felt I owed it to your mother to be discreet. It wasn't just you I was concerned about. Kay is involved with Mort and she didn't need him knowing she stayed at my place that night. It was sort of an accident…I mean, it didn't mean anything. And when I told you I couldn't remember anything about it, that was the truth."

"Sure, Frank." She was livid, embarrassed, humiliated. She felt like a total and complete fool.

"I was concerned about your mother, but that wasn't the only reason. I was afraid of what you might think of me."

"For good reason!" she shot back.

"I cared about you, Abby, even then. I was attracted to you, and because of the problems you and Kay had, I wasn't eager to tell you about our past."

"No, that's obvious, isn't it? But now that you've gotten laid, you can do the honorable thing, right?"

"Please, Abby, it's not that way at all. I care about you. That's why this is so hard for me."

"Don't give me that bullshit. You wanted to get me in bed before you gave me the news. You could have told me before, but you didn't. Do you know how humiliated I am? How stupid I feel?"

"What would you have had me do? What happened between Kay and me was before you and I became friends."

"Yes, but you hid it from me!" she cried, tears filling her eyes.

Frank sighed mournfully.

Abby was so upset she began trembling. If it hadn't been her car, she'd have gotten out and left. Half of her wanted to get out, anyway. She could barely make herself look at him, but she did.

"I want to know one thing, Frank Keegan, and I want it to be the goddamn truth. Does my mother know about us?"

He closed his eyes. He was in pain, but she didn't give a damn. She wanted to know.

"*Does* she?"

"She knows I care for you. Obviously she doesn't know we've been intimate."

"Oh, Jesus," Abby said. "You know what I feel like? A twelve year-old, a kid who's being parentified. Nobody wants to look me in the eye and tell me the truth."

She glared at him, her eyes narrowing with disgust. "I'd like to know how many people know about you and my mother. Is it the whole town? Am I the only one who didn't know?"

He groaned. "It wasn't common knowledge, but there

were quite a few people who were aware. The insiders—let's put it that way.''

"The insiders," she said. "Boy, isn't that an appropriate term." She shook her head, gazing out the side window.

"As far as the rest of the world is concerned, your virtue is intact," he said. "You may consider me a horse's ass, but I won't be going to the River Queen and entertaining the boys with the details."

Abby looked away with disgust. Neither one said anything as they each struggled with their thoughts.

"I'd hoped that maybe my feelings for you would be enough for you to overlook the past," he said, his voice gentler. "There was nothing I could do to change it. Kay and I were over and done with when I met you."

"She's my mother, for godsakes!"

His expression turned grim. "All right, Abby—I fucked up and you can't forgive me. That's obvious. Just tell me what you want me to do. Do you want me to get out of the car?"

He was either calling her bluff or shaming her. She wasn't sure which. The only thing she knew for sure was that she hated this. How could she look the man in the eye, much less have a professional relationship with him, knowing what she knew now? She couldn't be around him without thinking he'd made love to her mother, as well as to her. It wasn't a crime, maybe, but it wasn't something she wanted to endure, either. And it didn't seem to matter that she and her mother weren't at all close and that Kay had done precious little mothering over the years.

"I'd like a little time and distance from this," she said.

"I take it that means get out." He opened the door. "I assume you can drive, despite the foot."

"Frank, close the door."

"There'll be a phone booth nearby. I can get a taxi to the bus station."

"No," she said, "I'm not going to let you do that."

"You've got to get down to Daly City to see the priest. We're wasting time talking." He climbed out of the Bronco, opened the rear door and took out his overnight bag. Before closing the front door, he leaned in and said, "For the record, I want you to know I care for you more than any woman I've ever known. In some ways the last couple of days have been the best of my life. I'm sorry I hurt you. It wasn't my intent."

"Frank—"

"Just do your job, Abby. You don't need me."

With that, he closed the door and walked away.

For a moment she sat, stunned. The world she'd known ten minutes ago smashed to smithereens. She was alone again. Really alone.

A light rain began speckling the windshield. Down at water's edge she could see the angry, roiling surf. She thought of Frank's daughter being grabbed by the undertow and pulled into the sea. Tears spurted from her eyes and she began to sob. She cried for Beth, she cried for Sarah and she cried for herself. More than ever before, life seemed to her terribly, terribly unjust.

East Levee Road
Riverton

The town didn't have a bus station. With only four coaches winding their way through the Delta each day—two upriver, two downriver—there was no need for one. Passengers boarded and disembarked in front of the Aspeth Drugstore, which was located on the Bottoms side of the river, across from the bridge. There had been twenty or thirty passengers aboard when the bus left the Bay Area, but the count was down to three by the time Frank stepped onto the sidewalk in Riverton.

It was nine o'clock at night. Planes had flown from San Francisco to Boston and New York in the time it had taken him to get from San Francisco to the Delta. The old Chinese woman who sat next to him made the trip from Locke, the little town upriver from Riverton, into San Francisco every weekend to visit her daughter and son. Frank told her she deserved a medal. She disagreed, saying she liked the bus, especially in summer, because it was cooler than her house. It also gave her a chance to see the world. The comment made him realize how relative everything was.

A light rain was falling and Frank moved under the awning of the drugstore to make his decision about how to get home. Walking it would take the better part of an hour. The alternative was to go to the River Queen and see if he could find someone to give him a lift. There were advantages and disadvantages to each scenario. The rain convinced him the Queen was the way to go, especially when it began coming down harder. He pressed closer to the window and the cardboard Dr. Scholl's foot-powder display behind the glass, trying to keep dry. After several minutes the rain eased up and Frank decided it wouldn't be getting any better. He began walking the two long blocks to the Queen.

It had been a miserable day, and being home did nothing to raise his spirits. If anything, it made the agony of his rupture with Abby even worse. Having had plenty of time to think it over, he decided that her displeasure was inevitable and that it had been selfish of him to try to finesse his way past it. Maybe she was right; maybe he had been so eager to get laid that he'd rationalized. But it wasn't just sex, that much he knew. He'd wanted her like he'd never wanted any woman.

Monday nights at the Queen were slow except during football season when Kay tuned the big TV above the bar into the game. That and the network news were about the only things she put on. Kay didn't like television, but she liked the football crowd because they pumped up business on a slow night, and she believed that everybody should be informed about the goings-on in Washington. But football season was over, and thanks to the rain, the Queen was practically deserted when, dripping wet, Frank made his entrance.

Toad was tending bar. Seeing Frank, he gave him the high sign, tossing his head in the direction of the front booth, where Judge Fred Parker sat in a three-piece suit, studying his pocket watch. At about the same moment, the judge looked up and, spotting him, waved him over. Frank set his case down by the door.

"Toad," he called to the bartender, "bring me a double martini, will you?" Then he went over to the booth.

"Good, I was hoping you'd show up here," the judge said, offering his hand. The old man looked him over closely. "You're soaked. Where's your coat?"

"You know how it is with us farmers, Judge, we don't even notice the rain." Frank slipped into the booth across from him.

"A good way to catch your death. But that's another matter. I want you to know I tried calling your place, dropped by earlier this evening, all to no avail."

"What's up?" Frank said, noticing the watery glass of whiskey sitting in front of the old man.

"I've got an urgent message for you from Lloyd Witherspoon," the judge replied. "I must say I don't understand it, but Lloyd insisted I deliver it today, in person—for which I'm charging him handsomely, I might add."

"What's the message?"

"Lloyd intends to contest Chet's will unless he has your agreement not to publicly divulge any matter you've discussed with him this weekend. I trust that makes sense. It doesn't to me, but he wouldn't elaborate."

Frank reflected. "Yeah, I know what he's getting at."

"Are you in agreement?"

Frank thought some more. "Tell Lloyd I won't be blackmailed."

Judge Parker's brows rose. "Blackmail?"

"He'll understand, Judge."

"Shall I tell him your answer is no, then?"

"I'm not saying no, I'm not saying yes. Just let him know the case is going where the evidence takes it and nobody's getting preferential treatment."

"My, that does sound ominous."

"That's my answer," Frank said.

The judge consulted his watch again. "Well, I must telephone Lloyd and report. Then I'm headed for home and my nice warm bed. This is not an evening for an old man to be about."

"You're going to phone Lloyd now?"

"That's what he wanted—for me to call as soon as I have your response."

"Judge, is this threat of his serious?"

"From his standpoint or from the standpoint of the law?"

"The law."

Judge Parker rolled his eyes as if to say, "Of course not," but his actual words were, "Due to a potential conflict of interest, I'm not at liberty to say." With effort, he scooted from the booth. "Frank, my old bones are crying for relief. I'm making my call from the pay phone and I'm going home. Good night."

"Night, Judge."

As Fred Parker tottered off toward the pay phone in back, Toad arrived with the martini. Frank picked up the glass, measured it, then took a big slug. "Ah," he said as the sting made its way to his stomach. He hadn't had dinner and so he knew the martini would hit him right between the eyes. That was fine, though. At worst he'd be walking home drunk. Toad studied him with a bemused grin.

"How come you're so wet, Frank? Forget your umbrella?"

Frank took another gulp of his cocktail. "Wet, dry, what's the difference? Unless we're discussing martinis, of course." He cast a glance around the bar. There were a couple of old fellows sitting at the far end. The faces were familiar, but Frank didn't know them. "Kay off tonight?"

"Nope. She's back in her office, going over bills."

"*Is* she?"

"Yep."

Frank thought for a second. "Maybe I'll go back and have a word with her." He picked up his martini and finished the drink off, wincing. Then he handed the glass to Toad. "Bring another into Kay's office, will you, sport?"

"Sure thing."

Frank made his way back through the barroom. When he got to the alcove in back, the judge was just hanging up the phone. Nodding, the old man turned and went into the men's room. Frank continued on back, then rapped on Kay's door. While he waited he had a vision of Abby as she'd looked that afternoon when he'd told her his news. The horror on her face would probably stay with him until his dying day.

"Yes?" Kay called from inside.

He opened the door. Kay, in one of her sweaters, voluptuous as ever, sat at her desk, a lamp shining on the papers before her. Her hair was pulled back off her face. The image was terribly familiar, particularly with the ether of alcohol beginning to fog his brain.

"Well, look who the cat dragged in," she said, not sounding altogether displeased.

He leaned against the door frame. "Got a minute?"

"Is it business or social?"

"A little of each."

"Come in, then," Kay said.

Frank stepped inside, closing the door. He slumped into the chair across from her. "I fucked up," he announced.

Kay blinked. "Should I be alarmed?"

"Mainly I'm here to warn you so you can be prepared."

"Jesus. Prepared for what?"

He drew a long breath, but before he could speak Toad knocked and came in with the martini, placing it on the desk. He left without a word. Frank picked up the glass and drained the liquid partway down, then put the glass back on the desk.

Folding his hands over his stomach, he looked at Kay from under his brows. "I told Abby about us."

She studied him uncertainly. "You told her we…"

"…were lovers."

"Oh, God," she said, closing her eyes for a moment. "Why, Frank?"

"She was going to find out eventually, anyway, and I couldn't go on living a lie."

Kay didn't move or blink. "So, the two of you are having a relationship."

"*Were* having a relationship is probably more accurate."

She put her head in her hands.

"I was trapped, Kay. I didn't know what to do. I remembered you saying don't hurt her. And I also remembered you saying your relationship with her meant more than anything. I did what I thought was right, but it ended up pissing her off. God only knows how it'll affect you, but I figured you ought to know about it."

Her expression hardened. "You slept with her, didn't you?"

Frank took another swallow of his martini. "With all due respect, that's none of your business."

"Well, I know you did, otherwise she wouldn't have gotten so upset and you wouldn't be getting drunk."

He slurped more of his drink. "Women are too damned smart for their own good."

"Stupid is more like it."

Frank, getting tipsy fast, waved his finger at her. "There's nothing wrong with caring for a man."

"No, as long as you know you'll have to end up shooting him if you want to keep your self-respect. Damn it, Frank, how could you be so heartless?"

"The problem wasn't heartlessness, it was too *much* heart."

"Too much something else, more likely."

"Well, the point is, I've come to confess all so that you can do whatever you have to do to save your relationship with her. I'm putting you and Abby above everything else." He had another drink of his martini.

"What, exactly, did you tell her?" Kay asked.

"Just that we were lovers. I didn't go into your sexual preferences, if that's what you're worried about."

"Watch it, Frank. You're already in enough trouble."

He shrugged, feeling the effects of the vodka.

"Did you tell her I was at your house that night the girl drowned?"

Frank shifted uneasily. "I believe I mentioned that."

"Oh, shit."

"It was the truth, Kay. You were going to tell her yourself, remember?"

"There's a right time for the truth and a wrong time."

"What would you have had me do?"

She sighed. "I don't know. It's a tough situation. But I'm glad you told me. I guess I'll have to talk to Abby. She may end up hating me as much for this as she does you."

"Why? *You* didn't go to bed with her," he said, the vodka really beginning to hit him.

She shook her head, looking at him like he was a lost cause. Suddenly the door flew open. Frank, startled by the sound, whipped his head around. It was Mort Anderson.

"What the hell is going on?" Mort demanded, his face beet-red.

"Jesus Christ," Frank muttered. "Who'll be next—Santa Claus or the goddamn Easter Bunny?"

"Mort," Kay snapped, "what are you doing barging into my office like this?"

"No, the question is, what are you doing playing footsie with this bum?"

"Hey, wiseass," Frank said, bristling, "who're you calling a bum?" He started to get to his feet.

"Sit down, Frank, and shut up," Kay commanded. She turned her attention to Mort. "Do we look like we're playing footsie? We're discussing business. And I'll thank you not to question who I talk to."

"Keegan is interested in one thing and one thing only, Kay," Mort spat, his face still red. "Everybody knows that."

"I think I can handle it," she replied. "And I can also handle men who think that just because they're involved with me, they own me."

Mort frowned. "It's not that at all. It's this sonovabitch," he said, gesturing toward Frank. "Isn't it obvious what he's here for?"

"Mort, he's the one who's drunk, not me! Now if you don't mind, I'd like to finish my conversation. Will you please go?"

Frank reached for his glass, pleased to hear Kay giving it to Mort. He took a long swallow.

Mort huffed and puffed, but finally went to the door. "You don't know what a good thing you've got, Kay. It almost seems like you *want* to blow it!"

"Way to go, Mort," Frank said. "Threaten the lady. That'll make her swoon."

"Shut up, Frank!" Kay snapped.

Mort Anderson turned on his heel and went out, slamming

the door behind him. Kay leaned back heavily in her chair and sighed.

"Dear Lord," she murmured.

Frank appraised her. "Do you really like that moron?"

She shook a threatening finger at him. "I don't want to hear another word. You've screwed up enough lives for one day."

Her words sobered him. "Do you really think I've messed up Abby's life?"

"Women always survive bad experiences with men," she replied. "If they didn't the species would have died out long ago." She paused. "But don't worry about it. I'll see what I can do to repair the damage."

"For me?"

"No, for me." Then she added, "But if I can help you at the same time, I will."

He released a breath, feeling better.

"But don't count on anything."

"Hell, I know better than to count on anything, Kay."

She gave him a sad smile.

"I'm sorry about Mort," he said.

She shrugged. "He's the jealous type. Maybe I should feel flattered." Then, shaking her head, she said, "Now go on, get out of here. You've done enough for one day."

Frank considered mentioning he needed a ride, but decided not to press his luck. He got to his feet and went to the door. Opening it, he stood in the doorway, looking at Kay. "I love her," he said. "I really do."

Gathering himself as he went, Frank walked through the barroom. The two old guys were the only ones left. It looked like he'd be walking. He gave Toad a wave. Then, picking up his case, he went out the door. It was raining harder now. He squinted up at the black sky.

"Shit," he said.

Frank continued along to the street. Moving past a van

parked at the curb, he heard a sound behind him, but didn't have time to turn before he was struck on the back of the head, his legs giving way beneath him. Even before he hit the pavement, everything had gone black.

Watermark Slough

"I don't know whether to blame my horoscope or your daughter," Frank said, gingerly holding the ice pack to the back of his head as he turned toward her.

Kay, her eyes on the road, smiled. "Could be fate is trying to tell you something, lover boy."

"Yeah, like it's time to move to Arizona."

Kay lowered the volume on the radio. She'd put on the public-radio jazz station, her favorite. "You do seem to have made an enemy."

"I've got more than one. I know it was Mort who clobbered me tonight. Hitting a guy from behind is his style."

"You don't know that, Frank. Mort certainly had nothing to do with the car that tried to run you down in San Francisco. Or the gang that jumped you in Sacramento."

"Probably not, but this had his fingerprints all over it. The bastard was lying in wait because he was pissed about us conferring behind closed doors. The sonovabitch is a coward, Kay."

"But the other guys trying to get you were brave warriors fighting fair, right? Personally, I think you've got to take a hard look at what you've been doing and to whom."

"Abby was a target, too," he replied. "Unless her mistake just happened to be that she was standing too close to me."

"I hope you get to the bottom of this soon," Kay said. "Now I'm not going to be able to sleep nights."

He watched the wipers wag slowly back and forth across the windshield, brushing aside the light rain. "Abby's not new to police work, you know. She can take care of herself."

"I'm aware of that," Kay said, "but now she and I have a relationship—or we did until today."

"You haven't done anything wrong. I'm the bad guy, not you."

She sighed. "I hope you're right."

They were nearing Frank's place. It was late and he was more than ready for bed. Mostly, he wanted to get out of his wet clothes. Fortunately the old guys in the bar had come out a couple of minutes after he'd left and found him in the gutter, semiconscious. Toad and Kay had gotten him back inside. Sandy Mendoza, who was on the night shift, had come by, but there wasn't anything he could do. Frank hadn't seen a thing. It appeared to be the work of one guy. The weapon, found lying nearby, was a two-by-four. Frank's wallet was still on him, as well as his watch, so robbery wasn't the motive. An unprovoked assault.

It all pointed to Mort Anderson, but Frank hadn't said anything to Sandy—Kay would have been the one to suffer. "You owe me a ride home," he'd told her after Sandy had left to respond to an emergency call.

Kay slowed her Lexus as they neared his drive. "Isn't it coming up?" she said.

"Yeah, another hundred yards. You can let me out on the road," Frank said. "The drive's probably pretty muddy by now. You go down it, you might not make it back up."

"Just what I need—to get caught spending another night at your place. Concussion or not, I'll let you walk from the road."

"I didn't think the prospect of a night with me would please you. That *would* feel like incest."

Kay hesitated before speaking. "Frank, can I ask you something?"

"Sure."

"Did you mean it when you said you love Abby?"

"I was drunk and that's why I said it," he replied. "But

it also happens to be true.'' He gestured for her to pull over. ''There's my mailbox.''

Kay stopped the car. ''I've got to be honest,'' she said. ''I don't know how I feel about that.''

''I understand. I suppose I'd feel funny if you got together with my son—if I had one.'' He shook his head. ''I can't explain things like this, Kay. I don't know if anybody can.''

They exchanged looks, the looks of old friends.

''Well, it's late,'' he said. ''There's a wide spot another fifty yards up. You'd be better off turning around there.''

''Frank,'' she said, looking out her side window, ''I see a vehicle down by your trailer.''

''My truck.''

''No, beside your truck. Looks like one of those sport utility vehicles.''

''A Bronco?''

''I don't know.''

Frank leaned across her to get a look. It was difficult to tell in the dark, but it looked like Abby's Bronco to him. ''I think I know who it is.''

Kay squinted. ''Is it Abby?''

''Possibly.''

She gave him a look, shaking her head. ''Frank Keegan, you old son of a gun. What is it about you that makes it so hard for a woman to let go?''

''She might be waiting to hit me over the head with a two-by-four, same as Mort.''

''I don't think so, lover boy.''

Frank's spirits had taken an upward turn, but he wasn't about to get too euphoric. First, he couldn't be certain what was up, and second he was dealing with Abby's mother. The fact that she, too, had once been his lover wasn't the point at the moment. She was a mother—Abby's mother.

Kay sighed. ''Looks like maybe you'll be able to put in a

good word for me before I have a chance to put one in for you."

"Don't be too sure, Kay."

"After what you told me, that girl is here because she cares about you. Otherwise she wouldn't darken your door for all the gold in Fort Knox."

His heart really started to sing, but he kept a straight face and a calm demeanor. "We'll see." Reaching over, he patted Kay's hand. "Thanks, Kay. You're the best friend I've got."

Her smile was almost friendly. For the first time he looked at her thinking *mother-in-law*. It was weird, really out in left field to think in such terms, but possible—especially if Kay was right about why Abby had come. He couldn't wait any longer. He said good-night and got out of the car, grabbing his bag from the back seat. Kay drove on.

Frank descended the dark drive, his case in one hand, the ice pack in the other. The rain, not much more than a mist now, blew gently on his face. His head hurt, so he pressed the ice bag to the back of it. His foot slipped on the muddy gravel and he almost fell, but he managed to catch himself and continue on down the drive.

The vehicle was Abby's Bronco, all right. He was thrilled. But he couldn't see any sign of her. Then, when he moved around the driver's side, he saw her head wedged between the headrest and the window. She was sound asleep. Putting down his case, he rapped lightly on the window.

Abby jumped, awakening suddenly. What he hadn't seen was the gun in her hand—until it was pointed right at his face. She didn't fire, thank God. Instead, she rolled down the window.

"Frank, are you all right?"

The start she'd given him took his breath away. "I was until you almost shot me."

"Sorry, I thought maybe you were them."

"Them?"

"It's a long story."

"I've had a pretty rough night," he said. "I'd sort of like to get inside where it's warm and dry. You want to talk in your car or in my house?"

"Let's go in the house," she said, raising the window and removing the key from the ignition. "Lord, it's after eleven," she said, getting out. "Where have you been?"

"That's a long story, too."

Abby locked the car and they made their way to the house. He put down his case to unlock the door.

"What's that in your hand?" she asked.

"Ice pack. The crowning touch of my evening, so to speak."

They went inside. He turned on the lights in the front room and glanced around. The place was as messy as when he'd left. It seemed like ten years ago, but it was only a couple of days.

"What happened to your head?" she asked.

"A little more bad luck," he replied. "But don't you have a story of your own?"

Abby had a pained expression on her face. She lowered her eyes. "Before I say anything else, Frank, I want to apologize for abandoning you this afternoon."

"No need to apologize. I deserved it."

"No, you didn't," she replied. "I was completely out of line. Once I thought about it, I realized how childish I'd been. It was completely unprofessional. I should have been able to separate my hurt feelings from my responsibilities to you. Had you been any other member of the department, it would have been unconscionable to abandon you that way. After about five minutes I came to my senses and went looking for you, but you were gone."

"A taxi came along just as I stepped out of the parking lot," he explained. "But none of that's important. It's how you feel that matters."

"I'm still angry at you for not telling me about your affair with Kay. That really was inexcusable. I'm going to have to struggle with it for a long, long time. But that's another issue. I've been waiting here for three hours, worried sick about you. Where have you been?"

He ignored her question. "Why were you worried?"

"Because I saw the Chevy again in Daly City, the one that nearly ran us down on Lombard Street. I was afraid they may have come after you. Frank, somebody is definitely up to no good. They're after us, no question."

"I don't find that hard to believe, Abby."

"And that's not all—"

"Listen, sweetheart," he said, brushing her cheek with his fingertips, "I've got to take a leak and get out of these clothes. Will you give me a minute?"

"Sure, but I think you'll be happy to hear I've got the goods on our man."

"Biff?"

"Maybe Biff *and* Katerina. But go ahead, I'll tell you the whole story when you get back."

He gave her a warm smile that couldn't come close to expressing the relief he felt. It wasn't her apology so much as the fact she was friendly—practically the way she'd been before. Of course, her immediate enthusiasm was for the case, but that was all right. He sensed some forgiveness, and that was what he cared about most.

"I'll just be a minute," he said, heading for the bedroom. "Meanwhile, if you want to put some water on, we can have coffee."

"Have you eaten?" she called after him.

"No."

"I haven't, either."

"There might be a can of soup in the cupboard," he said, disappearing into the bedroom.

"I'll cook."

Frank closed the door, feeling great despite his throbbing head.

He put on his nubby cotton fisherman's sweater and jeans, having taken an extra minute or two for a quick shower to wash the dried blood out of his hair. The two-by-four and the martinis had done a number on him, but knowing Abby was with him, he felt giddy as a schoolboy.

Frank found her in the kitchen, stirring a pot on the stove. On the counter next to her was her service revolver.

"You expecting an Indian attack?"

"Maybe. I've been watching the road," she said, gesturing toward the window. "What looks like the same car has gone by three times. One headlight's a little funny."

"An old Chevy, maybe?"

"I couldn't tell, but after today I'd say it's entirely possible."

Frank went to the refrigerator to make himself a fresh ice pack. "So what happened in Daly City?"

"No, first you tell me what happened to your head."

He recounted the whole tale, including his conversation with her mother and the fact that Kay had brought him home. The last Abby pondered, her back to him as she stirred. He wanted badly for her to turn around so he could see her face.

"Do you suppose if my car wasn't here, she'd have wanted to stay and tend to your wound?" Abby asked.

"Absolutely not," he said. "*You* are Kay's number-one concern. I thought she was going to kill me when I confessed I'd told you everything. She didn't care if my head went rolling, but she was horrified at the thought I might have messed things up for her."

"That's not very Christian of her."

"Abby, she knows I'm going to land on my feet. You're her kid. She cares an awful lot about you."

"God, Frank, keep on and you're going to choke me up."

"There's some self-interest at play, sweetheart. I don't want your mother after my scalp for messing up things between the two of you. Besides, it'd make you look bad if she killed me."

Abby turned off the burner, giving him a look. "I was ready to kill you myself this afternoon."

"I know."

"But I've already made my feelings clear. There's no point in covering the same ground again."

Abby carried the pot to the counter, where she'd set out two bowls. "Just be warned I'm going to have to digest it for a while," she said. "That's the best I can do."

"I can't ask for more than that."

She ladled soup into the bowls. "We've got other worries, though. I should tell you about my adventure this afternoon."

"I've been dying to hear."

"Poor choice of words, Frank."

"Brushes with death are becoming daily occurrences," he said. "I hope it's no reflection on our chemistry."

Abby carried the bowls of soup to the table, where Frank was sitting and holding the ice pack to his head. "I can guarantee you, it's a reflection on Sarah Gibbs's death."

"Yeah?"

"Consider this. I arrive at Father Caratay's parish church. As I'm getting out of the car, I notice an old Chevy parked on a side street from a vantage point where the church can be watched. Looks like maybe a couple of guys are sitting in it. I decide to investigate."

"Without calling for backup."

"Frank, I wasn't sure it was the same car," she said, putting a couple of spoons and napkins on the table. "I wasn't going to make an arrest without involving the local cops, but I figured I'd find out pretty quickly if the guys were up to no good."

"And?"

"Well, they saw me coming and they took off like a bat out of hell."

"Get a description?"

"General. Hispanic or Asian probably. Twenties or thirties. Two guys, could have been one or two more of them slumped in back. I couldn't see. Anyway, I run back to my car, figuring I'll give chase. But just then a black-and-white comes up the street. I flag the patrol car down and we take off in pursuit. Trouble is the Chevy's got a pretty good head start on us. It makes a couple of quick turns, gets to a busy street and we lose it."

"And you've got some explaining to do to the cops."

Abby was back at the counter, taking some bread out of the nearly depleted cellophane bag. "Which wasn't easy, considering Mr. Model Citizen here didn't want to report the hit-and-run that morning in San Francisco."

"So, it's my fault, is it?"

She grinned. "Frank, you know it can't be the police chief's fault." She brought over several slices of bread on a plate. "This is stale, but I have a hunch you're used to stale bread."

"Ever the detective," he said.

Abby sat down kitty-corner to him at the small table. "So, I talked my way through that little mess with the Daly City police and got back to see the priest. Father Caratay's a very nice man, but wary as hell. Right away, I realize he's confused. The long and short of it is that Katerina Kreski had phoned him. Apparently the maid, Nedi, had told her about my conversation with her at the supermarket—at least that's my theory."

"Makes sense."

"It takes me a while, but I finally get the priest to tell his story. And it's pretty damning, Frank. Katerina offered him five thousand dollars to make himself unavailable when I showed up. Wanted him to go on vacation, disappear, anything to avoid talking to us.''

"But being a man of the cloth, he did his civic duty.''

"I don't know if being a priest had anything to do with it. He told me he became leery of Katerina after the previous maid, Evelinda, was paid fifty thousand dollars to pack her bags and leave the country.''

"Fifty?''

"That's right. The woman gets paid and twenty-four hours later she's in the Philippines.''

Frank stroked his chin. "The priest was promised five so that he wouldn't be around to tell you that, and the maid was given fifty to be unavailable for questioning. I'd say she knows something Biff might find embarrassing.''

"Want to hear my theory of the case?'' Abby asked.

"I'm on pins and needles, Chief.''

"Rance and Sarah split up. Maybe he threw her out, maybe Sarah got her fill of him. Either way, Sarah, desperate and alone, turns to Biff, the only guy in San Francisco who's shown her any kindness. Somehow the two of them end up in Ross. Katerina, obviously, isn't in. I didn't see the backyard, but there's got to be a swimming pool. Biff and Sarah do drugs, have rough sex, maybe in the pool. She drowns, maybe because he gets overzealous or angry, or maybe by accident. Because of the subsequent cover-up, I lean toward some form of homicide. Biff, in a panic, decides to dispose of the body in a way that will direct blame on someone else. He thinks of Chet, brings the body to the Delta and dumps it in the slough. Meanwhile, the maid, having witnessed the incident, tells Katerina, who decides to cover up the crime and get rid of the maid by paying her off.''

"Thereby becoming an accessory after the fact,'' Frank added.

"Exactly.''

Abby took a couple of hasty spoonfuls of soup as he pondered her theory. He couldn't see any obvious flaws. Everything seemed to hold together. Abby watched and waited, her expression so earnest and so adorable that he had trouble keeping his mind on what she'd said.

"Frank, what are you doing?"

She was looking at his bowl with disgust as he broke up pieces of bread, dropping them into the tomato soup. He pressed the bread chunks into the liquid with his spoon.

"Best use of stale bread," he said.

"Yuck."

"The secret of low-budget living is never waste anything."

"What do you do with your extra fishing worms?" she asked, making a face.

"There's some in the refrigerator if you'd like a little extra protein."

"I bet you're not kidding."

He grinned.

"So, what do you think of my theory?" she asked.

"Seems plausible to me. It'd be interesting to compare Biff's DNA with the DNA in the samples of flesh found under Sarah's fingernails."

"Wouldn't it, though?"

"You get the physical evidence and bring the maid back to testify against Biff, and you'd have a pretty strong case."

Abby watched him take a bite of the soggy bread. "Obviously talking to Biff again is a top priority."

"I agree a hundred percent, Chief."

They ate for a while without talking. Frank took a break, holding the ice pack to his head while Abby finished her soup. She had delicate hands and nice manners—he'd noticed that during their meals in San Francisco. Everything about her seemed to have a sexual dimension—either that or he was obsessed. Did he dare hope things were back on track?

Or was this all about professionalism and common courtesy? More important, where would the evening end?

"Your head bothering you?" she asked, setting her bowl aside after finishing her soup.

"It's felt better. How about your foot?"

"It's fine. I've got a nasty bruise, but nothing serious. I see your eye is healing nicely."

"Yeah, the ribs, too. If I could just shake the terminal cancer, I'd be in great shape."

"Frank, you nut."

He gave her his best smile, wanting to kiss her. Afraid to hope, but hoping just the same.

"Feel like some dessert?" he asked.

"What do you have?"

"I think there're some dried apricots in the fridge."

"That sounds appetizing."

"Actually they're not bad with Oreo cookies, but I think I finished the last of them a few days ago."

"I'll pass," she said, "but thanks."

"After-dinner drink, then?"

"What do you have?"

"Well, let's see. There's Bud and Bud Lite. Maybe a Heineken, if you want to go upscale."

Abby laughed. "You've been reading Martha Stewart," she said.

"The secret's out."

They exchanged long looks. Her eyes demanded something—honesty, maybe. She drew a careful breath. "Did you love my mother, Frank?" she asked.

He pushed some bread around in his bowl with the spoon. "Do you really want to talk about that?"

"Yes." She watched him shift uneasily. "I'm not asking you to betray any confidences. I want to know about your feelings."

"They say it's not good to discuss past relationships."

"Don't you think this is a little different? I sort of have an interest."

"What do you expect to gain?" he asked.

"An understanding of you."

He slowly nodded. "The easy answer, I guess, is yes and no. I loved Kay like a friend. And I was attracted to her. I'm not suggesting it was platonic or anything like that."

"But she was just the lady of the moment, not the woman of your dreams."

"That's as good a way to put it as any."

"Did she feel the same about you?"

"More or less."

Abby took a long, contemplative breath, mulling over what he'd said. "I suppose that shouldn't bother me. I mean, like you said, it was really before we—"

"But it does bother you, doesn't it?"

"It's kind of hard to get past, Frank, I have to admit."

"Maybe in time?"

"Maybe," she said.

Again they gazed into each other's eyes.

"I might have an after-dinner drink, after all," she said.

"There may be a little brandy around here somewhere."

"Bud Lite's fine."

"Sure?"

Abby nodded.

Frank got up and grabbed a beer from the refrigerator. He opened it and held it up for her to see. "Glass?"

"No thanks."

He put the beer in front of her, then took his seat.

"You aren't having one?" she asked.

"No, I've had enough already this evening. This debonair manner I've been treating you to is chemically induced, in case you hadn't guessed."

Abby gave him a delightful grin and took a pull from her

bottle. "You aren't expecting one of your girlfriends to drop by tonight, are you?"

"No. Why do you ask?"

"I wouldn't want to be here if one was. On the other hand, I really should get home and feed Tristan. The poor baby hasn't had fresh food in a day."

"Can't he wait for breakfast? It *is* the most important meal of the day, after all."

"Frank, your compassion knows no bounds."

"I'd do the same for him. Anyway, you look bushed. Why make the drive so late? You're safe with me."

"I bet." She drank more beer, eyeing him.

It wasn't exactly a seduction, but she wasn't running from him as fast as she could, either. It gave him hope. Still, he restrained himself from touching her. She seemed to vacillate.

"I would love a hot shower. You have a clean towel?" she asked.

"Clean towel *and* clean sheets."

"What more could a woman want?" She got up. "I'll let you do the dishes." Then, dragging her fingers up his arm as she moved past him, she headed for the bath.

Tuesday
February 25th

Watermark Slough

In the darkness of the night, Frank held her in his arms, her soft breasts against his chest, wisps of her hair across his cheek. She smelled of his bath soap and shampoo, but on her body the scent was extra special. He'd never endured such a throbbing headache while making love, yet he had still managed to find the experience divine. Abby Hooper was the most incredible creature he'd ever known. There was no doubt in his mind he loved her.

It wasn't a given they'd be intimate, though. In fact, it had surprised him because she hadn't started out with that intent. She'd been tentative, and after their first kiss she'd briefly resisted going further, calling him a bastard. But then she'd given in to her desire.

He'd made love with care, knowing she was still feeling angry and vulnerable. So he tried to show her how much she meant to him. And Abby had responded more generously than he'd thought possible. She was asleep now, but he was at peace just knowing she was beside him.

God in his compassion gave him this night, and Frank was grateful for it. But it was a vengeful God who cruelly shattered the moment. The crash of glass, followed the whooshing sound of flame made him sit up abruptly. His sudden movement jarred Abby awake.

"What's happened?"

The crackling sound and the roar of flames coming from the front room confirmed what he already knew. "Fire, Abby! Fire!"

"What?"

She looked about the dark bedroom, disoriented and trying to comprehend as he jumped from the bed and went to the door. He opened it a crack and saw that virtually the entire living room was in flames. He slammed the door shut.

"We'll have to go out the window."

Fumbling in the dark, he found his jeans on the floor and started pulling them on. Abby had gotten to her feet, her pale skin scarcely visible in the dim light.

"Get dressed!" he shouted.

"My clothes are in the living room."

"You aren't going out there."

The sound coming from the other room was a definitive roar. Darting to the closet, he jerked out a robe, tossing it to her.

"Put this on!"

Frank went over to the window, ripped off the curtains and slid open the glass. Cold, wet air was sucked right in, swishing over his face and bare chest. Abby had gotten the robe on and come to the window. Frank looked out, thinking he saw something move in the trees at the edge of the orchard.

"Wait," he said.

Scrambling over the bed, he got his gun out of the drawer in the bedside table, then scrambled back. Abby was leaning against the wall beside the window, peeking around the edge of the window frame.

"There're two of them," she said.

"I don't know about you, but when this tin can explodes, I'd rather be outside with a bullet in me than in here."

"Yeah," she said, "me, too."

"Your gun in the front room?"

"Yes," she replied.

"Looks like we're a one-gun family, sweetheart. I say we go out shooting."

"Sounds good to me."

The roar of the fire was getting increasingly loud.

"I'll pop off a few rounds and dive out," Frank said. "Once I'm on the ground I'll move to the left and fire a few more rounds. That should give you a chance to jump out."

"Fine, let's do it!" Abby cried.

Frank peered out the window, looking for a target. Before he could find one, a shot rang out and the glass next to him shattered. The muzzle blaze gave him his target. He fired a couple of rounds, then leaped out the window, landing in the mud and bringing return fire. He squeezed off another round as Abby hit the ground and crawled behind a bush on the other side of the window.

The next time he took a peek, the two figures were circling the house to the front. Judging by the way they were moving, it was a retreat. Frank took off after them, his bare feet slipping and sliding in the mud. By the time he got around the building, they were halfway up the drive. One was limping, the other helping him. Another man was up on the road, calling to them to hurry.

Frank went after them. The gravel in the drive was hell on his bare feet and he had to move to the edge. By the time he'd scrambled to the top of the levee, the trio was fifty yards down the road, the wounded guy with his arms around the shoulders of the other two and badly dragging a leg. They were approaching a car parked to the side of the pavement. Frank took off after them.

The men scrambled into the car. The engine started. Frank stopped, took aim and fired just as the car lurched into motion. The rear window of the vehicle exploded, then the car swerved violently toward the slough, went off the road and down the bank, rolling a couple of times before landing upside down in the water.

Frank jogged to the spot and stood looking down at the vehicle. All was still and silent. He turned and looked back down the road toward his trailer. It was enveloped in flames, the sky above it glowing orange. He glanced once more at the car in the water, then slowly walked toward his place. The rain fell on his bare shoulders and chest. He saw a figure in a white terry robe at the top of his drive. Abby was waiting for him.

"They went off the levee and into the drink," he said. "When they pull the car out, they'll probably find the driver has a hole in him. And I didn't yell, 'Halt, police!' once."

"They got what they deserved, Frank."

The two of them looked at his burning home. Abby's eyes were shimmering.

"I'm so sorry," she said.

"There are some photos I'll miss, but otherwise I'll be spared spring cleaning."

She put her arm around his waist. "Oh, Frank."

"There are advantages to not being sentimental," he said. Then he glanced up the road. "The fire department and one of your cops will be showing up before long. And you aren't exactly dressed for the occasion, Abby. Why don't you go on home?"

"Can't. Car keys are inside the trailer."

"Shit," he said.

"I can take it if you can."

Frank kissed her head. He shivered from the wet and the cold. "I think we're in for a long night, sweetheart."

Riverton Civic Center

"Coroner's office on line two, Chief," the dispatcher said. Abby took the call.

It was one of the deputy coroners from the county, a woman she didn't know. "We've got a preliminary cause of death on all three subjects," the deputy said. "Asphyxiation by drowning. Two had suffered gunshot wounds. One in the leg, the other in the neck. The latter was incapacitating, but not fatal. There were also broken arms, ribs, foot and a jaw. Lots of trauma, but it was river water that got them in the end."

"ID's?" Abby asked.

"On two of them. "Paco Ramirez and Johnnie Sales. Both ex-cons with a long list of convictions. Sacramento addresses."

"Sacramento?"

"That's right. The third we haven't been able to identify. Hispanic male, mid-thirties, five-nine, 160 pounds. Tattoos, scars—a whole host of distinguishing marks. We should be able to get something on him within a day or two."

Abby had taken notes. "Thanks," she said.

"We aim to please," the deputy said. "I'll send along the complete report when we're through."

Abby hung up. Ex-cons. But from Sacramento. That was the surprise. She'd have guessed the San Francisco Bay Area. That would have been more likely if Biff Roberts, or maybe Lloyd Witherspoon, were behind it. Regardless, a return trip to the city was in order. She'd considered questioning Biff further, but at the moment all they had was Katerina Kreski's apparent attempt to obstruct justice. Abby had talked to the D.A. earlier, and he felt that even if she was successful in linking Biff to Sarah Gibbs's death through physical evidence, there was still no proof that a crime had been committed. It was beginning to look like an eyewitness was essential, and their best hope for that might be out of reach in the Philippines.

Father Caratay had promised he'd try to track down Evelinda DeLeon through his contacts in Manila, but there was no way to be sure it could be done quickly, if at all. Abby worried that, without a witness, Sarah's death might end up as one of those murky cases where nobody knew with certainty what had happened, except, of course, the victim and the killer.

There was a light rap on Abby's door. It was Mae Brown.

"There's another TV reporter out front wanting to talk to you about the identity of Jane Doe," she said.

"It's only going to get worse. I better hold a press conference and talk to them all at the same time. There may be questions about the arson firebombing, too. Would you mind setting it up and making the calls?"

"No, Chief. What time?"

"We have to respect their deadlines, so it can't be too late."

"And we gotta give 'em time to get down here," Mae added.

"Let's make it three o'clock in the council chambers, if the room's available."

"I'll check it out."

"And would you have Charlene get the coroner's office to fax us everything they've got on both Jane Doe and the guys who drowned in the Chevy?"

"Sure."

Abby gave her a wan smile. "The way things have been going, we could use another six people around here."

"You know what they say, Chief—if it rains, it pours."

"Does it ever."

"Bring you a cup of coffee?" Mae asked.

Abby shook her head. "Thanks, but I've already had double my quota."

"Holler if you need anything else."

"Thank you, Mae."

The woman went off and Abby groaned. By ten o'clock

that morning everybody on the force and a fair proportion of the citizens of Riverton knew that she and Frank had been burned out of his trailer in the middle of the night, each of them wearing just enough to be legal. It was hard to know how people would react to that. Mae and a couple of the other women had been cautiously supportive, probably out of compassion. The effect on the male officers was still in doubt.

The town's reaction was anybody's guess. Most likely she'd be seen as a fallen woman. Had she been a man, her peccadillo would have been viewed as an indication of how macho she was. Nor would Frank be criticized for having seduced a female chief of police. It just proved he was a stud. On the other hand, a woman who'd seduced a male police chief would be seen as a siren, a floozie. So much for social justice.

Abby knew she had no choice but to deal with things as they were. Last night couldn't be undone. All she could do was be what she always was—professional and competent. That hadn't been easy in the small hours of the morning—not standing in the rain in Frank's bathrobe when Sandy Mendoza and the fire department showed up. She offered no explanation, quietly going behind one of the fire trucks to change into one of the sweat suits Frank had scrounged from the fire department. When Sandy went off duty and was replaced at the crime scene by Dix Fowler, she had Sandy drive her home. She'd just been through the most embarrassing experience of her professional life, and the only thing she knew to do was plow ahead confidently, hoping the scandal wouldn't bite her in the ass.

The fact that they'd managed to identify Jane Doe helped. It gave her something to focus on. Fortunately the press was regional. She could pretty well count on there not being any embarrassing questions at the press conference.

Frank, for his part, had been understanding. He'd arranged

to stay with Dix for a night or two. Knowing how embarrassed she was, he'd apologized profusely for her stay with him turning into a humiliating experience.

"Hell, it's not your fault," she said. "My dignity might have taken a blow, but you lost your home."

"I'm not sure I didn't get the better deal."

It was a kind thing for him to say, very understanding. But it didn't lessen her anxiety much. Abby was at a complete loss as far as the future was concerned—not only with regard to the department and the town, but with Frank, as well.

That morning she'd had Ed Goodwin, one of the newer officers on the force, drive to Tyler Island to pick her up. He was quiet as a church mouse on the way into town. Abby considered broaching the issue, but didn't have the courage. Instead, she talked departmental business, the discovery of Jane Doe's identity and the return of the reporters to town. Ed had seemed relieved they hadn't discussed the fire, and that wasn't necessarily a good sign.

The intercom buzzed again. "Suzanne Broussard on line one, Chief," the dispatcher said.

Suzanne Broussard. The name was familiar, but Abby couldn't place it. She picked up the phone, after a moment recognizing the voice on the other end of the line. It was Katerina Kreski's neighbor, the woman she and Frank had spoken with.

"You asked me to contact you if anything else came up," Suzanne said. "Well, my husband, Norman, got back from a business trip to Bangkok last night. At breakfast this morning I showed him that flyer you left with me." She paused. "Norman thinks he saw the girl, Jane Doe, at Katerina's place."

"Oh?"

"Yes, it was Valentine's Day night. He remembers because we had a fight and he stomped out of the house to cool off. While he was outside, a San Francisco taxi arrived, a girl got out and went to the house. Norman said she was in this little miniskirt and was quite young. She looked very much like the girl pictured on the flyer.''

The news sent a surge of adrenaline into Abby's veins.

"My husband wondered why a girl like that would be going to Katerina's, until he saw Biff come out in his bathrobe to pay the taxi,'' Suzanne continued. "Norman figured Biff must be having a party in Katerina's absence.''

"Did your husband say what time that was, Mrs. Broussard?''

"Yes, it was around seven-thirty. We had dinner reservations at eight and Norman remembered thinking we'd never make it, having only half an hour from the time he came back inside.''

"Did your husband see anyone else?''

"No, that was it. We were preoccupied with our argument, and we did go to dinner and were lucky not to have lost our table. At the time the girl didn't seem important, of course. It wasn't until Norman saw the flyer that he even remembered the incident. What stuck was the girl's age and the fact Biff was in his bathrobe.''

"This is most helpful,'' Abby told her. "I very much appreciate your calling.''

"We aren't the sort who get involved in other people's business, but neither Norman nor I have any use for Biff Roberts. This morning he backed into our mailbox. Norman was leaving for work himself and saw the whole thing. Biff didn't give a damn what he hit and took off up the street like he was late for his accident. Norman called me from the office and said to be sure and let you know about Valentine's Day.''

"I'm glad you did, Mrs. Broussard. Please don't hesitate to call again if either of you remember anything else.''

"We won't hesitate, believe me.''

Abby hung up the phone, excited. Now she had a witness

who could place Sarah Gibbs at Katerina's place with Biff the night she died, making him a liar. It still wasn't the smoking gun they needed, but the evidence was beginning to mount. Too bad there wasn't clear proof of a crime. If Abby had one major fear, it was they wouldn't be able to show criminal intent—at least not beyond a reasonable doubt. On the other hand, what they had going for them was that somebody had made a major effort to cover things up, which tended to show culpability. Unless Katerina Kreski simply did it to avoid embarrassment, that is. How far would the woman go, though? Abby had a hunch that would prove to be the question on which the entire case turned.

Dix Fowler came to her office next. It was the first time she'd seen him since he'd shown up at Frank's place to take over for Sandy. Dix wasn't one to gloat and he didn't stand to gain anything by seeing her down, but he was a man and part of him had to be chuckling to see the girl chief land on her face in the mud. For the first time since he'd died, Abby could actually say she was glad Chet Wilsey wasn't around. He would have had an absolute field day with this.

"What's up, Dix?" she asked.

"I took a call for you while you were on the phone, Chief. A Detective Owens of the Sacramento P.D. Special Investigations section. Said they may have one of the guys who jumped you and Frank in Capitol Park. A young Chicano showed up at a hospital in Bakersfield with a couple of days-old gashes and abrasions on his head. The gashes were badly infected. Claimed he'd been in an auto accident, but wouldn't give the particulars. The staff got suspicious and called the police. Somebody remembered the inquiry Sacramento had put out and called. Turns out their boy has a west Sacramento address. Two detectives are on their way to Bakersfield to pick him up. They may need you for an ID."

Abby shook her head. "You know, Dix, it wouldn't be

hard for me to start feeling paranoid. Is it the job or is it me?''

"I wouldn't take it too personally," he replied. "Several years back some con Chet had put away got paroled and came looking for him. The guy swore he was going to get every cop who ever nailed him. It was a week before Chet was due to go on vacation, so he went early. By the time he got back from his fishing trip, the con had shot a sheriff's deputy down near Visalia and they already had him behind bars.''

"What's the moral of the story? Discretion is the better part of valor?''

"Either that or sometimes it's better to keep your head down and let the storm blow over.''

Abby wasn't sure if he meant it that way, but his words could apply to her indiscretion with Frank as much as the bad guys who seemed to want to make them into poster children for victims of violent crime.

"I can't have the town thinking they've got a police chief who's a coward." She'd almost said, "a police chief who would rather make love than war," but caught herself. "No," she added, "I've drawn my gun. I've got to be willing to pull the trigger. Running from the situation's not going to do anybody any good, least of all me.''

Dix shrugged. "Don't say I didn't warn you.''

Riverton

Abby sat at a table in the Riverton Café, nursing a Pepsi and waiting for her sandwich. It was after one-thirty and the place was almost empty. She'd gone late, so she'd see as few people as possible. Not that she intended to hide forever, but time could be an ally in situations like this. Nobody had yet to say a word to her except hello, but she could sense an awareness, as if everybody was waiting to see what she'd do or say. She did her best to act blasé, but it wasn't easy. There had to be a certain amount of prurient interest involved—female police chief as sex bomb. If she had to guess, that was what people were thinking.

Frank unexpectedly came in the front door before her sandwich arrived. Abby's stomach clenched. She checked the other customer's reactions. An older couple in one of the front booths, a pensioner sitting at the counter in his John Deere baseball hat and Thelma were the only other people there. Thelma seemed to perk up, the others seemed oblivious, much to her relief.

"Hiya, Thelma," Frank said, chipper as could good be.

Abby could see he was decked out in new clothes. He had on a new pair of Levis and a khaki shirt, a crisp new beige windbreaker and new work shoes without so much as a mark on them.

"Sorry to hear about the fire, Frank," Thelma said from her perch up front.

Frank grinned as he made his way back to Abby's table. "You know what they say, Thelma—every once in a while you've got to burn off the deadwood if you want healthy growth. Needed to get rid of a lot of junk, anyway."

Abby knew she shouldn't be surprised by his cavalier manner. He had less reason to be embarrassed than she. To the contrary, he even had reason to gloat. After all, she'd beaten him out for the job of police chief, but he'd gotten her into bed, getting in the last shot, so to speak.

He was beaming as he approached until her saw her red face. "Abby? Something wrong?"

"Do you think it's a good idea for us to be seeing each other around town like this?" she said under her breath.

Her comment seemed to surprise him. "What do you mean? I work for you, don't I? Or are you trying to tell me I've been fired?"

"No, of course not."

"Can I sit down, then? Or would you rather I make an appointment to see you at the office?"

Abby glanced toward Thelma at the front of the café, realizing she was causing more of a sensation by arguing. "Yeah, sit down," she said.

Frank sat across from her and looked her right in the eye, which made her still more uncomfortable. "Am I an embarrassment?" he asked.

"You aren't personally," she said, lowering her voice. "The problem is what happened last night."

"People been giving you a bad time?"

"I wouldn't go quite that far. Everybody looks at me like I've got a scarlet letter tattooed to my forehead, though."

"I suppose you're going to tell me that's why all the TV crews are in town."

"No, they're here because I'm holding a press conference in an hour or so to discuss the Jane Doe case. Naturally everybody's clamoring to find out what they can about Sarah Gibbs."

"Better than questioning you about where you were last night."

"Who knows, maybe they'll bring that up, too," she said, not entirely facetiously. "All they have to do is a few man-on-the-street interviews and they'll hear the latest gossip."

"Abby, don't you think maybe you're blowing this out of proportion a little? I mean, this *is* a small town, but it's also the dawn of the twenty-first century. It's not like we're married to other people or anything."

"Easy for you to say."

"Want me to leave so a reporter doesn't catch you talking to me?"

He was needling her a little, but she deserved it. There was nobody else she could give a bad time over this and that was unfair to him. "No," she said contritely, "we need to talk about the case."

Abby saw he was having trouble keeping a straight face and that only made it worse, but she was determined to regain her dignity. She glanced up front again. The old guy at the counter was looking back at them, but didn't watch for long. She turned her attention to Frank.

"I guess I should be feeling sorry for you, instead of myself," she said, signaling an improved attitude. "Have you been out to your place to see the damage?"

"Ashes are about all that's left."

"Frank, I'm sorry."

"A guy's got to start over every once in a while. Divorce, fire, mudslide and earthquake seem to be the methods of choice. At least in this state."

"I'm glad you can joke about it," she said.

"It's not all fun. Spent damned near two hours in K-Mart. Cab of my truck looks like a booth at the flea market. You have any idea what it costs to get a whole new wardrobe in one fell swoop?"

"I haven't the faintest."

"Eighteen hundred dollars. Of course our buddy, Biff Roberts, probably spends that on one sport coat, but still…"

Thelma drifted up to the table. "Bring you anything, Frank?"

"How about a cup of soup and half a ham-and-cheese sandwich," he replied.

"Wheat, plenty of mayo, lettuce and tomato. Coffee, black."

"Hey, you know your customers, don't you, doll?"

"The predictable ones, anyway," she said, going off.

"You've got no secrets," Abby chided.

He rolled his eyes. "So, where were we?"

"You were giving me your wardrobe update."

"Yeah, the *GQ* man does K-Mart."

"Does your casualty insurance cover the loss?" she asked.

"Talked to my insurance guy this morning. Twenty thousand is all I'm getting for contents, including personal items. That doesn't buy a lot these days in the way of furniture, dishes, clothing, linens and so forth. I figure I'll come up five or ten grand light. But at least everything will be new.''

"What about your trailer?"

"That's a little stickier. Maybe thirty thousand if I'm lucky. And I have to find a place to live. Talked to Judge Parker and he said I could move into Chet's place and pay a nominal rent until the estate's settled and I get the house outright. Beats a high rent or living in the street.''

"You want to live at Chet's?" she asked, the mere thought making her quail. Her one and only visit to Chet's house had been the day his bloody corpse was found in that easy chair in front of the TV.

"Why not? Do you think the place is haunted or something?''

"No, but…''

"But what?"

"I don't know," she said. "It seems kind of creepy.''

"Maybe I'm not as sensitive about things like that as I should be.''

Abby realized he was dealing with his loss the way men do—rationalizing it away, denying the pain. "The important thing is that you get through this," she said.

"You're the one having a rough day. First you've hardly had any sleep, and now you've got to face the TV cameras. Not that I'm making excuses, but I'm kind of rummy myself." He reached into the pocket of his windbreaker. "Found a few of your things out at the trailer.''

Frank put her half-melted badge on the table in front of her. It looked like a coin that a steamroller had gone over a few times, enough so the design was little more than a vague impression. The leather case was completely gone, of course. From his other pocket he took out her service revolver. The metal was badly discolored, and Abby knew it would need work, if it could be salvaged at all. Next he put her key ring on the table. The rubber on the ignition key to the Bronco was completely gone, the metal of the keys discolored like her gun. Next was a little puddle of metal.

"I figure this was probably a lipstick," he said. "Soft metal. Didn't stand up to the heat. It was in the ashes with the gun, the badge and the keys where the purse must have been. Wasn't much else I could find that was recognizable. It was a hot fire. We were lucky we didn't have to go through it to get out."

Abby realized that was the salient point. All they were talking about was things. Frank either knew how to let go, or he was putting on a good act. "Salvage anything of yours?" she asked.

"One tackle box came through. All the flies and line inside were toast. A few hooks and lures survived. It'll be interesting to see if the fish notice the difference."

"That's all?"

"A frying pan made it and the blades to some kitchen knives. The silverware melted. Basically, it was a total loss." His expression grew sad. "The only thing I cared about were photos of Beth. But maybe I can get Arlene to make some copies of hers."

"Frank, I'm so sorry."

"Any word yet on who the men were who burned me out?"

Abby told him what she'd learned from the deputy coroner.

Frank's brows rose. "Sacramento boys, eh?"

Thelma brought Abby her sandwich. Frank told her not to wait for him. She began eating as he ruminated.

"What are you thinking?" she asked.

He leaned forward and spoke in a confidential tone. "I figure the odds are better than fifty-fifty that Mort clobbered me outside the River Queen. What I'm trying to decide now is if he'd be stupid enough to pay some guys to kill me."

"He'd have to be pretty jealous to get that upset over a simple conversation." Abby hesitated. "Unless you haven't told me everything."

"No, you know everything I do," he replied.

"I don't know Mort," she said, "but I'd be surprised if he's that dumb."

"You wouldn't think so."

It occurred to her then that Frank might not know everything that was going on between her mother and Mort. Kay could have said something that set Mort off, something Frank wasn't aware of—like the fact that she still loved him.

Frank had been watching her work through the problem in her mind. "What's your theory?" he asked.

"About the fire?"

"Yeah."

Abby dabbed her lips with her napkin. "I'd have thought Biff Roberts."

"Think he'd have come up to Sacramento to find his henchmen?"

"That does pose a problem," she admitted, "though not an insurmountable one."

"The possibility of it being Mort is eating at me," Frank said, "but that's partly because I hate the sonovabitch."

"Because of Kay?" she asked a little too quickly.

"No, it goes back a lot further than that. It's really not all that interesting."

"Well, I've got other news," Abby said, accepting his explanation.

Thelma brought Frank his lunch. Abby waited until the woman had gone before continuing.

"Remember Suzanne Broussard?" she said as he started on his soup.

"Katerina and Biff's neighbor, the one in the fashion jogging outfit who thought I was cute."

"God," Abby said, "what was I thinking when I told you that?"

"Trying to boost my ego, maybe."

"I don't think you have any problems in that regard."

"So, what about her?"

Abby recounted her conversation with the woman.

"Whoa," Frank said, "it'll be interesting to hear ol' Biff try to explain that one. Wasn't he insisting that the last time he saw Sarah was a week before she died, or is my memory playing tricks on me?"

"That's exactly what he said."

"Hmm. The plot thickens."

"I want to nail his ass, Frank."

He slurped his soup. "When?"

"Tomorrow?"

"By appointment or sneak attack?"

"Sneak attack," she said. "Preferably when Katerina's not around."

"Sounds like we should try him at his club. Assuming he still goes to work."

"When I get back to the office I'll phone and see if he's expected tomorrow."

Abby watched him finish his soup. His idiosyncracies were becoming familiar to her. Frank was without pretension. He knew what he wasn't and felt okay about who he was. She couldn't exactly say that made him more spiritual, but he seemed to have an uncommon relationship with the material world, sort of impervious to it somehow. It was odd how much she liked him. The fact that she could feel so comfortable around him—especially considering the conflict and adversity they'd faced—was very telling. Abby knew she had to be careful of her feelings, though. The events of the previous evening had been like a splash of cold water in the face, bringing her back to reality.

"Frank," she said, "there's something I want to say. I think we should put our relationship on hold until the dust settles. We've got a job to do and we should concentrate on that. I'm not about to change the way I run the department because of last night, but neither am I going parade my private life around town, throwing it in people's faces."

"I think you're being overly sensitive."

"Maybe, but that's the way I feel."

"You're the chief."

"It's just where I am right now, personally and professionally."

"I understand."

He said it with apparent sincerity, but she knew he didn't really understand. He would interpret it as rejection, but there wasn't anything she could do about that. Her feelings were her feelings, and the story about him and her mother wasn't easily digested. "So when are you moving into Chet's?" she asked.

"I don't know. Haven't gotten that far. I guess I'll have to have somebody go in there and clean it first. Meanwhile I'll probably hang out at Dix's place. He offered."

Neither of them had noticed Thelma had slipped up on them until she spoke.

"You kids want some dessert, or are you going elsewhere for that?"

Abby turned absolutely crimson. Frank looked sheepish. He seemed to realize that Thelma had unwittingly proved her point.

"I don't think we need anything, Thelma," he said.

"Except coffee, of course," she said, pouring more into his cup from the pot in her hand.

Frank took a new leather wallet from his pocket and gave Thelma a twenty. "Take both lunches out of this."

"No," Abby said, opening her purse. "Separate checks, please." She handed the woman another twenty.

"Yes, ma'am."

Thelma went off. Abby looked into his eyes. Frank stared back at her.

"I guess the next thing for me to do is to stand by and await orders," he said.

"Please don't hate me, Frank."

"How could I hate you when I love you?"

The Grove
Riverton

Frank's words were still haunting her when she pulled up in front of her mother's house on the swank side of the river. Abby had never been inside, having only seen the place when driving by. She didn't get out immediately, taking a moment to gather herself. Though feelings between them were improved, Kay Ingram remained a major issue because of their history. This wasn't about Frank, she told herself; it was about arson and attempted murder. It was about the present, not all those yesterdays.

Abby checked her watch. She wouldn't stay long. She still had the press conference to contend with. By all rights, she probably should have returned directly to the station and spent some time preparing, but this had been eating at her and she wanted to get it over with.

Kay came to the door in a flowered caftan, peering at her through the screen of the outer door. She didn't have on any makeup, and her hair was wet. Abby realized she'd made a mistake by not calling.

"Abby, what a surprise."

"I should have called before dropping in on you," Abby said. "I went by the Queen and they said you'd be coming in soon. I thought I'd catch you here."

"Well, you did," Kay replied, pushing the screen door open, "not quite in a state of nature, but close to it. Come in. I hope my old face isn't too much of a shock."

Kay did look older and far less attractive. Though her recollections were sketchy at best, Abby couldn't recall seeing her mother in any condition except all made up—mascara, eyeliner, shadow, blush, the works. Back when it was in fashion there'd been false eyelashes and powder that sparkled. The tinted hair had gone through various styles and incarnations, but it was always fashionably coiffed. This, though, was the woman without the glitter, the jewelry and the clothes.

"Part of building a relationship is putting aside pretense," Kay said, leading her to the seating area of the spacious front room. "I don't mind if you don't."

"Of course not."

"Consider it a compliment that I let you see me this way," Kay said. "You're among a select few who ever have."

They sat on facing flowered sofas.

"I'd be the same."

Kay laughed. "Sweetie, have you ever used anything besides a little mascara and liner?"

"Not often."

"Well, you're lucky. I was young in an era when natural beauty was irrelevant. A girl had to be painted, trussed and squeezed, no matter what. We got addicted to our facades like we did to cigarettes. You're growing up in a better age, Abby. But I guess you didn't come to hear an old lady's complaints."

"You're hardly old."

"Relatively speaking."

Abby wondered if they were already talking about Frank.

"But I do love it that you're my daughter and I can speak honestly. That's new for me and I like it."

Abby looked into her mother's eyes, her heart lurching

from past to present and back again. It seemed they'd made an awfully big jump, awfully quick. "It's a start," she said noncommittally.

She glanced around at the pastel room. It was like Kay—pretty and bold at the same time. Cheerful. A little showy with its enormous arrangements of dried flowers. The watercolors and Monet prints made the room seem more Southern California than Sacramento River Delta. This was the home of the queen of the Queen, after all, and it showed.

"So, are you here to talk about you, me, us or something else?" Kay asked.

Only then did Abby realize she may have had more than one reason for coming. "I wanted to talk to you about Mort."

Kay crossed her legs under the caftan and laid her hands on her knees. "Because of the fire at Frank's?"

"As a starting point."

"That's hardly the starting point, Abby. But then, I'm sure Frank's filled you in on the history of his relationship with Mort."

"Generally, yes. But I want to be clear about one thing. I'm not here at Frank's suggestion. In fact, he doesn't know I planned to come. I'm investigating a crime and the hard feelings between the two of them strike me as relevant. I called Mort's place, but got no answer."

"No, he left for Seattle this morning. On business. He'll be gone a while."

"I see."

Her mother contemplated her with maternal candor. "Do you want facts or opinions, Abby?"

"Whatever you have that would be helpful."

"I think there's a good chance Mort clobbered Frank with the two-by-four the other night. He's dumb enough to do that. But hire people to kill him? No. I don't believe it for a minute."

"Does he have reason to be that jealous?"

Kay smiled slightly. "We are getting to the crux of the matter, aren't we?"

"I don't mean to get personal," Abby said, "but we're talking crime and we're talking motive. Mort would have to have a damned good reason to go to those extremes."

"Let's not beat around the bush," Kay said. "Mort would have to think I still love Frank and that removing him from the picture would be the only way to avoid losing me."

"That would be an example."

"Well, it's not the case, Abby. Since Mort and I have been together, I've spoken to Frank. I regard him as a friend, as you well know. And yes, Mort is jealous of even that. I've never said anything to Mort to make him think I still care for Frank or otherwise given him a reason to want him dead."

Abby wondered if she should accept the statement at face value. Was this something Kay would lie about? Only if her intent was to save Mort Anderson's ass, it seemed. But if she cared that deeply for him, would she have been throwing Frank in his face? Logic indicated she would not, but logic wasn't always a controlling factor in such matters.

Abby nodded vacantly. "Well, I had to ask."

"You're the chief of police. You have a job to do."

For some reason, when she heard her mother say the words, Abby got a lump in her throat. It was because she didn't really have anyone to turn to, anyone she could spill her guts to, and now, here, for the first time in her life, she actually felt like she had a mother. She had a sudden urge to throw herself on her mother's breast and sob out all the anxiety, frustration and anguish she'd been holding in. Maybe this was the other, unconscious reason she'd come—to get some emotional support.

"The chief of police with a few problems of her own," Abby lamented.

"Care to talk about it?" Kay asked, understanding immediately.

Abby's eyes began to shimmer. "I suppose you've heard what the fire department found when they got to Frank's place last night."

"I heard you weren't dressed for the occasion."

"That's putting it mildly."

"These things happen. There's no such thing as perfect discretion."

"But I'm the police chief."

"You're human, like everybody else. Look at Chet, for crissakes! At least you didn't molest some kid."

"Women are held to different standards."

"Only if they let themselves be. If you feel guilty, people will think you are. Act like it and they won't try to talk you out of it."

"Don't you think the chief of police should be held to a certain standard?"

"When you took the oath of office, did you make a vow of celibacy?" Kay asked.

"Of course not. But that's not the point."

"What *is* the point?" Kay asked.

Abby stopped to think. That really was the issue. What was she afraid of? What did she believe? What did she want? What *was* the point? "I guess I'm not sure what I want," she said.

"Well, that's worth something," her mother said. "Now you know what to work on."

Abby looked down at her folded hands, embarrassed. "It's pretty obvious, when you stop to think about it."

"The obvious isn't always so obvious," Kay replied. "I'm new, in a way, at this mothering business, but I can see that part of it entails stating the obvious."

Abby smiled. "Thanks."

"Hey, we're friends, aren't we?"

Abby nodded. "I'd like to think so."

"Maybe I'll need *you* someday."

"And I hope I'll be able to help."

They looked at each other for a moment. Abby grew a bit self-conscious. She checked the time.

"Oops, I've got to get going. I'm holding a press conference in half an hour."

"Oh?"

"To discuss the Jane Doe case now that she's been identified."

"You know," Kay said, "I was so happy to hear that poor child won't be buried without her family knowing what happened. That was weighing on me. And a lot of other people in town, I think."

"Resolution is important."

"I was thinking we ought to have the fund-raising dance, anyway, give people a chance to do something charitable. What do you think?"

"It's a good idea."

"The high-school gym is reserved for a week from Saturday. And you'll be one of the stars of the show."

There was pride in Kay's voice and Abby was touched. Her feelings toward her mother were becoming more and more positive. "Well, I should get out of your hair," she said. "I know you have to get over to the Queen and I've got this press conference."

They stood up and went to the door.

"I'm glad you came by," Kay said.

"I am, too."

Abby started to go out the door, but gave in to her impulse, instead. She embraced Kay, and her mother hugged her back. Tears were running down their cheeks when they finally let go of each other. Kay smiled through her tears, touching Abby's cheek with her fingers.

"I have a wonderful daughter," she whispered.

Abby left quickly, before she really started to cry.

Wednesday
February 26th

Frank watched her parallel park the Bronco in a tiny space in front of Biff Roberts's building, slick as you please. Abby was nothing if not competent. The woman could handle herself. She was self-sufficient and she knew her mind. Odd how appealing he found that—especially for a guy who'd grown up in the fifties and early sixties, an era when women were still considered the weaker sex.

"If he's in Mexico or South America or someplace, I'm going to be pissed off," Abby said, turning off the engine.

"Me, too," Frank replied.

He understood her frustration. She told him she'd spent the previous afternoon on the phone, trying to locate Biff. He never showed up at his club, according to the manager. Abby talked to Nedi, Katerina Kreski's maid, who must have gotten a lecture about loose lips, because she clammed up. On an impulse Abby had given Suzanne Broussard a call, and Katerina's neighbor told her that the previous morning Biff had left the house in a huff with Katerina following him out the front door, screaming obscenities. "I was in my front courtyard stretching after my run when I heard the pandemonium," Suzanne had said. "Sounded to me like the definitive fight, the sort relationships end on, but you never know."

Abby had concluded tracking down Biff would be a challenge, but she decided to come to San Francisco, anyway, and give it a shot. She'd called Frank at Dix's place the previous night to make arrangements.

"Guess who we've just been watching on TV?" he'd said, coming on the line.

"God, which channel?"

"Three."

"I didn't see that one."

"You were great. Natural-born media star."

"Hardly," she'd said, embarrassed. But his praise had pleased her, he could tell. "At least there weren't humiliating questions about last night. The closest was when the *Bee* reporter asked if there was a connection between the Jane Doe case and the arson fire."

"And I liked your answer—'We have no reason to believe so at this time, but the matter is under investigation.'"

"What else could I say?" Abby had asked. "That my suspicion was so great that I slept with the occupant just to be around in case there was trouble?"

"How about you slept over because the occupant was irresistible?"

"If you want that out, you'll have to go on TV yourself, Frank."

He'd laughed and she'd told him she'd be at Dix's to pick him up bright and early. They'd ended up leaving the Delta at first light, hoping that even if they didn't find Biff, they'd find clues to his whereabouts.

Their visit to the club had been a bust. The staff confirmed that Roberts hadn't been around for several days. Frank suggested they swing by Biff's condo on the off chance he might be home. Repeating the drill of their last visit, they got the building manager, Mrs. Ungar, to let them in. The woman, again looking windblown, seemed glad to see them.

"I don't know what's wrong with Mr. Roberts, but he isn't himself," she said, unconsciously smoothing her flyaway hair.

"What do you mean?"

"He's been partying since yesterday afternoon like a wild man. A least three girls have been here, maybe more. Prostitutes is what they were, judging by their appearance and their clothes. The racket went on till four in the morning. The neighbors complained. I was ready to call the police and finally went up and told him so."

"You mean Biff is actually here?" Abby asked, surprised.

"Unless he sneaked out without me noticing."

"Just goes to show," Frank said, "if you can't find someone, try his home."

"It *is* rather clever of us, isn't it?" Abby replied.

"Personally, I think they were doing drugs," Mrs. Ungar said. "When I knocked on the door, I could smell marijuana."

"I think we have sufficient cause to pay Mr. Roberts a visit," Frank said.

"But not the breaking-down-the-door variety," Abby returned. "If he wants to flush his drugs down the toilet, it's fine by me. I just want to talk to the man. If you don't mind, Mrs. Ungar, I'd like you to accompany us and bring your passkey."

"Whatever it takes to stop the drugs and prostitutes from coming here."

They went up in the elevator to Biff's floor. Frank could smell traces of grass in the air.

"This is like being in college again," he quipped.

Abby gave him a look.

The mood between them was lighter than the day before. Abby seemed more relaxed, but still somewhat uncertain about what she wanted. He didn't press her, allowing her to take the lead. On the drive, they'd talked mostly about the case. She'd told him about talking to Kay, and though she'd drawn no firm conclusions about who was behind the arson, she was less inclined to suspect Mort.

They reached Biff's door. Frank knocked loudly. After waiting half a minute, he knocked again. "Open up!" he yelled. "Police!"

The ritual was repeated twice more, and when it didn't produce any result, Abby had the manager unlock the door. The apartment, so neat the last time they'd been there, was in shambles. Lamps were tipped over. Seat cushions were scattered about or were askew. There were glasses and bottles of booze, ashtrays full of cigarette butts and half-smoked joints, items of women's clothing, including underwear, strewn across the floor.

"Biff must have been a fraternity boy," Frank said under his breath.

The words were no sooner out of his mouth when he saw a woman's foot with a strappy sandal on it protruding from behind a chair. The flesh tone was ebony. Abby saw it at the same moment.

"Uh-oh," she said. She turned to Mrs. Ungar, who was standing at the door. "Please wait outside, would you?"

"And close the door," Frank added.

The woman did as they asked. He and Abby moved toward the chair, going around opposite sides of it.

She was a black woman—girl more accurately, considering that she appeared to be in her middle teens, despite the heavy makeup she wore—and she was naked except for her shoes. She lay on her back, her mouth sagging open. There was no sign of trauma. No wound or pool of blood. Victim of an overdose maybe?

"Is she dead?" Abby asked.

"You're right," he said softly. "No point in jumping to conclusions."

He bent over the body, pressing his finger to her carotid artery. To his surprise, there was a pulse. The girl moaned ever so slightly.

"She's alive. Reports of her death were premature."

"Do we need to call an ambulance?" Abby asked, squatting beside him.

"I think she's just stoned."

"Let's see who else is here and tend to her later," Abby said.

They checked out the rest of the apartment, finding no one until they got to the master bedroom. Biff was stretched out on the bed, naked as the day he came into the world. His snoring left no doubt he was still among the living. With his swollen belly and hairy torso, he was not a pretty sight.

Another young black woman was beside him. She, too, was nude. They didn't have to check her for vital signs, as she groaned and turned onto her side.

"The morning after one of Biffy's orgies," Frank said.

Abby looked disgusted. "This guy is a real scumbag."

Frank went over to the nightstand next to Biff. They'd been doing lines of cocaine. The floor was wet where a bottle of champagne had been knocked over. The place reeked of vomit.

"Actually, this might not be a bad time to question him," Frank said. "We've definitely caught him with his pants down."

The girl moaned more loudly, blinking her eyes open. It took a few seconds for her to register what she was seeing. "What?" she muttered incoherently. "Who you, man?"

"Police," Abby said.

"Oh shit," the girl said, closing her eyes and rolling her head back and forth.

Abby took the sheet and pulled it up over the girl's chest.

She put her hand on her shoulder and shook her. "Wake up. We've got to talk."

"Fuck, I don' know nothin', man. Leave me be. No shit."

Abby shook her again. "Come on, honey, wake up and talk to me or we'll have to take you downtown."

The girl squinted at her, rubbing her face numbly. "What you want?"

"What's your name?"

"Terrella," the girl replied.

"How old are you, Terrella?"

"Nineteen."

"The hell you are. I want the truth."

Terrella lifted her head and looked around, noticing Biff beside her, snoring away. "You gonna arrest me or what?"

"Depends if you cooperate," Frank said. "Answer the lady's question."

The girl squinted at him and groaned.

"How old are you?" he demanded.

"Seventeen."

Frank figured that was closer.

"How did you get here?" Abby asked. "What happened?"

"Me and my sister was just out lookin' for a good time and this man comes along in his big car and asks us if we want to party. We didn't know there'd be drugs. I swear. This guy, this one right here, he tricked us. He got us all drunk and made us fuck him. Me and my sister. An' some white chick."

"Is that your sister in the living room?"

Terrella lifted her head, suddenly concerned, but then let it drop. "I don' know what she do. Where is she?"

"Sleeping in the other room. What's her name?"

"Shawna. She okay?" Terrella said, lifting her head again.

"She's okay," Abby said. "How old is your sister?"

"Sixteen."

"Can you get up, Terrella?"

"I guess maybe."

"You come help me take care of your sister," Abby said. "Frank, see if you can wake our friend, Biff. Put him in the shower if you have to."

Abby helped the girl into the other room and Frank went to work on Biff. He managed to get him to respond, but he wasn't very coherent. It took a few minutes to get him into the bathroom. When Biff finally recognized him, he got scared. "What are you doing here? What's happening?"

Frank told him to get in the shower. The questions would come in time and he'd be doing the answering. Ten minutes later Biff was sitting on the bed with a towel around him. He was shivering and pale as a sheet. Abby brought the girls into the room, dressed now, more or less.

"Mr. Roberts," Abby said, "I believe you know Terrella and Shawna. They're seventeen and sixteen, respectively. Seems you provided them with drugs and alcohol and had sexual intercourse with them, oral copulation, sodomy and various and sundry acts of lewd and lascivious conduct. Is there anything I left out?"

Biff lowered his head into his hands.

"While you think it over, I'm going to read you your rights." She proceeded to go through the litany.

Biff looked up at her when she'd finished. "These girls aren't why y'all are here. What do you want? Why don't you get to the point?"

"Frank," Abby said, "while I see that these young ladies are comfortable in the front room, would you explain our concern to Mr. Roberts?"

"Sure, Chief."

Abby herded the girls out and Frank sat on the bed next to Biff Roberts.

"Here's our problem, sport," he began. "When we talked to you up in Marin, you told us the last time you saw Sarah

Gibbs was several days before she died. We accepted that because you seemed to be truthful and cooperative. You helped us find Sarah's family so that we could notify them of her death. That's all to the good. Meanwhile, though, we've learned from one of your fiancée's neighbors that on the evening of February fourteenth, the night Sarah died, she arrived at your front door in Ross in a taxi and was greeted by you in a bathrobe. Within hours Sarah was dead and Katerina's maid was on her way to the Philippines.''

Abby came back into the room as Frank said the last words.

"Seems to me we have a little credibility problem," Frank went on. "It's also starting to look like what happened to Terrella and Shawna last night happened to Sarah the night of the fourteenth—the difference, of course, being that Sarah ended up dead. I guess the most direct way to put this, Biff, is that we'd like the truth.''

"Are you going to nail me for last night?" he asked.

"I can be extremely tolerant of people when they tell me the truth," Abby said.

"If I tell you everything, you'll forget all this?''

Abby and Frank exchanged looks.

"*If* you tell everything," she said.

"Actually, what I told you before was basically true," Biff began. "Except about that last time I saw her. You're right about Sarah coming to Ross that night. Katerina was out of town. Sarah was in tears and begged me to help her. She told me Rance had left her and she had no place to go, no one to turn to. She asked if she could live in my apartment. She said she'd be my mistress, give me sex whenever I wanted. All she needed was a place to live.''

Frank saw Abby tense and for a second he wasn't sure whether or not she'd pop Biff in the chops. He did have a feeling Biff was spilling his guts, though. It almost seemed like, by readily sharing the gruesome details, he was giving proof of his credibility. Biff proceeded to describe how Sarah had seduced him in an effort to win his support. She'd prostituted herself and Biff had taken advantage of her.

"I resisted at first, but the kid was persuasive," he said. "I know that doesn't make it her fault and that I'm responsible, but I do want you folks to know she wasn't dragged off to bed kicking and screaming. The truth was, I said no at first. I said I'd give her bus fare home, but she didn't want money. She said she wanted to be my woman, my mistress. She said it was fine if I got married. She'd be available to me in San Francisco, whenever I wanted her."

"So she convinced you to take advantage of her," Abby said, her voice dripping with sarcasm. "Is that it?"

"I got drunk, we did a few lines of coke and I let that be my excuse. I'm not justifying myself, I'm just telling you what happened."

"Okay," Frank said, "you screwed her, got her drunk and high on drugs. Then what happened?"

"Well, I was pretty far gone myself. Maybe even in worse condition. I remember her saying she wanted to go in the hot tub. And I remember going out in back and getting in the spa with her. We weren't in there all that long when I told her she'd have to leave pretty soon. She started crying. I felt like shit," Biff said, lowering his head, "but I knew I couldn't help her. Money was all I had to offer."

"Did you argue?" Abby asked.

"No, I was in a funk, feeling like hell. The heat from the spa, the booze and drugs, all caught up with me and…well, I guess I passed out."

"You passed out in the hot tub," Abby said.

"That's right. I went out cold and didn't wake up until I was in bed in the Havallard Clinic up in Novato. The first face I saw upon awakening was Katerina's."

"You were with Katerina?"

"Yeah."

"What happened to Sarah?"

"I didn't know. When Katerina didn't say anything about her, I figured Sarah must have left before she got home. So I kept my mouth shut."

"Katerina had to wonder what was going on," Abby said.

"She knew I'd been drinking and doing drugs. She was pissed, but all she said was that she'd come home and found me passed out. She didn't mention Sarah and neither did I."

"That's it?" Frank said incredulously.

"Not quite. A couple of days later we read about a girl—Sarah—being found over in the Delta and that she'd died the night she'd been with me. Well, I couldn't handle that, so I broke down and told Katerina everything. She told me she already knew Sarah had been to the house, but since I wasn't directly responsible for her death, she was going to stand by me. But she made me promise I'd never tell anyone about Sarah coming to the house that night. That was the condition. She wouldn't be able to stand the notoriety and scandal. She said that even though I was innocent, my involvement with Sarah would have been enough to ruin our lives."

"What about the maid?" Frank asked.

"Yes," Biff said, nodding, "she was a problem. Evelinda was quiet and stayed in her room when she wasn't working. She normally went to bed early and got up early. Once dinner was over, she went off and I never saw her again. I guess I didn't give her a lot of thought when Sarah first got there. Until we got smashed, we were pretty discreet. But Katerina told me Evelinda had been aware there was a girl in the house, so Katerina paid her off and sent her away."

"That's the whole story?" Frank said. "You pass out and Sarah disappears mysteriously, only to turn up dead several hours later in Watermark Slough and you know nothing about it. You really expect us to believe that?"

"Whether you believe it or not, it's true. Ask Katerina. Hell, ask the people at the Havallard Clinic. They saw the condition I was in when I arrived. I'm telling you, the last thing I saw before I passed out was Sarah sitting in the hot tub across from me, crying. I wasn't conscious again until I woke up in the clinic.''

"And the only reason you didn't tell us all this before was because of your promise to Katerina?" Abby said.

"Mostly."

"And you're telling us now because you know we can put you away in the slammer for a few years because of last night?"

"Not entirely," Biff said, his face twisting with pain. "Katerina and I had a fight. I've been wanting to get it out in the open, but she's been adamantly opposed. She said we'd be prosecuted for covering up, for corrupting the morals of a minor, for drug offenses, obstructing justice and all the rest. We were innocent of murder, so there was no need to tell what happened that night Sarah came over."

"But you didn't buy it?"

"I was tired of hiding. I knew I didn't kill Sarah, so I didn't see what harm there was in saying what happened. I mean, we're talking about somebody's life. Katerina flew into a rage. 'What about *me?*' she screamed over and over. 'What about *me?*'"

"What was she talking about?" Abby asked. "The humiliation?"

"Yes. That's all she's cared about from the very beginning."

"So you had an argument and you left."

"Well," Biff said, "she tried to convince me it was all going to blow over, that we wouldn't be hearing any more about Sarah. I asked what she was talking about and she told me to trust her. The whole thing would die down. No more cops or questions."

"And what did you say to that?"

"I didn't believe her. I told her it was wishful thinking."

"Then what?"

"Well, she was livid, called me a coward, an ignorant fool. I told her I didn't care, that obviously things were over between us."

"And then you left?"

"Yes, but there was something else."

"What?"

Biff lowered his head.

"Come on," Frank said, "you've come this far. Don't start lying or hiding things now."

Biff nodded. Looking up, his eyes filled with tears, he said, "Katerina told me to go, to get out of her life, but she said if I ever talked to anybody about what happened that night with Sarah, she'd have me killed."

Abby, who'd been pacing in front of them, stopped in her tracks. "She threatened to kill you?"

"Yes."

"Since you didn't come to us, you must have taken her seriously."

"Katerina can be very tough. And she's not afraid to take matters into her own hands. A couple of nights ago I overheard her on the phone. I could only hear her side of the conversation, but it sounded to me like she was ordering that somebody be killed."

"Who?"

"I don't know."

"Do you know who she was talking to?" Frank asked.

"I have no idea. Her tone was cold as ice and I knew she was dead serious. When she threatened me the day I left, I truly believed her because of what I overheard."

"Have you talked to Katerina since leaving?"

"No."

"You've spent the time here, trying to drown your sorrows with sex, booze and drugs," Abby said.

"Look, I know I'm not a model citizen," Biff replied.

"Maybe I'm a shit, maybe I'm the scum of the earth, but I never killed anybody and I never had sex with anybody who didn't want it. I never pressured or coerced anybody. Maybe I should have said no when I said yes, like that last night with Sarah, but that's the worst I'm guilty of."

Abby stared at Biff, her hands on her hips. He looked back at her, unblinking.

"I'd like to ask a favor, though," he said. "Don't dick around with me. If you folks are going to run me in for what I did with those girls out there, just do it and get it over with. I don't want to live with this hanging over me."

"Mr. Roberts," Abby said, "I feel for you. I know how hard this must be. Hell, Alice Gibbs, Sarah's mother in Utah, knows what it's like to have to wait, not knowing what's going to happen. But in your case, it's too damned bad. I'm not going to accommodate you. I'm going to walk out of here and I'm going to continue my investigation of this case. And you, Mr. Roberts, you're going to just have to wait and suffer." She tossed her head. "Come on, Frank, let's get out of here."

He followed her into the front room where the two girls were waiting on the sofa, huddled together. They looked up at Abby with round eyes.

"All right, you two," she said, "get your asses out of here."

"You ain't takin' us to jail?"

"I'm giving you a chance to learn something, instead," she replied. "You were lucky you got a john who was only a party animal. He could just as easily been a psychopathic killer. You probably know you're taking your life in your hands, and maybe there's nothing I can say to get you off the streets, but if you want to live to see the other side of twenty, you'll stop this right now. Find yourself help, ladies, because if you don't, the morning will come when you won't wake up from the party the night before. The reason I'm here is because that very thing happened to a little girl who's in a refrigerator in Sacramento right now. It happens, believe me. And I'd just as soon the next body I put in a bag won't be yours."

Abby opened her purse and took out one of her cards. She wrote something on the back and handed it to Terrella.

"This is the name of a woman who works with girls like you. She's a cop like me and she has an office here in San Francisco. Do yourself and me a favor and call her, okay?"

The girls nodded.

"Now get out of here," Abby said.

The two got up and headed for the door like a couple of mice making their getaway. After the door closed, Frank put his arm around Abby's shoulders.

"Think they listened?" he asked.

"One chance in twenty," she replied sadly.

"Well, it was a hell of a speech."

"Thanks, Frank."

"How about some lunch?"

"I was thinking we ought to track down Katerina."

"You've got to eat."

Abby sighed. "All right. I'm putting myself in your hands. Take me somewhere."

Tiburon
Marin County

They had a window seat at Sam's, overlooking the marina. Their lunch dishes had been cleared and they were enjoying a leisurely conversation. The deck, normally crowded and sun-drenched on a summer day, was now empty, wet and uninviting under the slate-gray sky. The wind blew droplets of water against the pane of glass next to them. Abby stared at the monochromatic skyline of San Francisco in the distance—water, land and sky all different tones of gray. She shivered and watched Frank sip his coffee.

"If Biff is telling the truth—and I know that's a big if—then Katerina had to be responsible for Sarah's death," she said.

"Without saying it, he kind of made her out to be the bad guy."

Abby nodded. "Here's my revised theory—Katerina comes home, finds the two of them in the spa. Biff is doped out. Katerina goes into a rage, she and Sarah struggle and Sarah drowns."

"Accidentally or because Katerina wanted to kill her?"

Abby sighed. "Yeah, we have the same problem of proving a crime was committed, don't we? We need our witness badly."

"Unfortunately she's on the other side of the world."

"We also have to verify Biff's story about the Havallard Clinic," Abby said. "We need to drive up to Novato."

"Yes, if Biff was as incapacitated as he claimed, then Katerina had to be the one who dumped the body in the Delta."

"That doesn't prove she was responsible for Sarah's death."

"No," Frank replied, "but the evidence against her is mounting. That phone conversation Biff heard is pretty damning—if true, of course. She could have been talking to those guys in the Chevy who tried to kill us."

"What does that do to your theory about Mort?"

"Makes it a less likely possibility," he conceded. "On the other hand, of the two of them, who'd be more likely to hire guys out of Sacramento?"

"You're right about that," Abby said. "Sacramento doesn't seem like Katerina's kind of town."

"Not that I'm in a hurry to erase Mort from the list of suspects," Frank returned, "but neither one of them would lightly hire a gang of thugs to have a couple of cops killed.

I'll concede Katerina's in this thing up to her eyeballs. Figuring out exactly what she did, then proving it, will be the trick, though.''

Abby had a sinking feeling. Unless the maid, Evelinda, came through for them, this one just might slip through their fingers.

''Why so glum?'' Frank asked.

''I don't know. I'm getting a bad feeling, I guess.''

''About?''

''The case.'' She chuckled. ''What did you think?''

''Not to bring up a sore subject, but seems to me things between us have been a little up in the air of late,'' he said.

''I've been giving that some thought, too, Frank.''

His expression grew wary. ''And?''

''I like you. I like you a lot. And I don't want anything to get in the way of our friendship.''

He looked relieved.

''Which doesn't mean that I'm taking it lightly that you and Kay had an affair. Or that you didn't tell me sooner.'' She paused dramatically. ''But there's something I want to know. At Thelma's yesterday, you said you loved me. Did you mean it?''

''Would I lie?''

''I'm serious.''

''So am I,'' he said.

She struggled with her confusion.

''Don't ask me to explain,'' Frank said, ''because I'm not very good at looking beneath the surface of things. I know we're an unlikely pair. But I just can't get you out of my mind. With other women I'm as eager to get away after I've been with them for a while as I am to see them in the first place. You're different, Abby. Being with you seems so natural. You're sort of a part of me. Seems to me that must be love.''

Abby folded her hands on the table and stared at her fingers.

"What do *you* think?" he asked.

"I like being thought of that way. I like being with you, Frank. And I was very lonely last night. I've been alone most of my adult life. And you and I have only been together a few nights, but last night I really missed you."

Frank reached across the table and took her hands. "I had to fight myself to keep from driving out to Tyler Island. Even at three o'clock in the morning, I came this close," he said, holding his thumb and forefinger half an inch apart.

"I don't like the idea of you moving into Chet's place," she said.

"I've got to live someplace."

"What are you going to do, long-term?"

"I haven't decided. When I was awake in the middle of the night, I gave some thought to dropping by to see Constance Butterfield. It may be a pipe dream, but if I can, I'd sure like to buy her forty acres of pears."

"Maybe with the money you're getting from Chet."

"I don't know how much it'll be, so I'll have to wait and see."

"The coming months are going to be interesting," she said, her heart lifting as she considered the possibilities.

"Once we get this case behind us."

Abby had to admit the Jane Doe case held several lives hostage—not to mention the lives that had been lost. Chet was dead, Rance and some of the men in that cult and, of course, Sarah. Selfishness, greed, moral depravity and inhumanity had caused needless suffering and death. But there had been lessons learned, as well. Abby's life had changed because of Jane Doe, and so had Frank's. Much of Riverton had been affected, if only having been touched emotionally.

"There are several people responsible for Sarah's death," Abby told him. "Some have already paid for it, but I'm convinced the person most immediately responsible hasn't. I don't want this thing to go away unresolved.''

"Don't despair, Abby. We still have a few cards to play."

"Yes, but time is running out." She glanced at her watch. "Maybe we should get over to Katerina's."

"You *are* a dedicated little thing, aren't you, Chief?"

"Sometimes a person's strengths are her weaknesses," she replied.

Frank signaled the waitress for the check. "Then let's get hopping."

"By the way," Abby said, "how's that money holding up that Chet gave you?"

"It went up in smoke the other night with the rest of my things."

"Oh, no, Frank..."

He shrugged. "That's okay. It paid for a couple of the best nights of my life. How can a guy complain about that?"

Ross

"Lady go yesterday, she not come back," the maid said.

"But you don't know where she went?" Abby asked.

Nedi, all four feet ten inches of her, stood resolutely in the door like a guard dog. "Don't know."

"And you don't know when she's returning?"

"She not say nothing. Just go."

"Did she pack a bag?"

"What you mean?"

"Did she take a suitcase with her? Clothes?"

"Yes, maybe."

Abby gave Frank a look. He could see the frustration on her face.

Out of the corner of her mouth she said, "Does that mean yes or no?"

"Maybe yes," he replied.

Abby poked him in the ribs with her elbow. Nedi looked perplexed by the gesture.

"Okay," Frank said to the maid, "but you call us when Ms. Kreski comes home or telephones. Understand?"

Nedi nodded. "Okay." Then she closed the door.

Frank shook his head. "There's something about that woman that makes me want to call the Immigration and Naturalization Service."

Abby groaned her concurrence. "She knows who butters her bread, I guess. Shall we go up to Novato?"

"What say we have a look around back, first? We haven't seen this spa where Sarah supposedly died."

"Good idea," Abby said.

A light rain fell as they went around the side of the house where the driveway led to the garage. A high fence and hedge separated the parking area on the side of the house from the spacious back garden. They went to the gate, which opened just as they got there. A small Hispanic man in a rain slicker looked up at them with surprise. Behind him was a wheelbarrow with a couple of large shrubs in planting cans. He nodded and smiled, stepping back so they could come through. Judging by his manner, he didn't speak any English.

Seeing that the guy, who was obviously the gardener, would have to push his way through the gate with an awkward load, Frank held it open and gestured for him to go on ahead. The man, giving him a toothy, appreciative grin, lifted the handles of the wheelbarrow and started through the gate. As he passed Frank, the wheel hit a rock, throwing the wheelbarrow off balance and making it tip. Frank grabbed it, catching it before the plants tumbled out. In the process, the edge of the wheelbarrow banged his thigh.

As the gardener went on ahead with the wheelbarrow, Frank looked down at his pant leg, which had gotten smudged by the wet, rusty vehicle. He brushed at the spot, though it did little good. He glanced up at Abby, who'd witnessed the incident.

"Poor Frank," she said. "Try to be the Good Samaritan and you end up with a dry-cleaning bill."

"You suppose Katerina would pay if I sent it to her?"

Abby laughed. "Yeah, sure. With a check delivered by a hit man."

Frank flexed his leg. "Maybe I can sue her for pain and suffering."

"That'd be one way to get her into court."

They went through the gate to the back garden, a spacious, parklike setting with several large trees and enclosed with mature shrubs. The foliage and shrubbery were so dense that little more than the rooftops of the surrounding homes could be seen. There was a huge patio at the rear of the house. At the edge of it was a swimming pool with steam rising from it. They followed the flagstone walk toward it, stopping at the near end. Frank peered into the crystalline water.

"I bet Katerina pays more to heat this sucker than I pay on my mortgage," he said.

"Maybe she likes to swim."

The spa was at the other end of the pool, seven or eight feet of patio separating the two. A person could relax in the hot tub, then get energized by jumping into the relatively cool pool. Wasn't it in Sweden they did that? Or did the Swedes go naked from their saunas into the snow? Same concept, he decided.

The spa was covered, but steam rose from it nevertheless. Frank glanced up at the gray, misty sky, then at the house. French doors from what appeared to be a family room provided access to the patio. Off to one side was the kitchen, all lit up on this gloomy day. He could see Nedi at work in it, oblivious to their presence. It was difficult to tell what the room in the wing opposite the kitchen was, because the drapes were drawn. The rooms overlooking the patio and pool area on the second floor were most likely bedrooms.

"The spa is in plain view of several different rooms," Abby said.

"Yeah, I was thinking the same thing."

They looked in the direction of the neighboring homes. Roofs and chimneys were all they could see.

"If there were witnesses to what happened out here, they were mostly likely in the house," he said.

"Probably."

He glanced back the way they'd come. "I wonder how Katerina got Biff to the clinic."

"I never thought to ask," Abby said.

"Me, neither."

"He's a big guy, so she sure as hell didn't carry him, not without help."

"And if he was as out of it as he claimed, he didn't walk to a car."

"Maybe they'll be able to tell us at the clinic," she said.

"Are we finished here?"

"I am."

They began walking toward the gate. "So, when do we put out an APB on Katerina Kreski?" Frank asked.

"Let's see what they have to say at the clinic."

Novato

The Havallard Clinic was located on San Marin Drive on the northwest side of town. They'd gotten bad directions and it took a while to find it. The drive up from Ross had taken four times as long as it should have, and it was dark by the time they hit town. There had been a bad accident involving a semi-truck in San Rafael, compounded by the usual rush-hour traffic.

"What I can't believe is that people go through this every

day," Frank had said. "They really have to be addicted to their salary to put up with this bullshit."

"Everybody can't be a pear farmer, Frank."

The receptionist in the clinic directed them to the administrator, an officious woman named Mrs. Landour, who lacked both a sense of humor and any semblance of compassion. She was preparing to leave for the day and didn't appreciate being detained. The fact that they were police officers didn't particularly impress her.

"All information about our patients is confidential," she told them, "and can't be released without a court order."

Frank, who had little patience for the bureaucratic mentality, was annoyed. "We aren't asking you to divulge secrets," he said. "We'd just like to know if Biff Roberts checked in the night of February fourteenth."

"Look, Officer, this is a private clinic. People avail themselves of our services because they know everything will be kept in the strictest confidence, including whether they've even been here. Some very distinguished people pass through these doors, and we're not about to betray their confidence."

"Some sleazy criminals might pass through these doors also, lady. There's more than one way to be distinguished, you know. Besides, money and sainthood are not necessarily the same thing."

"Well, you can think what you wish," she said, looking down her nose, "but our files are still confidential. Now, if you'll please excuse me, our administrative office is closed for the day."

Frank and Abby retreated to the reception area where they sat in chairs to confer.

"Forgive me for saying so, but there's nothing I hate more than a snooty, self-important bitch," he said.

"She was unpleasant, all right, but it's also true that you catch more flies with honey than vinegar."

"You think I was unpleasant?"

"I've seen you more charming."

"So what are we going to do," he said, "get a court order?"

"Unless we can find another employee who's a little more sympathetic."

Frank glanced at the receptionist, a woman in her late thirties. She'd been accommodating when they'd arrived. He patted Abby's knee. "Let me see what I can do with a little honey," he said.

He crossed to the reception desk, noting the nameplate facing him. "Forgive me for interrupting, Monica, but when we were speaking to Mrs. Landour, we forgot to ask who was on duty the night of February fourteenth. Is there any way you can tell us?"

"I have no idea," the pretty brunette said. "The schedule's kept by the office."

He looked at her left hand and saw she wore no ring. "Gee, it's awfully important that we know who to talk to. Is there a way we can find out without waiting until the office opens in the morning?"

Monica, clearly wanting to help, looked at her calendar. "Let's see, what day of the week was the fourteenth?"

"A Friday."

"Oh, yes, so it was."

"I'm surprised you don't remember," Frank said. "That was Valentine's Day. At least five guys must have asked you out."

She smiled shyly. "Actually, I was home that night, watching a movie on my VCR."

"I don't believe it."

"It's true."

"You've been hiding, then, Monica. Nobody as pretty as you stays home on Valentine's Day unless she wants to."

She blushed, turning her attention back to her calendar.

"Let's see, this is Wednesday, same month. That means the same crew will be working tonight."

"No kidding. What time do they come on?"

"Eleven."

"Would it be possible to wait for them?"

"Visiting hours are over at nine and the front door is locked. But if it's important you could wait for them at the employees' entrance. There'll be three nurses, an orderly and two nurse's assistants."

"Monica, you're a doll."

She smiled at him. Frank turned to go, but stopped.

"By the way, you're cheating all the guys by staying home."

She bit her lip. "Thanks."

Frank went back to where Abby was waiting across the room, looking less than pleased. "Well?"

"Bzzz. Bzzz. Bzzz," he said. "Spreading a little honey works. Come on, we've got to kill some time until eleven."

"What happens then?"

"We interview the night crew."

After finishing dinner they decided to get a motel room. "We could always drive home," Frank said, "but we'd get in late and, who knows, maybe we'd get firebombed again."

"That's got to be the most creative excuse I've ever heard," Abby told him.

Frank beamed. "I don't know what it is about you and hotel rooms, sweetheart, but it's magic."

"No, it's sex."

Frank took her in his arms. "No, it's you, Abby."

They had two and a half hours to kill before returning to the clinic. Abby decided to take a bath and asked Frank if he wanted to join her.

"That's a question you'll never have to ask twice," he told her.

They took a long bath, titillating each other. When they got out of the tub, they dried each other off. Frank kissed her and carried her to the bed. They made love twice, once with energy and desperation. The second time was slow and affectionate. He told her again he loved her.

Around ten-thirty they got up to dress.

"I should have called the office today and didn't," she said, putting on her bra.

"It's never too late."

"Think I will, if you don't mind."

While Frank put on his shirt, Abby sat by the bedside phone and dialed Riverton. He liked it that she felt comfortable around him in her underwear. He listened to her talking to the dispatcher. She jotted down a note, then hung up.

"Crystal's been trying to reach me all day. Said it was urgent. Even though it's late, I'm going to call her."

Frank went into the bathroom to do something with his hair. Without a hair dryer it was tough to look halfway decent. He remembered with amusement the days back when he used to make fun of blow-dry guys. When he came out of the bath, Abby was putting on her blouse. She looked stricken.

"What's the matter?"

"Darren's disappeared and Crystal's worried. She's afraid he's gone looking for me and that his intention might be to hurt me."

"Why would he want to do that?"

"She told me he's been acting crazy. Apparently the police have come looking for him. My guess is the guy in the hospital in Bakersfield—the one who jumped us—implicated him. Crystal's afraid Darren's blaming me for all his troubles."

"So Darren was the one behind those guys at the Vietnam Memorial."

"Kind of looks that way," Abby said.

"I wonder if there's any chance he could have been behind the firebombing of my trailer, too. The guys *were* from Sacramento."

Abby gave him a woebegone look. "Frank, we've got way too many enemies."

"Yeah, well, I don't like the idea of Darren threatening you just because you won't go out with him."

"He's got serious problems, no question about it."

Frank went over to where she sat on the bed, took her face in his hands and kissed her on the lips. "I might insist on moving in with you for a while," he said, turning and sitting beside her.

"I've got Tristan to protect me."

"You prefer a dog to me?"

"Tristan's more socially acceptable, Frank. And he makes absolutely no demands except for an occasional pat on the head or getting his ears scratched."

"I may expect more, but just think how much more I have to offer. Am I a fun date or am I not?"

"Fun isn't the only issue," she said.

Frank shook his head, grinning. "Abby, we need a vacation. Someplace far away."

"Actually, that doesn't sound half-bad."

He leaned over and kissed her cheek. "Well, are you ready for another assault on the Havallard Clinic?"

"Sure, let's do it," she said.

He started to get up.

"Frank..."

"Yeah?"

"Look at your pant leg."

"I know. That's where Katerina's wheelbarrow bumped me."

"Yes, but look closely."

He peered down at his leg.

"What do you see?" she asked.

"Jesus," he said. "Rust and flecks of red paint."

The head nurse of the night shift was Mrs. Kajiwara, a middle-aged woman with a smiling face as round as a sunflower. She was very direct.

"Estelle loves her rules," she said of Mrs. Landour, the administrator. "And there's something else. Ms. Kreski and her father before her were major financial supporters of the clinic. Estelle believes our first duty is to protect our friends."

"There's a woman in Utah who'd like to know how her daughter died and who was responsible," Abby said. "We're investigating the possibility of Mr. Roberts's and Ms. Kreski's involvement. We'd appreciate any information you have that might help us understand what happened the night the girl died. What you tell us could be damning to Biff and Katerina, or it might exonerate them. The truth is all that matters. I hope the Havallard Clinic isn't afraid of the truth."

"I might discuss the matter with you off the record," Mrs. Kajiwara said, glancing at one of the other nurses who was walking down the hall.

They were standing at the nurses' station. Mrs. Kajiwara invited them into the supervising nurse's office and closed the door. "I don't know if I can help you, but I'll be glad to listen to your questions."

Abby explained the gist of the problem. Mostly they were interested in verifying Biff Roberts's story, especially the timing of his arrival at the clinic.

"I recall the evening quite clearly," the nurse told them. "Mr. Roberts has been in for treatment before."

Frank wanted to ask what for, but he knew that would be getting into a sensitive area, and their immediate objective was to keep the woman talking. Abby seemed to be doing well, so he let her continue the lead.

"What time did he arrive?"

"It was before our shift, but Karen, the supervisor who was on duty at the time, and I talked about it in detail because of Ms. Kreski's importance to the clinic. As I recall, Karen said they arrived around 10:00 p.m."

"And Ms. Kreski was with him?"

"She followed in her car. Mr. Roberts arrived by ambulance."

"An ambulance brought him to the clinic?"

"That's right," Mrs. Kajiwara replied. "In fact, the paramedics came back shortly after we were on duty because they'd left some equipment behind. I talked to one of them and he told me Mr. Roberts was in pretty bad shape, unconscious when they picked him up and incoherent when they got here. They wanted to take him to Ross General, but Ms. Kreski insisted they bring him here. When I first looked at him shortly after we came on duty, he was still out. I really shouldn't talk about the specifics, though."

"That's all right," Abby said. "The medical details are unimportant. He told us he didn't completely come to and know where he was until morning. Would you say that's probably true, based on what you saw?"

"I wasn't with him continuously, of course, but my impression was he pretty much slept through."

"And Katerina Kreski stayed with him?" Abby asked.

"She arrived with him and got him admitted, according to Karen. Once Mr. Roberts was settled, she left to get something to eat. She told Karen she'd been traveling and hadn't yet had her dinner."

"She left the clinic in her car?" Frank asked.

"I assume so."

"How long was she gone?" Abby asked.

"I first saw her here shortly before midnight, which would have made it about an hour and a half."

Abby looked at Frank as if to ask whether that was enough

time to drive to the Delta and back. It wasn't, and on reflection she seemed to realize it.

"Are you sure it wasn't longer?" Abby asked. "Say, two and a half, three hours?"

"No, definitely not. She brought a pie with her for the staff. I recall thinking how thoughtful that was. A nice coconut cream pie, one of my favorites."

Frank had that sinking feeling investigators get when things begin to unravel. Biff was unconscious and Katerina couldn't have gotten more than a forty-five-minute drive from Novato. Since Sarah was spotted in the slough during the small hours of the morning and had probably been in the water for a while before the kids found her floating by his dock, someone else must have dumped the body. But who? The maid?

Sarah's death hadn't been preplanned, so there couldn't have been arrangements in place for disposing of the body. Katerina would have had to organize things almost instantly, and it seemed unlikely she'd be able to call on outside help. How many people—like an innocent friend or neighbor— would agree to take a corpse, drive a hundred miles and dump it in a slough as a favor? Not very damned many. The maid must have been the one. The fifty thousand Katerina paid her had to be for disposing of the body, then getting the hell out of the country. Even so, Evelinda had to be pretty gutsy and tough to agree to something like that.

Abby was questioning Mrs. Kajiwara about Katerina's disposition, her attitude.

"She seemed very tired. As I recall, she said she'd started her day in Texas or someplace like that. She was worried about Mr. Roberts, I know. She asked several times if he'd awakened while she was gone, if he'd said anything. Otherwise she was considerate—for her—and in pretty good spirits." The nurse beamed a sunflower smile.

Abby glanced at Frank again, her expression indicating she

was completely deflated. "Do you have any questions for Mrs. Kajiwara, Frank?"

"No."

"We'll let you get back to work," she said to the woman. "And we appreciate your cooperation." Abby gave her a card and asked her to call if she remembered anything else from that night that might be of interest.

They left the clinic, returning to the Bronco. Once they were inside the vehicle, Abby slammed her fist on the steering wheel.

"Damn it to hell," she said. "I thought for sure Katerina was the one who dumped Sarah's body. Everything works but the timing. She put Sarah in the wheelbarrow, took her to her car, called the ambulance for Biff, and they convoyed up here to Novato. But she didn't have time to drive to Riverton and back in an hour and a half. She'd be lucky to *get* there in that time, let alone make the return trip. What are we missing, Frank?"

"It has to be the maid. She and Katerina put Sarah's body in another vehicle—either the maid's car or Biff's, and then Evelinda drove to the Delta."

Abby considered that. "You think a young immigrant would do something like that to accommodate her employer?"

"Fifty thousand, Abby."

She stared off into the night. "You know what that means, don't you? Evelinda's not coming back and probably won't talk to anyone. She's an accessory to the crime and a criminal herself."

He couldn't argue with that.

Thursday
February 27th

Novato

They arrived at the motel at about twenty after midnight. Abby pulled into a space near their room and turned off the ignition. She was beat and she was depressed. Frank must have felt the same because he sat there motionless, lacking the energy to get out of the car and go inside.

"Unless somebody lied to us, it's the maid," Abby said after a while. "You're right."

"Let's call the priest and run the question by him," Frank said.

"Now?"

"We're likely to find him in, aren't we?"

"It's after midnight, Frank. How about first thing in the morning?"

He sighed. "Yeah, I guess I can sleep another night without knowing."

They got out of the Bronco and went into the room. Abby went over to the bed and sat down heavily. She looked at the phone.

"It would really be inconsiderate to phone someone at this hour. I mean, this doesn't qualify as a life or death emergency, does it?"

"The more relevant question is if you can make it *sound* like a life or death emergency."

"Frank, you're evil, you know that? You've got a criminal mind. No wonder you were at the top of my list of suspects."

"And it's so much fun to lead you astray."

She gave him a telling look, then took her notebook out of her purse, found the priest's number and dialed. A sleepy housekeeper answered. She went to get Father Caratay. It took a couple of minutes for him to come on the line. Abby identified herself.

"I'm terribly sorry to call you at this hour, Father," she said, "but we're in hot pursuit of a suspect, and the degree and nature of Evelinda DeLeon's involvement has become critical. The evidence indicates she was an accomplice to what may now be murder."

"Evelinda involved in a murder? I don't believe it. She is a very religious person," the priest replied.

"Would she be capable of helping cover up a homicide?"

"She's human. She makes mistakes like everyone. But to intentionally break the law, no, it's not like her."

"Not even for fifty thousand dollars?"

"The money was compensation for the loss of her job and for giving up the opportunity to be in this country. I think the only reason she agreed is because her parents in the Philippines are so needy."

The priest's response lifted Abby's spirits. She pressed ahead hopefully. "Father Caratay, let me be specific. We believe that Katerina Kreski prevailed upon Evelinda to transport the victim's body to the Delta and dump it in a slough."

"Transport it? How?"

"Take it in the trunk of a car, for example."

"If so, it would have had to be in a taxi. Evelinda doesn't drive."

"She doesn't drive?"

"No," the priest replied. "She doesn't have a license and she has never driven an automobile. It was always a problem on her days off. It's difficult to get from Marin to Daly City by bus. But that's what she had to do."

Abby was stunned. She looked at Frank, who seemed to have gotten the message. He was as nonplussed as she.

"Then you're saying there's no way Evelinda could have taken the body to the Delta."

"Not unless somebody else drove. But I don't believe she would become involved in something like that, anyway. Truly."

"Father Caratay, it's more important than ever that we speak to Evelinda. Even if she wasn't an accomplice to a crime, she must know something terribly damning."

"I'm doing everything I can," the priest said. "But I will call Manila again tomorrow to see if there's been any progress on finding her. Eventually I will reach her, I'm sure. But these things take time. We're talking about a rural area, don't forget. When I started, I didn't even know where Evelinda was from."

"You're efforts are greatly appreciated," Abby told him. "Now I'll let you go. And again, I'm deeply sorry for having disturbed you at such a late hour."

"Both God and the law work strange hours," the priest said. Then he hung up.

Abby dropped the receiver into the cradle and turned to Frank.

"We're back to square one, aren't we?" he said.

"Yeah, but I have a feeling it's a good square one."

"Because…"

"Because this way we're more likely to hear from Evelinda."

Tyler Island

Abby drove along the fallow fields under the morning sun, headed for home. The gables of the Victorian could be seen for miles across the flat landscape. She was near enough that she could make out the distinctive roofline.

By the time they'd reached Riverton, the overcast had burned off, which she'd taken as a good omen. Even though both she and Frank were at a loss to explain what had happened the night Sarah Gibbs died, they sensed the mystery would somehow be solved.

Because they'd left Novato at dawn, it had been early when Abby dropped Frank off at Dix's place. "So, what are you going to do today?" she asked him.

"Think I'll have a beauty day."

"Beauty day?"

"Go fishing and relax. Get a little clean air in my lungs."

"How nice to be a man of leisure."

"You were the one who wanted to be police chief, Abby."

"And now you get the last laugh."

Frank had been audacious enough to touch her cheek affectionately, but mindful of the neighbors, he hadn't kissed her. "How about you?" he asked.

"I'll spend my day protecting the citizens of Riverton, of course. But not until I go home for a change of clothes."

"No leisurely soaks in the tub?"

She'd smiled. "Well, I'm not going to rush to the office."

"Have any plans for dinner tonight?"

"Give me a call toward the end of the day."

"Check."

Abby was already looking forward to the evening. Their easy camaraderie was awfully nice, something she'd never shared with a man before. She was certain now that they were headed someplace important. This was not just a fling.

Abby reached her driveway and turned off the road. As she approached the house she started getting a funny feeling. Then, when she stopped at the gate and Tristan didn't come bounding up to greet her, she knew something was amiss. Her pulse quickened.

Getting out of the Bronco, she scanned the yard. "Tristan!" she called. "Here, boy, I'm home!"

There was no sign of him.

When she opened the gate, she saw a smear of blood in the gravel. It looked as if someone had tried to sweep it or had dragged something over it. Then she spotted more streaks of blood leading off onto the lawn. Abby tensed, beginning to fear the worst.

She followed the trail to the nearby bushes, where she found Tristan. He was dead. The grizzly sight of her pet on the cold ground, his fur caked with dried blood, a bullet hole in his shoulder, sickened her. Tears filled her eyes. Even though she'd only had him a short while, Tristan had become her companion and friend, her protector.

Squatting beside him, she felt his leg. It was already stiff, the body cold, which meant he'd been dead for some time. The question now was if whoever had shot him was still around. Standing, she looked toward the house. The door and windows in front were intact. Of course, whoever it was could have entered in back. She decided to investigate. Since her home was in the county, the Sheriff's Department had jurisdiction, not the Riverton P.D. From their standpoint she was a citizen like any other, but it seemed more professional to know what kind of crime to report. She decided to check the outside of the house before making her call.

Stepping out of the bushes, she opened her purse and removed the replacement gun she'd gotten from Dix, a semi-automatic. She released the safety.

Walking slowly, Abby went around the side of the Victorian. In back, a car sat on the lawn—Darren Armstrong's red Corvette.

Abby's pulse went into high gear and her fingers tightened on the handle of the automatic. She glanced at the back of house and still saw no sign of a break-in. The car door was slightly ajar. The dew covering the windows prevented her from seeing inside. She considered retreating, calling for help, but decided to investigate first.

Abby inched forward cautiously, alert for the slightest motion. When she reached the car, she saw it was empty. Exhaling with relief, she lowered the gun, her shoulders drooping.

At that exact moment the voice from behind her hit her like a brick against the back of her head. "Don't move an inch, if you want to live to see my smiling face."

She froze.

"Now put your gun on the roof of the car and step back. Slowly!" he warned. "No sudden moves."

Abby complied.

"Okay, fine," he said. "Now turn around."

She did as she was told, finding Darren standing twenty feet away, the pistol in his hand pointed directly at her. Though he had a smug grin on his face, he looked like hell. His normally perfect hair was mussed. His eyes were glassy and red, and he badly needed a shave.

"What? No smile, no hello for the father of your child?" he said bitterly.

Anger began to replace her shock and fear. "Darren, what in the hell do you think you're doing?"

"Shut the fuck up, bitch!" he screamed, the gun in his hand shaking. "I didn't ask for a lecture. All I wanted was a simple hello."

She swallowed hard. "All right. Hello, Darren. Is that better?" She could see he was completely out of it, probably on drugs. He'd had his wits about him enough to get the drop on her, though. Whether he'd intended it as a trap or she'd just walked into it accidentally and out of stupidity hardly mattered at this point.

"Yeah, much better," he said. "Women should be gentle, Abby. Soft. It's much more attractive."

She couldn't decide what he was up to, but the gun pointed at her was not a good sign. She said nothing, figuring it was best to take her cue from him.

"So, where've you been?" he asked. "Playing house with the old fart?"

"I've been working on a case in the city."

"Oh, really?"

"Yes."

"With him?"

"Darren, is this doing anybody any good? Why don't you—"

"Goddamn it, shut up, Abby! I don't want to hear that! All I want coming out of your mouth is 'Yes, Darren.'"

She stood mute, her eyes narrowing. He glared back, angry, crazed.

"I have a feeling you won't have the sense to do this my way," he said. "So I'm not going to fuck around. It's cold out here. I've been freezing my ass off waiting for you."

Her glare hardened, but she was not at all confident of dissuading him from whatever it was he had in mind. Darren reached into his pants pocket and took out his car keys. "Here," he said, tossing them to her. "There's a bag in the trunk. I want you to take it out." He inclined his head toward the rear of the car. "Go on."

Abby, her knees a bit wobbly, went to the back of the Corvette. Her hands trembled enough that she had trouble getting the key in the lock, but she managed to open it. Inside she found a shopping bag stuffed with ropes and videotapes and a variety of sex toys. She looked back at him, beginning to understand.

"Yep," he said, answering her unspoken question, "you and me are going to have a party."

"Darren, I'm not going to have sex with you. You're crazy! You need help!"

He thrust the gun toward her, his face turning red. "What did I tell you before?" he said through his teeth. "'Yes, Darren,' is all I want to hear coming out of your mouth. All you need to know is we're going to have us another baby if I have to fuck you for a month."

He *was* insane. And Abby could see just what that implied. The man was a lot more dangerous than she could possibly have imagined. How would she stop him? He seemed so determined. Did she play along or make her stand now?

"If that expression on your face means you don't believe me, you'd better think twice," he said. "It can be nice or it can be not so nice. The choice is yours. Now take out the bag. We're going inside."

Hog Slough

Frank put a line over the side of his boat and lay back to soak up the morning sun. Fishing was the best way he knew to unwind. So he'd borrowed a rod and tackle from Dix Fowler and headed for one of his favorite spots. What could be better than the waters of the Delta, all that lazy blue sky and Abby Hooper to think about?

He'd had that conversation with himself that guys tend to have when they're getting serious about a woman. It had been forever since he'd thought of anyone that way. Everything felt so right he was afraid it might be too good to be true. His feelings for her couldn't lie, though. She really did it for him.

Fishing was not only good therapy, it gave a man time to think. Having parked his truck on the levee in sight of the charred ruins of his mobile home, he was reminded of the decisions he'd have to make. Abby hadn't liked the idea of him living at Chet's, but she hadn't exactly confirmed that she wanted him moving in with her. They had a day or two to play around with the possibilities, but their relationship would have to start moving in one direction or the other.

Abby had shaken things up, forced him out of the rut he'd been in. Contentment was no longer a goal, nor was it enough. He had desires now. And designs. What she'd done was take the complacency out of him and make him hungry again.

As he pondered his love for Abby Hooper, the insistent buzz of the engine of a small plane intruded. Frank squinted up at the sunny sky and saw a single-engine craft headed east on a descending glide path, probably on its way to Moke-lumne Airfield, which was situated on the edge of the Delta, six or seven miles east of Riverton.

When Mort Anderson had his plane, he kept it there. Back when Frank and Kay were still together, Mort had tried to get her to go for a ride, but Kay had refused, saying she never rode in little airplanes piloted by amateurs. A month later Mort had a minor crash and soon thereafter got rid of the plane. Though he was ashamed to admit it, Frank had often regretted the crash hadn't been a little more definitive.

The thought led him to the subject of rich guys and their playthings. Frank had rejected gadgets. All he'd cared about was having a place to sleep, a boat seaworthy enough to get him to his fishing spots, a TV, a VCR and enough cash for a few beers now and then. But, of course, that was probably all a reaction to Arlene.

Abby wasn't like his ex-wife, but she would undoubtedly have a few ideas about life-style. He'd noticed her checking out the houses in Ross, though he couldn't see her getting into that game. She wasn't a rich man's lady—not like Ka-terina Kreski and Suzanne Broussard. She didn't need big houses and fancy vacations and—

Suddenly it hit him—airplanes. He recalled Suzanne Broussard making a remark about Werner Kreski being a pilot. Suzanne had said Kreski had a couple of planes and he remembered her saying that Katerina had sold the jet. Did that mean she had a smaller plane? And more importantly, could she *fly* it?

Frank's mind began reeling with the possibilities. Katerina Kreski, a pilot! It was probably a long shot at best, but one thing was certain—flying between Marin and the Delta would be a hell of a lot quicker than driving.

Riverton

Frank pulled up in front of Dix's house, his mind still crackling with the possibility that Katerina was their man. Of course, there were still a lot of questions to be answered. All it would take was for one leg of the stool to break and his theory would go crashing down, but at least he had something to work on. Abby would have to admire his creativity, if nothing else.

He hurried to the porch, dumping the fishing gear by the door and ringing the bell. Cookie Fowler, a squat, round, twinkly-eyed female version of Dix, came to the door.

"Hi, Frank. How'd the fishing go?"

"Great."

"Where are the fish?" She wiped her hands on her apron and motioned for him to come in.

"Didn't catch any." He moved past her, smiling. "But I had a good time."

"That's what counts. How about some lunch?"

"Think I'll skip it, Cookie. I'm just going to shave, grab a quick shower and head over to the station to see Abby."

"You'd better call first."

"Why's that?"

"She's not there. At least she wasn't an hour ago when Dix phoned to see if you knew where she was."

"She was headed for her place, but she should have made it back to town by now," Frank said.

"Maybe something came up."

"She might have decided to take a nap."

He was disappointed. He'd been eager to tell Abby about his airplane theory, maybe have her call Suzanne Broussard to see if she could confirm the necessary facts. He didn't have the Broussards' number, but he might be able to get it from Directory Assistance. He decided to get cleaned up first. By the time he was ready, Abby might have shown up at the station.

Frank went off to the bathroom. Fifteen minutes later he entered the kitchen where Cookie Fowler was at work amid the alluring aroma of baking.

"Dix called while you were in the shower. I told him what you said about Abby resting. He'd tried calling but got a busy signal, so she's probably still at home."

Frank nodded. He could wait for her, or he could try to reach Suzanne Broussard himself. The notion of cracking the case and presenting Abby with the results had a certain appeal. "Mind if I use your phone to call the Bay Area?" he asked Cookie. "I'll leave a five to cover the expense."

"That's not necessary, Frank. Call anywhere you wish. Make yourself at home."

He did his thing and was somewhat surprised that the Broussards' number was listed. There was more good luck when he found Suzanne home.

"Oh, yes, the Riverton policeman with the blue eyes," she said. "What can I do for you, Mr. Keegan?"

Frank explained he needed information about Katerina Kreski's airplane.

"Norman would be much more informative," she said, "but I'll help if I can."

"Do you know if she has a pilot's license?" he asked.

"Yes, her father taught her to fly."

Frank's heart ticked up a beat. "Where does she keep her plane?"

"It used to be at Gnoss Airfield, where Norman keeps his plane. I assume that's still the case, but I couldn't swear to it."

"Where's Gnoss Airfield, Mrs. Broussard?"

"Northern Marin. Just outside Novato."

His heart soared. "Jesus," he muttered.

"Is it *that* remarkable?"

He laughed. "No, it's just that all the pieces are falling into place."

"Should I congratulate you, Mr. Keegan?" she asked, chuckling.

"Not yet, but soon, I hope." He paused a moment to think, then asked, "How would I go about finding out if Katerina made a flight between two points on a particular night?"

"Well, pilots frequently file flight plans and records are kept. But it's not mandatory. Norman thinks it's good policy, so he almost always does. It's one way people will know if you go down or are lost."

"But a person could sneak away in their plane for an hour or two and nobody would be the wiser."

"Sure, unless someone happened to notice them."

Frank considered that. His optimism was building, though it was still too early to declare a victory. "You've been a tremendous help, Mrs. Broussard." Then he said goodbye and hung up.

For a moment he pondered the situation. If Katerina flew Sarah Gibbs's body from Marin to the Delta, where would she likely land? There were several possibilities, but if she were to dump the body in Watermark Slough, it would have to be a field with easy access. Time would have been critical. It had to be Mokelumne Field.

Mokelumne Field

"The Kreskis have been flying in here for years," the airport manager, a man named Hatcher, said. "First Werner and now Katerina. They have a big ranch in the foothills, you know. I guess now I should say *she* does. This was where they liked to land because Werner kept his cabin cruiser at Popeye's. The field is between the marina and the ranch. Of course, if Werner was flying his Learjet, he'd go up to Executive Airport in Sacramento. Usually, though, they preferred the Cessna to hop, skip and jump over from the Bay Area. I'd see them at least once a month, maybe twice a month during the spring and fall. They've had a Land Rover garaged here at the field for years. That way they can get to the boat or the ranch without any hassle."

Frank couldn't believe how neatly it was all working out. "The Cessna is kept at Gnoss Airfield in Marin, right?"

"Yep."

"How long a flight is it?"

Hatcher, a longtime crop duster with a demeanor that fell somewhere between farmer and flyboy, lifted his baseball cap and scratched his balding head. "Twenty-five, thirty minutes, depending on traffic at the other end."

"Could a flight be made between Gnoss and here in the middle of the night?"

"It could for a qualified pilot. You see, Mr. Keegan, this isn't a controlled field. The landing lights are radio-operated. The pilot activates them himself. Of course, you have to be able to handle all that."

"Can Katerina Kreski do it?" Frank asked, warily waiting for the answer.

Hatcher thought for a moment. "I imagine she can. Werner did several times I know of, and she often flew with him."

Frank was on a real high. Katerina had the means, the ability and the motive to fly Sarah Gibbs's body to the Delta. She had a vehicle to transport it to the slough. The timing was such that she could have flown from Marin, done her thing and returned all in the course of an hour and a half. He figured he had it nailed. All he needed now was some physical evidence and maybe an eyewitness able to place her at either airport the night of February fourteenth. He decided to give it a shot.

"Mr. Hatcher, I don't suppose you have any idea when the last time was Katerina flew up here."

"She's here now."

"She is?"

"The Cessna's here. Has been for a couple of days." They were in Hatcher's little shack of an office. He gestured toward the window. "There in the tie-down area. See, it's the third from the right."

Frank felt a surge of energy. "Is she at her ranch?"

"I imagine so. I was here when she arrived. She headed in that direction when she left the field."

"I don't suppose you could give me directions."

Hatcher grinned, again lifting his hat to scratch his head. "Can pigs fly?"

Amador County

Frank's route had taken him east on Twin Cities Road until it became State Route 104 at U.S. 99. He'd gone from the low, flat land of the Delta to gently rolling, grassy hills, verdant in winter and studded with valley oaks and blue oaks and herds of cattle. He'd passed the Rancho Seco Nuclear Plant, now in mothballs, and he'd continued on toward the higher foothills and snow-capped Sierra farther to the east.

A few miles beyond the county line he came to the turnoff described by the airport manager. Following a single-lane, paved road for five miles, he reached the Kreski ranch. The entrance was rather unspectacular, considering the property, according to Hatcher, was several thousand acres in size. By all appearances it was a working ranch, which Frank knew to be entirely possible, even if Katerina didn't know a heifer from a bull. The ownership and operation of a ranch and farm land were becoming progressively separate. Gentleman farmers and ranch dudes bought these places as investments and for the wide-open spaces on which to locate a weekend retreat. Then they'd lease out the land for grazing or farming. Since Katerina was unlikely to do much roping, branding and riding, this was probably more a refuge than a home. And even more likely, it had now become a hideout.

Frank followed the gravel drive for three-quarters of a mile, going over a hill before reaching the ranch house. It was rambling, Southwestern in style, a place for Katerina and Werner before her to climb on a horse to unwind from the rigors of Montgomery Street with its faxes and e-mails and meetings and negotiating strategies.

Seeing the Land Rover sitting on the circular drive at the front door, Frank was relieved. He'd had visions of Katerina being gone and, though it was still possible, he felt he was in all probability closing in on his prey. The front door opened before he got there. The housekeeper, a pretty Chicana in her forties, told him Katerina had gone riding but was due back at anytime. Frank said he'd wait and headed for his truck.

As he walked past the Land Rover, he looked inside. The rear seats had been removed, which created a larger space for cargo. Glancing around and seeing no one, he opened the rear door of the vehicle, enabling the afternoon sun to spill inside. He bent close to the floor and after only a few moments of searching began to spot them—flecks of rust and red paint in the carpet.

Closing the door, he strolled along the drive, ruminating about his find. Katerina was his girl, all right. No doubt about it. And the ranch, located in the vicinity of Sacramento as it was, meant that a connection between Katerina and the three guys who'd firebombed his trailer was more likely than it had been only hours ago. She could have been involved in a murder conspiracy, in addition to any crimes she'd committed in connection with Sarah Gibbs.

When he came to a white board fence, Frank looked across the shallow valley at the low hill to the west. A horse and rider were making their way along the ridge, then they turned toward the ranch house. Frank watched their progress until they were close enough for him to see that it was indeed Katerina. When she was maybe two hundred yards away, she changed her course away from the barn and came directly toward him.

Katerina was in a waist-length leather jacket, turtleneck sweater and jeans. Her hair was pulled back into a tight chignon. She brought her horse right to the fence in front of him. Frank, who'd been resting his arms and chin on the top stringer, didn't move.

Katerina, her brow arched superciliously, said, "Well, it's the police. To what do I owe this unexpected pleasure?"

"I was in the neighborhood," Frank replied.

She gave him a half smile. "Without your boss?"

"You give away enough traffic tickets, they let you solo."

"I see."

"Nice day for a ride," he said, glancing out across the prairie.

"Look, Mr...."

"Keegan."

"Keegan," she said, "I'll give you two minutes, then I'm going to order you off my property."

"You put conditions on the conversation, Katerina, and I'll have to run you in so we can have a nice, leisurely chat at the county jail. The choice is yours."

She seemed amused. "I assume you know the consequences of a false arrest."

"I assume you know the consequences of a legitimate one."

Katerina's horse balked a little, tossing its head and stepping back. Frank held out a palm and the horse moved closer to the fence. He patted the animal's muzzle, then looked up at the woman. She gave him a steely glare, but he sensed her confidence was shaky.

"I'll get to the point," he said. "You're in deep doo-doo."

"Care to explain?"

"Here's my case. The night of the fourteenth you arrived at the Havallard Clinic, checked Biff in, then at around ten-thirty went to dinner. Instead of going to a restaurant, however, you went Gnoss Airfield where you removed the body of Sarah Gibbs from the trunk of your car and loaded it into your plane. The girl had drowned at your place in Ross, of course. To transport the body to your car you used the gardener's old rusty red wheelbarrow. Flecks of rust and paint got on the body.

"Now, with Sarah in the plane, you fly to Mokelumne Field, make a night landing with the radio-operated lighting system. The flight takes twenty-five minutes. You take the body out of the plane, put it in the Land Rover and drive it to Watermark Slough, where you dump it. Returning to the field, you fly back to Novato where you buy a pie for the staff and return to the clinic by midnight."

"You have a wild imagination, Mr. Keegan."

"It's not all hypothesis," he replied. "There're the flecks of rust and paint in the back of your Land Rover, for example. Unless you did a better job of cleaning the trunk of your car and the plane, they'll be found there, as well."

Katerina's stern visage began to show cracks.

"The list goes on and on," he said. "We've got Biff overhearing you ordering a hit. We've got phone records connecting you to the culprits." He was reaching, knowing some of this was pure speculation, but he sensed he had her on the ropes and he didn't want her to weather the onslaught. "Most damming of all," he said, "we got Evelinda DeLeon on her way back from the Philippines."

She smiled stiffly, maintaining her cool as best she could. "If you think you can pin a murder charge on me, then I *do* want to see you in court, Mr. Keegan."

"We've got enough to send you away for a long, long time, Katerina. Even without that."

She swung her leg over the saddle and dismounted. Then she lifted the reins over the head of her horse and began leading the animal along the fence toward the barn. Frank kept pace on the other side of the fence.

"Seems to me we're in the negotiating phase, Mr. Keegan," she said. "To make things simpler, why don't you tell me what it is you want? Biff's head?"

"Biff's?"

"That is what you're after, isn't it?" she said, looking over the fence at him.

Frank saw he had to give a little ground. "What I'd like is the whole story, beginning to end."

"Ah, so your omniscience isn't quite as complete as you would have me believe."

"There are a few blank spots," he conceded.

"So what are you offering?"

"What do you have to give?"

They walked in silence for a while. As they neared the barn, she said, "Let me explain my problem, Mr. Keegan. While you might not appreciate it, you have the power to ruin my life."

"I think we're way past that point," he said.

"Oh, don't be so sure."

"I'm listening."

They came to a gate. Katerina opened it and walked her horse through. Frank secured it behind her and she led the horse into the barn. He followed her inside.

Katerina tied the animal up in the saddling area. She removed the riding bridle and replaced it with a rope halter. Then she loosened the girth and took off the saddle and saddle blanket. Frank sat on a bale of hay and watched her pour some oats into a feeding bucket and hang it on the rail for the horse.

"Do you ride, Mr. Keegan?" Katerina asked him.

"No."

"Have any desire?"

"Not really."

"Tell me then, what do you covet?"

"Nothing in particular," he said.

She took a brush and began grooming her horse, brushing his back and flanks, shoulders and neck. "Money must interest you," she said.

"Do you have a point?" he asked.

Katerina stopped brushing the horse and turned to face him, her hands on her hips. "What you described earlier, the business about the plane, is basically what happened," she said. "I committed a crime. It's possible, though not a certainty, that you could get a conviction for that. I know that's not what you want, but it's the best you could possibly do because that's all I'm guilty of. When I got to my home in Ross that night, Biff had already killed the girl. Yes, he was out cold, but she was already dead. I can't say what happened because I wasn't there, but I do know this—he's had a convenient lapse of memory."

"Your story is changing again," Frank noted.

"Yes, I've foolishly tried to protect Biff from his own stupidity and culpability. Not for altruistic reasons, I freely admit, but to save my reputation. That was a mistake. And now you've got me dead to rights for trying to cover up a crime. I'll be blunt, Mr. Keegan—I can't afford even to go to trial, whether I was convicted and did jail time or not. So here's my point. I'm willing to pay handsomely for the matter to end right here."

"You want to bribe me."

"Yes."

"My, you are direct, aren't you?"

"I have no desire to play games. I assume your boss, Ms. Hooper, will have to be a party to our arrangement. You'll both be paid. I'm prepared to give you each half a million dollars."

Frank almost couldn't believe what he was hearing. "Half a million."

"That's right. You can buy pear trees until they're coming out your ears."

"You do your homework," he said.

"That seems to be a trait we have in common."

He stared at her and she stared back.

"It's the easiest money you'll ever make," she said. "And you don't even have to let a bad guy go free. What I did harmed no one."

"What about the attempt on our lives?"

"Were you hurt?"

"No, but we could have been killed."

"Mr. Keegan, I'm not interested in possibilities. I'm only interested in facts. How much did your loss amount to?"

"I don't know—sixty thousand dollars."

"I'll give you an extra hundred and you can keep the insurance money. That's my best and last offer, Mr. Keegan. You say no, and I hire myself a Johnnie Cochran and tough it out."

"There were tissue samples of Sarah's attacker under her fingernails."

"It'll match Biff's DNA, not mine."

"And the guys who firebombed my trailer?"

"They're dead."

"We've got Biff's testimony."

"Sarah Gibbs's killer? I wonder how credible he will be?"

Frank contemplated her. Katerina smiled.

"Six hundred thousand dollars, Mr. Keegan."

He rubbed his chin. "You really like to test a guy's mettle, don't you?"

"I like to keep things simple and neat."

He thought for a long moment, keeping her waiting. "You know, Katerina, I'm tempted. I really am. I won't pretend to be so virtuous that your money can't turn my head. But I think I'm going to pass. How could I ever explain driving a Mercedes in Riverton? Everybody who does is a thief. My friends would wonder about my character and soon I wouldn't have any friends at all. Seen it happen, honey, seen it happen."

"You're saying no?"

"I'm respectfully declining. Which means I'm going to have to arrest you." He got up. "Gather your things and let's go up to the house. I'll have to give the sheriff a call because I'm not equipped to drive you back to Riverton."

Katerina Kreski was incredulous. She turned red in the face. "Stupid fucking bastard!" she screamed. "Goddamn fucking moron!"

He sighed. Obviously she'd decided to go the Johnnie Cochran route. He jerked his head toward the house. "Come on, sweetheart, I've got things to do."

Frank sat in the front seat of the patrol car, talking to Dix Fowler on the radio. "She's still not in?" he said when Dix told him Abby had yet to show up.

"I've tried calling several times, but the line is busy."

"Maybe you'd better send somebody out there," Frank said.

"I would have already, but I've got a boating accident, an assault with a deadly weapon and a guy beating the shit out of his wife all at the same time, Frank. In fact, I'm on my way out the door myself to play beat cop."

"Then I'll go. We'll have to make arrangements to transfer

the Kreski woman later. Can I have the Amador sheriff call
you in an hour?''

"Yeah, barring an earthquake I'll be here. You go see
what's up with the chief.''

Frank ended the call, got out of the patrol car to speak
with the deputies, then got in his truck and took off. It was
damned near sunset, which meant Abby had been at her place
all day. She might have taken a nap, but not one that long.
Something was up and he didn't like it.

Tyler Island

As he sped along the road to Abby's place, Frank was
soaked with perspiration, his stomach in a knot. He knew
Abby could take care of herself and that she was probably
fine. But he wouldn't be able to draw an easy breath until he
knew for sure she was all right.

He wondered if Dix had thought to have somebody check
on the busy signal with the telephone company. The phone
could be off the hook or somebody could have ripped it out,
though he knew that a cut line would produce ringing, but
no answer. He'd run into that problem before.

Dusk had fallen, the setting sun glowing in the west behind
the shoulder of Mount Diablo. Frank was dying. Biff, Witherspoon, Darren, friends of the dead guys and no telling who
else had reason to go after Abby. Trying to kill her wasn't
beyond the realm of possibility. They'd firebombed his
trailer, for crissakes!

By the time he reached her drive, Frank could see lights
in one of the upper widows of the house. He didn't know
whether to take that as a good sign or not. If nothing else, it
probably meant someone had been there since darkness had
fallen. He knew to be careful, anyway, taking nothing for
granted.

Turning off his lights, he drove three-quarters of the way

to the house with nothing but the ambient light to guide him. Stopping there, he turned off the engine and got out. He left the car door ajar, knowing that if he shut it the sound would carry, then he jogged the last hundred yards to the gate. Parked outside it was Abby's Bronco, the driver's side door open. The interior dome light was burning, but it was so faint it was hardly visible. That meant the vehicle had been sitting like that for hours.

Seized by a terrible sinking feeling, he moved passed the vehicle and through the gate. The entire downstairs of the house was dark, but light still glowed from an upper window. He crept up the front steps and, trying the door, found it locked. Cursing under his breath, he wondered if he should force his way in or look for another means of entry. Deciding to check the perimeter of the building before resorting to forceful measures, he moved silently around the house, keeping his eyes on the dark windows.

In back he was surprised to see a Corvette on the lawn. He didn't know the car, but he sure as hell didn't like the looks of it. The light coming from a rear second-story window was more intense than the light in front. He climbed the back steps and found the door unlocked. He didn't like that, either. His stomach clenched and the adrenaline began to pump as he quietly let himself in.

He paused to listen, but heard nothing. From the enclosed porch he entered the kitchen. Seeing nothing unusual, he crept into the darkened back hall, which led to the front of the house. At the foot of the stairs he heard the sound of crying for the first time. A mournful but subdued sob that could have been Abby's.

His blood racing, he went up the stairs, two steps at a time, but as quietly as he could. Pleading with himself to be cautious, he moved toward the sound, which seemed to be coming from the room at the end of the hall, where light showed through a crack in the door.

He tiptoed toward the door as the sobbing continued, wishing to hell he had a weapon. Instinct told him he'd want to use it, whether he needed it or not. The choking sobs were more distinctive now. His breath racing, Frank clenched his fists and pressed his eye to the slight crack in the door. At first all he could see was the bed. A man was lying on it, naked and asleep. It was Darren Armstrong.

The sobbing continued. Frank carefully pushed the door open. Abby, completely naked, was hanging from a rope tied to her wrists and looped over an open beam in the vaulted ceiling. Her face was to the door, her backside to Armstrong. Though her feet were on the floor, much of her weight was being supported by the rope. She looked like she'd been there for hours.

When he saw blood running down her thighs, rage overwhelmed him. He was suddenly back in Vietnam, looking into the smoky interior of a hut. Morris, the fat sergeant who hated his guts, had backed a slender little girl against the wall while lowering his pants to rape her. Frank yelled at him to stop, but Morris ignored him. Instead, he threw the poor girl down on the floor and began hitting her. Frank grabbed him by the shoulders and pulled him away.

Abby's sobbing brought him back. He frantically looked around the room for weapons. There was a pistol and drug paraphernalia on the bedside table. He couldn't see anything else. Abby, sensing his presence, stopped sobbing and, lifting her tear-streaked face, saw him. Her eyes rounded in supplication and Frank put his finger to his lips, creeping past her to the table, where he picked up the pistol and stuffed it into the belt of his pants.

Armstrong, he could see, had a rubber tourniquet on his left arm, and a hypodermic needle lay on the bed beside him. Frank had half a mind to shoot the bastard right then and there, the way he'd wanted to shoot Morris. Instead, he returned to Abby and took his Swiss Army knife out of his pocket to cut her down.

"There's another gun," she whispered.

At the same moment Frank heard the bed creak behind him.

"Frank, watch out!"

Armstrong leaped, landing on him and getting his hands around Frank's neck as they fell to the floor. The rage Frank felt was the same rage he'd felt toward Morris that day in Vietnam. Once again, two guys and a helpless woman.

Frank brought his knee up sharply, smashing it into Armstrong's groin. Howling in pain, the naked man scrambled to the bed, reaching frantically under it, probably searching for the other gun.

Frank got there just as Armstrong pulled his hand out from under the bed, clutching a revolver. In his mind's eye, he saw Morris taking his .45 and shooting the girl before he could stop him.

The rage Frank had felt then coursed through him now. He stomped on Armstrong's gun hand, making him cry out in pain. Then he knocked the weapon aside with his foot. When Armstrong tried to get up, Frank pulled the semi-automatic from his belt and clobbered him on the side of the head. Armstrong went down with a thud and Frank kicked him in the ribs, twice, then aimed the pistol at his head. It was Morris's fat, angry face he saw before the sergeant staggered out of the hut, shouting obscenities and pulling up his pants.

"Frank, no!" Abby cried. "For the love of God, no!"

His brain locked with indecision, the adrenaline impelling him to shoot. All he could think of was the dead girl in the hut and Morris staggering down the village road, kicking away the chickens in his path. Two weeks later the bastard had gotten on a plane headed home, the girl he shot reduced to a statistic, another VC killed in action, the box of grenades by her lifeless body proof of the justice of her death. Frank's insistence that she hadn't been reaching for a grenade was ignored by the investigators, leaving him bitter and angry and sorry he hadn't pulled the trigger when he'd had the chance.

"Frank," Abby commanded, "put down the gun!"

Her voice finally brought him back. He hesitated, then let his gun hand drop to his side. He went to Abby then and cut her down. She collapsed into his arms and he held her, stroking her head.

Riverton

Kay Ingram carried the coffeepot from the table and refilled his cup.

"Damned good thing this is decaf," Frank said.

"You wouldn't be getting much sleep, anyway," she said, glancing at the kitchen clock.

It was after eleven-thirty.

"No, I'll probably spend the night wishing I'd killed the sonovabitch."

Kay put a splash of coffee in her own cup and returned the pot to the stove. Then she sat at the table. "Let's be glad you didn't."

"The only thing that kept me from doing it was Abby."

"She's strong, Frank."

He looked toward the door, then back at her. "Do you really think she'll be all right?"

Kay picked up her cup, pausing before taking a sip.

"She will be if you're loving toward her and understand her feelings," Kay said. "The important thing is to be patient."

Frank had that terrible, helpless feeling he'd had when Beth died. The difference was that this time there was someone to blame. Not that it made things any easier. It was still awful. But Kay had been great. Helpful to them both. Abby hadn't wanted to stay in the house, even with him there, so after she'd finished at the hospital and given her statement to the sheriff's deputies, Frank called Kay. She'd told him to bring Abby over.

Kay had been waiting anxiously when they arrived and the two women had immediately embraced, more truly mother and daughter than ever before. Kay had taken Abby to the bedroom, and he'd waited in the front room, knowing that what they were doing was very important. When Kay had come out, she said Abby was taking a bath. She'd taken him to the kitchen to make him some coffee.

Frank again looked toward the door. "You really think she's all right?"

"Yes, she'll come out when she's ready. You were a cop—you've handled rape victims before."

"Yes, but the victim's always been a stranger, Kay."

"Your role is a little different in this case, granted. Make her feel safe, Frank. She might be a cop, but she's human. She can be hurt. The important thing is she's dealing with it. She's not in denial."

"That's good, but would you check on her, Kay? Ask her if she wants me here. I just want to make it as easy as possible for her."

Kay got up, putting her hand on his shoulder in a reassuring manner as she headed for the bathroom. Frank glanced around the room, knowing it in a context that was so completely different from the one he was in now that everything seemed unreal. When the day started this had been the last place he would have expected to find himself at its end, particularly under these circumstances. He took a slug of coffee, then carried the cup to the sink where he rinsed it and put it in the dishwasher. He had what was for him a strange urge to clean up things, put them in order.

"Frank."

He turned at the sound of her voice. Abby was at the

kitchen door. She was in a sweat suit and gym socks, her damp hair slicked back, her face pink and scrubbed. Her demeanor was of an innocent child, a wounded, innocent child. He went toward her, her face crumpling as she tried unsuccessfully to smile. He held her and stroked her head, feeling her warm breath on his skin as she pressed her face into his shirt. He squeezed her tightly, determined not to let go until she wanted. If she cried, it was inwardly. Mostly, it appeared, she just wanted to be held.

When she did pull back she looked up at him, red-eyed, and whispered, "Thank you."

"Can I get you anything?" he asked.

"Do I smell coffee?"

"Yeah, Kay made a pot. Want some?"

"I'll get it," she said.

"I will."

"No, Frank, let me do it. Where does she keep the cups?"

He pointed to the cupboard. Abby poured herself some coffee, asserting her independence, wanting, he judged, to be self-sufficient. She was striking a balance, accepting her pain without going to either extreme—collapsing helplessly or rigidly denying it had happened.

"Want to go into the front room?" she asked.

They did. Some soft jazz was playing on the stereo. Kay was nowhere to be seen. Frank sat on the sofa, Abby next to him, close enough that their thighs were touching.

"I want to tell you what happened," she announced.

Frank's impulse was to say that she didn't have to. All that mattered was that she was all right. What had happened had absolutely no effect on his feelings for her. But he kept his silence, knowing that if she wanted to tell him, it was for herself more than for him. Anyway, he wasn't exactly sure what she meant by "tell you what happened," unless she'd forgotten he was right there when she recounted everything to the sheriff's deputies.

Frank had listened to her describe how Darren had tried to talk her into having sex with him, and how, when she'd refused, he'd tied her to the bed, then raped her. When he realized he'd accomplished nothing, he'd gone into a rage and strung her up to humiliate and torture her while he got high on drugs and abused himself. She'd struggled emotionally with the telling of her story, but being a professional, she'd gotten it all out, doing her duty and making it as easy as possible for the deputies to do theirs.

"There's more behind what Darren did than the usual power thing, the need to control by violence. He wanted to get me pregnant."

"What?"

Abby explained her past with Darren Armstrong, that she'd gotten pregnant by him and had an abortion. "For some reason that set him off," she said. "I guess it was the ultimate emasculation. I don't think he cared about children. He just didn't want me undoing his accomplishment—never mind the fact he'd gone off to Hollywood with his girlfriend and left me holding the bag."

"He knew, didn't he, that you thought he was a scumbag, so it's amazing he'd think you'd be interested."

"Darren's ego knew no bounds. When I didn't succumb, he couldn't believe it and flew into a rage. The fact that he's emotionally unstable and was drugged out didn't help."

"I hope you aren't making excuses for him."

"No, I hate him, Frank. More than ever."

"And the fact that you were strong enough to stand up to him must have set him off."

"Why are men like that?"

"We all aren't."

"Oh, I know," she said, taking his hand. "But too many are."

Frank kissed her temple. "The important thing is you don't blame yourself."

"The only thing I feel guilty about is letting him get the jump on me. Much as I hurt physically, and even emotionally, I think the deepest wounds were to my pride, Frank."

"Nobody's going to look down on you for this, if that's what you're worried about."

"It never would have happened to Chet Wilsey," she said.

"We're all human, Abby. Chet's frailties brought on an even greater tragedy, one that not only hurt him, but others."

"Maybe I'm lucky that my stupidity didn't result in some innocent woman getting raped."

"An innocent woman did get raped," he said. "But you can't beat yourself up for that. What happened didn't happen because of a failure of character—it happened because of circumstance. You'd forgive me, so you damned well better forgive yourself."

She rested her head on his shoulder. He rubbed her hand. They sat that way for a long time, listening to the music and the beating of their hearts.

Then she looked up at him, her eyes glistening. "I used to think people couldn't be both strong and needy, but they can, can't they?"

"Sure."

"Tonight I really wanted a mother, Frank, and when Kay and I were alone in her bedroom I cried in her arms like a baby. But that doesn't mean I can't be a good police chief."

"Of course it doesn't."

"People put a lot of pressure on themselves, don't they?" she said. "Needlessly."

"Yes."

"I guess it's okay to be less than perfect."

He nodded. "All we can do is the best we can, Abby."

She pressed his hand to her cheek. "What's your fear, Frank? What are you afraid of?"

He ran her question through his mind. "In one form or

another, I think everybody has the same fear—not measuring up.''

"I don't know what you have to worry about," she said. "You're the kindest, most special person I've ever known."

He laughed. "But what happens when you discover that ain't necessarily so?"

"Well, I'm not saying you're perfect. But you're comfortable with who you are and I like the result."

Frank Keegan smiled to himself. They were beginning to appreciate each other despite their flaws. That was important.

"Can I ask you something, though?" Abby said. "What were you thinking when you were standing over Darren with the gun in your hand, ready to shoot him?"

He drew a long breath. "I was wrestling with my demons, ones left over from Vietnam. And I was trying to decide which of us was stronger, them or me."

"*You* were."

He wasn't so sure, because only he knew how close he'd come to pulling the trigger. "Not until you reminded me."

"We all need a little help now and then."

"I'm glad you were there," he said.

She pulled his face down and kissed his cheek. "I love you, Frank Keegan," she said. "And I'm really glad you're in my life."

Saturday
March 8th

Frank pulled up in front of the River Queen at dusk. He didn't see Abby's Bronco, so he figured he must have beaten her there. She'd gone into Sacramento to meet with the D.A. for a strategy meeting. On Monday the court would be considering a motion by Katerina Kreski's attorneys for her release on bail, and decisions had to be made by the prosecution about additional charges. "I have this feeling," Abby had said that morning at breakfast, "that Sarah Gibbs's death is going to go unpunished."

"Something will break, sweetheart," he'd assured her. "This stalemate can't go on forever."

"I know I'm paranoid, Frank, but you have to wonder if Biff and Katerina still aren't in collusion."

What she'd been referring to was the fact that for a week they had been blaming each other for Sarah's death, while professing his or her own innocence. Frank and Abby were divided on the issue. He was leaning toward the theory that it was Katerina who'd killed the girl. Abby thought it was more likely Biff, though quite possibly unwittingly—perhaps while drugged out. Ironically, the debate between Biff and Katerina became their debate, as well.

Katerina, Frank maintained, had shown she had no compunction about using force, including a willingness to kill. "She's basically amoral and would do anything to advance her interests."

"Yes," Abby had countered, "that's the point. Katerina has ice water in her veins. She did everything in a calculated manner to save her own butt. At first she was trying to save Biff because she wanted to marry him, but when she decided he was a hopeless cause, she abandoned him and started looking out for herself. She didn't have to kill Sarah to accomplish her goal. The only clear motive for murdering Sarah would have been jealousy and/or rage. But Katerina wasn't there. It wasn't logical for her to kill Sarah."

"But she tried to kill *us.*"

"Well, she's denying that now. Anyway, we were a direct threat."

"Whether we'll be able to prove it is another thing, I grant you," Frank had said, "but we both know it's true. I honestly think Katerina is so evil that she'd stop at nothing. A life meant little to her, if it got in her way."

"Frank," Abby had said, "why are you protecting Biff?"

"I'm not protecting him—he's a bumbler. He's weak and selfish and he represents everything I have no respect for in a guy."

"Maybe that's the point. You make excuses for Biff because he's not personally threatening. But Katerina is loathsome because she's an independent woman and she's strong."

"Abby, you aren't saying you admire her."

"Of course not. She's also immoral unfortunately, so I can't approve of her actions, but she's definitely threatening to men, and that's probably what's behind your prejudice against her."

"What about *your* prejudice, Madam Police Chief? Biff's

a user. He exploits women, so in your mind that makes him not just a villain, but a killer.''

"Frank, I'm a professional. I can see beyond that sort of thing!''

"Well, I'm a professional, too!''

They'd gone back and forth that way all week as they'd been busy building their cases against Biff and Katerina. Abby had taken the Friday and Saturday off after she'd been assaulted, staying at Kay's. Sunday, Frank went with her to her house and they'd cleaned the place. She wasn't sure she was ready to stay there, but decided she needed to do it. "I'd like it if you'd move in with me, though,'' she'd told him. "Assuming you want to.'' He told her it was what he wanted more than anything, then got his things from Dix's. Abby reported to work bright and early Monday morning, immersing herself in her work. "Helps me to forget,'' she'd told him.

Their live-in relationship hadn't exactly begun under the best of circumstances, but it drew them closer. Frank was happy she'd attacked the case with determination, and he intentionally sparred with her to keep the competitive juices flowing. There was no doubt she'd been wounded, though. Twice during the week she'd awakened from a bad dream in tears. She was adamant about toughing it out.

Despite Abby's best efforts, being in the house was a problem for her. By the middle of the week she'd talked in terms of selling. "It's probably stupid and I will wait a while before I decide for sure, but I'm thinking it might not be a bad thing to start over in a new home. What would you think of looking for a place together?''

He knew she was aware he was thinking something more permanent than sharing a rental, but it was still early in their relationship and they'd been through a lot in a short period of time. He left things as ambiguous as she had. "Sure, sweetheart, I'm game.''

Abby had more to worry about than just her living accommodations, though. Crystal Armstrong had come to the house Monday night, and she and Abby had an emotional reunion. Frank grabbed his jacket and drove to the Queen so they could be alone. When he returned, Crystal was driving away. Abby told him what had transpired.

"The poor thing has been dying, certain I'd hold her responsible," Abby said.

"That's silly. She tried to warn you Darren was on a rampage."

"Still, he's her brother, and in her way she loves him. It's hard to love someone and know they've done something evil. Of course, he's sick and she knows it."

Frank had understood that, but he was still focused on his own hatred. And he was surprised Abby had shown so much compassion and forgiveness. It seemed to him it was healthier to hate passionately for a while. There would be time for forgiveness later.

If there was justice in the situation, it was that Darren's injuries were more serious than they'd at first seemed. He remained hospitalized a week later, drifting in and out of consciousness. Without exactly being proud of it, Frank didn't care what happened to the bastard. Truth be known, he was half-sorry he hadn't shot him when he'd had the chance. He didn't tell Abby that, though. She didn't need the burden of his hatreds.

Entering the Queen, Frank checked his watch. In a little more than three hours they had to be at the high school for the dance. The previous evening, Abby and Kay had gone to Nordstrom in Walnut Creek to look for dresses. Abby had come home in the best of spirits. She'd found a dress, but that was the least of it. She and Kay had had a really good time—"a real mother-daughter day with smiles, instead of tears," was the way she had put it. Though his past with Kay remained a touchy subject, Frank had been happy for them.

Abby and Kay needed each other, probably more than either of them fully realized.

There weren't many people at the Queen, considering it was a Saturday night, but it was probably because of the dance. Kay had planned to close the place down while the dance was on and had a big sign on the door to that effect. She wasn't there, apparently having left to get ready for the big evening. Toad was tending bar and Belinda Ramsey was hustling drinks. Frank asked her for a beer and slid into a booth. When Toad put the glass on the bar, Mort Anderson picked it up before Belinda could and brought it to Frank's table.

"Mind if I join you?"

Mort's earnest manner caught him off guard. "No, have a seat."

Mort looked him in the eye. "I'll get right to the point, Frank. Without prejudicing either your relationship with Abby or my relationship with Kay, it's obvious that one day you and I might end up related by marriage. Now I know that sitting down for Thanksgiving dinner with me would probably come low on your list of fun things to do, but it could happen. So I've been thinking it might be a good idea if you and I patched things up."

"That's very magnanimous of you, Mort."

"I'd be doing it for Kay more than anything, but hey, I probably deserve most of the blame for our problems in the past, so the way I see it, I owe you. I'm here to tell you I was the one who clobbered you with the two-by-four, Frank, and I want to make it up to you."

Frank almost couldn't believe his ears. "What did you have in mind?"

"There's a good-size pear ranch on Grand Island that'll be coming on the market soon. Over two hundred acres of mature trees, plus land for expansion. It's got a great building site for a house and it's less than fifteen minutes from Riverton. I'll help you acquire it, commission free, plus I'll kick in twenty-five thousand toward closing costs. That'll save you suing me for knocking you on the head.''

Frank shook his head with disbelief. ''Mort, your generosity stuns me, but you're talking big bucks for an orchard that large. Even if I got the most Judge Parker says is possible to get out of Chet's estate, plus a top-dollar settlement on the loss of my trailer from the insurance company, I wouldn't come close.''

''If Abby sells her place, she'll get a nice chunk of change. The two of you could come up with the purchase price for the land. Kay and I would be willing to make you a loan for construction of the house at a below-market rate.''

''Jesus, Mort.''

He smiled. ''Family's important, Frank.''

Just then Abby came in the door. Frank and Mort both saw her.

''Abby might have a thought or two about this,'' Frank said.

''Kay's been talking to her. My job was to broach the subject with you. There's no rush. You and Abby have decisions to make. I can keep this perking on the back burner a couple of months. Just wanted to plant the seed.''

Abby had reached the booth and Mort got up to let her take his spot.

''Hi, Abby,'' he said. ''You look like you want to talk to Frank, so I'll go on back to finish my beer.'' Grinning he added, ''See you later at the dance. Save one for me, will you, sweetie?''

He went off and Abby looked at Frank quizzically. ''What was that about?''

''I think your future father-in-law was trying to barter you.''

''*Barter* me?''

''Yeah, he wanted two cows and half a dozen goats for

you. I told him to come back when he was prepared to be more reasonable.''

"Like a pig and two chickens?''

"A *small* pig and two chickens.''

Abby gave him a look. "Well, I've got news. Lots of news.''

"Let's hear it.''

"D.A.'s decided they've got no homicide case against either Katerina or Biff. Monday she'll be free on bail. They'll prosecute her on everything else they've got, though. With luck, she'll do a few years in the penitentiary, but they told me not to bet the house on it.''

"What about Biff?''

"They've turned everything over to the San Francisco D.A. so they can look at the solicitation, corrupting the morals of a minor, the drug and other charges. Don't hold your breath on that, either.''

"They won't even wait for the DNA-test results?''

"I've got word on that, too. Report's in. The match was not with Katerina, it was with Biff.''

His brows rose.

"It was his skin under Sarah's nails,'' Abby went on, "but that's not good enough to prove he intentionally or even negligently drowned her. There's simply no proof that a crime occurred. The Marin D.A.'s got all the info, too, and has been studying it, but it's not likely they'll prosecute, either.''

They looked into each other's eyes for a long moment.

"You upset?'' he asked.

"Tomorrow I'm going to sit down and write Alice Gibbs a letter. I don't like having to say I don't know how Sarah died. It was my job to find out. I just wish I could tell her what happened whether I could prove it or not. Seems to me a family deserves to know the truth.''

Frank took her hands. "I know what you mean.''

"And I had lunch with Crystal,'' Abby said.

"How's she?"

"Relieved somewhat that things hadn't turned out worse for Darren. She was resigned to the fact he'll most likely spend a number of years in prison."

"How about you?" he said, rubbing her knuckles with his thumb.

"Darren is long since out of my mind. What he did to me the first time took a while to expunge. What he did this last time will take a while, too. But it will fade away, Frank—I'm hoping more quickly this time, because I've got you."

She smiled at him. Frank pulled her hands to his mouth and kissed them. "You look pretty enough to take to a dance. What do you say we go home and get ready?"

"Sounds good to me."

Frank chugged down a few gulps of beer and put three bucks on the table. They got up and were headed for the door when two smallish Asians, a man and a woman, came into the bar. The man wore a clerical collar.

"That's Father Caratay," Abby said, the surprise in her voice evident.

The priest saw her and waved. Taking the dazed-looking woman by the arm, he led her to where they stood. "Chief Hooper, glad I found you. This is Evelinda DeLeon. She arrived from Manila this morning. I thought you should hear what she has to say. At the police station they said you were at this establishment. So here we are."

Frank and Abby looked at the woman, who appeared to be both frightened and exhausted. Abby suggested they sit at the booth.

"Care for anything to drink?" Frank asked.

The priest and the woman both asked for soft drinks. Frank asked Belinda to bring a couple of Cokes.

Father Caratay, mid-thirties and earnest-looking, with thick glasses on his oval face, began the dialogue. "When I questioned Evelinda about the circumstances of her leaving Ms.

Kreski's employ, she told me something I knew you must hear for yourself." He turned to the woman. "Tell them what happened that night, Evelinda. Go ahead."

Evelinda DeLeon, a woman in her forties with streaks of gray in her black hair and a demeanor as earnest as the priest's, bowed her head contritely. "I am very sorry if this makes trouble for you," she said softly. "I did not know and I was very scared when I left to return to my country. If it is a crime, I am sorry."

"Just tell us what happened," Abby said.

"Well, I was in my room that night watching television when I heard the doorbell," Evelinda said. "It was maybe seven-thirty, something like that. I opened the door to my room and I hear voices. Mr. Roberts is talking to a girl and she is crying."

"Do you know what they said?"

"Only that she wanted to stay. I did not listen for long, because Ms. Kreski and Mr. Roberts often fight and I did not want to be a problem. I always stayed in my room if there was trouble. Then later, I heard voices through my door. Mr. Roberts and the girl were drinking and being very loud. I heard them in the family room, so I looked and they were naked. She was bent over a chair and he was having sex with her." Evelinda paused to cross herself.

"If I had known this was going on," the priest said, "I would not send my parishioners to work in that house."

Abby nodded. "So then what happened, Evelinda?"

"Soon they talked about going outside. Mr. Roberts was very drunk and perhaps he had drugs. The girl, who was very small compared to him, helped him out to the spa. I was afraid what might happen, so I went to the kitchen to watch. They were in the hot water and after a few minutes I could see Mr. Roberts was sleepy. I didn't know what to do, so I started back to my room. Ms. Kreski would come home soon, so I knew she would take care of the problem. But then the girl screamed. I returned to the window and I saw her on the side of the spa. She had Mr. Roberts by the wrists and she was trying to pull him out of the water. He was unconscious, I believe. Since he was so large she was having great difficulty. I ran to the family room to go out and help her, but as I got to the door, I saw that she had gotten him out of the spa. Only his legs were in the water. On her last pull, her hands slipped from his wrists and she went flying backward into the swimming pool.''

"What happened then?'' Abby asked, leaning forward expectantly.

Evelinda took a sip of her soft drink. "At that moment I heard Ms. Kreski coming in the front door. So I ran to tell her that Mr. Roberts was with a girl by the pool and that he was sick. But she was already upstairs, shouting Mr. Roberts's name, I think because she saw the clothes of the girl in the front room. I went up to tell her what happened, and when she saw me she was red in the face. I was very excited and I don't know if she understood me exactly, but she went to the window and looked down at the pool. She turned to me and ordered that I should return to my room, keep the door locked and not come out.

"I did as she told me. Later I heard an ambulance come, so I knew Ms. Kreski took care of everything. I did not see her until late the next morning when she said that she would give me money and that I should go to the Philippines. What happened was a great scandal that a naked girl should be at her house with Mr. Roberts. And so I left and did as she told me.''

"Did Katerina ask you what you saw?''

Evelinda drank more Coke. "Only if I saw them together. When I told her I saw them making love in the family room, she didn't want to hear more. You see, I didn't know that the girl also was hurt. I only saw her fall into the swimming pool. It wasn't until I talked to Father Caratay when I was back in the Philippines that I learned the girl died that night. I swear this on the Virgin Mary."

"So the last thing you saw was the girl fall into the pool?"

"Yes, I assumed she would get out. She was not so drunk as Mr. Roberts."

Frank and Abby exchanged looks. Abby shook her head mournfully.

The priest asked if there would be consequences for Evelinda.

"No," Abby told him. "It would be good if Evelinda writes down everything she has told us and sends it to me, but there should be no problem. Her story has been very helpful, though."

Evelinda seemed relieved. "Then I have made no crime."

"Not based on what you said," Abby replied.

There were thanks on all sides and Father Caratay took the woman's arm, telling Abby and Frank they still had a long drive ahead of them. "This has been a difficult day, but the truth is important," he said. Then they were gone.

Abby dropped back down on the banquette. Frank sat across from her.

"It was an accident, Frank. Sarah drowned because she couldn't swim."

"Yeah, Biff and Katerina were both telling the truth and each assumed the other was lying."

"Sarah was trying to save the bastard's life and she died in the process, being a Good Samaritan. She must have scratched him pulling him from the hot tub. That's how she got his flesh under her nails."

Frank shook his head, incredulous. "Who would have thought?"

"There may not have been a murder, but there were plenty of other sins committed," Abby said. "And plenty of crimes. We could have died ourselves."

"I just hope Katerina doesn't beat the rap altogether," he said. "But I'm not counting on a conviction."

"She may have lost something more important," Abby replied. "At least something more important to her."

Frank said, "You know what bothers me most is that Sarah's still the victim in all this. The poor kid was exploited from the very beginning by people she should've been able to trust—her father, her boyfriend, the others in her community. A number of adults were involved and every one of them let her down." He shook his head. "The big bad world must not have looked all that bad to her, not compared to the way things were at home."

Abby sighed. "Well, at least now I have something positive to say in my letter to her mom. Her child died trying to save another person's life. The basic goodness in her heart hadn't been destroyed. All the evil she'd seen, all the suffering she'd endured, couldn't snuff out the spark of decency in her." Abby's eyes glistened. "Makes you think about what's really important, doesn't it?"

Frank nodded. "Yeah, sweetheart, it does."

Abby wiped her eyes.

"Are you up to going to a dance?" he asked.

"I have to—I'm one of the featured speakers. I had a little speech prepared, Frank, but now I've got to change it."

"How so?"

"I want to share what I learned tonight. I want to tell people that the saddest life can still contain a spark of kindness. If good can survive a life like Jane Doe's, it can survive anything. We have a duty to try to save children like Sarah Gibbs, and I want the town to feel that way even if people think I'm preachy to say so. These last few weeks have to count for something."

Frank felt the emotion rise in his heart. He thought of his own daughter, of the peasant girl in Vietnam, of Frieda Benke, Chet Wilsey and, for that matter, Katerina, Biff,

Lloyd Witherspoon and Darren Armstrong. Life, he realized, could make a victim of just about anyone. Adversity couldn't be avoided. What was important was how you dealt with it. He squeezed Abby's hands and she squeezed back.

"So," she said, "are you taking me to the dance or not?"

"Sure," he replied. "But it'll cost you a pig and two chickens."

Abby rolled her eyes. "God, I finally find the man of my dreams and what does he turn out to be? Cheap!"

"But I'm warm on a winter night, my dear. Don't forget it's a cold, lonely world out there."

Abby laughed. "Not anymore, Frank. Not anymore."